Blorfindel Brighteyes
Part Two

Homecoming

Jonathan Gerkin

ISBN: 978-1-960647-02-3

Cover design by: Sean Bianchi

To my wife, Missy.

Acknowledgments

Tom Pray for providing the forum where the first character sketch of Blorfindel Brighteyes was introduced.

Roberta Gerkin, Colleen Chaffee, Mark MacDonald, and Nathan Smith for providing the forum and feedback on the design of the world and cultures presented in this work.

In addition, feedback from Sylvia D'Ambrosio was of great assistance in developing the final prose.

And, in everything, Missy Gerkin for being my sounding board, critic, inspiration, and motivation.

Table of Contents

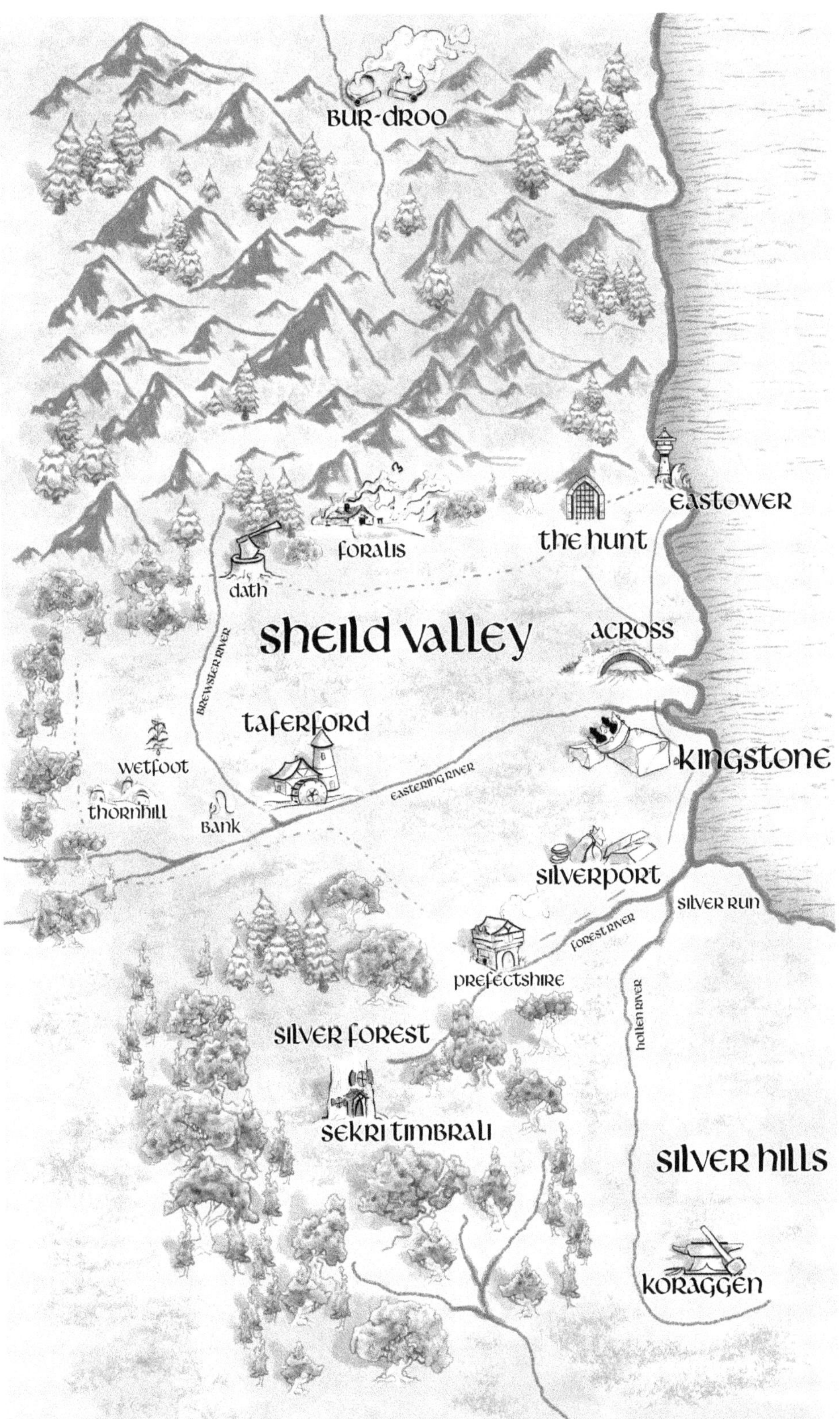

BUR-DROO
EASTOWER
the hunt
foralis
dath
sheild valley
across
BREWSTER RIVER
taferford
kingstone
wetfoot
EASTERING RIVER
thornhill
bank
silverport
SILVER RUN
FOREST RIVER
prefectshire
hollen river
silver forest
sekri timbrali
silver hills
koraggen

Synopsis

This is the second part of Blorfindel Brighteyes.

Blorfindel, a Fitheran, was orphaned at the age of 81 when the Wizard-King sent Kutel to attack his village of Foralis. Ammoss, a Tafer warrior, rescued Blorfindel from the pursuing Kutel. Ammoss and his wife, Shandi, adopted Blorfindel until he was captured by a Kutel and sold into slavery. Blorfindel was owned by the master of a traveling troupe of entertainers for decades.

When Blorfindel sang a song about a murder, he was branded an informant, or "Brighteyes," by the criminal organization in the city of Kingstone. The Knights Of the Circle rescued him from the would-be killers, but to protect him they locked him in their fortress. For years Blorfindel trained as if he would become a Tafer knight and wondered when he will be free to act like a Fitheran.

A Fitheran named Biolmi Yewstaff found him in the fortress and helped him escape to Sekri Timbrali, a city of Fitherani. There Biolmi taught him to be an archer in the Fithern tradition. Blorfindel met Afinlia and fell in love with the young Fitheresse from a wealthy family. Afinlia's father, however, is not at all certain that Blorfindel is a worthy suitor to Afinlia. He set a task for Blorfindel: he must make himself as wealthy as Afinlia's other suitors.

When a creature known only as a shapetaker began stalking innocents in Sekri Timbrali, Blorfindel, with the aid of his Fithern friends, set out to detect and capture the killer, saving the lives of several Fitheressi. The captured shapetaker turned out to be acting on orders from the Wizard-King with instructions to kill Blorfindel.

Though his people consider him a hero, Blorfindel is still too poor to be Afinlia's suitor. Impatient and afraid that he will lose her, Blorfindel marched back out into the lands of the Tafers to make his fortune the only way he knows how: with his Fithern bow and his father's sword.

On Fitherani

Fitherani are a long-lived people with a special love of trees and their forests. They tend to be fair skinned with light colored hair. Fitherani have distinctive pointed ears and very acute senses of hearing and sight. They average less than five feet in height, and are frequently less than 100 lbs. They are justly renowned for their archery, and all males are required to pass their archery test before their 175th year in order to become full citizens, simply known as 'archers'. A Fitheran allowed to live in peace might survive to two thousand years of age.

On Tafers

Tafers are a larger and faster-living people than the Fitherani. It is not uncommon for a Tafer to exceed six feet or two-hundred pounds, but rare for them to live to an old age approaching one hundred years. They are the most variable species of people, with no special leaning toward good or evil.

On Kutel

Kutel are a violent species. In size, they are nearly as large as the Tafers. They are the natural enemy of Fitherani, but their brutal tendencies make them the enemies of all people who value peace. Kutel are purple-gray, generally with purple scars. They are slow-witted but fast-breeding and their numbers combined with their natural aggression make them dangerous.

On Timbles

Timbles are a small, industrious, and humble people. An average Timble is three feet tall, though they tend to get rounder with age, if they can afford to. Many Timbles reach 100 years, though few 120.

Chapter 1

Nickadola

Blorfindel walked north a few miles out of Sekri Timbrali in the evening and spent the night under a tree. The air was clear and cool. He was glad to have two cloaks when he wrapped himself up to sleep that night. The next day he wandered generally north through the forest and wondered how he might earn enough money to impress Afinlia's father.

In the afternoon of the second day the trees began to become thinner. That evening he was descending through riverside farmsteads toward the Tafer town of Taferford. Though the sun was hardly below the horizon, the whole town seemed to be asleep. He slept on the riverbank, and the following morning he paid a Tafer three iron jertaks to ferry him across the Eastering River in a little fishing boat.

Taferford was a trading town at a river confluence. The Eastering River began at some unknown source in the mountains far to the west and made an easy trade route east to Across and Kingstone on the coast. The Brewster River joined the Eastering River from the north. A ford on the Brewster River allowed commerce between the Tafers on the east bank and the Timbles to the west. All of the lands north of the Eastering and west of the Brewster were populated by Timbles. They were nominally part of the Shield Valley and paid taxes to the king at Kingstone, but apart from that they were largely left to themselves. When the Timbles wanted contact with the outside world they would cross the river at Taferford.

The town had not changed much since Blorfindel was there with the troupe of entertainers six decades earlier. Taferford was really two towns in the same place. In the area of the river confluence was a trading town run mostly by merchants. All around was rich farmland. Tafer-run farms on the east bank of the Brewster looked at Timble-run farms on the west bank. Farther north and east were grazing lands for sheep, goats, and cows, as well as a couple of horse farms. The Sheildmaster of Taferford was responsible for the whole area.

Blorfindel wandered over to the Brewster river near the ford. The troupe used to cross here twice a year to visit the Timbles. The water was high, as it always was in the spring. He remembered floating the wagons across when the water was this high. He left his kit by the riverbank, took his boots off, and waded out until the river was over his knees. After two days of walking the cool water was very pleasant.

On the other side of the ford a Timble was putting things in a small reed boat – to a Tafer it would be a large basket. Blorfindel watched curiously as the naked Timble waded into the river pushing the boat ahead of him. Near the middle of the ford the water was nearly up to the Timble's neck. Suddenly, he slipped on a loose rock and fell into the river. Blorfindel splashed out and caught the boat just as the Timble resurfaced. Blorfindel met him at the riverbank.

"Thank you," the Timble said in Timbrali.

"You're welcome," Blorfindel said in the Timbles' language.

They both laughed.

"I am Nickadola Bretritich. How are you called?"

Blorfindel looked over his shoulder quickly to see if anyone else was in hearing distance. He replied in Timbrali, nonetheless. "I am called Blorfindel Brighteyes." He walked over to his kit on the riverbank and started arming himself. *I wonder if he knows what that means in Kingstone?*

Quietly the Timble began to unpack the load from his little boat. His clothes were common enough, but Blorfindel was surprised to see Nickadola put on armor much like his own boiled leather. He also belted on a scimitar which looked enormous on the three-foot Timble. His leather backpack had seen only slightly more wear than Blorfindel's. He threw a dark brown traveling cloak over all, and finally, from the bottom of the boat he pulled a leather-bound shield about two feet by a foot and a half.

Blorfindel was pulling his boots on. "You look like you're going to war."

"I might say the same to you. Are you on your way to Dath?"

"What do you know about Dath?"

Nickadola pulled a rolled up parchment from his belt. There was a dark band where the belt had pressed it into his armor. "They sent notices over the river, too."

"What notices?" Nickadola tried to hand it to Blorfindel, but the Fitheran was lacing his boots. He hoped that would cover long enough: Blorfindel had never learned to read. "What does it say?"

"'Let it be known that, as raids and villainy have persisted now around the village of Dath, Sheildmaster…' Oh, ah, the ink is running. Sheildmaster Terak of Dath is looking for help with Kutel raids. He'll pay room and board, plus whatever 'reasonable expenses' means, and we get to keep anything we take off the Kutel, unless they just stole it."

"'We?'"

"You're coming, right?"

"I'd like to see Dath again. Actually, this could be just the thing I'm looking for. I need to raise some money, I thought I could do it fighting Kutel."

Nickadola seemed very pleased. "So we might as well travel together. We'll most likely be fighting together once we get there, anyway: my sling, your bow, right?"

"Maybe. Why does the Shieldmaster have to put out notices? Shouldn't he be getting help from The Hunt or something?"

"I don't know. All I have is this notice. So are we traveling together? The Kutel may come south to try to cut the town off."

"Yes, I'll go with you," Blorfindel said. "I don't actually know the way."

Nickadola waved north with the rolled paper. "According to the notice, it's just up the river."

"Are you taking your boat?"

"The current is too strong for that. I'll leave it. Some Tafer kids will pick it up. I just made it this morning to keep my stuff dry during the crossing."

Blorfindel looked at the sun. It had been up for maybe three hours. "You did that this morning? That's fast."

"Reeds are my friends, so they help out when they can. It makes things go quicker." He started walking up the riverbank.

Blorfindel slung on his own pack and followed. "Will they help out when the Kutel attack?"

"Maybe."

Nickadola walked faster on his little legs than Blorfindel imagined possible. Even so, the tall Fitheran was moving at an easy pace. From time to time he would play his cittern as they went. Nickadola knew most of the lyrics, though he only sang along with the Tafer and Timble songs.

When they stopped for the evening Nickadola baited fish to the surface with flies. Blorfindel shot two of them. The Fitheran made a small fire and the Timble cooked the fish for dinner. That night Blorfindel slept under a tree by the river. Nickadola seemed comfortable in a small evergreen bush. It looked very prickly to Blorfindel.

Something woke Blorfindel. He rose silently and readied an arrow in his bow. He could see Nickadola's eyes in the bush, but the Timble made no sound.

They heard a howl.

"That's a wolf," Blorfindel breathed.

Nickadola's whisper was even quieter. "I know it's a wolf. What is she saying?"

"I don't know."

"Then be quiet and let me listen."

There was another howl, then another. A few minutes passed and then two more howls.

"They are re-establishing contact. Something split them up." Nickadola stepped out of the bush. "There are only two groups, maybe only two individuals."

"How far away?"

"They are both on this side of the river. Close enough. They'll find us if they want to."

Blorfindel saw one of them moving down the riverbank towards them with its head down. He drew his arrow.

"What are you doing? Wait! Don't shoot them! I want to talk to them."

"Talk to them? Wolves don't talk." All of the Timbles that Blorfindel had ever met considered wolves to be a danger to be driven off with slings or killed in traps.

"Sure they do, you just don't speak the language."

The second wolf came into view. It was to the east and closing rapidly. Nickadola began speaking in a language that Blorfindel did not know. *That does not sound like a wolf*, the Fitheran thought. Blorfindel took his eyes off the wolves for a second to see what the Timble was doing. He was waiving a dried leaf around in the air and still speaking gibberish. Then true to his word, he stepped forward and introduced himself to the wolves as plainly as if they were the Timbles next door. *He is insane.* Blorfindel drew his arrow to full length and took aim at the nearest wolf.

The wolf stopped and watched Nickadola, prancing nervously left and right. Blorfindel did not shoot because he could not anticipate where it was going to be.

"Will you put your bow away? You're making them nervous."

"Are you sure it's not you making them hungry?" Blorfindel said, but he thought, *He probably looks like a midnight snack to a pair of wolves.*

"Put it down! I haven't got much time. You're in no danger now."

That, at least, appeared to be true. Both wolves were now about forty feet away from the Timble and they were paying very little attention to Blorfindel. "Cruska!" He pointed the arrow down and relaxed his draw.

Nickadola seemed to think that he was having a conversation with the wolves. "Are you hunting tonight?" Then he would pause as if there was a response.

"How did you get separated?" Again he paused.

"How many Kutel?"

"How many in your pack?"

"I'm very sorry. We are going to fight the Kutel, would you like to join us?"

"But my friend has a bow, too. They can't fight us like they fight you. If it doesn't work you can run away again."

"Come and rest. I have some fish leftover. It's not much, but you can have all there is. We will get some more in the morning. You should get a drink from the river anyway."

"Yes, we'll rest together tonight, like a pack. Tomorrow we'll talk again." Nickadola turned his back to them and walked back to his sleeping bush.

Blorfindel stood slack-jawed. *Why did they not attack? Why not attack now, while his back is turned?* He spoke in amazement, "What's going on?"

"Kutel attacked their pack tonight. They shot most of them with black arrows, including Alpha and the Matriarch. They took the pups from the den. These two got away." Nickadola's voice broke. He was crying. It was as if he was recounting the greatest tragedy he had ever heard. "They're frightened and hungry. The Kutel were following them and keeping them apart most of the night. They just got together."

"Can you really talk to them?"

"Of course. What did you think that was? It's a spell. I thought Fitherani knew all about magic."

"I don't know. It looked strange to me. I mean, I've seen magic, but it's different."

"There are different types of magic. I am a follower of Dhu, Protector of the Innocent. He gives me spells to help me do his work."

As Blorfindel came to believe that the conversation really happened, he re-thought the story. Anger started to burn in him. "So the Kutel attacked them where they live, killed the defenders, stole the young, and these two had to run away to escape with their lives."

"Yes." Nickadola was unwrapping the leftover fish while the wolves nuzzled him.

"Story of my life." *I wonder if they feel like Jerhalli Quickshanks and Michido Lightshoe? I wonder what's happening to the pups? Do the Kutel make slaves of wolves, too?* Blorfindel's voice had steel in it when he spoke, "Tell them that we'll get the pups back."

"I can't. The spell is over. I'll have to tell them in the morning." He broke the leftover fish in half and gave each to a wolf. It was gone instantly. He stroked each of them under the chin and they went off to the river to drink. "Why the sudden change in attitude? You were ready to shoot them yourself a minute ago."

"It really is the story of my life. My village was attacked, only a few Fitherani escaped. I was taken prisoner by the Kutel when I was eighty-seven – a child – a pup by wolf reckoning. It was different, but the same, you know?"

"I'm sorry. I didn't know."

"I had to be rescued. One of the Tafers of Dath saved me from a bunch of Kutel and took me in. Those pups, they have to be rescued, too. I think I have to do it. I owe it to... the world?" Blorfindel did not really understand why, but he believed it.

"I should have known that there was more to the story when you didn't know the way to Dath."

"That came later. I was hit in the head and carried off. The next town I remember was The Hunt. I don't really know which way it was." Blorfindel did not really want to tell his whole story. He changed the topic. "Why do the Kutel want the wolf pups, anyway?"

"They will raise them – train them in a Kutel way. They keep them for battle. It does something to their minds, they aren't really wolves after that."

Blorfindel asked, "How long does it take?"

"I don't know. Months, I expect – it's not going to happen tonight. We should take watches. The Kutel may still be tracking these two."

Blorfindel climbed a few branches up the tree. "You go to sleep. They may be your friends and all, but I don't think I'll get much rest with two hungry wolves around."

"They'll be fine."

"And so will I. I'll be right here in this tree. If the Kutel come looking I'll see them long before they see us." Blorfindel pulled his bow and quivers up after him on a cord. He was used to spending the predawn hours in a tree. He had done this many times while hunting.

The first ray of dawn seemed to wake the Timble. "Have you been up all night? I can watch for a while if you want to get some rest."

"It's only been a couple of hours since the howling woke us. Besides, we need to get some food for the wolves before they forget who their friends are." As he spoke a rabbit stood up on top of its hole and sniffed the morning air. Blorfindel drew an arrow. "Are rabbits your friends, too, or can we feed them to the wolves?"

"Wolves eat rabbits. It's the natural order of things."

The arrow struck the rabbit before Blorfindel spoke again. "So that means I can shoot it, right?"

Nickadola laughed. "What difference does it make now? Did you miss?"

Blorfindel was climbing down. He was also a little insulted. "I did not miss. How many rabbits is it going to take?"

"They'll eat all you get, I expect. Two rabbits each would be a decent breakfast, though four might make you more comfortable around them."

An hour later Blorfindel returned with five rabbits, two pheasant and a crow. He lost one arrow trying to take another crow in flight. "Share as you like, but one of the pheasants is my breakfast."

"You're that hungry?"

"Well, maybe I'll have something left over for the wolves. You know, this is great small-game country."

"Why don't you get some sleep while I cook the pheasants? I should have got a fire going, I guess."

Blorfindel looked at the wolves tearing into the rabbits. He thought, *I hope they remember where it came from.* He lay down under the tree again. "Save the feathers if you can."

"Of course."

Nickadola had to wake Blorfindel when the birds were cooked. "I'm sorry, I don't think I really got the fire hot enough. They dried out a bit."

The wolves were both lying nearby watching the meat with intent. Blorfindel scolded them. "You've already had yours!" The pheasant was quite good. Nickadola had picked some wild herbs nearby and even had a little breadcrumb stuffing from the dry bread in their traveling rations. Nickadola gave more than half of his pheasant to the wolves. Blorfindel had very little left over. When he finally gave up the scraps he said, "Let's go find those Kutel while it's daylight."

"Wouldn't it be easier to sneak up on them in the dark?"

Blorfindel recited from his lessons: "Kutel don't like daylight. It hurts their eyes and blurs their vision. They don't look around as much and most of them will sleep by day. They are much more dangerous in the dark." He went to the river to wash and drink. "Can the wolves follow them?"

"We had a little talk while you were sleeping. They will come with us. They should be able to follow the Kutel by scent."

"Did they tell you how many Kutel?"

Nickadola winced a little. "At least fifteen. Maybe twenty-one."

"We better catch them sleeping," Blorfindel said. "I can't shoot twenty-one Kutel before they overrun us. They don't fight well in the daylight, but they're not blind."

"We just sneak into their camp and sneak away with the pups. Oh, and remember the wolves are afraid of bows. Try not to spook them again."

"I never thought a wolf would be afraid of me."

"You don't know much about wolves."

Blorfindel thought to himself, *I don't know much about anything. I need to learn a lot to make sense of this.*

They packed up and started walking north. It was clear that the wolves wanted to go faster than the Timble could walk. "They're big enough to carry you," Blorfindel suggested.

"They're wolves, not ponies."

They walked at the Timble's pace all morning and into the afternoon. They moved north and east, following the wolves. Trees grew closer together here and the forest rose above them to the north. The wolves became more animated as they approached a thick stand of old trees. Suddenly a flock of crows flew out of their shade. The birds made one half circle and went back in.

"You know what makes crows gather?" Blorfindel asked grimly.

"Carrion. It's the den. The Kutel will have left a mess."

"It's also a nice, dark place on a bright, sunny day," Blorfindel thought out loud. "The Kutel may still be there."

"Something disturbed the crows."

Blorfindel unslung his pack. "At least one Kutel is moving."

Nickadola looked the Fitheran over. "How stealthy do you feel?"

Blorfindel laughed. "If I can't sneak up on a Kutel in the daylight, I might as well turn around and go back."

They both moved through the undergrowth toward the den. The Timble made no more noise that the Fitheran as they approached. Nickadola could move faster in the short cover because he did not have to crawl to stay low. Blorfindel more than made up for it when he could put a few trees between himself and the den. Still, they took nearly an hour to close five hundred yards. The wolves followed.

Blorfindel spotted a Kutel. *That must be a sentry.* He signed to Nickadola that he had eyes on one Kutel. He had to repeat himself. *Maybe Timbles use different signs.* Blorfindel continued to close unseen on the Kutel. *I can put an arrow in him from here, but if there is another sentry he might see this one fall.*

The sentry got up and walked back into the trees. Blorfindel used the opportunity to dash to a tree on the edge of the grove. *I can shoot from here.* Nickadola did not dash, but was still moving slowly and silently closer. Blorfindel heard a Kutel speak, "Your turn for watch." Blorfindel had been taught the Kutel language as a child.

"Too early. You're lazy."

"Get up or I'll piss in your mouth!"

"You have to sleep too, stupid. I'll get you then! Cruska! I'm awake now anyway."

Blorfindel smiled. *Only one on watch at a time, unless the other watch changed quietly? Probably just one.* He waited for the sentry to settle and the other Kutel to fall asleep. The sentry walked toward the edge of the trees to relieve himself. *That is just too easy.* Blorfindel shot an arrow through its throat. The only sound the Kutel made was kicking in the wet leaves.

They better all be asleep. Blorfindel moved quickly into the camp. He drew his sword when he found the sleeping Kutel. Suddenly one of the Kutel sat up. Before Blorfindel could react one of the wolves dashed in and tore its throat open. A fountain of dark blood sprayed across the sleeping Kutel, disturbing their sleep. *So the stealth plan did not work.* Blorfindel moved through the camp killing prone Kutel quickly as he could. Some were waking, some were fast asleep. The wolves were less neat and methodical, but no less deadly. He quickly lost count of how many Kutel had died.

One of the Kutel stood up and raised a sword. Nickadola's sling howled through the air. A lead sling bullet hit the Kutel in the forehead, knocking it off its feet. One of the wolves jumped on it and it did not rise again.

Two more stood up. One went down with a sling bullet and a wolf. The other shouted, "Fitheran!" and jumped at Blorfindel with a back iron mace. Blorfindel was not there when the mace fell. He was already behind the Kutel and his backhanded slash opened a cut on the Kutel's thigh. The Kutel spun around and swung the mace in a wild arc. Blorfindel leapt back out of reach until the mace past, then his leg uncoiled like a spring as he thrust his sword point through the Kutel's hide armor and into its chest. Blorfindel retracted the sword almost as quickly. The Kutel was still spinning from its the wild attack when it hit the ground.

Blorfindel turned to see that the last three Kutel were on their feet. One had a sling bullet bounce off its armor as it drew a sword. The other two were using spears to keep the wolves at bay. Blorfindel tossed his bow out of the way and drew his dagger with his left hand. The sword-Kutel smiled cruelly. Blorfindel knew that he would be fighting for his life, but so would the Kutel. *What have you got to smile about?* He closed on it with caution.

It thrust at the Fitheran. Blorfindel felt himself moving as though his body knew how to fight better than his mind did. Hours and weeks and years of training animated his muscles to fight more quickly than even Blorfindel could imagine. He turned the Kutel's sword with his dagger and flicked his own sword point across the Kutel's face. It flinched out of the way and used a wild slash to force Blorfindel to step back. It recovered quickly and slashed up toward the Fitheran's armpit. Blorfindel spun around to the left to turn the sword with his own and tried to slash around with his dagger at the Kutel's neck in the same motion. The Kutel threw himself at the Fitheran when his back was turned and instead of cutting the Kutel's throat Blorfindel struck it in the side of the head with his elbow. This did no harm to the thick-skulled Kutel but Blorfindel's hand went numb and he dropped his dagger. The Kutel had launched his shoulder into the Fitheran, intending to overbear him and take him to the ground. Blorfindel simply continued his spin and landed on his feet. Off balance, the Kutel landed heavily on its right shoulder.

A sling bullet went by and hit one of the other Kutel.

Blorfindel stabbed down at the Kutel on the ground but it rolled away. Instead of following it he made a flying lunge at one of the spear-Kutel who was occupied by a wolf. Dropping to one knee he thrust his sword under its armor and deep into its side. Now that one spear was out of the way, the wolf leapt at the back of the other spear-Kutel. To Blorfindel, everything seemed to be happening at once.

The sword-Kutel rolled to his feet and tried to lunge at Blorfindel. It was hit in the thigh by a sling bullet, forcing it to skip just to keep its feet. Blorfindel pulled his sword from the dying spear-Kutel and struck the sword-Kutel in the face with the pommel in the same motion. When Blorfindel came on-guard the Kutel was looking over its shoulder at Nickadola. Blorfindel waited just the tiniest moment. When the Kutel turned its head to face him, Blorfindel thrust his sword point into its right eye socket until it hit the back of the Kutel's skull.

Blorfindel withdrew his sword and looked around. The wolves were still tearing at one of the Kutel, but it clearly would never recover. The others were dead or dying. The crows settled on the carcasses almost immediately.

Blorfindel recovered his dagger and heard a faint whining over the growling and the groaning. "The pups are here!"

Nickadola came running. "Stay away from them! They're probably scared to death!"

Blorfindel cut a relatively clean strip of cloth from a Kutel's tattered blanket to clean the blood off his sword. "You're the expert."

While Nickadola and the wolves looked after the pups, Blorfindel went over the bodies. The sentry had broken his arrow thrashing around on the ground. The Kutel had some arrows, but Blorfindel did not want to take any of their poisoned shafts. He used them to start a fire, instead. He found three wolf pelts in good condition and set them aside. He also collected the Kutel weapons and made a pile of them. Most of the Kutel also had some coins. He counted them out and divided them into two piles on one of the pelts.

The ferocity and pace of battle was waning from him. He fought to keep from shaking. His mind caught up with him again. He looked at the pile of weapons, then over the crow covered corpses. *This is about as ugly as it gets. Should I be sick or something? I do not feel anything. I should feel something.* He walked around again and counted the corpses. There were eighteen dead Kutel, though two were not fresh kills. *So we just killed sixteen Kutel, most of them in their sleep. Is not that wrong? Should I feel guilty?* There were also the remains of eight wolves. The Kutel had skinned and butchered them. He looked away. *Why do I feel badly for the wolves and not for the Kutel?*

Blorfindel was absentmindedly putting a spiked club and a spear shaft on the fire when Nickadola returned with the two adult wolves and five pups. "I don't feel anything. I just murdered all those Kutel. Shouldn't I feel something?"

"Triumphant? Victorious? This isn't murder. This is war."

"What's the difference?"

"The eagle kills the snake, or the snake eats the eggs. You kill them so that they can't kill you. The Kutel would hurt you if they could. Did you hear that one with the mace when he saw you? He didn't care about me or the wolves, he didn't care about self-defense or any of his fallen comrades, he wanted to kill a Fitheran. They killed all of these wolves. They'll be killing Tafers in Dath soon if no one does anything about it. The Kutel chose their side long ago, we can either fight against them or be their victims. There really aren't any other choices."

"Why don't they just leave us all alone?" Blorfindel glanced over the corpses again. "They keep dying. Don't any of them think, 'Hey, maybe I shouldn't go fight?'"

"I don't know. Kutel are pretty vicious. Maybe some of them don't want to fight, but the rest make them anyway. I don't think a softhearted Kutel would live long enough to grow up. They kill their own young if they aren't vicious enough, or tough enough, or whatever. The Kutel are born to destroy. If they aren't stopped, they will keep on destroying."

"How many Kutel have you killed?"

"I don't know. I think that one that I hit in the head over there was dead before the wolf jumped on him, maybe. You got one with an arrow, right? You got two by yourself, if you don't count the sleeping ones."

"That's right, you distracted the one with the sword, so that was two-on-one. This is your first battle?"

"Yes, but it worked! We must have killed a dozen Kutel among the four of us!"

Blorfindel spoke as if to the fire. "Sixteen."

"Sixteen, really? That's great! Just think about how much havoc sixteen Kutel could be causing in Dath tonight."

"I guess so."

"And just look at these little guys." He picked up one of the pups. "We couldn't just leave these guys with the Kutel, could we?"

"They are pretty cute." Blorfindel reached out to pat the pup. One of the adult wolves growled and Blorfindel retracted his hand as if he had been bitten. "All right, hands off, I get it." He turned back to Nickadola, "You'd better put that pup down before you hurt yourself. It's nearly as big as you are."

"I'm not as weak as I am small." He put the pup down anyway. "I was afraid they might be too small for solid food, but they'll be fine. I'll just have to cut it up small." He walked over to one of the Kutel and cut it open from the buttock to the back of its knee. The pups wandered over and watched curiously as he cut off small pieces of meat.

"You're going to feed them Kutel?"

"Why not? It's fresh. You think we should leave it all for the crows?"

Blorfindel set one of the Kutel shields down next to the Timble. "You can use it for a cutting board. I'll be over there finding something else to look at."

"Wait. Help me cut this up. We need to feed them and get out of here. These Kutel may be missed, and I don't want to be here for the third ambush at this den in the last two days."

They kept cutting meat well after the pups had lost interest in the food. They packed it into one of the sacks that the Kutel had used for packs. Blorfindel rolled up the Kutel weapons that looked valuable in the wolf pelts and put them across his shoulders.

"Isn't that heavy?" Nickadola said as he slung the bag of fresh Kutel meat over his own pack.

"Yes, but some of these swords are worth sixty stowsaw. Oh, yeah, and I have some money for you, too – from the Kutel." He started walking west toward the river and Dath.

Nickadola walked beside him. "We won't get anywhere near sixty for a Kutel sword. Still, it's all money. I wonder if bullets and arrows count as 'reasonable expenses'?"

"I guess we'll find out. Can we make it to Dath this afternoon?"

"I don't know. They look like fuzzy bundles of energy right now, but the pups will get tired quickly."

"Are they going with us to Dath?"

Nickadola walked backwards to face Blorfindel when he asked, "What else are we going to do with them?"

"They're not going to be very popular with the farmers. I mean, the pups we might get by with, but two wolves? I don't know."

"They better get used to the idea." The Timble turned to walk forward. "The notice says room and board for Kutel fighters and they qualify."

Fatigue mounted on the pups quickly. Before long the adult wolves were carrying them in shifts. When they got to the river Nickadola called a halt. "We're running them into the ground."

Blorfindel dropped the bundle of weapons and started to unstrap his pack. "I'm ready for a break." His voice sounded exhausted.

The Timble offered some of the meat to the pups but they all preferred sleep. "We're not going to get to Dath today."

Blorfindel looked up at the sun. "The Kutel will be out after the horizon crosses the sun. If they find us out here by the riverbank they'll have us surrounded pretty quickly. Are we ten miles away from the battle site?"

The Timble shook his head Tafer-style. "Maybe seven. Why don't we let them sleep for a while and head for Dath after sunset? The Kutel won't instantly appear as soon as it gets dark."

"You might as well get some sleep, too," Blorfindel said, "I'll wake you for the sunset."

"You should sleep, too. You stood watch last night.

"Wake me half way."

The trees and meadows ignored them as they rested by the riverbank. Blorfindel put a small bag with half of the Kutels' coin next to Nickadola. He was already asleep. Blorfindel tried to figure out how much money he should be able to make from the Kutel weapons, but he kept rethinking his estimates. He woke Nickadola after his turn at watch and lay down on the wolf pelts in the sun.

Blorfindel had missed the best part of the sunset by the time Nickadola woke him. The Timble shrugged, "I thought you'd rather sleep."

Blorfindel stared out over the river. "When the sun sets over the river in the spring, it's worth missing some sleep."

Chapter 2

Lantid and Alehra

They packed up and headed up the river in twilight. It was three tedious miles to the first farms of Dath. More eyes than candlelight peered out through shuttered windows. No one was on the paths or streets. It was another two miles before the buildings drew close enough to call it a village.

Blorfindel startled Nickadola and the wolves by dropping the Kutel weapons in the street. A torch came around a corner ahead. Blorfindel shot two arrows into the torch bearer before Nickadola realized it was a Kutel.

"I thought the Kutel didn't need torches."

"They don't need them to see. They need them to light fires." Blorfindel shrugged off his pack and readied another arrow. The sputtering torchlight ruined his night vision but he could hear running steps coming closer. *Are you Kutel or Tafers?* A Kutel stepped into the light and tried to pick up the torch on the run. Blorfindel's arrow grazed off its back. Nickadola's bullet rang off its helmet and it went down hard. It fell on the torch and did not lift itself. Blorfindel could hear it sizzle.

The footsteps were closing faster than the Fitheran's eyes were adjusting. Figures were closing but he could not tell whether they were Kutel or Tafers. The silhouettes were too similar. He set his bow down on his pack and drew sword and dagger.

Nickadola readied his scimitar and shield. He stood in front of the pups and shouted, "The Shield!"

The first one to come was a Kutel. It tried to hack the Fitheran with a battle axe as it ran past. Blorfindel ducked under the clumsy swing and laid its thigh open with his sword. One of the wolves jumped it as it stumbled.

A light appeared from down the street but it gave them only more silhouettes, and there were a lot of silhouettes. It was not a torch, but a lamp of some kind. The light was coming closer, too. Someone else shouted, "Dath and The Shield!" The voice sounded like a Tafer. Blorfindel could hear metal armor ringing on some of the runners.

The next four figures were all Kutel. The first one tried to run past to the right of Blorfindel. The Fitheran swung his sword at its knees as it went by. It jumped over his blade but landed shield-down with its face in the street. A wolf jumped on it instantly.

The next Kutel was coming straight for him with a sword raised over its head. The Fitheran lunged at the Kutel with his dagger and shouted, "Foralis!" The Kutel brought its shield up, but Blorfindel struck with such force that the heavy dagger burst through the wooden shield and into the Kutel's hide armor. The dagger did no harm but stopped the foe cold. The Kutel's sword went over Blorfindel's back and struck his armor. It did not have enough force to penetrate.

A Kutel with a mace tried to run down Nickadola. Two quick passes with the scimitar made it stop and reconsider. It smashed down with its mace but the Timble turned the blow on his shield.

The next Kutel had been trying to run around the battle to its left. When it heard Blorfindel shout it stopped and tried to stab him with a spear. Blorfindel turned the spear with his sword but it still came close enough to trace a line across his armor. The next silhouette stuck a sword into the spear Kutel's back. *That must be a Tafer.*

Blorfindel kicked against the sword Kutel's shield and withdrew his dagger. In doing so he sent the spear from the now-dead Kutel clumsily into the air. The Kutel knocked it away with his sword and squared off against Blorfindel. It smiled for just a moment before a Tafer arrived behind it and split its helmet and skull with a single blow of a heavy sword.

Blorfindel stuck his dagger at the Kutel with the mace. It was watching Nickadola, but it was moving and its shield got in the dagger's path. When it felt the attack the Kutel turned to see Blorfindel. Nickadola slashed his scimitar up between its legs as soon as it turned away. Mercifully, a wolf jumped on it and killed it quickly.

Blorfindel looked around. None of the Kutel were still standing. A lantern was sitting on the street about sixty yards away. A Tafer was kneeling in front of it. He looked almost like a skeleton or a wraith in the strange light. A number of Kutel lay on the street. Blorfindel watched the Tafer cut one of their throats with a dagger. The Tafer got up and moved to another Kutel and shouted as he went, "Give me a hand! <wheeze> They'll wake up in minute!"

Blorfindel jogged toward the prone Kutel, as did the figure in the shadows to his right. Blorfindel looked over to see who had saved him from the spear-Kutel. "You're a Taforam!"

"You were expecting maybe a Fitheresse?"

"A Tafer?"

"Most of the Tafers in this town aren't worth a pinch of salt in the driving rain – present company excluded, of course," she said.

The Tafer with the dagger wasn't paying attention, anyway. "Take one alive <wheeze> for questioning."

The Taforam drove her sword into the back of one of the Kutel as he spoke. It convulsed and then lay still. "Not this one."

Blorfindel walked up to one of the Kutel. It was snoring. He kicked its sword away from its limp hand then sheathed his own sword. "What should I do with it?"

"Tie it up." The Tafer cut another Kutel's throat. "We'll kill the rest."

Blorfindel cut the shield straps off the Kutel's arm and sheathed his dagger. He shouted to the Timble, "Nickadola! could you bring me the rope out of my pack, please?" The Kutel did not wake up. He shrugged and pulled its clawed hands together behind its back. That woke the Kutel. It struggled to its feet and tried to pull its hands free.

"Al, give him a hand! <wheeze> He's not going to be able to hold it!"

Blorfindel put his shoulder between the Kutel's shoulder blades and ran it face first into a wall. "I've got it!" He held both of its wrists and pressed it into the wall with his shoulder. He held the squirming Kutel there until Nickadola arrived with the rope.

The Timble coiled the rope around the Kutel's wrists. "Be a good boy and you might be alive when the sun rises."

"I don't think it speaks Shield." Blorfindel shoved his shoulder in harder and repeated the sentence in Kutel.

"I don't think he can breathe like that."

"After you've got its hands and feet tied I'll let it breathe again."

"What if I take too long with the knots?"

"Then we don't get to question this one."

When the ropes were secure Blorfindel stepped back and let the Kutel fall to the ground. It gasped and started coughing.

"What did you do to it?" the Tafer with the lantern wanted to know, "It's coughing up blood. <wheeze> It may not live long enough to question."

Blorfindel shrugged. "It's just from its nose. Once it remembers how to breathe properly it will be fine."

The Tafer with the broad sword walked over to them. He kept looking over his shoulder at the wolves. They ignored him and stayed with the pups where the battle began. "I am Terak, Shieldmaster of Dath."

"Blorfindel Brighteyes, at your service." Blorfindel used his stage bow.

The Tafer with the lantern and the dagger said, "Brighteyes? Don't say that in Kingstone."

"I'll try to remember that."

The Taforam asked, "Why not?"

Shieldmaster Terak ignored her. "Have you come to help fight the Kutel? You seem to have arrived at a good time."

Nickadola waved the notice from his belt. "Yes, we're here to help. I am Nickadola Bretritich." He held out his hand.

The Taforam took his hand and shook it. "I'm Alehra. Call me Al." She pulled her sword from a dead Kutel. It was long and light like the Fitheran's. She wore a mail shirt and a round shield that was much broader than she. Two daggers and a war hammer hung from her belt. She seemed to notice Blorfindel's gear at the same time. She laughed. "We'll have to be careful not to get our weapons confused." Brown hair hung down in a single braid from under her oddly-shaped helmet. Her clear, bright, brown eyes looked out of place on her blood-smeared face. In another guise she might have been pretty.

The Tafer with the lantern wiped his small dagger off on the struggling Kutel and sheathed it. "I'm Lantid." He wore a tan robe of undyed wool which hung from him as if he were a cloak-peg. He was only an inch or two taller than Blorfindel and he looked like he might weigh no more than the Fitheran. His black hair was haphazardly shorn at his neck. His cheeks were dark and sunken which contrasted with his otherwise pale skin. His brown eyes looked almost like burn holes in his face. The lantern light flickered as he coughed a deep, dry cough. If he had introduced himself as a vampire, Blorfindel would hardly have been surprised.

Nickadola turned to the Shieldmaster and said, "It's been a long day for us, and the pups are exhausted. Is there someplace where we can get some rest?"

"Alehra, Lantid, show them to the barn. Bring your prisoner, too. I'll get some people to clean up this mess."

Alehra objected. "Hey! We're entitled to the spoils – all of us, I guess."

Shieldmaster Terak sighed impatiently. "I'll see that you get them."

Lantid said in way of apology, "She's Mikenuran. You get used to her."

Blorfindel asked, "What does that mean?"

Alehra laughed and walked with them to their bundles. "Nothing, as far as he knows. I'm from Mikenura. He thinks that I'm some kind of barbarian, but he doesn't know what he's talking about." Lantid was guarding the Kutel. She had to shout the last part to be certain that he heard it.

Blorfindel did not know anything about Mikenura, but he did not want to sound stupid by asking. Nickadola had no such problem. "Where's Mikenura?"

"If you could go west over The Spine you might get there. I came north around the Hollenwae and Kutel lands by ship."

"What brings you here?"

"Same as you, I expect: too much curiosity for my own good."

Blorfindel joined in, "Not me. I just need to get enough money together to get married."

"That's commitment for you. How long does a Fitheran marriage last? A thousand years?"

"More, I hope."

"Damn! Tafers don't know any more about commitment than these wolves."

Nickadola corrected her, "Actually, wolves mate for life."

"Lucky bitches."

Blorfindel and Nickadola gathered their things. Nickadola asked, "So you and Lantid aren't together, then?"

"Lantid? No. He's a brave guy and all, but damn!" She shook her head as if Blorfindel and Nickadola should understand. She gestured to Blorfindel's bundle. "Do you need a hand with that?"

"I've brought it this far."

"Anyway, I don't think Lantid is going to live long one way or the other. I try not to talk about it with him, but that cough is pretty bad. I think he's just decided that he'd rather die fighting Kutel than die in bed."

"Maybe I shouldn't be the one to talk," Nickadola said, "but he doesn't look like much of a fighter."

"He isn't, but he'll flick his throwing knives in whenever he gets a chance, and it was his sleep spell that stopped most of the Kutel – well, a bunch of them, anyway."

"So it was magic. I thought there were a lot more of them running at us."

"They were running away from us. We thought we were driving them out of town. We didn't expect you to be here."

"All of those Kutel were running away from the three of you?"

"Pretty stupid, huh? We jumped three of them and one got away. It ran screaming something. Anyway, the Kutel that heard it turned and ran, too. The crowd of them just kept getting bigger. We probably wouldn't have chased if we had known how many there were. Until tonight, they had been coming to town in twos and threes." They rejoined Lantid at the captive Kutel. Alehra untied its feet and took up the rope which was still tied to its wrists. She pulled its wrists up behind its back until it got to its feet. "This way." She pointed over its shoulder with her sword. It just stood there.

Blorfindel barked out in Kutel, "Walk!" It stumbled forward.

Lantid walked beside it with his dagger in one hand and the lantern in the other. "I was kind-of counting on the idea that you spoke Kutel. <Cough, cough> All Fitherani do, don't they?"

Blorfindel nodded. "I learned Kutel when I was a kid."

Alehra said, "So you're an archer?"

Lantid answered before Blorfindel, "Of course he's an archer! Don't be rude! It's insulting to a Fitheran to even ask."

"Maybe here it is. The Fitherani of Sekri Tao don't care."

Blorfindel was surprised to hear the name. "You've been to Sekri Tao?"

"No, but I know some Fitherani from there. My bow's from there – you'll see when we get to the barn."

"There has been no contact between Sekri Timbrali and Sekri Tao for so long we weren't sure if it still existed."

"Are you from Sekri Timbrali?"

Blorfindel sighed. "No, I'm from Foralis."

"Where's that?"

"About twenty miles east of here. The Kutel burned it almost a century ago."

"Damn."

The nearest barn to the center of town had been partially given over to the Kutel fighters. The animals inside panicked and bolted as soon as the wolves came to the door. The slowest was a gray goat. One of the wolves caught it by the throat and dragged it back in.

"The farmer's not going to be happy," Alehra observed.

Nickadola said, "Room and board for Kutel fighters, right?"

Lantid smiled. "I can't wait to hear Terak explain that to the farmer. <wheeze> The best sleeping is in the loft, though I guess the animals won't bother us in the night anymore." He made a cough that might have been a laugh.

Blorfindel carried his bundle into the loft and unrolled it.

Lantid hung the lantern from the rafters. "Hey, that's a pretty good haul. Where'd you get that?" While Blorfindel told them about the earlier battle, Nickadola used the pelts to make a place for the pups to sleep on the barn floor. When he was done Lantid said, "You should do pretty well. Terak has a bounty of sorts on Kutel weapons – I guess he'd rather pay for them than let more Kutel get them."

Alehra took the free end of the rope and ran it over a beam. The Kutel was bent over and nearly hanging by its arms backwards. Its head dangled forward. She pulled the rope extra tight before tying it off.

"<Cough> His arms aren't supposed to bend like that."

"What? Are you going to report me for cruelty? He'll be lucky if the wolves don't bite his stones off for a midnight snack, anyway. You're the one who wanted to keep him. He's already stinking up the barn. Who'd have thought it could get worse in here? Do you think he knows anything?"

"We might as well ask him now. <wheeze> Blorfindel, could you ask him where the Kutel camp is?"

Blorfindel climbed down to the Kutel and drew his war hammer. He used the weapon to prop the Kutel's chin up so that he could look in its eyes. They were dead-black. Even with the lamp it was dark enough in the barn that the Fitheran could see the heat flowing out of them. "Where's your camp?"

The Kutel spit a gob of blood and mucus at him. Blorfindel dodged and it missed. Alehra was impressed. "Damn, you're quick."

Blorfindel smashed the Kutel's left foot into the hard-packed dirt floor with his war hammer. The Kutel's scream distracted the wolves from their dinner for a moment. Blorfindel propped its chin up on his war hammer again. "Where's your camp?"

It was gasping for breath and crying a bit. "The boss' house."

"Where's the boss' house?"

"Outside of town."

Blorfindel stepped on the broken foot. "Which direction?"

"Don't… don't know direction."

Blorfindel turned to Lantid. "He says they camp is at the boss' house, outside of town, but he doesn't know which way."

"I bet he'd know which way to limp if we let him go. <wheeze> OK, repeat after me. Close your eyes." It did not close its eyes until after Blorfindel ground his heel in. "Now let's pretend. Pretend the boss got you up really early for a raid, and the sun is still up. You face away from the sunset because it hurts your eyes. Which way is it to town? It is over your left shoulder, or your right shoulder?"

"No shoulder. Straight ahead." Blorfindel translated verbatim.

"He's lying. They'd be on the other side of the river."

Blorfindel crushed its other foot. "This how it works. Every time you give me the wrong answer, I'm going to break something." He pushed its chin up again. "Which way to the boss' house?"

"Moonrise. Follow moonrise."

Blorfindel said, "East," to Lantid.

"How do you find it?"

"Follow the path."

"You made a path from Dath to the boss' house?"

"Tafer path, not Kutel path – very old."

"What does the boss' house look like?"

"Bigger on top than on bottom."

"Just on one side or all the way around?"

"All around."

"Kutel house?"

"Tafer house – very old. No one goes there."

"Where does the boss get water?"

"Well in the bottom of the house. I'm not allowed. I have to go to the stream."

Blorfindel had not been translating. Lantid was growing impatient, "What's he saying?"

Blorfindel continued asking the Kutel, "Are the out-buildings still standing?"

"Fall down, bent. Stupid Kutel stay in them – not smart, like me. They fall down soon."

"A barn and a smoke house?"

"I don't know! What barn? What smokehouse? Old wood leans over. Fall down soon. No smoke, no fire, just old. No roof on big one, already fall down."

Blorfindel turned to Lantid. "I know where it is."

"You've been talking long enough you should know how many windows."

"Four small ones on the first floor: two south, one east, one west. Ten on the second floor: four south, two east, two west, two north. Two more small ones in the gables east and west. The smokehouse is falling over and the roof has already caved in on the barn. There are two stone chimneys on the north side of the main house."

Lantid laughed. "Somebody give him a pen so he can draw us a floor plan."

"I think remember the floor plan."

"Now you're just fooling around. There's no way he told you the floor plan."

Blorfindel said coldly, "I lived there for six years."

Alehra was shocked. "What?"

Lantid put the pieces together quicker. "You're from around here. I forgot. So is the boss a Kutel?"

Blorfindel translated back and forth, "Yes."

"How many Kutel are there?"

Nickadola laughed, "He can't count that high."

"Ask him anyway."

The Kutel could not count that high. They discovered that the boss had five bodyguards, and that there were four groups of raiders each with its own leader. The groups were all about the same size.

"<Cough, cough> That's too many."

Alehra looked at Lantid. "How do you know? He didn't say how big the groups are."

"All the groups are the same size. So they're the same size as the one we fought tonight."

"Maybe that was more than one group?"

Nickadola agreed with Lantid, "One group. There was one group that attacked the wolves, too. Call it fifteen to twenty Kutel per group."

"That's eighty-six Kutel, worst case. We can't touch that."

Alehra was still catching up. "Eighty-six?"

"Four groups of twenty plus the boss and five guards. Blorfindel, ask him if he counted his own group in the four."

Blorfindel asked. "He did."

"So there's three left. It's still too many."

Nickadola disagreed, "He can't know about the group we killed, yet – the one with the wolves. That was just today."

"We still can't attack forty-six Kutel. That's almost twelve to one."

"Eight to one." Nickadola gestured toward the wolves.

"What about Terak?" Alehra wanted to know.

"He'll never leave the town undefended. <Wheeze> It doesn't matter, getting it down to six or seven to one is still not good enough. <Cough, cough>"

Blorfindel asked, "He should be able to get help from the king, though, right?"

"The King <wheeze> isn't sending help to Dath, at least not soon. The Kutel are pressing hard at The Hunt and Eastower. <Wheeze> The Putnu even landed a handful of ships on the coast near Silverport." He was unable to continue due to a coughing fit.

Alehra commented, "I don't think the King of The Shield Valley cares very much about Dath right now. What's a hundred farmers to him?"

"Putnu?" Nickadola was confused. "That's just Kutel for pimple, right? Who landed near Silverport?"

Alehra answered, "Putnu are little Kutel – sort of. A big Putnu is four feet tall. They're weaker and maybe even dumber than Kutel except for one thing: they understand ships pretty well. Back home we have more trouble with Putnu than Kutel since they can sail around the point."

Blorfindel asked, "So what do we do about the forty Kutel up the road?"

Lantid suggested, "We could try to attack the camp while the raiders are away."

Nickadola did not like that idea. "They'd be here burning Dath while we're attacking their camp. It's a bad trade."

"Ask the Kutel if they have a shaman, or any kind of spell-caster."

Blorfindel asked. They did not.

"Why do they come in four raiding groups? Why not all together? The town would be crushed."

Blorfindel did not bother to ask the Kutel. "They can't stand each other. They fight too much among themselves."

"You didn't ask him."

"You didn't listen to him describe the other groups."

Nickadola said, "We have to keep picking off one group at a time, maybe even part of a group if we can. I don't think we want to face the boss and his bodyguards with even another ten Kutel backing them up. They've got to be the toughest Kutel for miles around."

Alehra added, "Lantid can just knock 'em out with his spell. I bet they're not so tough when they're asleep."

"It doesn't work like that. The spell works great on rank-and-file dimwits like this one, <wheeze> but not so good on bigger, smarter, or tougher things. Besides, they would all have to be pretty close to each other."

Nickadola asked, "How often can you cast the spell?"

"I might survive casting it twice in the same day. There would have to be six hours in between for me to even have a chance."

Alehra drew her sword. "Do we have any more questions for this one?"

Nickadola and Lantid looked at each other. They both shook their head, "No."

Blorfindel said, "Wait! Don't kill it!" and headed up the ladder to the loft.

Lantid tried to reason with him. "What else are we going to do with it? We can't just let it go, and we can't keep it prisoner."

Nickadola agreed, "Even if we did let it go, it wouldn't last long with two broken feet. The Kutel won't nurse it back to health."

Lantid picked up where Nickadola left off. "If they did it would just come back here with another one of the raiding parties."

Nickadola took over again. "Kutel can't be reformed. They are born evil. It's not like a Tafer who can choose to be good if it wants to. They were created to be evil from the beginning."

Alehra was curious. "What do you mean, they were created evil?"

Nickadola answered, "Many of the things that are were created for good or evil, for order or chaos in the beginning. Each of the gods made their own puppets and they had absolute control over them. After a few generations some things started to drift away from their original purpose. The great wolves of order eventually became wolves as we know them today. When this sort of thing happened the creator gods tried to destroy them. This is when Dhu made his presence known. Dhu is The Protector Of The Innocent. He protected these rebel creatures so that they could grow into whatever best suited them without the influence of the other gods. The Kutel have not broken free from their creator, nor have the Fitherani, for that matter. Baett made the Kutel to hate – especially to destroy the Fitherani and this still lives in their minds. So you see, Blorfindel, there is no helping the Kutel. If they overflow into the world around their lands they simply have to be destroyed."

Blorfindel descended the ladder with a Kutel battleaxe. "We can still make it quick, right?" Without waiting for an answer he swung the axe in a great arc and struck the Kutel on the back of neck nearly severing its head.

Lantid coughed, "Oh, that's fine. Could you clean that up, please?"

Blorfindel and Alehra dragged the corpse out the barn and out of town. Shieldmaster Terak was in the barn when they returned. He was counting out coins. "Two hundred fifteen stowsaw, sixty-four ardiv – that includes the value of their arms."

"What about expenses?" Nickadola wanted to know, "I've lost half a dozen sling bullets, and Blorfindel has got to be missing some arrows."

"And he should get a patch sown on the back of his armor," Alehra added.

Terak held up his hands. "We can handle that in the morning, right?"

Nickadola did not let it go, "I'd hate to run out of bullets if the Kutel attack again tonight."

Terak gave up. "Six lead sling bullets and how many arrows?"

"Four – no, five. Thirty inch draw, please."

"I'll see what I can do."

Blorfindel added, "What about the weapons we got from the other band of Kutel?"

"That can definitely wait until morning."

"But you'll buy them, right?"

"Yes. I have a standard schedule for redeeming Kutel weapons, so make certain that you collect them all. Did you learn anything from your prisoner?" The bloodstain on the floor was obvious enough.

Lantid answered, "We know where their base is now."

"It's probably a trap, or at least a lie," the Sheildmaster said.

"I don't think so. Blorfindel recognized the place."

"Been doing some reconnaissance?"

Blorfindel shrugged, "I used to live there."

"What? You lived at the Kutel camp?" Terak did not believe it. "They'd eat you alive."

"They're staying at Ammoss and Shandi's house."

The Shieldmaster shrugged. "Who? Those don't sound like Kutel names."

"They were Tafers. Ammoss was a great Kutel fighter. They lived in a big house outside of town. They took me in after I ran away from Foralis."

"You said that name during the battle. What's Foralis?"

"It's where I'm from. It's only twenty, twenty-five miles east of here. It hasn't even been gone for a century yet."

The Shieldmaster laughed. "Not even a whole century? How could I have forgotten? I must be getting absent-minded in my old age."

Blorfindel had not forgotten how short Tafer's lives were but he had expected some record of Foralis, or at least Ammoss, to have survived. *Foralis will be remembered.* "If Shieldmaster Roun of Dath had come to help us when the Kutel attacked, there would be a forty Fithern archers to help you now instead of just one. Perhaps you'll get that much help from your own king?"

Lantid pressed on before the sarcasm got any worse. "We may have cut their strength nearly in half today."

Again, the Shieldmaster did not believe it. "There were only fifteen, so sixteen Kutel including your captive. He told you there were less than forty Kutel? He was lying."

Nickadola said, "We got sixteen more this afternoon, and the wolves got another two last night."

"'We?' You're telling me that you and the Fitheran killed sixteen Kutel this afternoon? What do you think I'm stupid?"

The Timble shot Blorfindel a look to say, 'Don't answer that,' but the Fitheran was climbing the ladder to the loft. "Blorfindel, the wolves, and I, yes, killed sixteen Kutel this afternoon."

Blorfindel threw the pile of weapons to the floor with a crash. Terak looked at them for a moment, counting. "Just because you have their weapons… They killed each other, right? Tell the truth now. They fought among themselves and you picked up the pieces."

Blorfindel leaped from the loft. He drew his sword and dagger in the air and landed at the Shieldmaster's feet. Terak took a step back and drew his own broad sword while raising his shield. Blorfindel said, "You think because we're smaller than you that we can't fight!" but he said it in Timbrali and only Nickadola understood.

Alehra moved to break it up but the Timble waved and the wolves jumped in front of her and growled. "Let him be," Nickadola said in Shield. Alehra stopped.

Lantid tried to say something but a coughing fit stopped him.

Blorfindel feinted with his sword toward the Tafer's leg. Terak lowered his shield to parry. Blorfindel thrust high with his dagger but the Tafer caught the blade with his sword. Blorfindel lowered his hips, put his right shoulder against the Tafer's shield, and shoved with both arms and his body together. Shieldmaster Terak landed on his backside with his head against the barn door. Blorfindel stepped on his shield, guided the Tafer's sword away with his dagger, and put his own sword point to the Shieldmaster's throat. He spoke in Timbrali again, "I'm quicker than you are. I'm stronger than you are. I'm better than you are."

Nickadola repeated, "Blorfindel, the wolves, and I killed sixteen Kutel this afternoon."

Blorfindel switched languages to Shield. "If the Tafers of Dath had kept faith with us, there would be forty more Fithern archers here to take on the Kutel. We would overrun this 'boss' in a single day. Every one of my people is an archer, a priest, or a wizard. How many Tafers of Dath were in the battle tonight? Two? We're fighting for their homes and they won't even show themselves." Blorfindel took a step back.

Terak did not get up. He sat there dazed.

There was a long silence before Alehra said, "Damn! When you took the Kutel to the wall I though he was just a shingus. How strong are you?"

"I am Blorfindel Brighteyes, son of Lalliam Steelhand and the last warrior of Foralis, until we rebuild it. I am the biggest Fitheran you'll ever meet." Blorfindel's tone lightened. "What's a shingus?"

"Uh… a not-so-strong fighter, sort-of."

Nickadola said, "Not all people are built the same. The muscles on a Fitheran are different from a Tafer. He carried all of his gear plus those weapons all afternoon without slowing down, and he still fought well when we got to town."

Terak steadied himself on the door as he rose to his feet. "You've proven your point. I'm glad you're on my side, both of you, and the wolves. We'll settle up with the weapons in the morning. Good night." He slumped out the door.

Chapter 3

Ambush

Blorfindel awoke the next morning to soft, oddly high-pitched growling. He looked down from the loft to see two wolf pups pulling on the end of a green rag. The other end was tied to a piece wood which Nickadola had clenched in his own teeth. He was on his hands and knees pulling and shaking his head more than the wolves were. The Tafers were still asleep. Dust danced in the sunbeams cut by the gaps in the planking and the angle indicated that the morning was quite old.

Nickadola took the toy out of his teeth long enough to say, "Don't wake them. They kept watch all night. They took me to breakfast when I got up."

Blorfindel climbed down to the Timble before replying. "That hay is more comfortable than I thought. How's the 'board' part of the deal?"

"Basic Tafer food: last year's oats boiled with some fat. Tafers aren't very good at first meal. Maybe things get better as the day goes on."

"I wouldn't count on that." Blorfindel arranged his gear and headed out the door. Nickadola gave him directions. He was surprised to find that Sheildmaster Terak did not live in the same place that Shieldmaster Roun had.

Blorfindel got his bowl of oats cold. It was nearly hard enough to be a biscuit. Terak gave him a dozen arrows and a big, ugly wooden talisman on a green cloth strap. "It's your badge of office: to show the townsfolk that you're here to fight the Kutel." Blorfindel realized what Nickadola had been using to play with the wolf pups. "Bring in the Kutel weapons that you captured, and I'll pay you for them." He also gave Blorfindel directions to a Tafer who could patch the cut in his leather armor. There was no mention of the shoving and shouting from the night before.

Blorfindel dropped his armor off to be mended and took his breakfast north out of town. He had to do a bit of looking but before too long he found some nearly ripe raspberries to make his breakfast more palatable. Those berry bushes were on the riverbank so he had fresh water, too. He remembered Biolmi's words. *"If you're willing to put your life on the line, eat hardtack and sleep in the rain, you can make big money and do the world a favor at the same time."* I have a barn roof, oats and berries. I guess this is luxury. Maybe that is why the money is so light.

When he got back to the barn Nickadola and the Tafers were gone. He wondered if there might be trouble, but the wolves were still there. He collected the weapons and went to the Shieldmaster's house. The others were sitting in his front yard eating lunch. Allegedly there was some meat in the broth. Blorfindel declined. On his way out he split the weapon money with Nickadola and said, "Why don't we go have a look at the Kutel camp?"

"Because if they see us, we'll be in the stew." The Timble swirled the broth with a wooden spoon. Eventually a carrot turned up and he fished it out.

"I can outrun a Kutel," Blorfindel said.

"I can't."

Alehra and Lantid did not respond. Alehra's armor slowed her down too much to be sure. Lantid could only run for very short distances before he ran out of breath. There was a long pause before Alehra offered, "Maybe we could set up an ambush."

"We can't ambush forty Kutel," Nickadola and Lantid said in unison.

"What if Blorfindel sneaks up and puts an arrow in a guard, then runs away? They won't all follow him. If he does it during the day, most of them won't even be awake, right?"

Blorfindel liked the idea. "If only a few of them come, we ambush them. If they all come at once then we just run away."

Nickadola was not convinced. "Do you think this is magic stew? I still can't run that fast."

Lantid was warming to the idea. "You don't have to. It's going to take time for them to get all the Kutel together and moving in the right direction. If only the ones that are awake chase him then he leads them to us and we jump them. If he sees that there are too many, he runs back to town by a different path. They won't even know we're there."

"What if they follow him all the way to town? It would be Blorfindel and Terak trying to hold off forty or fifty Kutel."

Lantid was not ready to give up. "They may do that anyway, if they can. The boss has to know that he lost two groups. At best he'll wait out tonight to see if anyone is coming back. I know he's a Kutel, but is he stupid enough to keep losing them like this?"

Blorfindel added, "I can outrun them, for certain. They'll have to slow down to follow a track."

"They might just be smart enough to guess you came from town."

Lantid disagreed. "Why? He's a Fitheran. There are no Fitherani at Dath – at least as far as the Kutel know. So long as he doesn't run straight for town I think our odds are still good. <Cough>"

Alehra asked, "Have you got a better idea?"

Nickadola shrugged. "We can keep defending the town. That's worked so far."

She shook her head. "We got lucky last night. The Kutel got spooked and ran away from only three of us. Even so, if you hadn't shown up they probably would have lit the town on fire."

Lantid was convinced. "It's a good way to take them on less than twenty at a time. <Wheeze> Even if Blorfindel just gets one before he runs, it's something."

"What if they don't chase him?"

Blorfindel laughed. "Then I keep shooting them. I'll come back when I run out of arrows. Come on, it's no more dangerous than when we jumped the first group."

"Except there's twice as many, plus the leader and his guards." The other three just kept staring at him. "All right, all right, let's try it tomorrow."

Blorfindel was impatient. "Why not now?"

"I have to change spells. I won't be ready until tonight at the earliest, but we want to do this in daylight."

Blorfindel asked, "What do you mean, 'change spells?'"

"Every morning I prepare for the spells that I might use that day. I expected to be ambushed, not to do the ambushing."

Lantid asked, "How many do you get each day?"

"Two, and I've already used one to talk with the wolves. I'll be ready tomorrow."

Blorfindel turned to Lantid, "You only get one, right?"

Lantid shook his head. "It's different. Nickadola gets his spells from Dhu, so he has to ask for them well in advance, and the god decides how many he gets. <Cough, cough> I cast mine on my own, which is harder and takes a lot out of me, but I can choose on the spot. Part of the problem is that I have to learn my spells, so he probably has more options to choose from."

Alehra frowned. "I though all you could do was the sleep spell."

"It's my best attack against the Kutel. I mentioned it works well on stupid targets, so long as they're not too big. I have a protection spell and a fire spell, too. I also have more scholarly magic that won't help much in battle."

"On the subject of sleep," Lantid continued, "we should stay awake for the rest of the afternoon and try to sleep through as much of the night as we can." Blorfindel looked confused. "We've been sleeping days and watching nights for the Kutel."

It was the next morning. The sun was strong and the clouds were few and small. Blorfindel dashed from tree to tree. At each piece of cover he would stop and listen, then slowly look around for signs of Kutel. Finally he would pick his next tree and dash again.

He was moving generally north. He knew that he was south of Ammoss and Shandi's house, but he could not be certain that he remembered exactly where it was. The forest had changed a great deal since he was here last. Many of the old trees remained, but there were many young ones who did not know him. He did know that he had not crossed the path yet. He also knew that he had not seen a Kutel yet. He had passed some footprints and some damage to the forest that was probably caused by Kutel, but that was all too old to be of any use to him now.

Nickadola, Alehra, Lantid and the wolves were southwest of him. They had good cover and could wait all day if they had too. Blorfindel was supposed to make contact. The ambush site was on the slope of a hill. At the bottom was a swampy area with a few drowned trees. Blorfindel was counting on those trees to get him over the worst of the swamp without getting stuck. The hill climbed out of the swamp into a rocky area with thick bushes that left only a few good paths through. Toward the top of the hill there were sturdy trees. His friends were waiting in those trees. They would have a clear view of the Kutel as they approached. If too many Kutel followed Blorfindel he was to run past without turning up the hill. That was the sign that they should go quietly back to the village. The agreement was: if Blorfindel turned up the hill then the ambush was on.

Blorfindel continued to dash and cover. The morning was wearing on now. The sun was as bright as it would get all day, and he knew that the Kutel would be hiding from it if they could. At each stop he forced himself to rest. He was impatient, but the other three had each warned him to save his strength for the run back – a run that might be a long loop all the way back to Dath if too many Kutel pursued.

He crossed the path. He did not notice until he was at the next tree, but when he looked around the path was behind him. *Is that the path to Dath or Foralis? Am I east or west of the house?* He stopped to listen but the forest sounds did not indicate Kutel in either direction. He crossed back to his former cover. This time he was careful not to step in the path where a footprint might be seen.

He stood with his back to the tree and looked at where he had come. He had to remember the way back to the ambush well enough to get there with Kutel on his heels. Without any real evidence he turned east. After three or four more dashes he began to recognize landmarks. *The dog, Truck, liked to lay under that boulder on a hot day like this. This is the way.* The hole she had dug had filled in, but the boulder had not changed.

Two hundred yards later he could see the house through the trees. He circled around so that he could approach from the south as they had originally planned. Nickadola was concerned that the Kutel might think Dath was involved if he approached from the west.

Things had changed. The way Blorfindel remembered it, a visitor would have to be very close to the house to see it through the trees. The Kutel had cut many of those trees down. They had built some rudimentary shelters in the clearing with some of the logs. Most of it appeared to be firewood. Some of the biggest trees were still rotting on the ground. *What a waste!* Blorfindel remembered climbing those trees.

The clearing did give him much better shooting lanes than he had expected, and the leafy crown of a recently cut maple gave him perfect cover. He could see two sentries. *There are probably at least two more on the other side.* They were remarkably attentive. They walked back and forth in front of the house. Blorfindel had expected them to be goofing off in some way. *Have they heard something?* He waited silently for a few minutes. He could see movement on the other side of the clearing. *There are four more sentries and all of them are alert. They cannot know that I am here: they have not raised an alarm. Can it be that they keep good watch all the time?*

The two sentries nearest Blorfindel crossed paths less than thirty yards away from his hiding place. Blorfindel readied an arrow and waited. He wanted them to cross again so that they would be back to back when his first arrow arrived. He shot quickly without taking careful aim. *I just need to get its attention.* As usual, his aim was better when he relaxed. The arrow stuck in the Kutel's throat and it dropped almost silently.

Blorfindel stood with his mouth open for just a moment. *If I get this one too, then I can get into the camp and do some real damage.* Blorfindel took careful aim at the other sentry and loosed his arrow to intercept it just before its turn. The arrow struck the Kutel high in the back but its armor took most of the force. It spun and yelled for help.

The other four sentries came running. There were more shouts as well. Blorfindel held his position and shot another arrow at the wounded sentry. The arrow went in its open mouth and silenced it.

Blorfindel continued to hold his position. *They have to see me.* None of the sentries seemed to know where he was. He shot a fourth arrow. One of the sentries saw it in flight and raised its shield. It might have done some good if that Kutel had been the one that the arrow was aimed at. The arrow pinned a different Kutel's sword arm to its armor. Blorfindel was impressed that it did not drop the weapon.

Now the sentries saw him. They shouted, "Fitheran!" in unison and charged at him. Blorfindel had another arrow ready so he shot it. He took too long to aim and the Kutel were only about ten yards away when he let it fly. It punched through the Kutel's heavy wooden shield, but did no other harm. Blorfindel ran away. Things were going according to plan. *One, probably two are dead already. The third might bleed out.*

Blorfindel ran two hundred yards before checking on the Kutels' progress. They were falling well behind him. Their bulky hide armor inhibited their running and the rough terrain favored the graceful Fitheran. He drew an arrow. *I might as well take the shots they give me.* All three Kutel took cover and held their positions. Blorfindel waited for a minute to see if they would break cover and give him an opportunity for a shot. They did not. *What do I do now? If I run I will get away and they will not come to the ambush.*

Blorfindel saw the Kutel with the wounded arm nearly catch up with the others before it, too, took cover. *I must not have gotten much of the arm.*

He put his arrow back in the quiver. One of the Kutel shouted and they all ran at him. Blorfindel stood there in indecision for precious seconds as the Kutel closed. *Do I shoot or run?* He drew an arrow. All of the Kutel dove for cover again. He got his arrow off before the last one made it to its rock. The arrow hit something but continued on. The Kutel was behind the rock that same instant. *It probably just got a piece of his armor.*

Blorfindel turned and ran. The Kutel shouted as they ran after him. Even over their voices he could hear them trampling the forest floor with their heavy boots. Twice more on the way to the ambush site he stopped. Each time the Kutel took cover as soon as he drew an arrow. Each time when he put the arrow away he let them close some of the distance before he ran. This way he kept from outrunning them. He came to the little swamp at the base of the hill. He had not seen more than four Kutel on any of his stops – the perfect ambush. He turned up the hill. He saw Lantid step behind a tree as he approached.

The Kutel had fallen behind again and would have lost the Fitheran in the woods. The swamp gave them a longer field of vision and the turn gave them an angle to cut. They shouted and redoubled their efforts only to be bogged down in the swamp.

Blorfindel made a show of getting caught in the brush for a short while so that the Kutel did not lose sight of him. Only when they were nearly out of the swamp did he slip into one of the paths and run for the trees. *When I stop to shoot they all take cover, but the brush is not good enough cover to wait in. They will have to charge on unless they think the brush is going to stop my arrows.*

Blorfindel stopped in plain sight and turned to shoot. He could see that he had actually passed Alehra's hiding place. Now she was slightly ahead and to his right with her back to him. She had her own bow ready but she did not step out.

True to form the Kutel looked for cover when Blorfindel turned. Three of them realized that there was no cover to be had. Thinking that this was the Fitheran's ploy to catch them in the open they raised their shields and charged up the hill. Blorfindel could hear one say, "Get it before it shoots us all!" The fourth Kutel was closer to the edge of the brush and tried to dash into the trees to the left of the ambush area. Blorfindel shot at that one first. Their shields covered from head to thighs. Four arrows and one sling bullet left one Kutel dead, one incapacitated and one wounded.

Nickadola readied his scimitar and shield. The remaining two Kutel were getting close. Blorfindel thought, *Unless both Alehra and I score solid hits at least one of us will be in hand-to-hand before we draw steel.* Blorfindel drew sword and dagger. Alehra drew her sword and swung her shield around. She barely had grasped the handle when the Kutel arrived.

Blorfindel and Nickadola ran down the hill engage. Alehra had stopped one and Nickadola was charging it unseen, hidden by the Kutel's own shield. The Kutel coming up the hill at Blorfindel raised its axe high and tried to run down the lighter Fitheran with its shield. Three throwing knives flashed by from its unprotected right side. Two stuck in its hide armor but the third passed between armor and shield and cut a gash in its left bicep. Distracted, the Kutel did not react fast enough to Blorfindel. In an instant it was bleeding from three new wounds and sliding down the hill on its back.

Blorfindel turned to see Alehra's sword glance off the other Kutel's helmet while Nickadola cut most of the flesh off its left calf. Metal sang on metal as the Kutel's sword drew across her back. It did no more than leave a bright line across her armor. With her own shield against its shield she shoved it back down the hill. A throwing knife lodged in its cheek when it landed. Another struck its throat before it could try to rise.

Blorfindel turned in the direction of the Kutel which took cover. The wolves were there tearing at it. All he could see of the Kutel was one boot and the part of a calf that stood out of the wolf's month. He judged that the other wolf had it by the head or neck. The Kutel at his own feet was still struggling on the ground. Blorfindel finished it.

Lantid looked around before he started retrieving knives. "Four? Is that all?"

"There were six sentries. I got two before they knew where I was. I'll try to bring more next time."

"Four at time is just fine," Nickadola said.

Lantid agreed, "I just wanted to be sure we accounted for all of them. Blorfindel, Al, move the bodies under cover. We may want to use this spot again."

Alehra grabbed the legs of the Kutel at Blorfindel's feet. "You guys didn't even use any magic."

Lantid was wiping off his knives. "It takes me all day to recover from casting a spell. We may need it tonight."

Blorfindel and Alehra started to drag the body up the hill and out of sight. Nickadola shouted, "Cover! Take cover!" At the same time a bow string sang. Blorfindel and Alehra dropped the body. She took cover behind a tree. He ran for his bow.

The wolves were running back up the hill. Two more arrows took flight before Blorfindel had his bow up and looked down the hill. Three Kutel archers were at the far edge of the swamp. There were more Kutel crossing the swamp – a lot more. One of the wolves was wounded. Blorfindel could see a gash open and close on its side with every bound; still it ran.

Lantid was crouched behind a rock. He hissed, "They must have been following the first four. Get down! They don't know where we are!"

Blorfindel stood straight and took aim. "They know where the wolves are." He let fly at the Kutel who looked most ready to shoot. Arrows passed in flight. Blorfindel's arrow lodged in its chest. He shot another arrow at the next Kutel. The arrow struck in the middle of its chest but appeared to do no harm. Its thick hide armor saved its life.

The Kutel seemed to just notice him. "Fitheran! It's the Fitheran!"

"They're his wolves!"

"Get up there, you idiots, before he shoots us all down!"

Blorfindel told the others, "They think it's just me and the wolves. Maybe we can spring the ambush again." He loosed another arrow for a scratch hit on an archer.

The Kutel archers were pushing through the swamp now, too. The Fitheran was too high and too far away for them to shoot back from where they had been. They also tried to get lost in the crowd of Kutel so that they were no longer choice targets.

Lantid hissed, "We can't ambush thirty of them! <Wheeze> We have to get out of here!"

Blorfindel shot another arrow at an approaching Kutel. When it fell the Kutel behind it trampled it into the swamp.

Nickadola whistled for the wolves then said, "I can't run away from them, and neither can you, I expect. Blorfindel and the wolves could. Maybe Al too, if we hold them up a bit."

Alehra was not having any of it. "No way! We all stay or we all go."

Lantid insisted, "Chrushk! I'm dying anyway! Just go, all of you! I'll cast the sleep spell when they get close and <wheeze>…"

Blorfindel shot another arrow. The Kutel caught it on the shield. Nickadola launched a sling bullet. It hit the same one in the groin. It fell to its knees and stayed there. As Alehra ran for her bow she hissed back at Lantid, "You can't make us run!" She snatched the bow off the ground and ran behind a tree to draw.

Blorfindel reached for another arrow. The quiver on his hip was empty. He drew from his second quiver which was on his back. Alehra released first. Blorfindel's arrow was in the air before hers struck. Both arrows struck the same shield.

As Blorfindel took aim again he said, "Lantid, if you're just going to hide there go in my pack and get my extra arrows. There should be a half dozen in there." Lantid crawled off.

Alehra and Blorfindel shot in unison. Her arrow stuck a Kutel in the eye. His landed harmlessly in the swamp. She asked, "Do you think we'll have time to use all we've got?"

A sling bullet hit one of the Kutel archers. It fell but got back up slowly and pressed on.

The Kutel shouted, "Fitherani! It's an ambush!" They all tried to take cover, but there was not enough for all of them in the swamp.

Blorfindel let the others know, "They finally figured out that there's more than one of us." Alehra shot an arrow into the archer who had just gotten up. It stayed down this time. Blorfindel hit another Kutel in the throat as it struggled to pull its foot out of the mire. "Yes, I think we might get a chance to use all our arrows."

One of the Kutel crushed another with a cruel-looking mace. "Get up the hill, you cowards! You sack-biting lice! I'll kill you myself! Now run!" Blorfindel's arrow hit it in the mace-arm, Alehra's arrow hit it in the thigh and Nickadola's bullet hit it in the mouth sending tooth fragments through its cheek. The Kutel did not seem to notice. All of the Kutel broke cover and started across the swamp again. The front runners were nearly to dry ground.

Alehra's next arrow hit a shield. Blorfindel waited until the first Kutel stepped onto dry ground and nailed its foot down with an arrow. He smiled at Alehra, "They won't think you're a Fitheran much longer if you keep shooting like that."

Once again they shot in unison. Alehra's arrow missed. Blorfindel put an arrow in the forehead of the one whose foot he had wounded. Alehra said, "Hey! I was doing pretty well until just now! Do they really think I'm a Fitheran?"

Nickadola's bullet bounced off a Kutel's armor doing little more than knock it off stride. Blorfindel shot it in the top of the head as it stumbled. "You're too small to be a Tafer."

"So Ilsorma has given me one blessing," Alehra said as she shot. Her arrow might have scratched a Kutel on the way by.

Lantid stuck some arrows in the ground in front of Blorfindel. "There were seven arrows, not six. I suppose we could call that a blessing from Hytrem?" Lantid used his coughing laugh again.

Blorfindel and Alehra shot again. Each arrow hit a Kutel in the helmet. Alehra's ricocheted off. The Kutel just shook its head and kept coming. Blorfindel's arrow dented the Kutel's helmet and the Kutel fell.

Alehra said, "How about sharing some of that blessing over here? My quiver's getting awfully light." She had one arrow in her quiver and one in her hand. Blorfindel nodded but Lantid was already bringing her four of the arrows.

Most of the Kutel were in the paths through the bushes now. Blorfindel thought, *We might not get to shoot all our arrows after all.* His next arrow stuck in a shield. Alehra's missed the Kutel that she was aiming at and grazed one behind it.

Nickadola's sling was silent. He was casting a spell.

One of the Kutel archers stopped to shoot. The arrow stuck in Blorfindel's armor but did not scratch his skin. The Fitheran did not stop to take it out before shooting back. Both he and Alehra hit the same Kutel archer. It fell.

Suddenly the bushes started to reach out and grab at the Kutel. At first Blorfindel thought it was just the Kutel being clumsy, but there was no mistaking that the plants themselves were trying to hold the Kutel down. He shot one in the armpit before turning to Nickadola. "Bushes are your friends, too?"

"Yes," Nickadola said as he shot his sling again. The nearly immobile Kutel were easy targets. The bullet broke a Kutel's jaw.

Alehra's arrow stuck in armor.

Blorfindel said, "You sure have got a lot of friends." He shot an arrow into a Kutel's chest. At this range his bow was too strong for its armor. The bushes still held it up, but it quickly stopped struggling and went limp.

Some of the Kutel were close enough for Lantid's throwing knives now. His first two were deflected by the brush. "Can you teach your friends to duck?"

The writhing plants and chaotic movement of the Kutel trying to break free made it impossible to count how many Kutel were coming up the hill, but Lantid tried to count. "I don't think there's twenty left. Maybe as few as a thirteen."

Alehra shot an arrow into a Kutel's forearm. Lantid's third knife caught the same one in the other wrist. The bush held it fast while it bled out.

Alehra drew her sword and swung her shield around. "They're coming through."

The first Kutel out had to leave its shield stuck in the bushes. Blorfindel shot an arrow into its neck. It fell nearly at his feet. Alehra intercepted the next one. Lantid hit it in the thigh with a throwing knife as it approached.

The wolves started growling and snarling from the top of the hill. Nickadola shouted, "Behind us! Where did they come from?"

Blorfindel did not turn. A Kutel threw a spear at him. He knocked the point aside with his forearm at the last moment. The shaft hit him sideways causing him to drop his arrow. His wrist was bruised and bleeding, but he did not have time to be concerned. He drew another arrow and took aim at the Kutel who tried to spear him. At the same time another Kutel drew a bow. Blorfindel changed targets and hit the archer in the left hand. Its arrow flew wild.

Lantid turned and ran up the hill. The wolves were rapidly giving ground before ten Kutel. He cast his sleep spell. Eight of them fell asleep. The wolves counter-attacked immediately. Lantid drew his dagger and dashed in among the sleeping Kutel while the wolves kept the other two off him.

Alehra wounded a Kutel. It fell back and got stuck in the bushes again. "You know, I really thought we might make it when they stopped in the swamp."

All of the Kutel who could were hacking at the bushes to free themselves and their comrades. Blorfindel shot his last arrow at one of them. The arrow glanced harmlessly off its sword. He tossed his bow out of the way and drew his dagger and war hammer. "We're not dead yet."

Alehra took on the next Kutel to come out of the bushes. The exchange left marks on both their shields but neither Alehra nor the Kutel was harmed. As they dueled on, she said, "There's got to be ten of them left in the bushes. I wonder how many are behind us?"

Blorfindel threw his war hammer at the next Kutel to come free. The Fitheran was drawing his sword even as the hammer smacked into its shield. "I can still hear the wolves. That's a good sign." The hammer did not slow the Kutel and it immediately faced Blorfindel. It already had blood on its mace, and blood was running from its mouth.

Another Kutel came free of the bushes.

Nickadola tried to pick off one of the Kutel who were fighting the wolves but his shot was a clean miss. Lantid was going carefully from one sleeping Kutel to another, cutting throats. He was slower than he wanted to be because he could not risk waking them up or getting caught in the combat going on only a few feet away. The wolves were holding their own. One was wounded and bleeding. One of the Kutel was also wounded – a bite on the wrist as a consequence of an overextended strike.

Alehra gut-wounded the Kutel in front of her. It fell down the hill and struggled to crawl away.

Blorfindel cut the nose and cheek of his opponent open. It was bleeding from one arm, one leg, its mouth and its face, but still it battled on. The next Kutel tried to spear him but he turned the thrust with his dagger. He slid between the two Kutels' shields and got some scrapes as they tried to crush him between them. They were too slow to crush Blorfindel, but the Kutel with the mace pushed so hard that he tipped the spear-Kutel off balance. The Kutel with the mace tried to gather for an attack, but Blorfindel kept his sword against the mace shaft and interfered just enough. Twisting, he drove his dagger into the spear-Kutel's back as he ran a circle to retake the high ground. His sword slowed the mace enough for him to easily avoid harm.

In turning to face Blorfindel the mace-Kutel turned its back to Alehra. She stuck her sword in the back of its neck with such force that the point came out the front. As Blorfindel took position to her left he said, "If they keep coming out of the bushes slowly, we might just make this work." Three more Kutel broke free. "Crushk!"

Lantid shouted to Nickadola, "Help me with these! They're going to wake up before <cough, cough>… before I get them all!" The Timble drew his scimitar and joined the Tafer in the slaughter. The wolves were having a deadly dance with the two standing Kutel. The Kutels' weapons gave them much longer reach, but the wolves were faster and fiercer.

Blorfindel and Alehra were doing all they could just to slow the Kutel down. They were giving ground now, and apart from a small scratch they caused these three Kutel no harm. They were able to protect themselves as well, but the longer the battle lasted the more Kutel came free of the bushes. It was five on two when Alehra found an opening and cut a Kutel's cheek off. Even as she did so one of the other Kutel struck her leg with a spear shaft. She fell and rolled back to her feet. Blorfindel had to parry a Kutel sword for her as she came up. He ducked another sword aimed at his own head and with his dagger parried yet a third away from his stomach.

Alehra was favoring her right leg when she came up. Blorfindel swirled his sword over and cut a gash open from ear to nose on the Kutel that stabbed at him. Two Kutel with half a face fell back. Two more Kutel came up from the bushes. Blorfindel and Alehra had to go back-to-back. "This is where it gets ugly," he said.

"You mean, not pretty like a minute ago? Damn!"

Lantid looked up from another dead Kutel to see a wolf leap. The Kutel facing it stepped aside and swung its sword down towards its spine. The Tafer launched himself at the Kutel's sword arm. The crossguard struck him in the shoulder before the blade laid him open from shoulder blade to hip. The wolf tore the Kutel's wrist open and then ripped open its throat.

Nickadola ran screaming at it, but too late to do any more. The other Kutel panicked when it realized that it was alone facing two wolves and the Timble. It tried to run. It had not the slightest chance of outrunning the wolves who tore it to pieces within five strides.

Nickadola went to Lantid. The Tafer did not rise but waved him off. "I'm alive <wheeze>. Finish the Kutel before they wake up and kill us both!"

Blorfindel and Alehra were desperate to take down a Kutel and even the odds but they just could not move quickly enough to parry all of the attacks and get a counter-attack in. Blorfindel parried two swords with his own and struck his dagger through a Kutel's armor. Before he could recover one of the others struck him in the head with the edge of its shield. He did not even remember falling to the hard ground. It was all he could do to get to his feet and parry again before they could cut him apart. Blood was running into his eyes now.

Alehra had her back to him. "How are things going back there?"

"I got one. One got me. I'm standing and he's not. I can't see very well, though."

Just then one of the Kutel in front of Blorfindel disappeared in a gray blur. Half a heartbeat later the next one did the same. When he wiped the blood from his eyes he could see the wolves rolling down the hill with them. He turned to face the Kutel that were fighting Alehra.

Only a moment before, the Kutel were fighting five on two with hope of reinforcement from the other side of the hill. Now only two Kutel stood in front of Blorfindel and Alehra. They broke and tried to run. Alehra stuck one in the back as soon as it turned. Blorfindel switched hands and threw his dagger at the other. He cut its arm open but it did not stop running. He drew one of Alehra's daggers from her belt and ran down the hill towards the wolves. Alehra was only one step behind him.

Neither of the other Kutel ever regained their feet. Blorfindel and Alehra looked around to find a half-dozen wounded Kutel retreating across the swamp. Without a word the Fitheran and the Taforam started back up the hill, she was limping and he was holding the skin on his forehead. They were a few moments before they realized that they could still hear the sound of steel on steel. They dashed up the hill.

Blorfindel crested the hill only a few bounds behind the wolves. Nickadola was fighting a single Kutel scimitar to sword. The Kutel looked up as the wolves approached. Nickadola used the opening to slash open its thigh. When it bent down to grab the wound, he slashed its throat. The wolves leapt on it anyway.

The Timble went immediately to Lantid who was face down among the dead Kutel. Blorfindel ran over as soon as he could see. The Tafer was still alive, but bleeding badly. They poured half of their fresh water on him and tore his robe to ribbons in order to make bandages enough to stop the bleeding.

Nickadola bound Blorfindel's forehead and wrist as well. "These ten had us flanked. He put his sleep spell on them and all but two went down. We didn't kill the sleeping ones fast enough. The last one woke up after I sent the wolves to help you." He took two weary breaths. "We should get back to town as soon as possible."

Lantid whispered, "Don't hurry on my account. Half an hour one way or the other isn't going to make any difference. How many did we get?"

Alehra looked a Blorfindel but neither had kept count. "I don't know."

"Well, go count. While you're at it, you might as well see if they have any coin."

Blorfindel volunteered. "I'll go. Al, you stay here. You probably want to rest that leg anyway." She was already sitting next to Lantid.

Nickadola picked up his scimitar. "I'll go with you. No one should be alone out here." The Timble was not injured, though his shield was a good deal smaller than it had been.

They returned a few minutes later with a bag of coins and a head count. "Thirty-seven," Nickadola announced.

"Plus the two back at the house, that's thirty-nine," Blorfindel added.

"Too bad we can't take the weapons with us."

Lantid wanted to know, "Did any get away?"

Alehra answered, "Oh, yeah – at least five."

"You should have gone after them. They'll tell the boss all about us."

"Who should have gone after them? I can't run and Blorfindel can't see – or couldn't, anyway. I've only got one arrow left. Have you got any?"

Blorfindel pulled two part-way out of his quiver. "I found them on the ground. I didn't take time to try to recover any more." He returned her dagger. He had recovered his own as well as his war hammer.

Nickadola handed Alehra a Kutel spear. "You can use it for a walking stick."

"We can use it for a stretcher pole." She gestured at Lantid. "He can't walk."

Blorfindel used one of the Kutel axes to cut the heads off the two longest spears. With the spear poles and a couple of cloaks they made a makeshift stretcher for Lantid. The worst part was when they rolled him onto it. The pain made him shout, the shouting made him cough, and the coughing disturbed the wound causing more pain and spasms.

Nickadola and the wolves led the way back to Dath. Alehra limped along at the front of the stretcher. Blorfindel took the rear of the stretcher and hung both Tafers' packs from the poles at his end. Every time the stretcher jostled Lantid would shout and cough some more.

The Timble tried to take his mind off the pain. "You saved the wolf's life, you know. I never would have guessed."

"There were two Kutel <gasp>. We needed the wolves to keep them busy while we killed the sleeping ones <wheeze>. I can't go <gasp> toe to toe with a Kutel. It was better for me to go down than the wolf."

"It was a very brave thing."

"It gave us a chance <wheeze>. With the wolf dead, we would have never made it. <Cough> Crushk! <Cough>"

It was a long, slow trip to Dath.

They were walking into town before Blorfindel thought to ask, "How are we going to get him into the loft?"

"We're not," Nickadola said. "We're going to get him a bed with clean sheets. We're not going to put that wound in some dusty hay loft."

Alehra said, "We should ask the Shieldmaster. He should have thought of this. We're defending his town, after all."

They went directly to the Shieldmaster's home. Terak met them outside. "What happened? He's not–"

"<Cough, cough> Ow! I'm not dead yet, if that's what you're asking, though every time Al stumbles I wish I was."

Alehra looked back over her shoulder at him. "Thank you very much."

Nickadola started to say, "He needs a–"

Terak turned and reentered the house. "Bring him in."

Nickadola took the packs off the end of the poles so that they could get the stretcher through the doorway more easily. Blorfindel was surprised. "How much do you weigh?"

"Now's an odd time to ask. You can manage another few feet, right?"

"Actually, without the packs hanging off the back you don't weigh a thing."

Alehra groaned. "I was just about to say he got heavier somehow."

Lantid closed his eyes. "I did, for you, and I got lighter for him. It's all about balance. I'll explain later, if you like."

Terak had them put Lantid in his son's bed. His wife was protesting but he cut her off. "We can find somewhere else for Teral. He can sleep at the mill, if he wants to. This Tafer needs a proper bed until his wounds heal. Oh, and make certain that there's silverseeds in the meals until they're all healed."

That was a new word to Alehra. "Silverseeds?"

Nickadola explained, "Silverseeds, Frenlias' Gift, the plant grows wild just about everywhere. They don't taste like much, but they speed healing. Anything that doesn't kill you you can recover from in a month with silverseeds – even one a day. He'll be on his feet in a few days."

Blorfindel laughed, "I'll take longer than that, even with Frenlias' Gift."

"Yes, that's an odd thing about silverseeds: someone like Lantid will heal faster than someone like Blorfindel. They give more virtue to someone who is frailer."

Alehra understood now. "Oh, 'bloodseeds' we call them at home. I thought I was going to have to use the ones I brought from Mikenura." Blorfindel had a two-dram bag of them in his pack, but he said nothing.

The Timble continued, "They grow everywhere that I know of. There are actually a few different plants, all of one family. The seeds lie in the ground for two years before they sprout, so you can even dig them up if they're out of season. I was surprised that you didn't know the name. You can bet that the Kutel who got away are already eating theirs."

"I thought it was a good plant. Does it heal evil creatures?"

"Anything that has blood. The wolves will eat a few when they're injured, though I don't think they like the taste. I've been told that you can even feed them to fish."

Terak interrupted, "Did you say the Kutel got away?"

Blorfindel responded, "Five or six of them. We got nearly forty – that is, we counted thirty-seven bodies, and made certain they were past the aid of Frenlias' Gift before we left them. There were two more, one with an arrow in its throat and another with an arrow in its face – I think they're dead, too."

"Forty? If your prisoner was telling the truth then that's nearly all the Kutel around. They should pack up and go."

Lantid shook his head gently. "The wounded might desert, but the boss isn't going anywhere. He's got a stronghold and he's been living off your town all spring. So long as there's a chance of food and plunder, he'll get more foot soldiers. The question is: how quickly can he reinforce? Does anybody know where the nearest Kutel town is?" No one knew, and that was the end of the speculation.

They left Lantid in the Shieldmaster's care and went back to the barn. Nickadola killed a goat for the wolves and crushed some silverseeds over the meat. The injured wolf would not even let the Timble near its wound. The gash on its side was certainly made by an arrow. It did not look deep but it was nearly six inches long.

"You know, Kutel use poison on their arrows," Blorfindel warned.

"I know, but the wound is pretty clean and she hasn't shown any ill effects – except the bleeding, of course. She'll recover like the rest of us. Maybe the poison will slow the effects of the seeds, but that's all, I think."

As predicted, Lantid was on his feet in two days and he moved back into the barn. He was ready for action in two more. The wound on his back still showed a red line, but it did not cause him too much pain or threaten to break open when he moved. Alehra's limp was gone by then but she still did not dare to run on it. Blorfindel and the wolf both needed more time before they would be in full fighting form.

Shieldmaster Terak replaced the spent arrows, sling bullets, and even Lantid's throwing knives. He also got Lantid a new robe and gave him some cloth suitable for use as bandages. He made certain that their armor was mended.

Nickadola got a new shield made at the Shieldmaster's saw mill. He was shaken when he came back. "I've never seen so many mutilated trees in my life. They use the river, like a grist mill, but they have it rigged up to pull a saw back and forth. They shove trees into the blade to cut boards. It's not right."

Blorfindel asked, "How do they check the grain?"

"They don't! The just hack it apart! There's got to be thirty dead trees waiting to be fed to this thing! It's not right and there'll be Raiden to pay! The Tafers think that the trees are just here for their benefit!"

Alehra shrugged. "They replant after they cut."

"If the Kutel took good care of the orphans would it be all right to kill all the adults in town?"

Alehra opened her mouth to reply but stopped when Lantid shook his head. "Trees are his friends, too."

After dividing the coins from the Kutel, each person's cut still did not total the value of five silver paddiban – less than one gold malstren. Blorfindel was concerned. *Two hundred weeks like this will be a long time to wait, if I survive at all. At least I am getting some cittern practice in.* He complained about the take at the barn.

Lantid was not concerned. "The boss will have the good treasure. He'll only give his soldiers as much as he has too. You can bet he has a lot more. We just have to go remove him from it."

It was a full six days after the battle before all of their wounds were healed and their gear was mended or replaced. During that time the Kutel did not attack. The question on everyone's mind was: had the Kutel reinforced, and by how much?

"We'll just have to go check," Blorfindel said.

Lantid frowned. "We'll have to do something a little different. They may be stupid, but the boss has got to be smart enough. He'll have changed something. I wouldn't be surprised to find the Kutel had hidden watches or something now. They will set traps if they can."

Alehra disagreed. "They can't set traps everywhere. There's only a handful of them left – or there was. Besides, they have to get in and out somehow. Even fortress walls have gates."

Nickadola joined in. "We can't wait for the Kutel to attack here again. If we let them reinforce then our ambush did us no good."

"I didn't say we shouldn't go. I just said we need to do something different."

"The old Foralis road runs right by the house. We could try that. Maybe they won't expect us to come from the northeast."

"We should go have a look anyway."

Chapter 4

The House

The following morning found them on the north side of the path a half a mile beyond Ammoss and Shandi's house. Blorfindel was kneeling by a thorn bush on the side of the path. The others stayed in the woods. What they found there surprised them. "This path has been used recently." The way was cleared of trees and trodden bare. The middle of the path was several inches lower than the forest floor.

"I can see that from here. The question is, why?" Lantid looked up and down the path but saw nothing.

"The Kutel are using it."

"Of course the Kutel are using it. Why are they using it? What's at the other end? You're the local."

"Foralis. It ends there, or it used to."

"The town that burned a century ago? I don't think the Kutel are going back and forth on sightseeing tours. There's got to be something else."

"I don't know."

Alehra asked, "Can you tell anything from the footprints?"

"There really aren't any footprints to see; the ground in the trail is so hard packed I'm not sure a cart would leave a track."

Nickadola offered, "We could just watch the path for a while and see."

"They won't come out until dark."

"So we watch at night. The white moon is nearly full, even you should be able to see tonight. Blorfindel and I can watch until the moon rises."

Alehra asked, "What if the Kutel attack the town while we're here?"

"Maybe they'll burn the sawmill."

Lantid was not amused. "Very funny. Still, they haven't attacked for a few days, maybe the Boss will keep them a few more. I guess our options are to wait here, wait at Dath, or go to the camp."

Blorfindel offered, "I can go check on the camp. I'll just come at it from a little further north."

Lantid agreed, "If there are only a few Kutel at the camp today then they probably won't attack at night. If there are a lot of Kutel there, maybe we should get back to Dath."

Blorfindel's reconnaissance mission did not take long. Soon he was reporting back to the group. "There are only two sentries in the clearing. There are a few Kutel asleep in the barn. I could only see three, so I don't think there are very many. The smokehouse has fallen over. They can't be in there."

"What about the house?"

"I saw movement in the windows on the second floor."

Lantid nodded. "That makes sense. The Boss probably hasn't got his reinforcements yet. He has the survivors from the ambush on watch and living in the barn. Two out, three in, that's the five that you said got away. Then he has five bodyguards, so he has one or two of them on watch all the time from the house."

Nickadola said, "They're not going to attack Dath. Even if they all go, that's a smaller force than the one we crushed in town. Actually, it's smaller than any of the groups we fought. If the Boss has any brains at all he's not going to get caught out when he's that vulncrable."

Alehra said, "Why don't we attack the house today? We can probably get the two outside sentries and maybe even clean out the barn before the Boss and his guards form up. Like you said, it's smaller than the other groups."

Blorfindel added, "You can walk right up to the barn if you time it right. The outside sentries walk all the way around and you can't see over the barn from the house except where the roof has fallen in."

"How close did you get?" She asked.

"I got to the barn."

"Damn. We can do this."

Lantid was not sure "How are we going to take the house? It's easily defended. The wolves aren't going to be much help breaking down a door."

Nickadola shrugged. "If they don't come out after us, we can just leave. If we get all of the sentries today he'll have to do something different tomorrow."

Alehra smiled grimly. "If they won't come out we can burn the house down around them."

"Not if they shoot from the upper windows."

"We might as well get the sentries, anyway, right?"

They all looked at each other. No one could come up with a reason why not.

Blorfindel was at the last tree at the edge of the clearing. The rest of the group was hidden behind one of the Kutels' own brush piles. Blorfindel waited for the sentries to walk to the other side of the house and waved Nickadola over to him. The Timble's dash brought him to cover long before the Kutel came around the other side.

"You and the wolves should be able to get to the barn without the sentries knowing. See that hole where the planking has rotted away on the bottom? Something has dug out underneath. I think it's big enough for the three of you to get in. I'll shoot the sentries as they come around the barn. If they go down quietly we'll all meet you inside. If not, you can get started on the Kutel before we lose surprise. We'll join you as soon as we can."

"What about the Tafers?"

"They're too noisy. If any of the Kutel in the barn are awake, they'll hear them coming. They'll have to wait until we've cleared the barn."

"We don't even know how many Kutel are in there."

"They'll come running if we shout. It's probably no farther for them to come from the trees than for the Kutel to run around the barn from the door."

Nickadola waited for the sentries to walk behind the house again and ran back to the wolves and the Tafers. He updated them on the plan before the sentries made their next round. The Tafers did not like the plan very much, but they were not going to take the time to change it.

"What if there are more Kutel in the barn than we think?"

"Then you better come quickly."

When the sentries passed behind the house again Nickadola and the wolves dashed for the barn. Blorfindel joined them on the way. He stopped twenty yards from the barn in a place without cover. The Kutel would still have to walk around the barn to see him. *If they see me they will not bother to look for Nickadola and the wolves.* He aimed an arrow just past the corner of the barn. If the Kutel walked around in the same path as before he could shoot one before it even turned its head.

Alehra moved up to Blorfindel's old position and prepared her bow.

The wolves had to dig a bit to get under the boards. Nickadola followed them in.

A Kutel sentry walked around the barn. Blorfindel's arrow struck it in the neck and it fell.

The second Kutel sentry came around the other side of the barn at almost the same time. Alehra's arrow hit its shield. Before either could shoot again it screamed and ran back around the corner. Blorfindel ran to get an angle on the remaining sentry. Alehra and Lantid ran for the barn.

Blorfindel turned the corner. The Kutel was running for the front door of the house. He shot it in the back. It did not move from where it fell. At almost the same time an arrow came from the house. Blorfindel ran back around the corner. The black arrow missed.

Lantid had his back against the barn. He was panting and wheezing.

Alehra wanted to know, "How do we get in there?"

Blorfindel leaned out and shot an arrow at one of the windows on the second floor of the house, then ducked back without seeing what the arrow hit. "The door is on the other side, but there is a Kutel shooting from the windows."

Lantid drew his dagger and started prying at a board. "We'll <wheeze> have to <puff> break in <wheeze>."

Blorfindel looked around the barn again. Another arrow came from the house. He had to duck back without shooting.

Alehra found that she could get further around the other side of the barn without being seen by the Kutel archer. "I can see the door from here. It's closed."

Blorfindel ran over to Lantid. He smashed through the weather-weakened planking with his war hammer.

Nickadola was waiting with blood on his scimitar and a bruise on his cheek. "There were five in here. One of them woke up. They're all dead now." The Timble and the wolves came out through the new hole in the wall.

Alehra shouted, "Yah!" as an arrow stuck her shoulder. It did not pierce her armor but she fell back out of sight of the archer. "He finally spotted me."

Blorfindel took up his bow and went around the other side of the barn. It was a moment before an arrow came. He was ready for it and jumped back around the corner.

Nickadola went back into the barn. From inside he could see out through the cracks and knotholes without making himself a target. "They opened the door."

A black arrow skimmed passed the corner of the barn. Blorfindel had not been exposed. A moment later another flew by the other corner. Alehra was also out of the way. "Who is he shooting at?"

Nickadola answered, "He's just trying to keep you from shooting at the door. Something's coming out."

Both Blorfindel and Alehra broke cover and shot at the door to the house. Something was coming out, and it was not a Kutel. A black arrow came at Blorfindel and he jumped back without really seeing clearly what it was. Alehra shouted, "That looks like a giant!"

Nickadola shouted, "It's a Cral! It can barely squeeze through the doorway!"

Blorfindel had never seen a Cral before. Stories of their appearance varied widely, but they were always too big, too tough, and too strong. He stepped out to have a good look. It was enormous. Hunched over, its back scraped the top of the overhang which was over seven feet high. It was very broad. If it had been only Blorfinel's height it would have outweighed him by twice and then some. Blorfindel guessed that if it stood straight, it would have been at least nine feet tall. Its skin looked like nothing Blorfindel had ever seen. It was light blue-grey on its forehead and got darker as it went down. Its feet were unshod and black. Legend had it that a Cral's hide was as hard as the stones of a mountain. Blorfindel could see that both he and Alehra had hit it in the right breast with their arrows. Neither shaft had penetrated beyond the arrowhead and the Cral did not seem bothered by them at all. Its eyes were big, runny, and red where Blorfindels' were white. Dark green hair grew from its head like an unruly shrub. It carried a wooden hammer so huge that even the Cral had to use it two-handed. Blorfindel could only guess at the weight of the stump that made up the hammer head.

He shot it again. This time his arrow hit it in the cheek and drew dark, oily blood. It roared and charged at him.

The Kutel archer shot at Blorfindel again. The black arrow hit the corner of the barn before striking the Fitheran's armor. It did not have the power to penetrate and fell away.

When the Cral ran at Blorfindel, Alehra could see past it to the door. There was a Kutel coming out. She shot her next arrow into its gut. Its armor slowed the arrow point but could not save it from a wound. It drew a scimitar and ran at her.

Blorfindel withdrew behind the barn. "The Cral is coming."

Lantid said, "I heard. Al! Get back here. We can at least make their archer break cover to shoot at us!"

Nickadola was still watching, "One, two, three, four, five Kutel. I think the archer's still inside. I don't see a bow."

Lantid said, "Well, that's good news."

"Why is that good?"

"I was afraid that all of the Boss' bodyguards might be Crals."

"Keep thinking those happy thoughts."

"What do we do now?"

The Cral turned the corner and charged at them. Alehra shot it in the mouth. It bit the head off the arrow and spat it out, but there was blood, too. Blorfindel drew sword and dagger and braced for its arrival.

"That wouldn't have been my first choice." Lantid dashed out of the way and threw three knives in rapid succession past Alehra. They were aimed at the Kutel with the scimitar who had just turned the corner behind her. One went over its head, one stuck in its shield and one stuck in its thick forehead. It did not drop. "Crushk!"

Two more Kutel turned the corner behind Alehra. The wolves intercepted them as she drew her sword and swung her shield around. "How about putting the Cral to sleep?"

"It's too big!"

Blorfindel slashed at the Cral's belly as he rolled away from the hammer. His sword did not draw blood. He could feel the air pushed by the hammer as his head came up. Even as he got to his feet the hammer smashed into the ground between them. It left a hole in the earth a foot deep.

Nickadola came out of the barn behind it and opened a small cut on the back of the Cral's knee with his scimitar. He ducked back into the barn. The Cral's hammer smashed a hole through the barn wall. The Timble was already gone, but not far enough to avoid scratches from the splintering wood of the old planks.

Alehra saw a fourth Kutel come around the corner then three of the Kutel fell asleep. One of the wolves did, too. Lantid shouted, "Help with the Cral! <Wheeze> Nickadola isn't big enough to leave a stain on its hammer!"

When the Cral's back was turned Blorfindel lunged with his sword. The sword did not strike deeply, but at least this wound bled.

As the beast spun back to face the Fitheran its hammer struck Alehra on pure luck. Thought it was only a glancing blow it took her off her feet and she landed four feet away. The Cral saw her prone and raised the hammer over its head for a killing blow. Both Blorfindel and Nickadola attacked its flanks. The Fitheran's sword dug into its right ankle even as his dagger glanced off its buttock. The Timble's scimitar opened another small gash on the back of its right knee. Alehra rolled away before the hammer fell. The motion of the hammer strike brought its elbow in contact with Blorfindel's shoulder. It was enough to knock the Fitheran off his feet.

Before Blorfindel could spring up a Kutel with a bow came around the same corner of the barn as the Cral had. Nickadola, being the only attacker on his feet, was its target, but he was on the other side of the Cral. Its first arrow struck the Cral in the calf as it turned. The point bounced out of its flesh and caused no harm. The Kutel's second arrow hit the Timble in the foot. Blorfindel rushed at the Kutel archer and slashed open its right wrist as it dew another arrow. As it flinched he stuck his dagger in its throat.

Alehra had not regained her feet. She was doing everything that she could to avoid the repeated blows of the Cral's hammer. The monster seemed to have forgotten about all the others as it tried time and again to crush the Taforam. When she rolled inside a strike it lifted its foot to stomp on her. She stuck her shield under the arch of its foot edgewise and it tripped. Alehra's wrist twisted violently as the shield pushed away. She could not longer hold the shield properly when she stood up.

A large Kutel burst out through the hole in the barn. Nickadola was bent over to pull the arrow from his foot. The Kutel swung a six-flanged bright steel mace at his exposed back. A wolf bit the Kutel's arm in mid-swing but could not stop the blow. There was a hollow thud and Nickadola fell to the ground. The Kutel struck the wolf on the head with the edge of its shield and the wolf, too, went to the ground.

When Blorfindel turned Nickadola and both wolves were on the ground. Alehra was standing one-on-one with the Cral and Lantid was charging at the over-sized Kutel. The Fitheran charged at the Kutel but only feinted with his sword. Spinning, he lashed out with his dagger, but the Kutel ducked back out of reach. The Kutel swung its mace up between them to force Blorfindel to back off. Blorfindel continued past the Kutel and stuck his sword into the Cral's back again. He did not penetrate its hide.

Alehra ducked under the Cral's arcing hammer and brought her sword point to its shoulder. The force of its own swing helped the weapon penetrate. She shouted to Blorfindel as she withdrew the blade, "I can handle it! Get the Boss!" Then she jumped back to avoid the hammer's return swing.

Blorfindel turned to face the Kutel leader. Its mace was high in the air and coming down on him even before he turned. Blorfindel threw himself down to his knees, coming inside the crushing blow and pressing his face against the Kutel's shield. He reached behind the Kutel's legs with his sword and lifted. The Kutel was forced to take the power out of his attack to save his own legs. The mace struck Blorfindel's armor and caused only a bruise underneath. Blorfindel's sword drew only a small cut across the Kutel's calves as it somersaulted away, backwards.

The Kutel brought its shield up as Blorfindel tried to follow up with a sword-lunge. It brought three quick swings across the Fitheran's body which did not land, but kept Blorfindel out of dagger range.

Alehra lunged inside the Cral's reach only to have her sword point turned by its hide. It drove its hammer handle at her head but she was already stepping back. Her helmet rang and pulled her hair but it did no great harm. She drew her sword across its wrist as she backed away, but again its hide was proof against her blade. It swung again and forced her to take another step back. She stabbed at its hand when it reversed the swing and cut one of its fingers open. Though the cut was small, she was glad to see that she had caused it some harm.

Blorfindel stabbed down at the Kutel's foot. It stepped out of the way and jabbed at his head with its mace. When Blorfindel parried the mace with his dagger the Kutel stepped in and struck the Fitheran's sword arm with its shield. Blorfindel raised his knee between the Kutel and its shield. He jabbed at its face with the dagger which forced it to raise its shield, then he brought his sword under and stabbed inside its guard. The Kutel spun away from his sword point as it punctured its left arm. As it did so it brought the mace around in a powerful arc. Blorfindel did not try to parry the weapon. He continued to move inside the Kutel's reach and threw the Kutel off balance. Blorfindel hooked his dagger behind its shield and pulled it out. To the surprise of both combatants a wolf bit the Kutel's thigh from behind. Blorfindel delivered the killing blow with his sword across the Kutel's neck.

Alehra stood still for just a moment. The Cral swung its hammer down in a quick overhead stroke. That was what she wanted. She stepped in, stabbed it in the armpit, and caught the handle of its hammer on her shield as she ducked under its arm and away. The shock to her left wrist made her see stars, but the damage to the Cral was clear. Oily blood was streaking down its side now and it had to swing the hammer with just its left arm. When Alehra came on-guard on the other side of the Cral Blorfindel was standing next to her. "Good hit."

The Cral's hammer came down. Alehra shifted to her right and stabbed at its elbow joint, drawing no blood. Blorfindel hopped left then jumped on top of the hammer head and stabbed at its face even as the Cral was lifting hammer, Fitheran and all, with just its left arm. Blorfindel guided his sword point to the wound in its cheek that his arrow had made. The Cral swatted at him clumsily with its right hand. Blorfindel dove down, rolled between its legs and got up onto one knee behind it. Looking down brought the monster's face low. Alehra stabbed it in the eye. Now behind it, Blorfindel stuck his sword point in the back of one knee and his dagger in the other, both into cuts it its hide that Nickadola's scimitar had opened. As it stumbled forward its own weight drove Alehra's sword point into its head. She had to jump quickly to avoid being trapped under its bulk. It fell and did not rise.

They turned to see Lantid kneeling over Nickadola. One wolf also lay inert. The other nuzzled it. Blorfindel and Alehra both ran to Nickadola. "How is he?" they asked in unison.

"He's alive <cough>. He has a good chance if the poison doesn't kill him <wheeze> and there are no more Kutel around to finish the job. The arrow went in and out. I got it all out and the wound is as clean as I can get it. Hasn't he ever heard of boots?"

Blorfindel shrugged. "Timbles go barefoot all the time. Why not, nearly everything else does? Besides, your boots wouldn't stop a Kutel arrow. How's the wolf? I thought they were both down."

"One was just asleep <cough, cough>. It was too close to the Kutel when I cast my spell. The other one is alive, at least, but I don't know for how long <wheeze>. I didn't see what happened and the other wolf... well, I'm not going to tell it to let me look <wheeze>. There's blood, but I'm not certain if it is from the wolf or the Kutel – probably both."

Alehra looked around. "We're going to have to get permission if we're going to get out of here. Can we carry them both?" She opened and closed her left hand around her shield handle; even that much movement made her wince. "I don't know if I can carry a stretcher this time."

"We can stay in the house." Blorfindel picked up his bow. Alehra followed but did not change weapons. Her wrist was too sore for archery.

"Be <cough>, be careful. There may still be more Kutel around."

Lantid waited with Nickadola and the wolves while Blorfindel and Alehra investigated. The waiting was difficult. There were screams and some sounds of battle but he did not leave the wounded. It was only a few minutes later that Alehra returned. She was spattered with even more blood. Lantid asked, "Where's Blorfindel?"

"He's dragging the bodies out of the house."

"How many more were there?"

"A dozen or so – all females and kids – the Boss' harem, I guess."

"You killed them all?"

"You want to keep them? Do I look like a Kutel nurse to you? If we let them go they're going to go find some males and tell them what happened here – maybe tell them that we're pretty beat-up, you know?"

"I guess so. Yes, you're right. I'm only used to seeing the warriors."

She took one of the large Kutel shields. "We can put Nickadola on this and carry him in. I don't know what to do about the wolves."

"We can lean some of the boards over the wounded one so at least it'll be out of the weather <cough, cough, cough>. Give me a hand. We should do that first, no sense in leaving Nickadola on a hard shield any longer than we have to."

The wolf seemed to understand that they were trying to help. She remembered that Lantid had jumped between her and a sword to save her life. She watched anxiously as the Tafers built a Tafer-den over her wounded comrade. She was more concerned when the Fitheran came and took Nickadola away. He said something to her, but she could not understand. *They will take care. They are a pack.*

Nickadola was light enough that Blorfindel could carry him on the shield without help from the Tafers. Blorfindel put the cleanest Kutel sleeping mat on top of the softest one and covered it all with his new cloak. He called it a bed and slid Nickadola onto it.

Lantid called down from the attic, "Hey, there's a strongbox up here! It's probably got the Boss' treasure!"

Alehra answered, "We saw it. It's locked."

"I bet I know who has the key!"

Lantid returned to the house a few minutes later with a key and a kerchief full of coins. "I picked over all the bodies while I was out there – just the normal stuff. We almost left one of them alive in the barn. That could have been bad." He started up to the attic. Blorfindel and Alehra looked at each other and smiled. She was sitting on the box. "Where is it? <Cough, cough>"

"We brought it down."

"Why didn't you say so?" He came back down.

They made him look around for it before she got up and gestured to the box. He was too excited to complain. He unlocked the lid and opened the box. Inside was a variety of coins, but most of it was copper. Lantid started sorting the coins on the floor.

Some of the coins were of a type that Blorfindel had not seen before. "What are those?"

"That is what the Conjinese call a soldier. It's worth a bit more than a stowsaw. And this is a Colonel, which is smaller than a paddiban."

Alehra burst out, "Hey! that's a Mikenuran talon!"

"What are they worth?"

"About half a paddiban, I guess."

Most of the coins were struck in the standard weights used in The Shield Valley and Sekri Timbrali. Still, the sorting and dividing took a while. Blorfindel left Lantid to it and went to check on Nickadola. He was still unconscious. Then he started making rounds of the second story windows and keeping watch. All the while, he tried to imagine how the pile of coins could add up to enough for him to go back to Afinlia.

Lantid came to relieve him a couple of hours before sunset. "You should get some sleep. If the Kutel come it will be at night, and you have the best night vision. Al will take over after the white moon rises. Oh, yeah, the total is about two hundred forty paddiban – sixty each."

"Twelve malstren?" *I have a long way to go.*

"It's a start. <Cough>"

"What are you going to do with yours?"

"I'm saving up for a spell."

"Getting bored with the sleep spell?"

Lantid smiled. "Maybe I'll buy some that I can cast someday. I'm saving up to have a spell cast on me. There's a priest in Kingstone who can cure me of this cough."

"The priest charges money for that?"

"Why not? People want to be cured <wheeze>. He can't cure everyone, so why not cure the rich ones?"

"How much?"

"Thirty malstren."

I thought I needed the money! "Two more like this?"

"Not like this one. <Cough, cough> This one was too close. Get some sleep. <Wheeze> We need you to be alert tonight."

Blorfindel's turn at watch was uneventful. When the white moon was big and bright over the treetops he woke Alehra. "It's been quiet so far."

"You've just been watching from the windows?"

"Yes."

"They could sneak up on the other side of the barn, like we did."

"Not with the wolves there."

"I'd forgotten about them. I wonder how they're doing? Have you checked on Nickadola?"

"Not yet. I wanted to get you up and watching first."

"I can take a hint. I'm up." She shrugged on her armor and belted on her sword. Her left wrist was nearly twice the size of her right, but she took her bow and quiver with her upstairs.

A few minutes later Blorfindel joined her. "Nickadola's still out, but he's stirring a bit. I guess that's a good sign."

"I hope so."

"I'm going to check on the wolves – bring them some water. I guess I should crush some 'seeds over one of the dead Kutel for them. What do you think?"

"Nickadola would."

"Yeah."

"There are a couple of spare Kutel helmets downstairs. They should work for a water dish."

Blorfindel was back in a few minutes. Alehra whispered out the window as he came to the door, "How are the wolves?"

"Alive at least." He went inside and up the stairs to speak with her again. "They didn't drink while I was there. I think they were both awake, though."

"That's a good sign – I mean, the one was unconscious before."

Blorfindel nodded Tafer-style. "I talked with Lantid earlier. He says he's saving up for a spell to get that cough cured."

"That's a good idea."

"It costs thirty malstren."

"Malstren are the gold coins?" When Blorfindel nodded again the Taforam did some mental arithmetic. She was not yet used to the coins of the Shield Valley. "The take was worth more than that, right?"

"The whole thing. Each share was only worth twelve. What were you planning to do with yours?"

"I don't know. I'm not really in it for the money. I guess I'd save up and get better armor. You should too, you know. That leather is good for sneaking and running, but it won't stop much. I'd like to think you had at least a helmet. You think we should pitch in for Lantid's cough?"

"I will if you will. Nine malstren each will give him enough."

"I thought you were saving up for a wedding?"

"I need two hundred to prove that I am a worthy suitor, but I'm not going to let Lantid die to get it. He can pay us back later. The rest of the money will come faster if he's still helping. I wouldn't be this far along without him, or you, or Nickadola."

"I hope he's all right."

"Maybe we'll find out in the morning." Blorfindel turned to go.

"Yeah, I'll pitch in for the cure. That should still leave you enough for a decent helmet. Your fiancée would approve. Who wants to spend a thousand years with a husband with a cracked head?"

"Afinlia's not my fiancée, yet." *If Lantid can pay me back, I will only need to do this another fifteen times or so.*

The next morning Nickadola was conscious long enough to take some water and a silverseed. He started to ask about something when he drifted off again. Everyone agreed that this was a good sign.

The wounded wolf had its eyes open when Blorfindel refilled the water helmets but it did not appear to have moved. The other wolf had cleaned it so he could clearly see the wound on it head. He tried to give it a silverseed but the healthy wolf growled when he got too close. Blorfindel dropped the seed on the ground and backed away.

When Blorfindel returned to the house Lantid was going through the Kutels' food stores. The Fitheran asked, "Are you going to eat Kutel food?"

Lantid laughed and coughed. "Most of it came from Dath, anyway. I've been throwing out anything that I don't recognize. I think I found the Shieldmaster's daughter's cat." He gestured to a pile of rubbish on top of a Kutel shield. "Take this out and dump it somewhere. Bring the bucket with you, <wheeze> you're going to need some water to clean up the kitchen before I start cooking."

"Why should I clean it up?"

"You made the mess, at least some of it." Kutel blood was spattered around the kitchen. "I cook. <Cough> You clean. Fair's fair."

"Where's Al?"

"She's on watch."

Blorfindel spent most of the morning cleaning the kitchen. Even after all of the damage from time and Kutel, it still brought back memories of

Shandi. The brick ovens, the stone countertops, and even the rusted fire irons reminded him of how things used to be. Blorfindel felt strangely guilty that he could not get the kitchen clean enough for her.

Lantid was impressed with the kitchen in spite of its condition. "If you would have told me that the Kutel lived like this, I'd have called you a liar."

"It's not like they built it."

"There's still some dishes in the cabinet that haven't been broken. Too bad none of the chairs have survived."

"It looks like the Kutel broke them up for firewood."

"The counters must have looked too much like work." He laughed that coughing laugh again. "Oak with marble tops? There was gold leaf on these plates once. You lived here?"

"It was Ammoss' house, but Shandi's kitchen. She was a Shieldmaster's daughter – that makes her a princess, right? They took me in after… well, after Foralis burned, after my parents were killed. I didn't know it at the time."

"You never told me you lost your parents. I should have known. 'The last warrior of Foralis' – that's what you said. What happened to them?"

"They died defending Foralis."

"I'm sorry. I haven't spoken to my father in years. He doesn't like me very much, I'm afraid." Lantid tossed a dented pewter pitcher out of the way. Blorfindel snatched the pitcher out of the air. It was the pitcher that Shandi had used for cold tea. Lantid watched as Blorfindel set the pitcher on the counter reverently. "Sorry. I guess you remember some of this stuff, huh? It all looks like junk to me."

"I used to think my father didn't like me either. When he left me here, that is, when he didn't come get me, I thought he just didn't want me around. I didn't know, but he was already dead."

"My father's not dead, and when I left he made it perfectly clear he did not want to see me again."

"That's terrible. I'm really sorry Lantid."

"He couldn't stand having a weakling for a son. If he knew I was hiding behind a Fitheran and a Taforam in battle…" Lantid looked down for a moment, "I guess that would be just what he expects."

"It's not your fault, Lantid. You've hardly been hiding, anyway. If you were a Fitheran you'd get an exception for your cough. No, actually, you wouldn't need one, you could pass the wizard test."

"An exception?"

"Most Fitherani are archers. Fitherani who can't take the archery test because of something like your cough get an exception. They aren't archers, but it doesn't have the same… uh, meaning."

"Stigma?"

"Yeah, stigma. Anyway, you wouldn't need an exception because you could pass the wizard test, which is just as good as the archery test."

"It's not good enough for my dad."

"I don't know what his problem is. How many other Tafers are helping to defend Dath? What do all of their fathers say? Where was he when the Kutel came, anyway?

"At The Hunt. I'm not from Dath."

"Oh. I thought… I guess I just assumed you were. Anyway, you're braver than everyone in town. You're brave enough to stand in battle. You're body just isn't up to it."

"That would be the part that bothers my dad. He wanted a big, strapping son to inherit my great, great grandfather's sword <cough>. I just don't fit the description."

"Is that why you want the cure so much?"

Lantid made the coughing laugh again. "No, it's too late for that now. <Wheeze> I just want to be able to breathe. Al told me about your plan. I'd like to be noble and tell you to keep the money, but this breathing thing is pretty important. Thank you. You can still hold on to your share of the money for now. If we all get out of here – that is, will you come with me to Kingstone to get the cure?"

"Sure."

"Thank you. Oh, and by the way, I wasn't joking: don't call yourself Blorfindel Brighteyes in Kingstone. 'Brighteyes' means something different there. The Amada in Kingstone will pay big money for the head of a Brighteyes."

"I know. I really am a Brighteyes – in Kingstone, I mean. I had to be held in the Fortress of the Circle to protect me from the Amada. If you were to kill me now and bring the Kels my head you could afford your cure and have plenty of gold leftover."

Lantid laughed and coughed so hard he had to hold onto the counter to keep from falling down. When he could breathe again he turned his attention to the stew. "It should be ready soon. You know, I've been in the kitchens of two Shieldmasters: in Dath and in The Hunt, neither one was this nice – well, not as nice as this one was."

Even in Shandi's kitchen, the food did not remind Blorfindel of Shandi. *She would not even have fed this to the dog.* Still, it was at least as good as what Terak's wife had been providing and they were all hungry. Blorfindel took his with him upstairs to eat on watch. He sent Alehra down to get hers while it was still hot.

They went on keeping watch for Kutel from the second floor and taking care of the wounded as best they could. Nickadola came to in the middle of the night. They gave him something to eat and got him back to sleep.

The next morning Nickadola insisted that they take him out to see the wolves. He crawled in to see the wounded wolf and held its head in his lap as it drank from the Kutel helmet. He even got it to eat a silverseed.

Time passed and their wounds healed. Nickadola kept re-injuring himself to take care of the wolf. Blorfindel and the Tafers could not talk him out of it. After three nights the wolf was on its feet and Nickadola was not. Only then were they able to talk him into staying in bed.

"What about the pups?"

"What?"

"The pups! We left them in the barn! How long has it been? I've got to–"

Blorfindel restrained him as he tried to rise. "I will go back to town and make certain that Terak is taking good care of them."

Alehra ran in to the sick room. "You need to rest. Every time you move you're back starts swelling up again. Just lay still."

"You're going to check on them?"

Blorfindel still held the Timble down. "I will check on them."

Alehra walked out with Blorfindel. "You're going back to town to check on the pups?"

"It's only a couple of miles. The sun will still be up when I get back."

"Be careful, and don't pick a fight with Terak when I'm not around to watch." She smiled.

Blorfindel smiled back. "I'm just going to check on the pups."

It was just before dusk when Blorfindel returned with all five pups following behind. They looked tired.

"How did you do that?"

"Mostly I ran around after them. Eventually they all got too tired to fight and came along."

"And Terak?"

"Let's just say I won't be getting Shieldmaster Terak a puppy for Arienic's Night."

"We'd better not tell Nickadola about that."

"Between that and the sawmill he'd probably cut Terak off at the knees. Oh, by the way, we're fired."

"What?"

"Terak figures that since all of the Kutel are gone from the camp that he doesn't need us anymore."

"That ungrateful bastard! No wonder his wife's mad all the time!"

"He told me to say 'thank you.'"

"Thank you? He can go–" Alehra switched into her native language. Blorfindel had never heard Mikenuran before. It sounded angry.

Lantid came downstairs. "What is going on? I saw you bring the pups in <wheeze>. You're not upset about that?" Blorfindel brought him up to date. "Well, I guess I should have seen that coming. We'll just have to find the next hot spot."

"The road to Foralis," Blorfindel said.

"What?"

"The road to Foralis. The Kutel have been using the road to Foralis. Why? I want to know. The Kutel can't just keep walking over my home town. I won't have it. It's like admitting defeat. Maybe on one day they can get lucky and take Foralis, but they can't keep it. I won't have it."

"It's as good a place as any. We can use this as our staging base. First, we have to get Nickadola back together."

Alehra switched back to Shield, "And get your cure, and Blorfindel's helmet."

Chapter 5

A Cure

Late that night Blorfindel was awakened by a shout. He tried to shake the clouds from his head as he rose. He had only got off watch an hour before. He found his bow and a quiver.

Lantid's voice cut through the fog. "Are you up? Say something! There's something coming!"

Alehra responded before Blorfindel. "I'm up. What is it?"

"I don't know. It looks like maybe a group of Varren."

Blorfindel heard her armor ring as she put it on. "What? How many?"

Lantid's voice dropped. "Four of five. They slowed down. They might hear us."

Nickadola whispered, "They smell the dead Kutel. How could they help it?" His voice was too low for the Tafers' ears.

Blorfindel's whisper was louder. "Come on, we'll catch them."

Alehra was putting her helmet on as she got to the door. "Which way are they?"

Lantid kept his position in the window. "East. They're on the path. Be careful. All I can see are little shadows."

Blorfindel belted on his weapons and nodded to Alehra. She opened the door and ran out. He followed and quickly overtook her. He stayed on the edge of the path hoping that the Varren would not see him until it was too late.

The Varren were still moving towards the house, but very cautiously. The healthy wolf was out and growling: warning them off the make-shift den. They did not know why the wolf was there. No one had told them that this outpost had wolves, but Kutel only told the Varren what they wanted to, and that frequently left gaps. They could smell dead Kutel, but that did not tell them very much either. The Boss here had been asking for reinforcements for some time, so they expected casualties. Things did not seem right but nothing in particular was very wrong. Then the arrow came.

The first Varro's back sprouted an arrow point. The remaining four stopped and stared at it for a second as their leader fell over, dead. They looked up and located its source. They saw two figures on the path. One was shooting; the other was charging with a long sword held high. They were too small to be Kutel or Tafers and too big for four Varren to deal with. They shouted, "Fitherani!" as they turned to run.

Blorfindel's second arrow shattered a Varro's hip. It still tried to crawl away. Alehra slashed its arm open on her way by. She was now in the Fitheran's shooting lane, so he charged forward. They had nearly caught up with the Varren when he caught up with her again. He paused long enough to shoot down one more.

The remaining Varren split up, turning left and right off the path. Alehra went right so Blorfindel went left. He shot as soon as he had a lane. The arrow was deflected by a low tree branch. He ran parallel to it and shot at the next clear lane. This arrow staked its kidneys together. He turned to help Alehra.

She came out of the woods carrying a dead Varro. "Where's the other one?"

"In the woods."

"Well, don't just leave it there. Go get it."

He shrugged and went back after it.

One by one they went over the bodies and threw them on the pile of dead Kutel. The one with the arrow in its hip was still alive when they got to it. Blorfindel stabbed it with his dagger before going over its possessions.

Alehra clucked with her tongue. "You should have left it alive for questioning."

"Too late now."

The first one had a rolled up skin tucked in its belt. There was writing on it. Blorfindel took that with him. Alehra collected a pouch of coins. "It's mostly iron jertaks. It might buy us each a beer."

When they got back to the house Alehra took watch so that Lantid could look at the scroll. He lit a candle and unrolled it on one of the kitchen counters. "I think it's in Kutel." He looked at Blorfindel.

"I speak it. I can't read it."

Lantid shouted to Alehra, "Do you see anything else coming?"

"All clear!"

He took wheezy deep breath and cast a spell. He started reading:

No more Kutel for you, Jurtha. You wait. Keep your group strong. Use the Varren to find the Fitherani. How many Fitherani are there? You send me the answer before you attack. Send breeders to Jun to grow babies. If you want more warriors you must grow babies. When we have victory in the east then I will send you Kutel. Stay strong. Raid and run. Do not give battle. No burning. Let the Tafers raise crops. Raid again after the harvest for food. The food is not for you. Hunt your own food. The food is for me. I will send Crals to come get it. You better be ready when they come or you will be food.

"There is no signature. Jurtha must be The Boss." Lantid took out a pen, ink, sand, and paper and started writing it out in Shield.

"I wonder when those Crals are coming?" Blorfindel said.

"After the harvest. We've got plenty of time. I'm more concerned about 'victory in the east'."

"Foralis is east of here."

"So is most of The Shield Valley. Unless some Fitherani snuck back to Foralis I don't think that's his target. He's got to be talking about The Hunt or Eastower, or both. The Kutel must have a strong leader if they are going to try to conquer either of those towns. Those were built to stop the Kutel."

"He's a wizard. He sent a shapetaker to Sekri Timbrali and put it under a curse."

"That makes sense, at least."

"Do you think the wizard wrote this message?"

Lantid did not think that was likely. "This is a field commander. The Kutel king or wizard or whatever won't stick his neck out that far. He's safely behind walls somewhere."

Blorfindel thought about the message. "He doesn't sound too smart."

Lantid disagreed. "I don't know. I think he may just be talking down to Jurtha. He tells him to hold his ground and keep his raids light. <Cough> He's thinking ahead to feeding his army this fall. He thought to remind him about breading soldiers – they say that's the key to a strong Kutel leader. If he takes The Hunt and Eastower he can move troops by sea and maybe cut the Eastering River. The Hunt is the key to The Shield Valley for the Kutel, <wheeze> that's why they attack there all the time. Eastower guards the seacoast."

"So Across will be under siege before the rains come?"

"That's what he's hoping. The Kutel have attacked The Hunt hundreds of times, <wheeze> at least a dozen times when I was growing up, and we still hold it. I expect that each of those Kutel commanders thought he was going to win, too."

"So what do we do?"

"We can turn in a copy of the message when we get to Kingstone."

"That's it?"

"Sure. I guess we know what they're using the road for, now."

"What?"

"The couriers use the road. It must connect this outpost to the main Kutel force, or at least Jun <wheeze>, wherever that is. Have you ever heard of Jun?"

Blorfindel shook his head.

"They probably all came down the path to find <cough> Dath."

"So they're walking over Foralis every time?"

"Probably. We can do something about that." Lantid smiled. "Jun is probably just out of striking distance from The Hunt. The Shieldmaster there likes to take convicts on long patrols to push the Kutel back."

"Is The Hunt full of convicts? I mean, I know there are some families there, but are they, well..."

"No. Most of the town is a regular farming community. The Shieldmaster keeps the convicts separate, but they can get married and raise families if they want to <cough> legally, anyway. <Wheeze> The sentence is just to fight the Kutel. Some of them live a long time."

"I knew someone who was sentenced to The Hunt. He didn't last long."

"Really? What was his name?"

"I can't remember his real name. We used to call him Hairy-Ass. That would have been sixty, maybe seventy years ago."

"I guess I never met him, then. My grandfather would have been young then."

***

It was three more days before Nickadola could hobble around without re-injuring himself. He brought the pups out to the wolves and had a private conversation. When he came back he told the others, "The wolves will be staying here. They've found a place under the old smokehouse to make a den."

Blorfindel was disappointed. "That's it? They're leaving? I mean, they're not going to keep fighting the Kutel?"

"It's not their fight. They need to raise the pups. This last battle was too close. The pups were left alone for days and one of the wolves nearly died."

"You weren't looking too good yourself, there, for a while."

"I think I'm done, too. When my foot heals up enough I'm going home."

"Oh, I thought… I was kind of counting on you to help us find out what is going on in Foralis."

"I don't think so. When we got started I thought it would be a grand adventure. Now even the Tafers we saved don't want us around. I wonder how many people in town would even remember our names? To think, we just made it safe for them to go butcher more trees."

Alehra put her hand on his shoulder. "We'll go with you as far as Taferford. We're going to Kingstone to get a cure cast on Lantid."

"Yeah <cough>, they're giving up their share of the money to help me pay for it. Very nice of them, I should say."

"Hey, count me in! I'll buy a piece of that. You deserve it. I won't have much to spend the money on back home anyway."

"Will you come with us to Kingstone?"

"Yes. I might as well see the city once. They tell me I won't like it."

Blorfindel laughed. "It's mostly rocks and rats and Tafers. It's worth looking at the sea, though."

Lantid said, "And the market is as good as you'll see anywhere. Maybe you'll see something you like."

Alehra said, "You should see the market at Wazikama! And the sea, it's so beautiful off the beaches at Sami, when the sun sets over the water... I miss that a lot."

"Shouldn't you be on watch?"

It was three more days of hot meals and silverseeds before Nickadola's foot healed. All of the other wounds were healed by then. Blorfindel shot two rabbits as a parting gift to the wolves and the four of them set out for Kingstone.

They did not stop at Dath. They passed through without stopping to speak to anyone and turned south down the Brewster River. They spent one night on the riverbank and reached Taferford the following afternoon. They stayed in a tavern there called The Bee Hound and Blorfindel played his cittern and sang for the crowd.

Spirits were high and hangovers mild the next morning. They paid passage on a raft heading down the Eastering River. In two lazy days the spring-flooded river brought them to Across. They walked over the river on the stone bridge that led to Kingstone. They stopped in the middle of the bridge for nearly an hour. On one side Nickadola got his first good view of the ocean on the horizon. Then they turned to watch the sun set over the river.

They stayed at an inn on the outskirts of the city. Again, there was much merriment, and Blorfindel played and sang until his throat was sore. There was an uneasy undercurrent in the crowd, though. Soon all of the patrons seemed to be looking over their shoulder for something to happen.

They learned that the Knights of the Circle had sent a large force north to fight the Kutel somewhere. People in the city were concerned how much it weakened their defenses. There was a rumor that The Hunt had been burned, but no one had any solid information. Lantid worked the crowd pretty hard before giving up and going back to the table.

"No one really knows. <Cough> The Knights didn't just leave on a pleasure jaunt, though."

"Victory in the east?" Blorfindel said.

"Maybe."

"The Knights can do some serious harm. I lived with them for a while, too. All they do is train and fight."

"The Hunt has never needed them before, <wheeze> not since before my great, great grandfather's time, anyway. Whatever happened, we should be able to find out tomorrow."

"How are we going to do that?" Nickadola wanted to know.

"Like I said, you can buy just about anything in the market. Information will be for sale, too. Oh, yeah, and I got us a room. We should keep watch tonight. This place is cheep, but there's a reason, you know?" Lantid shot a meaningful look at Blorfindel.

In the morning Lantid woke the group. "We should get going."

"What's the hurry?"

"Early in my watch someone tried to come through the window."

"What happened?"

"The lunatic got as far as the windowsill and stuck himself in the eye with a throwing knife. The body is still at the base of the wall."

"Really?" Alehra stuck her head out the window to look at the corpse.

Blorfindel pulled her back in. "Put your helmet on before you do that again."

Nickadola was doubtful. "He stuck himself with a throwing knife?"

"That's the story I'm going to tell anyone who asks. Let's get going <cough, cough> before people come asking." On the way out he whispered to Blorfindel, "I don't know what you let slip last night, but don't do it again."

"It's how I got in trouble with the Amada the first time: singing."

The marketplace had grown up around the temple of Feadin. They bought fresh tarts and sweet wine for breakfast as they made their way through the crowd. At first Nickadola objected to wine for breakfast, until Lantid told him that the only way to get clean water in the city was to catch the rain as it fell. As if on cue, it started raining.

Stepping out of the marketplace and into the temple was like stepping into another world. They were an odd group, and fully armed, but in the jaded streets of the Kingstone marketplace that did not buy them much room or respect. The temple grounds and the thick walls were enough to keep most of the street noise away. The soft spring rain that pattered noisily on the metal roof drowned out all other sound.

The acolyte had to repeat himself, "May righteousness guide your footsteps. Can I help you travelers?"

"Thank you, yes. My name is Lantid. I <cough> was here about a year ago. Someone said that the high priest could cure my cough."

"Unfortunately, High Priest Litne is a busy Tafer and can not attend all of the sick–"

"I have the thirty malstren, that is, we have thirty malstren worth of coin."

"I'll see what I can do."

He returned a few minutes later with an older Tafer. His robe was as plain as the acolyte's, but Lantid recognized the scepter of the High Priest. Only Blorfindel could hear the acolyte talking as they approached. "…It seems like an odd group. I thought they had just come in to get out of the rain. The one, Lantid, said he had been here before. They don't look like the kind of people to have that kind of money."

Blorfindel stepped forward and shouted above the rain, "Litne? Is that you? Do you remember me? I was Ghinlihil! You don't remember me, do you?"

Lantid, Alehra, Nickadola, and even the acolyte gaped at him. The high priest raised his voice above the rain, but still did not seem to shout, "I do not remember you, Ghinlihil. Help me. When did we meet?"

"I saw you the day you were born! You were with the troupe when it broke up! Dond and Pelli, your mother's name was Pelli."

"I'm sorry, but you're mistaken. My mother's name was Thernas."

"Thernas? Thernas was the priestess?"

"That is correct."

"No, Pelli was your mother. Thernas took you in, I think. I don't remember what happened exactly – it was a long time ago." Blorfindel kept talking faster, "You don't remember? You were maybe three years old?"

"I know that you believe what you say, but I have no memory of this Pelli."

"Do you remember the troupe? We used to go from town to town, performing. That all ended here, though. Joikim was killed. They took us all to the fortress. You left with Thernas. They kept me for over a decade."

"I remember the fortress – of course I do, I been there many times. What I mean is, I remember being a child in the fortress when I was very young. I remember crying. There is one room in there that has always made me sad, but I don't really know why. I thought it was a nightmare. A big scary man, like an evil knight, reached out for me. I was in my mother's lap. Somehow I knew he was going to take me away from her. No, it's a dream. I've had the dream many times. I know it's a dream."

"It really happened! I don't know. I wasn't there when they took you away from Pelli. I just know Pelli had a son named Litne, and Thernas left the fortress with him, that is, you!" Blorfindel had unpacked his cittern as they spoke. He played the lead-in that the troupe had always used. It got no reaction. He played the theme they used for the fortune teller. He got it wrong the first time and had to try again.

"I remember that!"

Blorfindel played the fortune teller theme again.

"Yes, that!"

"That was the theme we used to introduce Pelli. She told fortunes."

"Thernas was not my mother? I don't look like the rest of the family. Tell me about Pelli. And Dond, who was Dond?"

"Your father–" *At least he said he was.* "Dond took care of the wagons. He was a guard, too."

Lantid coughed. "Excuse me, your Excellency."

Blorfindel maintained his enthusiasm, "I'm sorry! My friend, Lantid, he has this cough. We came here to get a cure. We brought money."

"Keep it." Litne laid a fleshy hand on Lantid's shoulder and cast a spell. It seemed to take a long time to cast. When the high priest took his hand from Lantid's shoulder they both drew a deep breath.

"Your hands look like Dond's." Blorfindel was surprised. Like most of the troupe, he did not believe that even Pelli had known who Litne's real father was.

Lantid was not distracted. "I can breathe! Of course I can breathe! Thank you! Thank Feadin!"

Litne looked him in his sunken eyes. "I've seen you here before."

"Yes. I lived in Kingstone while I was studying. I used to come here when I could. Feadin helps me... with my father."

"She helped me with my father, too. Or, at least, the Tafer I thought was my father. He wasn't really my father. He took me into his home and raised me with his own children. I owe him so much, but I always thought... That doesn't matter now. What about your father?"

"He is my real father, or he was. He disowned me. My mother gave me the money to study. She had to sneak it by him. I'm all right now. I learned my lessons and I can cast my spells. We four have been fighting the Kutel together in a little town called Dath. And now I can breathe! I should go back to The Hunt soon. I could face him now, if I had to. I should speak to my mother."

Litne bowed his head. "If your mother was at The Hunt, I am afraid I have bad news. The Kutel have overrun the town. They broke through the fortress. I don't know the whole story. The Knights of the Circle have gone to retake the town. Brother Fargus – one of our own – has gone too, to help with the wounded that remain."

Lantid was shocked. "Overrun? When?"

"I don't know. The courier arrived two nights ago. The Knights left yesterday morning. Brother Fargus was not ready until this morning."

"The Hunt is less than a full day's ride for a courier. He was on horseback, right?"

"I did not speak to the courier. I assume so."

"A runner could have made it in a day, too, I think."

The high priest tried to calm him. "They are not all dead, by any account. I don't know if anyone is. Please don't be too alarmed. You will see when you get there."

"We can be there in two days."

"Calm yourself. The knights will drive the Kutel out of town. I would have heard by now if they suffered a reverse. Brother Fargus will do everything possible for those who remain. Is there a healer among you? I did not think so. There is little you can do now."

"We can follow the Kutel."

Alehra tapped Lantid on the shoulder. "Can we wait long enough to get Blorfindel some armor? Since we have the money left, he should get some metal on. He's not dressed for the battle line."

Litne held up a gentle hand. "Yes, please prepare yourselves properly. I would hate to think that I sent you away too hastily for your own safety."

Blorfindel asked, "What about Foralis?"

Lantid turned to face Blorfindel. "Foralis can wait, can't it? I mean, there are Tafers – people – at The Hunt."

Nickadola agreed, "Live Tafers take precedence over dead Fitherani."

Alehra turned to the Timble. "I thought you were going home?"

"That was before I heard about The Hunt."

Lantid held out his hand to Blorfindel. "Come with me to The Hunt. If you help me clear the Kutel from my home town, I will help you clear yours. I swear, in Feadin's holy temple I swear that as long as these lungs hold breath I will go with you."

Blorfindel took his hand and shook it. "I will go with you to The Hunt."

"Our paths cross at a place called Jun somewhere in between, anyway."

"That's right."

Alehra clapped them both on the shoulder. Lantid staggered sideways as she spoke. "Let's go buy some armor!"

Litne said, "Yes, that's very wise. Go to Herik on Bass Street in the Fishers' Row. Tell him that I sent you. He is not the least expensive in Kingstone, but he will not cheat you."

Lantid nodded, "I know where that is."

"Good. Meet me here when the sun sets. You four will be Feadin's guests tonight. For my part, I have many questions for you, Ghinlihil."

"I'm called Blorfindel now."

"Of course, I am sorry Blorfindel. I will see you at sunset?"

"Or earlier! I never thought I'd see any of the troupe again!" They were all glad to have the invitation. The high priest walked them to the door.

Herik bit his lip when Blorfindel asked him about armor. "I can make you some, certainly. I keep a good selection, but not in your size. Maybe a mail shirt?"

"I was really looking forward to plates for the arrow-proofing. Are you sure you haven't got anything? I'm really big for a Fitheran."

"I guess you are, but I don't get a lot of Fitherani in here looking for any kind of plates. Mostly I get recent convicts heading for The Hunt who need something in a hurry, or something like that. I wouldn't be able to afford to keep this kind of inventory at all, but I'm an official armory for the king." He shook his head. "I have a set you can try on, but it's going to be too big."

Blorfindel tried it on. It was too big. He was about to try a mail shirt when Alehra had an idea. "Try it on over the leather."

The armorer did not think much of that idea. "That leather isn't going to stop anything that gets through those bands."

"Maybe not, but it can't hurt."

"Yes, it can. It's extra weight he doesn't need to carry, and it will be hot."

Blorfindel started layering on the armor. "I was going to carry the leather anyway, for scouting and things."

"You can sleep in the leather, too," Nickadola suggested.

The armor fit perfectly over his leather. It was bulky, but he could still move well. He sparred with Alehra for a while to be certain that it did not get in the way. He could still run faster than the Taforam could with her mail shirt and round shield. The armorer was impressed. "That's not too heavy for you? Put the greaves on. I've never seen a Fitheran wear fifty pounds of armor. Still, with the leather underneath you shouldn't have a problem with pressure-points. You carry it well." After Blorfindel tied the greaves on the armorer grabbed by the armor and shook him. "It feels good. It's not moving on you, is it?"

"No. I think I'll take it. How much?"

"Wait!" Alehra injected. "He needs a helmet, too."

The armorer found a skullcap and mail coif that fit the Fitheran well. When Blorfindel complained about his hearing Herik made an immediate modification. He cut some of the rings out of the coif so that Blorfindel could put his ears through. "It's less protection, I know, but this is how most Fitherani want it. Just remember, if you get shot in the earhole it isn't my fault."

Alehra stepped back to look at him, "Now you look ready for battle."

"You should get some, too."

"No, I like the mail shirt. It goes on quick. Besides, the shield more than makes up for the difference in protection. A set of those greaves would be nice, though. Do you have some that are brighter, you know, like my armor?"

"I have some polished. They haven't acquired the same red-brown accents as your mail yet, though. Did you ever think of having the rust rolled out? It can be ready before you go."

Blorfindel turned to Lantid, "How about you? Don't you want some armor? It would have been nice on top of the hill."

"I can't. That is, I can't cast spells in armor. It has something to do with the energy flow – I don't really understand. I just know it doesn't work. I don't think I'm strong enough to carry it around, anyway."

"Nickadola?"

"It's forbidden. No metal armor, Dhu's orders. I can't even have a metal shield boss."

The armorer shrugged, "I haven't got anything in his size anyway."

Blorfindel was surprised that when the haggling was over he still had a few coins left. He had expected to borrow money from the others. As it was he had enough left to replenish his supplies and get some spare cittern strings. He worried, *Now I am back to the beginning. I suppose if I survive twenty campaigns like that without needing to buy new armor, I will have enough to win Afinlia.*

Nickadola recommended that they buy a lot of other things in the Kingstone market. "Whatever they have at the Hunt now, they're going to need it. We should be sure to bring extra ammunition: arrows, knives, bullets, and pack all the food you can carry. The Kutel will have taken all that they could from The Hunt."

"And ruined anything they left behind," Lantid agreed.

In the end, Lantid decided to buy a pack mule. Nickadola interviewed them before he made his selection. The dealer was surprised, but could think of no reason not to allow the Timble to speak with his stock. When the shopping spree was done they picked up Alehra's armor and went back to the temple.

A different acolyte answered the door, but she had instructions. She sent another acolyte to tend to the mule as she led them to a large back room. Litne joined them soon after. "You're early. That's good. There are a thousand things I want to ask Blorfindel, but first, I have some news. The Knights of the Circle are sending a supply caravan to The Hunt. You should travel with them. You can help protect the wagons and the knights can help protect you. I still don't have a clear picture of what happened, but the Kutel do not hold the town. The knights are in control now. They will stay until order is restored."

Lantid asked, "What about the Shieldmaster? He's not in charge?"

"He would not command the knights. I think the Shieldmaster of The Hunt is missing or possibly dead, though I must stress that I have no information to back that up. He would have been leading the defenses during the Kutel attack. I hear that he leads from the front."

"He does," Lantid confirmed. "Sometimes he forgets that he is supposed to be in command. He spends too much effort fighting and not enough leading."

"There are worse ways to lead soldiers in battle."

"I didn't say he was a bad leader. I just think… I don't know. He's the Shieldmaster and I'm just Lantid. He can charge into battle if he wants to. His men, the convicts too, they all follow him and they always win – up until now, anyway. Sometimes I think he could do better if he tried to outthink the Kutel every now and then."

"Well, you obviously know more about that than I do. From what I hear, the fortress at the Hunt is in good condition. The knights do not expect difficulty holding it, though I don't why not."

Nickadola asked, "Where did you hear all of this?"

"I went to the Fortress of the Knights Of the Circle after speaking with you. I wanted to borrow some of their records about what happened there fifty-five years ago. Their records are a bit more complete on the topic of my birth parents than I might like, I must admit."

Alehra said, "You mean the story of your parents was there for you to read all the time, and you never went to look?"

"I did not know there was anything to look for until this morning."

They spent the rest of the afternoon going over Litne's childhood. Lantid, Alehra and Nickadola were all excused. Acolytes showed them each to a small bedroom where they were invited to stay. When they rejoined the high priest and the Fitheran for dinner they were still talking about the troupe. Litne forced conversation back to the present for the duration of the meal, but then it was back to fake fortune tellers and abusive knife throwers. He did not allow Blorfindel to talk late into the night, however. "You'll have to be up early to be ready when that caravan leaves."

The caravan consisted of six wagons pulled by two oxen each. Teamsters ran the wagons. A silver knight was in command and there were four copper knights as escort. They accepted Litne's recommendation to include the four adventurers and their mule. The silver knight thanked Lantid for a copy of the Kutel message that they had captured.

Blorfindel did some slow arithmetic as he walked the length of the caravan. After spending the previous day in the Kingstone market, he had a much better idea what things cost. *The caravan and everything in it is worth about one hundred malstren – half of what I have to raise.*

Blorfindel found a surprise on the last wagon. "Ichassi!"

"Blorfindel! Is that you?"

"What are you doing here?"

"I was in town when the news came in. They'll need archers for the walls at The Hunt. I couldn't go with the knights, so I'll ride in the wagon."

"They're not still mad about… you know?"

"All is forgiven, or at least forgotten. It's been nearly half a century, after all. How many of those knights will still be here?"

"Ichassi, I want you to meet my friends: Nickadola, Alehra, and Lantid. We've been fighting the Kutel together." The Fitherani had been speaking in Timbrali. He switched languages back to Shield so the Tafers could understand. "This is Ichassi Quickstring, one of the best archers of Sekri Timbrali."

Nickadola gestured to the pack mule. "This is Sturdifoot."

Lantid asked, "Have you heard anything about The Hunt?"

"Only that the knights are holding it. That can't be good. They tell me that it's been a long time since the Kutel did this much damage."

"Not since before my great-grandfather's time."

"Well, anyway, don't tell them, but the knights aren't very good at holding ground. As Blorfindel knows, they can't even hold their own fortress against a determined attacker."

Blorfindel said, "That was different."

"Was it? I don't know what the Kutel have backing them up. The knights are really good at taking ground. They need someone like us to hold it."

Lantid asked, "Any idea of how much damage the Kutel did? I mean, were a lot of Tafers killed?"

"I don't know. I've never heard of the Kutel winning a bloodless victory. We'll see when we get there. There isn't anything we can do until then, is there?"

"I guess not."

"You cast spells, right?"

Lantid nodded.

Blorfindel asked, "How did you know?"

"Anyone who looks like that and runs toward Kutel is either a wizard or a fool. I just wanted to be sure. Two archers, a Taforam warrior, a wizard and a Dhu worshiper, we might be able to hold the walls for a while. We'll have to see what the Kutel have to throw at us."

Lantid sighed. "And what there is left to hold."

The trip went slowly for Lantid. It took nearly all day to get from the Kingstone market to the north side of Across. They spent the night with the wagons at the north gate. The city guard was not pleased with that, but they were not going to tell a silver knight to get out of the street. Once they were on the road it was clear that they were still two days out from The Hunt. Lantid fretted but did not complain. The pack mule was little faster than the wagons.

The third afternoon the caravan approached The Hunt. Lantid wanted to run ahead but Nickadola called him back. "We're in more danger from the Kutel now than anywhere else on the journey. You can wait another hour or so."

When the wagons got close to town the group was assaulted by the stench of smoke and decay. There was no mistaking the destruction. Even the outlying farms had been burned. Piles of Kutel bodies were smoldering here and there. They added to the general look of destruction. Some of them had been reduced to piles of ashes, but most of the fires were not hot enough. There were Tafers walking around who seemed to be in a daze. Every now and then one of them would pull something out of the wreckage that might have some value. Much of the time they would just stand and stare at something like a burned-out house or a bloodstain on the ground or maybe nothing at all.

When the caravan pulled between the first two fires Lantid ran ahead. Alehra followed him. Blorfindel and Nickadola stayed with the wagons for the hour that it took to reach the fortress. Lantid and Alehra rejoined them as they pulled inside the stone walls. They did not speak. Lantid's face looked even worse than when he was coughing and writhing in pain on the stretcher.

The fortress itself was in good condition. The curtain walls had not been breached, and the gatehouse was standing. The heavy wooden doors were scorched, but intact. There was damage inside. The knights had put up a pavilion in the courtyard and their horses were also inside the fortress. There were groups of refugees clumped together in the corners and against the walls.

The silver knight reported to the gold knight in charge. Without any permission or making any introduction Ichassi climbed the stairs to the curtain wall with bow in hand and began scanning the world outside the fortress.

Blorfindel, Nickadola, Lantid, and Alehra were standing waiting for the silver knight to finish his report so that they could introduce themselves to the commander. While they were waiting a Tafer strode hurriedly up to them. He was armored much like Blorfindel, but his helmet and shield bore a white bird on a green field – the symbol of Feadin. He had a large mace in his belt, but both weapon and armor seemed out of place with his manner. "Thank Feadin you've come! We've been waiting. The knights won't follow without their tracker, and the Kutel must be far away by now."

Blorfindel stared at him. "Their tracker?"

Nickadola explained, "I don't think we're who you think we are. You're Fargus, right?" The Tafer nodded. "I'm Nickadola, this is Blorfindel. That's Alehra with the shield, and Lantid is the one with the long face. We just traveled with the caravan. That's Sturdifoot, over there."

Blorfindel asked, "What happened here? How did the Kutel take the fortress?"

Fargus shook his head. "I don't really know. The Shieldmaster gave–"

Lantid interrupted him. "You don't know how?" His voice was more bitter than the stench of burning corpses. "I'll tell you how it happened." He ran up the stairs to the top of the wall. He was shouting as the others followed. "The Kutel approached through the woods over there, after dark, before the moonrise. They put as many light skirmishers as they could, maybe fifty, in that stand of trees over there – it's called Talor's Stand. The main force set up over there, in the open, and started lighting torches. The commander made certain that some Crals could be seen in the lights. Naturally, the Tafer population panics and runs for the safety of the fortress. Rather than charging to cut them off, which the defenders expect, the Kutel hold their positions. When all eyes were on the fires a strong Kutel lieutenant with picked troops moved around the town to the south not far from the road. As you can see, there is no cover around that way, so to cover their maneuver a Kutel leader shows himself and advances his main force toward the fortress. The defenders have been waiting for this. The Shieldmaster masses his forces and essays from the gate. He keeps his best troops around him to punch a hole through the Kutel lines. He plans to kill the leader himself. He thinks that if he kills the leader, the rest of the Kutel will scatter – they usually do.

"Things go exactly according to the Shieldmaster's plan. His Tafers hold two lines to maintain a corridor back to the fortress and he kills the Kutel leading the advance, except that's not the Kutel commander. It's some patsy they set up to look like a leader. The Kutel break and run and the Shieldmaster and his warriors pursue. When they get about there – you see the little rise there – the Kutel rally. There are Crals anchoring both ends of the Kutel's lines and the real Kutel commander is up there on that rock. He signals the skirmishers in the woods and they run out behind the Shieldmaster and his warriors, cutting them off from the fortress.

"The remaining defenders in the fortress charge out to force open a corridor through the skirmishers. The second opening of the fortress doors is the signal to the Kutel to the south. They charge quietly at the fortress and, because no one is looking for them they arrive at the doors and attack the rear of the second group of Tafers and hold the door open. All of the Tafers are now surrounded and the Kutel have control of the gatehouse." He spun around and faced his audience.

Fargus said, "You sound like you were here. I've spoken to most of the survivors and they don't even know what happened."

There was ferocity in Lantid's hollow eyes. "What they said matches my version, though, doesn't it?"

"I guess so. The Kutel certainly got into the fortress when the second group of Tafers was leaving. You're a magician, right? Did you check a crystal ball or something?"

"That's exactly how the Kutel caught Shieldmaster Talor in the open nearly a hundred and fifty years ago; except Talor cut his way through to the stand of trees and rallied there while his reserves fought their way back into the fortress and the Taforam held the gate. The Kutel still burned the town before he could push them back.

"Shieldmaster Lorten uses only farmers for reserves. He doesn't care if his watchmen are all looking in the same direction, either. I told him to cut down that damn stand of trees years ago and got my butt whipped for it! 'It's a historic landmark,' he said! The trees in that historic landmark have gotten bigger and darker than they ever were in Talor's time. If an eleven-year-old kid could figure it out, the Kutel were bound to figure it out eventually."

Fargus bowed his head. "Shieldmaster Lorten paid the price for it, anyway. He's missing – either dead or captive."

"And how many others paid, too? He's supposed to be in command. He's supposed to know what he's doing. He's supposed to be smarter than a Kutel, but he isn't!"

Fargus spoke quietly, "There are fifty missing that I know of. Some are probably dead, but we know that the Kutel took captives."

One of the local Tafers spoke from the stairs behind them, "Lantid? Is that you Lantid?" He was short and squat and had a dirty bandage on his right hand.

"Bron?"

"It is you! You came back!"

"Not soon enough."

"You were right, you know: Lorten took all of his warriors with him on the first charge. We tried to win back to the gate but… Some of the people inside got over the wall to safety before the Kutel got to them."

"Sural?"

"The princess? I'm sorry Lantid, she's dead."

Lantid sat on the wall and buried his face in his robe between his knees. The squeak of his voice said he was crying. "Are you sure?"

"She killed herself."

Fargus picked up the story. "I heard that part. The Kutel captured her. She threw herself on one of their spears rather than be a prisoner. There are other prisoners, though, and the Kutel are getting away with them. Princess Sural must have been a remarkable girl, all of the people of The Hunt are mourning for her, but the others are still alive. The knights won't follow them until their tracker arrives, but the trail is clear enough so that even I could follow it, and they're getting away. Who knows what the prisoners are enduring?"

Lantid spoke through the cloth robe. "Sodri? Is Sodri here?"

Bron answered, "She's gone, too. She was alive last anyone saw her. We could hear her scream when she saw Sural die. I'm sorry Lantid, there was nothing—"

"There was nothing you could do, Bron. It's not your fault. You weren't cut out to be a soldier, either. Lorten's shoulders are broad enough to carry all of the blame." There was a long pause before Lantid wiped his face on the hem of his robe and stood up. "You're right, Fargus, we have to do something about the living. That's what we said, right Blorfindel? Living Tafers are more important than dead Fitherani? They have to be more important than dead princesses, too."

Chapter 6

Fargus

Blorfindel, Nickadola, Alehra, Lantid, Fargus, and the mule named Sturdifoot began following the retreating Kutel army. Ichassi thought it was a good idea in principal, but he would not leave the surviving townsfolk. "There's maybe fifty captives who might not even still be alive. There's a hundred Tafers here who have a good chance if we defend them. If they get some more defenders here then I'll catch up."

The knights had a similar view. The gold knight was waiting for reinforcements, including a tracker, before he would split his force. "We have to stop the Kutel here. If they get free into the valley they can break into raiding groups and we'll never catch them all."

They had spent only one night in the fortress at The Hunt. There was no more comfort there than on the trail, anyway. Lantid spoke to a few old friends before they left but no one was in the mood for a joyful reunion. He did not even ask any of them to follow the Kutel.

They were climbing through low mountain passes. The terrain was heavily forested and the slopes gentle. The landscape was little different from Foralis and only slightly more rugged than around Dath. The Kutel army had left only the trees in their path, all other growth was cut or trampled down. The damage to the countryside made Nickadola as sick as the destruction at The Hunt. Blorfindel was reminded of his time with Lalru the Kutel chief, who had taken satisfaction in killing green living things.

Fargus proved to be a capable campaigner, or at least he could suffer in silence. He carried his own pack and tramped along in his armor like the rest of them. If anything, he appeared to be more motivated than any of them. He even hurried them a bit if rest stops took too long. He was careful not to push too hard. He was very aware that he was the outsider in this group.

"How long have you been fighting together?"

Alehra answered, "Just this spring."

"And you've been fighting Kutel?"

"Yeah. We were defending Dath."

"Where is that?"

Blorfindel answered, "Where the Brewster River meets the forest."

"Oh." Fargus had no idea where the Brewster River was, either, but he did not want to belabor the point. "How many Kutel were there?"

Alehra said, "Less than a hundred, maybe eighty? No, maybe a hundred with the females and young."

Nickadola said, "Plus the Cral and five Varren."

"You fought a Cral?"

"Al did, yeah. The rest of us were busy with the Kutel."

Alehra would not take all the credit. "Everybody helped with the Cral."

Lantid said, "Not me."

"If you hadn't put the Kutel to sleep, I'd have never gotten free to fight the Cral."

Fargus cut them off before they started arguing. "Al, you're the front-line fighter-type, right? And Blorfindel is more of an archer?"

"We can both go either way."

Nickadola added, "I'm much better with my sling than my scimitar."

"Timble slings are almost as famous as Fithern bows, and you have the Dhu magic. Lantid, you have wizard spells?"

"Sleep, shield, and fire, and some non-combat stuff. Two per day."

"Hey!" Alehra objected, "I thought you could only do one per day!"

"I'm getting better. Practice makes perfect, you know. I could have cast another spell after the battle with the Cral – not right after, but in a few hours. Now that I've been cured I can go even sooner, I think."

Nickadola said, "Dhu was pleased when we set the wolves up with a safe home. I have more spells, too."

Alehra turned to Blorfindel, "Do you feel left out? I feel like my sword should get sharper or something."

He shrugged, "You got new greaves."

Lantid laughed. "And you learned how to kill a Cral. Oh, yeah, and Fargus, I throw knives, too, but I'm not getting much better at it."

"I don't really have a ranged attack, myself. I got a little combat training this spring, so i can use the mace if I have to and my armor is good enough so I can hold the line in battle, but I won't be knocking heads off." The group had more or less figured out that Fargus was not a warrior. "I have healing magic, though, so if you're hit sing out – especially if you're hit badly."

Blorfindel sang, "Ow, I've a sword in my head. Darn, there's a sword in my head. Please take the sword from my head." They all laughed, even Lantid.

Lantid asked Fargus, "How many healing spells – you know, each day?"

"Three. I can take other spells instead, of course, but right now I think we're most likely to need the healing. Let's hope it's only for the captives."

Lantid could sense Fargus' anxiety. "Don't worry, we're catching them. Armies move slowly, and the captives are slowing them down even more." He laughed bitterly. "Just think how much time it takes them to stop and cut down every bush they pass."

"Thank you," Fargus replied. "You know, I'm not very good at this."

"Good at what?" Blorfindel asked.

Fargus gestured at the world around them. "All of this. I've never been outside Kingstone before. I saw the sunrise from the bridge once."

"Your doing fine," Lantid said. "Just watch and listen."

"Why did you leave Kingstone?" Blorfindel asked.

"I was cleaning the audience chamber when the news came – you know, that the Kutel had attacked The Hunt. They asked for a healer. Litne said no one was prepared to go. I volunteered. I don't really know why; I suppose it's just something I think shouldn't be ignored."

"A strong choice," Lantid said, "but not a popular one. Did anyone else come – other than the knights?"

"Not in the first group – sortie – whatever you call it. When we got there, the town was still burning. The people had given up and were huddling in the keep. I never saw anything like that. With the Shieldmaster missing and the princess dead, no one was in charge. Then there were the ones looking for people, the missing. That might be the first thing that I actually did: try to help people find each other. Some families were just separated, but mostly, we found corpses."

Alehra asked Lantid, "This princess, what's-her-name, was she your sweetheart or something?"

"Sural. Her name was Sural. She was seven years old the last time I saw her."

Fargus was surprised. "Everyone said how beautiful she was, I thought she was older."

"I've been gone for over ten years. I thought you had met her."

"No, they had already buried her when I arrived. They asked me to say some words over her grave." Lantid was crying. Fargus' eyes were glazing over, too. "I'm just a brother at the temple, I never had to do that before. I'm afraid I made a mess of it. She clearly deserved better. All the people loved her."

Lantid bowed his head. "I had to sneak into the fortress to see her the last time. I knew it would be a long time before I saw her again. I never thought it would be the last time."

Blorfindel asked, "When did you and your father, ah…"

"The last time I spoke to my father I was thirteen. That was fourteen years ago. I wasn't banished or anything, but it was still hard to go to The Hunt. I had to sneak around him. I didn't want to see him again. I was afraid that he'd say something again. You know, I still am. I'm kind-of afraid that he'll be one of the captives. Isn't that strange? He's either captive or dead. I don't wish him death, but I'm afraid he might be a captive."

Blorfindel said, "I didn't know. Of course, you must of asked about your family when you ran ahead."

"It's not my family anymore. He made that clear years ago."

"Your mother?"

"Also missing."

"Do you have any brothers or sisters?"

"Dead." He walked a few steps before continuing, "My brothers all died young. Two were sickly, like me. One was killed by the Kutel – that was after I left. My sister didn't make it though this last attack. I think it's better, maybe. If she was a captive they'd... It would be worse for her, I think."

Alehra swallowed hard. "That's why the princess, Sural, killed herself?"

"I think so."

Fargus quietly disagreed, "You're wrong, Lantid, and so was she. I'm sure the captives are having the worst time of their lives, and some of them probably wish they were dead by now, but when it's all over it will be better."

"You think they're going to get over it? You're crazy. Do you know what they're doing to them? Did you ever think about where Half-Kutel come from?"

"I know what they're doing, and if there aren't enough Taforam to go around then they'll use Tafers, too. No, they won't get over it completely, maybe not ever. It's still better than giving up. Some people live their whole lives as Kutel slaves. It's still better than being dead. What, were you thinking of killing the captives when we caught up with them?"

"No."

"That's right. We're going to bring them home. They will start healing and get on with their lives."

Blorfindel said, "I was a Kutel captive once."

"Would you rather be dead now? That's what you're saying, Lantid, he'd be better off dead."

"That's not what I meant."

"I am sorry, Lantid. I know you've been through a terrible time, and not knowing about your parents must be very hard. I just want everyone to understand: we're going to rescue the captives, not put them out of their misery. If we have to make a choice between getting them killed or letting the Kutel keep them, then the Kutel can keep them."

Nickadola was the first to say, "Agreed." Lantid was the last.

Chapter 7

Chase

The sun was high overhead when they came to an abandoned Kutel campsite under a tall cliff. Lantid looked up the mountainside. "They must have been tired to stop here. There's no cover from the noon sun."

Nickadola said, "Tents."

"You think so?"

"They notched the trees to hang them. Some of them will survive, but not all."

Fargus was confused. "Some of who?"

Blorfindel was looking at the notches, too. "Some of the trees. There must have been a lot of them. They put up a lot of tents – big ones. Some of these notches are ten feet in the air."

Lantid bit his lip. "No fires. They must have been concerned that someone would see them. I wonder why? They would have been here the day after the attack. They still held the fortress at the time. They would have been breaking this camp when the knights got to town."

"The damage is older than that," Nickadola said.

Lantid snapped his fingers. "The retreating Kutel didn't make this camp!"

Alehra threw up her hands. "There's another couple of hundred Kutel around?"

"No – maybe, I don't know. No, they made this camp on the way <u>to</u> The Hunt. They didn't light fires because the defenders didn't know they were here yet."

Fargus asked, "So what does that tell us?"

"Nothing. We're wasting our time. Let's go."

They went another five miles on the trail. Blorfindel held up his hand and strained his hearing. "Crows. Something disturbed a flock of crows."

"How far away?"

"Close enough. I'm going to have a look." He took his new armor off. "I'll be back."

Blorfindel was walking casually when he came back. "It's a bear. There are some corpses and it's eating them. It must have shooed the crows away. It's a big one, not like the bears around Sekri Timbrali. My parents had a bearskin… uh, never mind."

Nickadola started down toward the path. "Maybe it saw something." Blorfindel put his armor on and caught back up with the group before they saw the bear. Nickadola was impressed. "He's a beauty! Eight, maybe nine hundred pounds!" The Timble ran toward it.

The others followed more cautiously. Lantid could not get the pack mule within sixty yards of the bear. Fargus looked back at them. "That mule has more sense than we do. That bear could swat the face off a Cral."

Nickadola cast his spell and spoke with the bear.

Once Blorfindel was satisfied that the bear wasn't going to attack Nickadola, he started looking at the corpses. He made certain to stay at least ten feet away from them so that the bear did not get the wrong idea. He shouted back to the others, "It looks like they're mostly Kutel. I think there's one Tafer, though. They're in pretty rough shape, it's hard to be sure. It looks like another campsite, but not so big."

Eventually Nickadola came back and reported to the group, "The Kutel stopped here for the day. They left corpses. He wasn't here when they died, but the bodies were still a little warm after the Kutel left. There were seven Kutel and two Tafers."

Lantid stared at the bodies. They were too far away for detail. "Can we look at them?"

"It's been a week, Lantid, and the animals have been here often. You're not going to be able to tell who they were. Even the bear thinks it's nasty now. It wasn't eating those corpses. There are some fresher Kutel corpses here, too. Some Kutel have come by alone or in smaller groups. The bear killed two."

"Did you ask how many Kutel there were in the big groups?"

"More than ten. Bears can't count very high."

Fargus asked, "Which way did they go?"

"He wasn't here, but there are two trails. One goes north, the other goes west – more or less."

Lantid said, "The captives went north. The group headed west is going to raid Dath. They may even be there by now."

Blorfindel quoted the message, "Victory in the east."

Lantid nodded. "We'd have to be able to fly to even get a message to Dath before the Kutel get there. Hopefully they also have orders to keep the town intact until the Tafers get the harvest in."

"It also means fewer Kutel are with the captives," Alehra added. "That's going to help."

They circled around the bear to the northwest and picked up the trail going north. It was clear that they were no longer following the army's path: the swath of destruction was much narrower and less complete. They traveled nearly another ten miles before the sun set behind the mountains. Fargus said, "My, it gets dark quickly here. This must be Kutel land."

Blorfindel said, "The Kutel may like the dark, but they don't command it. The mountains just pass in front of the sun. It's a lot different than watching the sunset over the valley from the Kingstone walls, though."

"Yes, yes it is. You seem used to it."

"Foralis is like this."

"Foralis?"

"My home town. We're going there after we're finished here."

Alehra explained to the confused cleric, "The Kutel burned it. He thinks they're disrespecting his ancestors or something."

Lantid led the mule up a gentile slope away from the trail. "We should camp off the trail. Who knows how many groups of Kutel are out here?"

They each took a turn at watch. When Alehra woke Fargus for his watch he asked, "How do I know when to wake Lantid?"

"When that star sets – well, goes behind the trees. No, that one. See it?"

"Yes, thank you."

"You're not used to this, are you?"

"I've never been so far from Kingstone in my life."

"You're doing pretty well then. Don't worry about it. Keep your eyes and ears open. If you see or hear anything strange, wake Lantid. He'll know what to do."

There was nothing for him to report. The night passed peacefully.

The next morning they spotted another Kutel campsite. They were surprised when a Kutel jumped up and ran. Blorfindel shot it in the back as two more jumped up. Blorfindel and Alehra both shot the same one and the third was off and running. As soon as Blorfindel had a clean shooting lane, it was over. The arrow struck the Kutel in the back of the neck. It was still struggling when he arrived. His sword put an abrupt end to its suffering. Blorfindel and Alehra hid the bodies off the trail.

"They'll be no hiding them from the crows," Fargus said.

"I know, but maybe any other Kutel around won't know we're here."

"Are they a rear guard? Just three of them?"

Lantid shook his head. "They're deserters or stragglers. The bear said there were smaller groups. One of them was wounded before Blorfindel shot him. The good news is that this camp is so close to the last one. I don't think they made fifteen miles that day."

"I don't understand. Why do we care how fast the deserters move?"

"It's not just their camp. These three didn't do all this damage."

Nickadola agreed, "Most of the damage to the trees was done days ago."

Fargus had to agree that there was a lot of damage for three Kutel. "You think we'll catch them, then?"

"That depends on how far we can move in a day, and how far they have to go. They have a big lead. We don't really know where they're going."

"Then we should go." They silently agreed and continued on.

They passed another Kutel campsite that afternoon. This one was unoccupied. It gave them all hope that they were catching up. Fargus worried, "Do you think that they're going slow because the captives are so badly wounded?"

Blorfindel said, "I think the captives that were slowing them down are back with the bear."

Lantid agreed, "They may have sent the wounded Kutel back with the captives. That would explain the dead Kutel, too. Anyone who was too wounded to walk they just left there."

Blorfindel agreed. "It's a Kutel thing to do."

They camped off the path again that night. Blorfindel woke Alehra early for her watch. "There's something on the trail. I'm going to check." As soon as she had her armor on, he snuck away. He did not like how loud he was. *This metal armor makes too much noise. I don't have time to take it off. Maybe Alehra has a point, that mail shirt goes on and off easily.*

There were Kutel voices ahead. "Come on! Nugrot won't wait forever. We have to catch him if we're going to get paid for this disaster."

"What pay? Nugrot doesn't have any metal. He left just as quick as he could, cowardly pussbag!"

Blorfindel closed on the sound at a run. *So long as they are shouting at each other, they won't hear me.*

"You mind your manners! Nugrot will hear about your mouth someday. I wonder what he'll use to fill it." The Kutel laughed.

"He won't hear nothin' that you don't tell him. He won't be a big-Kutel after now, anyway."

"He's big enough for you! He's still got all the boys he sent off after the burning, and he's got money coming for the captives, and I want my share – and yours, too. You owe it to me."

"I don't owe you cruska! I owe you a slap on the head!"

"You'll have to catch up, first! You owe me for getting you out! The metal-skins would have you now if it weren't for me – them or the bear. Even if you did get away, you'd be lost out here! You can't find your own ass without a guide!"

"You can find it with your tongue easy enough!"

Their conversation was starting to turn Blorfindel's stomach when he broke into the open. He was only a few feet away from two Kutel. Blorfindel dropped his bow and arrow and drew sword and dagger. The first Kutel never came on guard. It just stood there with his mouth open until Blorfindel stabbed it in the throat.

Blorfindel immediately turned to face the other Kutel. It tried to draw back far enough to put its spear point between itself in the Fitheran. Blorfindel followed the Kutel to stay inside its guard and stabbed his dagger into its armpit twice. When it dropped the spear he let it fall back a step and cut its throat with a sword slash.

He turned to recover his bow and saw that there was a third Kutel. It was quietly limping down the path away from him using a battleaxe like a cane. When Blorfindel picked up his bow it jumped behind a tree.

Blorfindel approached with an arrow ready until he was about three strides from the tree. *No sense in wasting an arrow on this one.* He put his bow down to draw his sword. The Kutel broke cover as soon as he put the bow down. It hopped toward him on one leg and the edge of its shield. It shouted as it came. It might have been comical if it had not been for the battleaxe that it held over its head.

Blorfindel drew and threw his war hammer at it with an awkward underhanded flick of his left hand. It hit the Kutel in the face and knocked it off its bizarre balance. It caught itself with the axe, but Blorfindel ran it through before it could fully recover.

He picked up his bow and arrow as quickly as he could and looked around for another target. When he could not see one, he listened for a few minutes. There was nothing. He recovered his war hammer and started walking back to camp. He heard a bowstring. Reflexively he threw himself to the ground and listened to the arrow go by. *It went the wrong way.* The sound of the bowstring was up the hill from him and the arrow went past toward the path.

The arrow hit its intended target, however. A fourth Kutel was on the path. It had hidden itself, but left cover to go over the bodies of its fallen comrades when the Fitheran walked away. Its armor saved its life, though the arrowhead penetrated enough to stick into its back. As Blorfindel got his bearings another arrow flew at the Kutel but it brought its shield up and intercepted the missile.

Blorfindel realized that the arrows were friendly and the Kutel was the target. He drew his sword and dagger and charged the Kutel. It picked up the battleaxe from the dead Kutel and turned to meet him. The Fitheran had to give way before the ferocity of the Kutel's attack. For the moment he resigned himself to just avoiding the mad axe.

The Kutel gained confidence as Blorfindel parried and dodged. It started to smile as the Fitheran danced around the battleaxe. It fell like a marionette without strings when Alehra stabbed it in the back of the neck.

"Who's on watch?"

"I woke Fargus. You need to be more careful. That one almost got away."

"Yeah." Blorfindel looked around. "Is that all of them?"

"I think so. That one was nearly enough. I thought you were going to dance with him all night."

"I was waiting for you. I got three. This one was yours."

"Right."

In the morning Blorfindel told the rest of the group about the Kutel conversation. Fargus took some hope from it. "They think this Nugrot character will be waiting for them. That sounds like good news. The longer they delay, the more likely that we can catch them."

Lantid nodded. "And the captives are worth money, which means that they'll at least try to keep them all alive and intact. It also means that their leader is with the captives, maybe. That will make this trickier. He's not as dumb as your average Kutel."

Blorfindel said, "Dumb or smart, he's going to be tougher than average. I don't know how 'big' a Kutel has to be to command and army, but I bet he's pretty tough."

***

That morning they came to another campsite. This time they were more cautious with their approach, but it was empty. Lantid shook his head. "Another fifteen miles. It's a good thing it's springtime."

Alehra asked, "Why?"

"Because the days are long and the nights are short. We have more time on the trail than they do. Even so, if this keeps up, it will take us another five to seven days to catch up."

Fargus was not ready to get discouraged. "But the others said they were waiting somewhere."

"Let's just hope they're not waiting in Bur-Droo."

"We've been turning a lot. Maybe they're lost? I am. It seems like we've been turned around a dozen times."

Nickadola said, "We've been turning a lot to get around the mountains but we've been heading just east of north since we left the bear."

Lantid frowned at the mountains on the left. "We'll have to turn west at some point. Al, you've sailed around the point. The Kutel valley is on the east side of The Spine, right?"

"The Spine is bigger than you think. It took us days to sail around it. Once we left Haafven we stayed as far out to sea as the captain dared. I didn't see much of the Kutel lands."

Blorfindel said, "We can't cut the corner anyway, even if we knew they were going west. There isn't any other trail through the mountains and we can't risk losing them."

Late that afternoon the trail descended into a river valley. They could see a camp by the river from a mile away. A large area had been cleared, though there was no sign of what happened to the trees. The camp itself consisted only of tent canopies.

The group took cover and stared down at the camp. Alehra said, "So the Kutel were right, they are waiting. We should get ready to attack soon, before the sun sets."

Fargus disagreed, "As much as I would like to see the captives freed, I don't think we have much chance of saving them all with an ill-planned attack." Lantid and Nickadola nodded.

Blorfindel started taking his armor off. "I'll go have a look."

Lantid was staring down at the river valley as he spoke, "Be very careful, and don't engage them – not even if you're sure you can get away clean. We have to surprise them when we attack. Anything we can do to make them feel safe, we should do."

Nickadola laughed. "Should we bake them a cake or something?"

"I'm serious. This isn't going to be like before. We must have total surprise and get it over with quickly. If they realize what's going on they may try to kill the prisoners. With only five of us it's going to be hard to stop them. Fargus, that means we kill them – all of them: no prisoners, no sermon, no mercy. If you get a chance to kill one it his sleep, when his back is turned, or when he's relieving himself, do so, and don't hesitate. We won't have time for people to hesitate."

"I get it. I don't see any prisoners down there, do you? I mean, would Kutel put the prisoners under a tent?"

"Maybe if it made them easier to guard. No, I wouldn't expect it, but we're too far away to know for sure. Blorfindel can tell us when he gets back."

Alehra shrugged off her pack and her armor and lay down with her shield over her eyes. "Wake me when he gets back."

It was fully dark when Blorfindel returned. He was surprised to find only Fargus was awake. He was not surprised that he got behind the cleric and into their little camp unnoticed. He sat and had a drink of water and watched the Tafer's back for a minute. Then he quietly woke Nickadola, Lantid, and finally Alehra. She jumped up and came on guard, startling Fargus.

"What? Oh! What happened? Were did you come from?"

"Behind you. You need to look around more when you're on watch."

"I'm sorry. I thought I was watching the camp."

Nickadola sighed. "Our camp, not theirs."

Blorfindel smiled. "Don't feel too badly about it. The Kutel had four sentries and they did no better."

"So what did you see?"

"No Tafers. I didn't cross the river, but there are none on this side. The river's bigger than it looks from here, by the way, easily a hundred fifty feet across. The Kutel have been in the river, though, and probably to the other side. They've also been up river but I don't know how far."

"How many?" Lantid wanted to know.

"Thirty, maybe more; I didn't go from tent to tent. Some of them are wounded."

"So they're resting here?"

"Resting and fishing. They have a bunch of fish drying all around the camp – some other meat, too."

Fargus started to say, "You don't think–"

Lantid interrupted him. "Not so long as they're worth money."

Blorfindel continued, "Anyway, we should be able to surprise them tomorrow. There really aren't too many of them, and if we get the sentries–"

Fargus asked, "What about the captives? Where are they?"

Lantid said, "Up river. I told you they had to go west at some point. This is it. We'll have to deal with these Kutel later, not now."

Alehra did not like it. "So we're going to just leave these guys behind us? They get stronger and heal up while we get tired climbing these mountains? It doesn't sound like much of a plan to me."

Fargus agreed with Lantid, "We should concentrate on the captives. If the Kutel get them to Bur-Droo, or wherever they're going, we will lose them forever."

"Do you think we're going to sneak fifty refugees past them? What if they don't stay here all that time? What if they're going up the river while we're coming down? They could meet us at night in our camp."

Lantid spoke calmly. "They could, and that would be bad, but we still have to leave them."

"But–"

"How much food are you carrying?"

"What?"

"How much food?"

"I don't know. I still have more than half, maybe two weeks if I'm careful. You said to pack heavy."

"How far do you think that will go among fifty people?"

"I thought the food on the mule was for them."

"It is, but it's not enough. It won't get us all back to The Hunt, not even at the rate we're going now. We'll slow down when we have the others, and every day we have to go to catch up with them is at least another day to get back."

Fargus caught on. "So we leave these Kutel here, fishing. When we get back we take their fish and we have enough food to get back to The Hunt."

"I hope it's enough. Maybe we'll do some fishing, too, or something, but I don't want to stay in the mountains any longer than we have to. We've been lucky with the weather so far. We may need their tents as much as their fish by the time we get back."

Blorfindel had his armor on by now. "Well, I hope everyone else had a nice rest."

Fargus asked, "What's that supposed to mean?"

Lantid answered, "It means that we're moving on."

"In the dark? Why not camp here?"

"Because we're too close to the Kutel. Now that it's dark they'll be active, and if they spot us here all of our options are bad. Also, we need to catch up to the captives as quickly as we can. We've been stopped for too long. Don't worry, Alehra, Nickadola, and I will stand watch tomorrow night. You two can rest. Fair's fair."

They stayed high on the mountain until the Kutel camp was hidden behind it, then made for the trail. They managed five miles in the dark before they made camp for the night. The morning came too soon for all of them.

Nickadola asked, "How long do you think we can keep this up?"

"Until we quit," Lantid answered. "If we can't cover more ground than they do, we might as well go back."

"It's a horrible strain on Sturdifoot. How heavy is his load?"

"As heavy as I dared. You're right, though, now that we have eaten some of our own rations we could take some of the weight off him." They redistributed the load of provisions. Lantid checked everyone's pack. "Blorfindel, Al, are you sure you want to carry that much? You've got the heavy armor and all."

Blorfindel said, "I can manage." Alehra just strapped her pack on and stood up.

Fargus looked around. "I may be just the new guy, but if we're coming back this way couldn't we hide some of it somewhere?"

"We might need it all to get back here. We don't know how far we'll have to go to catch up."

That morning they found that they had camped less than a mile downstream from a Kutel camp. Lantid was not happy to find it. "Crushk, I thought our forced march last night would have put us further ahead." They tried to move more quickly after that. When after only five miles they found another camp, he was confused. "This isn't right. Who made this camp? They can't have slowed to five miles a day."

Blorfindel suggested, "Maybe they're fishing too, or they were."

"Why? They had all the stores of The Hunt when they left. They could have taken all the food they wanted and made the captives carry it. They know how far they are going, or should know."

Fargus suggested, "Maybe they really are lost."

"No, their path makes sense up until now. They weren't wandering. Every day on the trail to the river they were making fifteen miles. The terrain here is easier, but they slow down? It doesn't make sense."

Alehra said, "If they're really only going five miles a day now, we should be catching up quickly. This could be the break we need."

"I still wish I knew why."

They passed two more Kutel camps spaced about five miles apart. Lantid started doing some calculations in his head as he walked. "Crushk!"

Alehra asked, "What?"

"I've been trying to work out how close we are. We won't catch them today. If they keep up like this we should catch them tomorrow. The question is, did they stop at the first camp on the river?"

"We know they didn't, we found their first camp."

"Maybe not: the camp we found would be about five miles from the one we avoided – one day for them at this rate."

Nickadola slapped his own forehead. "The trees!"

Blorfindel looked at the trees around them. They looked normal to him. "What about them?"

"The trees down by the first camp on the river! They cut them down!"

"It's a little late to be upset about that now, isn't it?"

"Did you see any wood when you were in their camp, or evidence of big fires?"

"No, not really. There was plenty of brush around, though."

"Where did the trunks go?"

"I don't know."

"Lantid! I think I know why they're so slow!"

"What? Why?"

"They're carrying logs."

"That's stupid. I'm sorry, but there are trees everywhere, why would they be carrying logs?"

"I don't know why, but they are. They cut down trees at the river, but the logs aren't there. Now they are moving really slowly. They have to be carrying the logs."

Lantid still did not believe it. "It doesn't make sense. Why carry logs when you can cut trees anywhere?"

Nickadola shrugged. He did not have an answer.

Five miles later they came to yet another camp on the river. They did not get another five miles before darkness fell. Lantid was not happy. "We're falling off the pace."

"Does that mean we won't catch them tomorrow?" Alehra asked.

"We should, if they keep going slow like this."

"Then I'm stopping here. I think my shoulders are bleeding under these straps."

Nickadola said, "Not here. Let's go away from the river. If that Kutel group below is following us I don't want to get caught tonight. Besides, that's not a sunset, that's a storm coming over the mountains. The river may rise tonight." Alehra grimaced and shrugged her pack into a slightly different position. They all climbed out of the river valley.

Nickadola asked Blorfindel to help him gather firewood. While they were away from camp, Fargus cast one of his healing spells on Alehra. A few seconds after he laid his hand on her, her shoulders were back to normal and the blisters on her feet were healed over. "Hey, that's nice. I could get used to this."

"Don't get too used to it. If there's a battle tonight I'll be short one cure."

"You should check with Blorfindel first, you might be short by two."

When Blorfindel and Nickadola arrived with the first armloads of wood Lantid frowned at it. "If we light a fire the Kutel might see it."

Blorfindel disagreed, "From where? They'd have to be right below us to see the light, and the dry wood won't smoke much."

Nickadola added, "There's a storm coming. We're going to need the heat tonight if we're going to keep pushing like this tomorrow."

Even Fargus was for the fire. "If we wait to light it until the storm is close, maybe they'll think it's a lightning fire."

Lantid gave up. While the Timble and the Fithcran went out to find more wood, the Tafers put up some shelters. Mostly they cut evergreen boughs and leaned them facing the unlit fire. Lantid tied a piece of canvass between two trees to form a wind break for the mule. "There, now you've got as much shelter as any of us." He turned to Alehra, "I've been traveling with Nickadola too long. Now I'm talking to the mule!" She was already asleep.

When Nickadola woke Blorfindel for second watch the wind had started to pick up. The Timble said, "I'll light the fire now. If we wait much longer we won't be able to get a fire lit at all."

"Lantid has a fire spell."

"Let's not wake him to cast it."

It took the Timble many tries, but eventually he got a fire lit underneath his cloak and was able to get the campfire going. He nestled under cover and wrapped himself tightly in the cloak. "Once the storm starts there won't be anything to see. Just concentrate on keeping the fire going. There's no point in you getting soaked so that you can see another three feet."

"Right."

"Tell Al the same thing when you wake her."

Nickadola was wrong. There was plenty of lightning to see. Even the roar of nearby thunder could not wake the sleepers, though the mule twitched and shivered. Blorfindel used nearly half of the dry wood to keep the fire burning hot in the deluge. The storm was over before Blorfindel woke Alehra for watch. He did not put out the fire. They were all wet and cold, especially Sturdifoot.

In the morning the fire was still burning low. Lantid did not wake the others for the dawn. Even fatigued as they all were, the damp woke them up eventually. One by one they gathered around the fire. They all needed it. They had their first hot meal since leaving The Hunt.

Lantid said, "We should catch them today, unless they speed up."

Nickadola climbed on the mule's back and stroked it to dry it before its burden went on for the day. "How far away do you think they are now?"

"That depends on a couple of things. Did they stop at the first camp or cut the corner?"

"They stopped at the first camp and cut trees. They are carrying logs, remember?"

"Maybe. It still doesn't make sense to me. If that's true, then they were probably close when we camped last night – less than ten miles away."

"But they will have moved away during the night, so they're fifteen miles away now?"

"Maybe. Maybe not. Did they move in the storm? If not, did they move afterward? When did the rain stop?"

Blorfindel answered, "Well before midnight, anyway. Did it rain at all on your watch, Al?"

"No, just tree drippings."

"So maybe they only went half a nights march. That puts them anywhere from six to twenty-one miles, depending on whether and how fast they were moving last night and the night before. We should catch them today."

They walked another three miles up the riverbank when they came to a Kutel camp that bore out Nickadola's theory. There was evidence of several very large fires, but no trees were cut in the area. There were some big logs in the ashes, only partially burned. They were clearly too big to have been collected on site. Lantid bit his lip as he looked around. "You were right. I still don't see why they did it, but you were right."

Fargus was concerned. "What if they made some sort of sacrifice? Karakak is supposed to require burnings."

Alehra had to ask, "Who is Karakak?"

"The Kutel god of lightning and random destruction."

Nickadola did not like it. "If they sacrificed to their lightning god, maybe they got what they asked for. That storm seems like an odd coincidence."

Lantid half smiled. "If they asked for that then they're even less intelligent than I thought. We wouldn't have caught them last night in perfect weather. We all needed the rest. But the Kutel probably had to wait out the storm."

Alehra stirred the ashes and found glowing embers, "This is still burning! They were here last night!"

Lantid said, "Yesterday or the day before, at the latest. No one was tending these fires during the storm, though."

Blorfindel had pushed on up the path a short distance. When he came back he said, "The river falls down from the mountainside just a little further on. The trail doesn't go that way. I think they went over that pass." He pointed to a saddle between two mountains.

Fargus asked, "Why there?"

"Because they've been going west, and that's the easiest way to go west. At least it looks that way from here. We'll still follow their trail, anyway."

Lantid said, "But they aren't carrying the logs anymore, which means they will have sped up. We'd better go."

After a two or three miles they were winding up the mountain towards the pass. Sturdifoot the mule proved true to his name and plodded faithfully behind. At a rest break Lantid said, "There won't be a five mile camp today. They must have pushed all the way over the pass in one trip, however far that is."

Blorfindel said, "We'll have to be careful when we cross the ridge. There isn't much cover up here and we don't want them to see us. They're close."

Nickadola confirmed, "These plants were cut after the rain."

"A silhouette on a ridge is pretty easy to pick out from below, but if the Kutel have to look at the sun to see the ridge, they probably won't. We want to crest the ridge with the sun still at our backs." They all got back on the trail.

Their shadows were getting short when Blorfindel came back from the ridge. "This is it. The path falls away from here. I think they're camped below us, someone is. There's something else – something you ought to see."

"What is it?"

"I think it's a town. Come and see, but don't stop on the ridge. Leave the mule for now."

One by one they each followed the Fitheran over the ridge. He lead them on an awkward path that kept them off the ridge most of the time. The wind that they had been listening too all morning was blasting them in the face as soon as they crossed to the west side of the pass. At first it was refreshing. When they stopped in the shade of a boulder it was cold.

Lantid stared down into the valley. "That's not a town; that's a city!"

"Bur-Droo? A river runs by, on the other side." Fargus asked.

"Who knows? It doesn't matter; you can bet it's not friendly."

Alehra was staring, too, "It's got a wall. If they're in there, we'll never get 'em out."

Blorfindel took a few steps forward and pointed more sharply down. "They aren't there yet. If you come here you can see a camp, but stay low. We're in plain view from here." They all came forward. "See there, that red thing under the trees, that's got to be a tent, and next to it there's a black one. Can you see it?"

Lantid said, "I can see the red one." He looked over to the city again, "What do you think? Are they ten miles away from the city?"

"Oh, yeah, ten anyway, maybe fifteen. They're only four or five miles form here, though."

"But they'll be settlements outside the city, maybe even patrols. The Kutel have to know how close they are. They'll start early tonight and be in their own beds by tomorrow morning."

Fargus laughed ruefully. "Did you have to mention beds?"

"What I mean is: we have to catch them today and stop them today. Tomorrow is not an option."

Nickadola asked, "Do you think they're in contact with the city already? They might have sent a runner or used some kind of signal."

"They might have. There's nothing we can do about it now. Our best chance is to get down there as soon as we can and get the captives back before they get to the city or get reinforcements. We don't even know that the captives are still there."

"So, what's the plan?" Fargus asked.

Lantid crouched down and started scratching in the dirt. "We want to get the captives out of there before the Kutel know that their leaving. That's the hard part. If we can do that, we can draw the Kutel into an ambush."

Chapter 8

Rescue

Blorfindel was creeping toward the Kutel camp from the southwest. There was one sentry between him and the captives. The plan said that he had to kill this one as soon as the trees moved. Alehra was approaching another sentry to his right with the same orders. If they were successful there would be a gap for the prisoners to escape through. Fargus was between them and slightly behind to lead the prisoners out.

Normally he would have thought this was an unacceptable gamble. Both he and Alehra were wearing their armor and making noise despite their best efforts. Nickadola had enlisted the aid of a few noisy birds who were now moving in and out through the Kutel camp and generally being a distraction. Blorfindel was afraid that they might wake some of the other Kutel, but the others thought it was their best chance of getting close enough to effect a rescue.

Lantid and Nickadola were north and south of the camp, respectively. They each also had a sentry to eliminate, but they could use spells to do it. Both were very confident that they would succeed in taking down the sentries.

The tricky question was: could they get the prisoners safely away before the sleeping Kutel reacted? There were forty or so Kutel in the camp. Nickadola said the trees might stop them, but there would probably be some that got away. The trees would probably wake all of them, though. He also warned that the trees could not tell friend from foe, so he could only use them against one sentry without getting the captives caught.

Blorfindel moved into position behind a rock, readied an arrow, and watched the trees. They seemed to wait for a very long time. Blorfindel allowed his gaze to wander for a moment. One of the sentries was very close to the captives. It was the one that Nickadola was responsible for. *He probably doesn't want to take a chance in getting the captives in his spell.*

When it started to step away Blorfindel concentrated on his own target. It was watching the birds fly around. It switched its spear to its shield hand and picked up a stone from the ground. It threw the stone at a bird, but missed. The other sentries laughed at it. The trees started moving.

Blorfindel shot his sentry in the back. It died quietly. Alehra's target was masked by its shield. She had to shoot it in the leg to get it to move before she could finish it. Naturally, it cried out in pain in between arrows. Blorfindel cringed at the sound, but there could be no helping it now.

The other two sentries were screaming as well. Nickadola's was hanging from a tree and struggling to free itself. It had no chance of overpowering the spruce. Lantid's sentry was loudest of all. It burst into flames. Unfortunately for all involved the spell did not instantly kill it. It screamed and ran around like a grotesque torch. The trees, of course, shrank back from the burning Kutel, but it was no danger to the captives, and that was the point.

Fargus broke cover and ran towards the captives. He did not shout to them. The plan called for him to get in and get out without the Kutel noticing him. So far it was working, the Kutel had plenty of other things to occupy them.

Both the captives and the Kutel began to wake up. Most of the Kutel were snatched up by the trees as soon as they moved, but not all. The others were secondary targets for Blorfindel and Alehra, at least until Fargus got the captives out past them. Blorfindel had to maneuver to his left to get a clear shooting lane. He did not want to shoot over the captives.

Lantid passed behind him. This also was part of the plan. He was to lead the captives away while Fargus, Blorfindel and Alehra formed a rear guard to keep the Kutel back. Nickadola was to move into position where he could use his sling.

One of the captives, a big, bald Tafer, picked up the sword that Alehra's sentry had dropped and shouted, "The Hunt and The Shield!" and charged at the Kutel.

Fargus shouted, "No! Follow me! This way!" but either the Tafer did not hear or did not listen.

Another Tafer picked up the spear from Blorfindel's sentry and followed the first. Yet another found the axe that the burning sentry had dropped and joined them. A fourth started in that direction but Fargus caught him, spun him around, and shoved him the other way. "Out! Get out, all of you! Now! Follow Lantid!" He pointed at the wizard who was now looking down at the camp from the path. "If you're fit enough to fight, you're fit enough to help the wounded! Now help someone up and go!" He drew his mace. Some of the Tafers might have thought it was to reinforce his orders, but he turned to protect the three that were already in battle.

Nickadola had to shout to him, "The trees! Stay back!"

The first Tafer got to a Kutel and slashed it's chest open with a sword before the trees grabbed him. The other two did not even close with their foes before they were caught.

The trees were catching the Kutel, too. Some had three or four in their boughs, but some of the Kutel were dodging and weaving their way through. Blorfindel shot one. It ducked to get away from a tree limb and nearly escaped the arrow. It was bleeding from the back of its scalp but it kept moving.

Alehra shot one of the Kutel that was held before she saw any of the ones that were moving. When she saw the Tafers get hung up she shouted, "Get them out of there! Call the trees off!"

Nickadola replied, "I can't! Not without letting all the Kutel go, too!" Nickadola had been clear, the trees would not kill, only hold. When he had first explained this, Blorfindel had been disappointed; now that there were Tafers caught in the trees he thought differently.

Fargus stood there watching. He was only ten feet away from the nearest of the held Tafers, but he could do nothing. Even if he could get to them he had no way of freeing them from the trees. He took a quick look over his shoulder and saw that a number of the captives were still there, torn between helping and fleeing. He shouted, "Get out! There's nothing you can do here! Help the others get away!" Reluctantly, they turned and ran.

Blorfindel kept shooting at the moving Kutel. Their erratic movements and the movements of the trees shielded them from his arrows. He dropped only two with four arrows. Nickadola, targeting held Kutel with his sling killed as many.

Alehra ran into the camp and stood to Fargus' right. When a Kutel tried to kill the bald Tafer she shot it through the heart. Blorfindel moved slowly to take up a position on Fargus' left. This was the plan for the rear guard, but they were supposed to be withdrawing with the captives, not standing in the Kutel camp. He shot and wounded another Kutel on the way.

From somewhere in the trees a Kutel gave orders, "Get out there and get those damned archers! You can kill the ones in the trees later!" The Kutel tried to obey.

Blorfindel, Alehra and Nickadola kept shooting. Nickadola used his sling to knock out the Kutel in the trees as fast as he could. Blorfindel and Alehra were targeting the free Kutel and dropping them almost as fast as they came. Alehra smiled and said, "Sort of reminds you of the ambush on the hill, doesn't it?"

Fargus intercepted the first Kutel to come free. While it parried his mace Blorfindel shot an arrow through both of its thighs. Then he answered, "Except we didn't have Fargus to pick up the leakers, and we didn't have Tafers in the line of fire."

Three more Kutel came free. Alehra shot one in the throat. Fargus could only intercept one. Blorfindel tossed his bow out of the way and drew his sword and dagger. He had to jump away from a Kutel axe before his sword was out. Another Kutel got out. Alehra's arrow hit its shield and she too had to draw steel. "We got to do more shooting from the hill, too."

Blorfindel stepped back out of reach of a downward chop. He stepped onto the axe handle and stabbed high and low with his sword and dagger. The Kutel raised its shield to turn his sword away making an opening for the dagger. It penetrated between the bones of the Kutel's forearm and he drew the weapon down until the Kutel struck him with its shield, knocking him away. His new skullcap prevented a nasty knock on the head. The Kutel fell back, weaponless, and could do nothing more than shout when Blorfindel pulled its shield down with his dagger and delivered the coup de grace.

Alehra was locked in a sword duel with the Kutel on her side. Blorfindel saw one of the Kutel who was working its way towards them pause long enough to stab its spear into a Tafer who was now helpless in the trees. Blorfindel held sword and dagger in his left hand and threw his war hammer at the offending Kutel even as it prepared to kill another of the held Tafers. The hammer head struck it just above the ear and lodged in its skull.

Alehra shaved the skin off her opponent's shin with the edge of her shield. When it flinched she stepped to the side of its shield and stabbed it in the ear. She closed with the Kutel fighting Fargus. Blorfindel tossed his sword back to his right hand and approached from the other side. It had been doing well with Fargus and had even landed a few blows – none of which penetrated the cleric's armor. It had no hope whatsoever against all three of them. It was able to parry Alehra's sword for a moment with its shield. Fargus hesitated, concentrating on the Kutel's sword. Blorfindel drove his sword through its armor and into its lung. When the pain held it in place Alehra cut its throat.

Another Kutel stepped out of the reach of the moving trees only to find that it was facing three armed opponents. Alehra shouted across to Blorfindel, "We've got this one. Get you bow singing." The Kutel had other ideas. It focused on the Fitheran and tried to put the other two behind its shield. Fargus' mace rocked the shield and made it step back. Alehra cut its calf open. It stumbled. She stabbed again at its neck. Fargus' mace struck the top of its head immediately after. The Kutel's bloody sword fell from its nerveless hands at Blorfindel's feet.

Blorfindel sheathed sword and dagger and picked up his bow. He could not see any more Kutel moving through the trees. He began shooting Kutel that were held. Alehra joined in a few seconds later. They had to move carefully around the trees to get shooting lanes, and the branches even tried to catch the arrows out of the air. Even so, nearly every arrow was a kill.

Fargus waited at the edge of the moving trees. "Are you going to shoot them all like that? They can't even move!"

Alehra shouted back, "In a few minutes those trees are going to let go. All of the Kutel who are still alive are going to hit us then. The three of us – plus the crazy Tafers in the trees – aren't going to stop them."

Blorfindel shot another Kutel before he shouted back across the trees, "The only other option we have is to leave these two and follow the original plan!"

Alehra shouted back, "I'm not leaving them! I came here for a rescue!"

Fargus looked into the trees. "I think… It looks like only one is still alive." He shouted at the trees, "Are there any Tafers still in there?"

A single voice responded, "The Shield!"

Blorfindel shot another Kutel. "I see him! It's the same crazy Kutel's son that charged in in the first place!"

Alehra shouted back, "I'm still not leaving him! Not unless we have to." She shot down a Kutel.

Blorfindel moved sideways as he replied, "I'm still here!"

Nickadola moved closer behind Fargus to get a clear shot. "The trees won't hold much longer anyway." He slung a bullet. "Everybody come back! We need to close in! The trees are going to let go soon!"

Alehra got one more arrow off before she dashed back. Blorfindel was already standing next to Fargus. The cleric shouted into the trees, "The trees are going to drop you! Get back here as quick as you can. We'll hold the line. You have to get back here!"

A voice came back, "I will not retreat before these Kutel!"

"Don't be stupid! Come back here where we can protect you! We have our weapons and armor! We are ready for them!" The trees let go. "To me! Now!"

Blorfindel heard the Kutel commander shout, "There's only four of them! Attack!" A dozen Kutel hit the ground running.

Fargus' eyes got wide, "Can you handle twelve at once?"

Alehra and Blorfindel each shot one arrow. Blorfindel's hit a Kutel in the eye. Alehra's deflected off the rim of a shield. They both said, "No."

Nickadola drew scimitar and shield and stepped up to the line. The Tafer in the trees held his ground. The Timble stepped forward beside Blorfindel, "We're going to have to go get him." Alehra and Blorfindel left their bows and drew as they advanced.

Fargus kept pace with them and held the line. He said under his breath, "If we live through this…" They all stopped when they got to the Tafer. Fargus shoved him in the shoulder with his mace head. "Stupid!"

The Kutel charged them. When they were two steps away the first seven Kutel fell flat on their faces. Blorfindel and Alehra leaped over them to engage the remaining four. Nickadola shouted to Fargus, "Kill the sleeping ones before they wake up!" and ran around them to engage one of the ones that was still on its feet.

Fargus stood there with his mouth open for a moment, then began to crush the skulls of the sleeping Kutel with his mace.

The first Kutel that Alehra caught was not ready. It tried to level its spear but she easily knocked it away with her shield. She kicked the bottom of its shield and stabbed over it. The Kutel was stone dead before it hit the ground.

Blorfindel ducked between two Kutel and charged past, turning a sword each with his sword and dagger. The remaining Kutel stabbed at him with a spear. He jumped over the attack and landed with both feet on the spear shaft. It fell back.

Alehra engaged the Kutel to Blorfindel's right. Nickadola took on the Kutel to his left. Blorfindel followed the spear-Kutel. It drew a sword and came on guard as he approached. It smiled cruelly. Blorfindel smiled back. "You're the leader," he said in Kutel, "the one called Nugrot?"

It was surprised to hear the Fitheran try to talk to it. It swung its heavy-bladed sword at Blorfindel, intending to take his legs off at the knees. He blocked it with his own sword and stepped quickly left while stabbing with his dagger. The Kutel's armor stopped the blade. It spoke, "I'll kill you. Nugrot will pay me for your head. You should have run away."

"I came for Nugrot." Blorfindel stabbed down at its foot with his sword. It moved, but too slowly: it's foot was bleeding now. It stabbed at his chest. He turned the blade with his dagger, but the point still scratched his armor. "I'll have Nugrot's head. Too bad you can't run and tell him, messenger-boy! Now that you've got a hole in your foot you're no good for anything. Your never going anywhere again."

It stepped in and struck him on the sword arm with its shield then punched him in the jaw. "Fool! Fitheran! I'll roast you alive!" Then it swung its sword backhanded across the Fitheran's throat.

Blorfindel allowed himself to fall backwards and lifted the Kutel's shield with both of his legs. With all of his weight on his shoulders Blorfindel stabbed his sword into the Kutel's groin. Then he shifted his angle on the shield and pushed the Kutel over backward.

When he jumped to his feet Alehra and the unknown Tafer were standing there facing another Kutel. The Tafer shouted, "He's mine!" but Blorfindel knocked its sword away with his dagger, jumped on its shield and stabbed it in the eye with his sword. He turned around. Ignoring the Tafer he joined Nickadola and Fargus to help with the sleeping Kutel, but they were all dead when he got there.

Fargus wiped the blood away from his mouth with the back of his hand. "I didn't think we were going to make it."

Alehra smiled, "You forgot Lantid. Speaking of Lantid, he's probably waiting for us."

The bald Tafer spoke to Blorfindel, "In the future you would be wise to do as you're told."

Alehra answered before the Fitheran could react, "Who on Yultif's good earth are you to be telling Blorfindel what to do? You're the one who made a mess of the plan to begin with!"

"I am Shieldmaster Lorten of The Hunt. You will remember that when I give you an order."

Alehra was unimpressed. "Yeah, right, whatever." She turned to Fargus, "You should see if the other two are alive."

"I already did. They're quite dead. They were both stabbed in the chest." He looked around. "Someone should go get Lantid. He may want to change the plan now that all the Kutel are dead."

Lorten spoke, "Lantid may have led you here, but I am in charge now."

Alehra said to his face, "Lantid got us here. He'll get us out. You just button up."

"Now you just listen to me–"

Fargus interrupted, "I've watched you get two Tafers killed who listened to you. You just keep quiet and do as you're told. We'd be gone with all of the captives by now if it weren't for you. We can't have two leaders. Every time you give an order you get in the way. We can't be forever debating about it."

Lorten was not finished. "I don't know where you're from or why you never learned what it means to obey orders, but you're going to learn now–"

Blorfindel put his fist in the Tafer's shoulder and shoved him around so that they were facing each other. They both still had weapons in hand. The Fitheran's voice was low and dangerous. "If you give one more order I'll kill you myself. Two Tafers are already dead. We took on forty Kutel just to pull you out. You could have gotten us all killed – would have if Lantid hadn't come back to cast his spell. So I'm telling you right now, the next time I hear you give an order I'm going to silence you forever and just assume that I'm saving lives in the process."

"It is against the law to even threaten a Shieldmaster!"

Nickadola and Alehra smiled. Blorfindel laughed in Lorten's face. "What's the punishment? Having your town burned and everyone you know sold as Kutel slaves?"

"Death."

Much to Lorten's consternation, Blorfindel laughed again. "Do you know who I am? Do you know what I am?"

"You're a crazy Fitheran on his way to the block – if you live that long."

"I am Blorfindel Brighteyes. That's right, I'm a Brighteyes. I've been under a death sentence for sixty years. Do you think you're going to collect? If it's illegal to threaten a Shieldmaster, then I'm already guilty of that, too. In fact, the last Shieldmaster I met lost the duel and could barely walk away. If you think that here, within sight of a Kutel city, I'm afraid of your Tafer law, you're crazier than a sun struck squirrel." Blorfindel's smile vanished. "Now if you want to enforce your law, or try to take command, you might as well start here and now." Blorfindel came on guard.

When the Shieldmaster hesitated Alehra and Nickadola drew as well. The Taforam spoke first, "Give it up. You have no chance."

Nickadola said, "We're all together on this. You had your chance to lead and failed. The Hunt is a ruin because of it. There are going to be some tough situations ahead, and at least one battle. You will do as you are told and you will not get in the way. If you're going to challenge our leadership then you're a liability – more dangerous than the Kutel. If Lantid tells you to go, you go. If he tells you to stop, you stop. If he says piss on your own foot then you better have been drinking your water. And, if once we're back to The Hunt you decide to take put the law to any of us, you'll have to deal with all of us. Right now I think we could take over your whole town, if we wanted the crushk-pile."

"I am the Shieldmaster of The Hunt. Leadership is my birthright."

"My father, Laliam Steelhand, was the leader of the archers of Foralis, does that make leadership my birthright, too?"

Fargus interrupted. "None of that matters. Birthrights won't get everyone back to The Shield Valley alive. Even if your parentage did make you Shieldmaster of The Hunt, this isn't The Hunt. By the time we get back to The Hunt... You know, I think you should consider abdicating. You got your command destroyed, after all. It will take a long time to rebuild the damage, and that is going to take a leader who knows about more than just charging into battle. If the Kutel come back during the reconstruction, the town will be much harder to defend that it was when you lost it. If you're going to try to stay the Shieldmaster of The Hunt then I am going to have to recommend the King find someone to replace you."

"You're going to recommend?"

"Do you want your name to be remembered as the Shieldmaster who got the town burned and became the enemy of the temple of Feadin at Kingstone?"

Nickadola picked up the lecture. "Even that doesn't matter now. We have to get back to The Hunt before that matters. What would you do, Shieldmaster? If you were in command, do you know how to get back?"

"We can follow our own path."

"And the Kutel band that is barring the way?"

"We'll have to fight our way through."

"Just like you did at The Hunt? They are the same Kutel that defeated you before and they know it, and they're rested. What about food? What would you feed your people on the way home?"

"We could hunt."

"Hunt what? The Kutel have driven all of the game away from the trail and hunted this ground themselves. You'd have to spread your group thin to find enough food."

"Then we spread thin."

"Thin enough so that small Kutel groups could pick you off in ones and twos? They are out here, you know. We have caught a couple of groups."

"So there will be losses."

"You say that much too easily. You don't have a plan. You don't know what to do. You don't even know where you are. How fast do you think you could move and hunt? How long before the Kutel caught you? We just fought a battle within sight of Bur-Droo. Don't you think they'll send someone to investigate?"

"I didn't think about that."

Alehra said, "Lantid did. He's the one with a plan. Even if he doesn't have all the answers I at least trust him to think our way out. I've only known you for a couple of minutes and you have done nothing but make mistakes."

"That's all Lantid does, sit around and think. There's no action in him!"

Blorfindel laughed again. "He was the one who got us here in time – if it wasn't for him we'd have spent a day fighting another Kutel group and you'd be in Bur-Droo before we caught up. He accounted for a fifth of the dead Kutel here, and he broke their charge when they were about to run us down. That was after he led the other captives away. You've got a lot of action to do before you come even with Lantid."

Alehra continued, "I don't know why we even bother. You will do as you are told. If you get in the way, it will be a race between Blorfindel and I to see who kills you."

"You have all the advantages against me." Lorten dropped the Kutel sword.

Fargus pointed to the weapon. "No one said you had to be a prisoner. Pick it up. We may need the help in battle coming up, just be ready to follow orders." He turned to the others. "I think we should take a quick look at the dead Kutel and take what we can. There are some of the other captives who are fit enough to fight in self-defense."

Nickadola agreed. "And they might have some food. I'll go catch up with Lantid and the others, maybe we'll send back some of the Tafers to help carry."

They made two litters of spears and shields and piled the best of the Kutel weapons on top. Alehra and Blorfindel also recovered as many of their arrows as they could. There was very little food, but they took what there was. Lantid sent a few able Tafers down to help carry, leaving the rear guard to concentrate on being a rear guard. They got back to the rendezvous point without further incident.

Lantid was in a hurry. "Let's go. We have to get back over the pass. The Kutel will come after us when the sun goes down. We need to stay ahead of them."

Fargus said, "Some of these people need rest. The Kutel nearly walked them to death."

"Remember: every day that we sit still may means a day on the trail without food. We just don't have options. I think we'll spend all day and all night on the other side of the pass. That will have to do. We'll still have to find a place we can defend from either side. There's no guarantee that the other group is still fishing. They may be waiting for us when we come over."

Blorfindel said, "Nugrot's still out there somewhere."

"He's probably fishing. He's smart enough to know that they need food – remember the note? He's smart enough to regroup and gather the stragglers. He's probably healing his wounded up, too. He doesn't even know we're here and he's making the right decisions. He can play a waiting game and we can't."

Chapter 9

Pass

The sun was below the level of the pass when they crossed back over. Their world instantly fell into shadows. The captives had been resting most of the day and the rescuers were crossing the high pass for the second time that day, but it was Lantid pushing the crowd forward. "We can't stop here. No, get up! Get up and walk. You'll freeze up here in the wind if you stop. We can light a fire on the other side and have a proper camp."

Someone said, "Who'd have thought it would be Lantid walking us into the ground?"

A Taforam's voice said, "You're breathing much better than usual, Lantid."

"I got cured at the temple of Feadin in Kingstone. Come on, people, I'm as tired as any of you – this is my second time over this pass today – but we can't let the Kutel catch us tonight."

Even with Lantid pushing everyone on, it was after midnight when they got to the Kutel camp. They stirred ashes and found orange glowing coals. Fargus put a hand on Lantid's shoulder, "We need to stop. They need the heat."

"What if we're being followed?"

Blorfindel answered, "We're not. They didn't come over the pass, unless they snuck over, I've been watching. I can set up out by the falls and watch. Unless it clouds over I'll see them on the ridge."

"Take someone with you. Nobody should be out here alone."

Fargus added, "And don't let yourself get cold."

Lantid squinted at the Fitheran, "What happened to your jaw?"

"I got hit by a Kutel."

"Fargus, why don't you cast one of your heals on him?"

"What about the captives? Most of them could use a heal."

"So long as they can walk they don't need a heal. Blorfindel may be in combat later. If he goes down the Tafers aren't going to fill the gap. That goes for all of us. You can use what's leftover on the rest of them, especially the ones with leg and foot wounds."

Fargus healed the Fitheran. The spell cured the damage from the Kutel's fist and many of the blisters and bruises from the trek. Even Blorfindel's loose teeth tightened up. "That's nice, thanks."

Nickadola volunteered to sit with Blorfindel, "I don't want to watch the trees burn, anyway. What a waste. Oh, yeah," he tapped a random Tafer on the hip, "what happened to the trees? What were the Kutel doing?"

"The Kutel leader was footsore when we got to the river, so he made us build a raft and pull him up the river from the shore. We had to pull it out of the river and carry it up here so they could burn it."

Lantid said, "You're lucky. If you hadn't been pulling the raft we wouldn't have caught up with you. Blorfindel, don't kill yourself out there. If they don't come over the pass in the next couple of hours they won't get here tonight. Don't forget to look the other way every now and then, that other group may try to by-pass us and go over the pass."

After their watch Blorfindel and Nickadola tried to sneak back into camp but Fargus saw them this time. Blorfindel smiled. "You're getting better."

Fargus laughed. "That's funny, 'cause I feel worse. At least I got an hour's sleep. Sleep wherever you want. Lantid made them set up all the tents, so there's plenty of room. I think he wants to make us look like more than we are."

"How many are we?"

"I don't know. I'm too tired to count. We'll figure it out in the morning. You know, we forgot the two bodies."

"Forgot? Oh, that's right, Tafers want funerals. Fitherani don't do that."

"Timbles have funerals, too. Still, we couldn't have taken the time to bury them."

Fargus shook his head. "I don't even know their names."

Blorfindel said, "The Shieldmaster better know them. He better not forget them, either."

Fargus rubbed his eyes. "You know, he hasn't said a word to Lantid. I don't think Lantid spoke to him either, except when he was talking to all of us."

"I don't think they like each other very much," Blorfindel said.

Nickadola smiled. "Hatred might be a better word."

Fargus snorted. "Everyone knows it, too. I mean, they weren't there when we told him off, neither was Lantid. I don't think he's spoken directly to anyone."

"Weren't his parents in the group?"

"I don't think so. The Kutel didn't save many people that were that old."

Nickadola took a slow breath. "No wonder he's been driving so hard. He's trying not to think about it."

"Lorten's that old, isn't he?" Blorfindel asked. "It's hard to tell with Tafers, they get old so fast."

"They saved the Shieldmaster and his wife. I think they were trophies rather than slaves. She's having a hard time. She's the one they carried up from the path. He's physically fit. Mentally, well, you know."

"Lantid was right. The Kutel commander back there was smarter than this Shieldmaster."

"Get some sleep."

The sun was high over the river when Nickadola woke Blorfindel for watch. Half-asleep, he spoke in Timbrali, "We're still keeping watches? Did I miss a day? What?"

The Timble replied in Timbrali, "You haven't missed much. We're not moving today so we started the watches over again when the sun came out from behind the horizon. The Tafers need to get used to being awake in the daylight again, and we all need the rest. Lantid got a count, there are twenty-nine of them. I did get one juicy piece of gossip, though."

"What's that?"

"Lantid's parents are here. They just won't talk to each other. Even after all this, he and his father can't get along. I think his mother wants to talk to him but his father won't allow it."

Blorfindel started putting on his armor. "Who is it?"

Nickadola waited until the Fitheran looked him in the eye. "It's Lorten."

"The Shieldmaster? I don't believe it. There's no way that squirrel-brain had a son as smart a Lantid."

"I guess Sodri, that's Lantid's mother, is pretty smart."

Blorfindel laughed. "She made a cuckold of him with her teacher or someone."

"Don't talk like that! Not even in Timbrali. Who knows if any of the Tafers speak it?"

"If you say so. How did you find out?"

"All of the captives know – all of the ones that are old enough to remember. They're all shocked that he came. They're less surprised to see a Timble, a Fitheran, and a Taforam in the rescue party. They expected him to be dead by now."

"So what do we do?"

"I don't know. I don't think there's anything we can do. Lorten knows where we stand, assuming that he isn't dumb enough to forget your threat yesterday. He's been arming his people this morning. Keep an eye on him, I don't trust him. Oh, and guard the stores. We have to ration the food, at least until we get some more. Some of the Tafers wandered towards it, but they turned around when I gave them the eye."

"Because you look so dangerous."

"Very funny. We got the job done, didn't we? They know we beat the Kutel, anyway."

"I guess we did. We've still got a long trip back."

"Yes. I'm going to wander down to the river and see if I can see any smoke or maybe a sign of the other Kutel group."

Blorfindel had just woken Alehra for watch when Nickadola came back. "They're still fishing."

"You didn't see anything then?"

"I asked a duck to fly down to take a look. Her memory's a little shaky, but there's only one Kutel group on the river, and it's closer to the coast than it is to us."

"How many are there?"

"If a bear can't count them do you think you're going to get accurate numbers from a bird? She saw the fish, though."

"How far is the coast?"

"I don't know, but its got to be at least a little ways downstream from where we met the river or we would have seen it." He looked at the Tafers milling around, "Has Lantid opened the stores?"

"He's still asleep."

"I think I'll see if some of the Tafers want to go fishing. We're not moving today, we might as well see if we can raise our stocks a bit."

"Fish aren't your friends?"

"That's one of the problems with being able to talk to plants and animals: sometimes you have to eat some of them. By the way, ducks are off the menu – I made a deal."

"Of course."

"Besides, if we catch some of the big fish maybe we'll save some ducklings. You should see the fuzzy little peeps."

They spent all day and all night at the camp. Blorfindel decided to break out his cittern. The Tafers seemed to hang on every note, and through the music they realized that they were free of the Kutel. Most of them had been in shock or too fatigued to realize what was going on. The bright, happy sounds seemed miles away from their nightmare trek, and the ordeal to come.

Nickadola's fishing trip brought back enough meat for everyone's dinner and some to spare. They were all glad to have it, though even the Tafers who were too sore or too tired to fish spent most of the day cleaning and boning them. They asked Blorfindel to keep playing rather than help them. They seemed to need music more than food.

Chapter 10

The Crusher

The following morning they were back on the trail. Blorfindel and Nickadola were leading the way with one of the Tafers. They were scouting well ahead of the rest of the group, and the Tafer was supposed to run a message back to the main group if they found anything. Even though they were moving with caution and some stealth, they kept pulling ahead. They made only twelve miles that day.

First thing the next morning Nickadola got a message from a duck. "The Kutel are at our last camp. They're following us."

Lantid bit his lip. "Well, I guess we expected it. They'll catch us at this rate, maybe tonight."

Lorten said, "We'll just have to move faster."

Fargus shook his head. "The wounded can hardly keep up as it is. We'd be walking them to death." He drew his mace. The action was not lost on Lorten. "We agreed, if it's a choice between captured and dead, we let the Kutel have them."

"We'll die fighting!" Lorten insisted.

Blorfindel looked the Shieldmaster in the eye and said quietly, "You first."

Nickadola said, "We don't have time for this! We've got enough problems with the Kutel."

Lantid nodded. "We'll fight them. We have to. We'll look for a good spot to ambush them today. I think I remember a narrow pass ahead.

Lorten, you will take anyone who can't fight and keep going while the daylight holds. We'll catch up to you after the battle if we can. If we're not back by morning, don't wait for us."

"That's Shieldmaster Lorten, Lantid!"

"Sixteen years ago you told me that if I wasn't fit to lead Tafers into combat then I wasn't fit to be Shieldmaster. Well, you're not fit to lead Tafers into battle. You're mentally deficient. You've proven that time and again with your childish tactics and disregard for battlefield discipline. This time you got caught by a force with superior numbers and in spite of having every other advantage – high ground, superior cover and position, superior supplies, superior weapons, and operating on the same ground your troops train on every day – you lost. In the last battle you made another mistake and got two more Tafers killed when it was totally unnecessary to put them in harm's way. I will never call you 'Shieldmaster' again, just like you'll never call me 'son' again."

"Lantid, I–"

"In a few hours we're going into battle against a foe of unknown strength. They will probably have us vastly outnumbered. They will have better supplies, they will not be burdened by the wounded, and they have us caught between two forces, either of which has sufficient strength to wipe us out in a fair fight. We're not going to give them a fair fight. If we can manage it we're not going to give them a chance at all. I've changed my mind. I want you with me where I can see you. Sodri can take command of the others for a day." He stormed off without giving anyone a chance to reply.

Alehra tapped Lorten on the shoulder with an arrow. "I'm watching you." She ran to catch up with Lantid.

"She's awfully mouthy for a Taforam."

Blorfindel laughed. Nickadola said, "That Taforam killed a Cral in hand to hand combat. I, for one, think you should frightened."

When they caught up with Lantid he was going over the armed Tafers. He had already sent the non-combatants forward. There were fourteen left, but Fargus did not like some of his choices. "You can't let him fight, Lantid, he's just a child."

The little Tafer proved his point by shouting, "Am not!"

Lantid said, "He's not going to fight. What's your name, kid?"

"Ritt."

"Ritt, you are our signal-Tafer. Also, help with the wounded – get them out of the fighting and get a bandage on them."

Fargus had not lost momentum. "And him? His right arm's a mess. If I heal him now I won't have anything left for the battle. You said heal the ones with leg wounds first."

"He can stand in the back and make it look like we have more soldiers." Lantid started pulling things from his pack. "Here, you with the sling, take these bandages. You'll be behind the lines all the time, so you're the first one to help the wounded."

"Right."

"Ritt, can you start a fire? You know, with flint and steel and tinder?" The child nodded vigorously. "Here's my tinder box and take this lantern and oil. Don't light anything until I say, and don't fill the lantern until you're in position or you'll spill the oil all over."

"Yes, Shieldmaster."

"It's Lantid, Ritt, just Lantid."

One of the older Tafers spoke up, "I thought you were taking over as Shieldmaster."

"You're Kochie, right? Listen Kochie, nothing has changed between me and Lorten, except that right now we're doing things my way. Anyone who'd rather follow orders from him might as well go now and catch up with the others; we don't have time for politics." He paused long enough to look each of them in the eye. Many of them looked beyond him to Lorten, but no one walked away.

One of the Tafers spoke up, "You've come a long way, Lantid."

"Longer than you know, and we've still got a long way to go. Come on, we need to get going, too. If you see anything that can be cut into a sturdy spear-shaft, stop and cut it. It's got to be straight for at least ten feet. Sorry, Nickadola, but we're going to have to cut some live wood."

"What for?"

"Stakes. You'll see. Trust me, I wouldn't do this if I didn't think it was important. We're not building a raft or taking them to the sawmill." Lantid went over his plan in his mind as they walked. "Nickadola, can you get us a fast messenger, preferably a bird?"

Nickadola had to stop and wake an owl along the way to enlist his aid. As payment the Timble killed two squirrels with his sling.

The spot Lantid remembered was only three miles downstream. The riverbank here was a steep rocky slope that slid fifteen feet down from the path to the river. The path itself was about twenty feet wide. On the other side a mountain rose. On the west face there was a small cliff and some debris where a rockslide had fallen. The north slope, facing the path, was steep and rocky, but not a wall.

Lantid called a halt. "Everyone with poles set them up here. They need to point up the path and have the points between waist and chest high. Leave enough space between them so that you can move in and out. No, sharpen them after they're set."

"The ground's too hard to drive them in here."

"Then block them up with rocks."

Lorten said, "You don't really expect the Kutel to throw themselves on these things, do you?"

"That is exactly what I don't expect them to do. Listen, everyone, these poles are to make the front of the Kutel line slow down. That's all. The fighting line is going to be too thin here to stop them if they charge. The stakes will stop the charge. Now get it set up, your lives do depend on it.

"Not you, Ritt. I want you to go up the slope and build a little fire above the cliff. Stay back from the cliff, but close enough so you can see up the path, right?"

"Right!"

"Nickadola, you go with Ritt and help him find some nice dry deadwood. You've got to have enough to keep a little signal fire going all night."

Lantid turned back to the Tafers. "When the Kutel come Nickadola will pull some fog out of the river and onto the path for you. He's going to use this line as a guide. Don't go into the fog! That means you, Lorten! It will probably be after midnight by the time the Kutel get to you. You will not be able to see at all in the fog. Even the Kutel won't be able to see what's going on in the battle line from two or three ranks back. That's important. They won't be able to tell how thin you are here."

"You sound like you're not going to be here."

"We're going to be further up the trail. We'll hit them from behind as soon as they commit to attacking here. We will take out their leaders. The Kutel won't march through a wall of magical fog to attack an unknown force without a strong leader to push them. When the front ranks hear the back ranks panic, they'll probably run away. Do not chase them into the fog. Your job is to hold this line. If you don't kill a single Kutel, that's fine so long as the line doesn't break. Does everyone understand?" He paused to look everyone in the eye again. In turn, they each nodded. He had to hold Lorten's gaze for a few heartbeats before the Shieldmaster accepted his role.

"When they break they will either run toward us, in which case we'll kill them, or they'll run into this side canyon past the cliff. Once the path is clear of Kutel we can all follow them in and finish them off."

Blorfindel said, "When you're done with the stakes, why not pull some loose rocks out of the river or that rock pile and put them in the path were the fog is going to be? That'll slow them down."

"Good idea. Are you ready to go scouting?"

"Just give me time to get out of my armor."

"Right. We'll be up that slope waiting for you to come back."

Fargus said, "Don't forget to bring something to eat; it could be a long wait."

Blorfindel took his hiding place about a mile up the path from the line. He made himself comfortable and the warm sunshine put him to sleep almost immediately. A night chill woke him. He checked to see that the path was clear and then stretched as well as his cover would allow. He looked at the stars; it was well after midnight. He worked on a little hardtack and water while he waited. *So this is what Biolmi meant about eating hardtack and putting my life on the line. It's a good thing that it's not raining. I wonder how my sentry would do in the rain?*

He saw the owl approaching even before it called. He waved back. That was the signal. The Kutel were close. The owl turned and found some rising air. Blorfindel packed up and got ready to move. When the Kutel got close enough to hear he crawled under the boughs of a young fir tree. *Just like during the archery test, only I'm closer to the Kutel.*

He watched many walk by in silence. A few of them grumbled as they went. It was some time before any of them spoke loud enough to be heard. "We should look for a camp soon."

"Tired already, puss-feet? There's a lot more walking for you before you can sleep."

Blorfindel made a note of that one. *He must be a leader.*

"Why are we chasing these Tafers, anyway?"

"Because I said so."

"Well I say my boys and I are going to stop right here."

Blorfindel thought, *Two leaders.*

"I'll knock your fat, useless head off your narrow shoulders if you do. We're going to catch those Tafers tonight even if we have to march in the daylight."

"Why?"

"Because they've got all the stuff that Nugrot took from the Tafers, that's why."

"How do you know that?"

"You're so stupid, I don't know how you remember to take your pants off to…" They were moving out of earshot. Blorfindel decided not to risk breaking cover to hear the rest of their conversation.

He watched the rest of the Kutel go by and waited a few minutes to be certain. Then he finally broke cover and followed them. He climbed a low mountainside and sprinted by to get in front of them again. None of the Kutel heard him over their own tramping feet. He was back down in the path and still moving quickly when he came around a mountain and saw the signal fire. He worked back off the path so that his silhouette would not be visible to the Kutel. A few minutes later he met Lantid, Alehra and Fargus at their hiding place. "Where's Nickadola?"

"He has to be down by the river to pull the fog out."

"Well, I picked out two leaders. One is tall and broad and carries a heavy bladed single-edged sword – like a giant cleaver. The other is a little shorter and has a big head. He has a bear skull helmet over it which makes his head look as big as his shoulders. He carries a mace. The one with the cleaver is stronger, but maybe not by much."

"How many Kutel total?"

"A lot. I don't have enough arrows."

Alehra handed him a bundle. "Here, I packed extra."

Lantid was more concerned about numbers. "'A lot?' What are you, a duck now? How many were there?"

"I'd say the weak leader's group is in front – that makes sense, right? There are about forty of them. The strong leader has at least fifty. They're not far apart, not so you'd notice a gap. They don't have a beater and the leaders don't seem to have shield-bearers."

Alehra asked, "Where were the leaders?"

"In the middle. They were arguing when they went by me."

Lantid said, "They'll move around once they think they're getting into battle. I think they only use beaters and shield-bearers against the Fitherani. I've never heard of them before."

Blorfindel smiled. "That's because you Tafers don't know how to lay a good ambush." He started to put on his armor and pretended not to hear their replies.

It was not long before they could hear the Kutel walking the path below them. They all stayed out of sight from the path. Blorfindel tried not to stare at the signal fire. *I will need my night vision when the shooting starts.* A Tafer with an axe walked in front of the signal fire. He made a perfect silhouette. "Who is that?"

"That's the signal. The lookout just saw the Kutel. He's going down to join the others."

"All the Kutel must have seen it too. Shh, listen, they saw him."

"They're supposed to. Hopefully the Kutel will think he was the only lookout up there. The kid will light the lamp when the Kutel engage the Tafer line. If the line breaks he will put all the lights out and hide. Try to look up every now and then.

"Get to your shooting positions. Remember, once they're committed to the attack, silence the leaders. Don't wait for the fog. We have to shut them up before they can turn their forces on us. Neither of our groups can stop either of theirs if they fight intelligently."

Alehra said, "Don't worry, we'll dumb them up for you – or is that dumb them down?"

Blorfindel said, "I've got Cleaver, you take care of Big Head." She nodded as they split up.

The big-headed Kutel leader was forming his troops into lines when Blorfindel and Alehra got into their shooting positions. One of the shaky parts of the plan was the Taforam's vision: it was too dark for Alehra to see properly. She would be shooting at a dark spot on a dark trail. The task would have been impossible if it was not for the river sparkling in the starlight on the other side of the trail.

Blorfindel had no trouble picking out his primary target. He was at the very back of the Kutel group haranguing his troops. The Fitheran's night vision was good enough to pick out a vital area.

They waited.

Eventually the leader at the rear became impatient and had his troops push the other group forward into battle. The Kutel battle line was in disarray by the time they had taken their third step, but they were still bearing down on only thirteen armed Tafers.

The Kutel, however, could not see through the Tafer lines to know how thick they were, and all of these Kutel had been over the battle site on the other side of the pass. Every one of them remembered that there were over forty dead Kutel bodies there and only two dead Tafers. The Kutel in the front line very much wanted to be somewhere else. By the time they got to the stakes many of them were only moving forward because they were being pushed from behind.

Blorfindel took his shot. The arrow struck the Kutel in the neck. The Fitheran watched in amazement as the Kutel pulled the arrow out and started giving orders. Blorfindel was not too amazed to shoot again. The Kutel turned and raised its shield. Blorfindel expected this and shot low.

The arrow struck its thigh. The Kutel seemed to ignore the wound and continued to give orders. Blorfindel shot lower still, this time the arrow passed through its left foot into the rocky trail. The Kutel merely stooped to pull the arrow out. While it was bent forward Blorfindel put his next arrow over its head and into the gap in its armor at the back of its neck. Its right arm went instantly limp, but it still fell slowly.

He looked over to Alehra's target. The big-headed Kutel leader was still alive, cowering under its shield. Four arrows stuck out of the heavy oak target and one more out of the Kutel's helmet. Her arrows were having the desired effect, it could not direct the battle, but that would only last for so long. Eventually it would get the help that it was screaming for. Blorfindel hesitated for just a moment. The Kutel in the front group were trying to withdraw back to their leader while the rear group pushed on through them. He could not see through the fog to the Tafers' battle line, but the second light was lit. He shot at the second Kutel leader. It had no idea where he was and his angle was much different than Alehra's. While its shield completely covered it from her direction, Blorfindel put an arrow in its right eye. Again, the Kutel leader did not drop. *What are they made of?* Blorfindel wondered. He shot it in the throat and it fell over. It was still kicking but it could not give orders. Alehra had put two more arrows into its shield in the meantime. Blorfindel had to shout over the Kutel voices for her to hear him, "It's down, change targets!"

"I can't see."

Even as she spoke a torch arced over their heads and landed on the side of the path below. In a few moments the sputtering torch relit and illuminated some of the Kutel in the back ranks. Blorfindel tried to concentrate his arrows on the Kutel further away from the torch. Alehra shot at the Kutel in the light. Fortunately the rank-and-file Kutel were not as tough as their leaders.

Six arrows and four Kutel later, Lantid slapped Blorfindel on the shoulder as he went by. The Fitheran could see Fargus doing the same to Alehra. That was the sign to go close off the path. *This is where it gets really dangerous.* The plan said that the Kutel would panic and most of them would run south. The real situation was that there were still far too many Kutel for them to deal with. If even a quarter of them held together the Kutel had a good chance of a breakout.

Fargus and Lantid ran down the middle of the path. Blorfindel stopped ten feet up the slope above. He shouted to Alehra as he shot, "Stay up-slope if you're going to keep shooting. Remember, there are Tafers on the other side of that fog." Instead of stopping on the slope she ran across and started shooting from the riverbank. She was careful to only target Kutel on the right side of the path.

Their arrows dropped five more. It was only after Lantid threw the torch forward again that some of them got the idea that the arrows were coming from behind them. Since the four adventurers were on the other side of the torchlight the Kutel did not know how many there were.

Eight Kutel convinced each other that there were only a couple of archers. Blorfindel heard them and shot one before they started towards them. Both he and Alehra moved onto the path to either side of Fargus. They kept shooting and took their chances that they would not put an arrow past the Kutel to the Tafers. They each dropped one Kutel when Fargus stepped forward into the edge of the torchlight. He raised his mace and shield and waited.

Blorfindel shot another Kutel down as they passed by the torch. Alehra's arrow stuck in a shield. When the remaining four Kutel put the torch behind them and saw Fargus they all stopped. One of them shouted, "It's The Crusher!" right before Blorfindel's arrow silenced it forever. The other three turned to run. Alehra shot one in the ear as it turned. They each shot one in the back. Alehra's arrow got caught in its armor and it staggered ahead.

The other Kutel who heard the cry turned to look. They saw one wild-eyed Kutel running for its life and four more strewn out on the path. Due to the torch on the ground between them they could only see Fargus. Most of all they could see his mace held high. One of them shouted, "Run! Aaigh!" as an arrow stuck it through the arm. The panic and despair in its cry seemed to run through all of the Kutel. Some of them jumped into the river. Some of them ran into the fog. Most of them bolted into the canyon to the south.

Lantid calmly said from the darkness behind, "That was easy."

Alehra was still shooting into the rout. "What did they say?"

Blorfindel was shooting, too. "They think Fargus is 'The Crusher,' whoever that is." He turned to shoot at a Kutel in the river, but a sling bullet hit it and it went limp before he could take aim.

Blorfindel, Alehra, Fargus and Lantid began to advance slowly. The archers took shots whenever they could. When they passed the torch Lantid picked it up and held it low behind Fargus' back. He hoped it made him look frightening. They were a hundred yards away from the fog when they heard Lorten shout, "That's done it! They're running! Let's go!"

Blorfindel held his breath for a second before he heard another Tafer shout, "Hold the line!" Then again and again different voices shouted,

"Hold the line!" Blorfindel kept shooting. *If Lorten charges into the fog, it's his own fault if I get him with a stray arrow.*

Kutel started to come out of the fog. Blorfindel and Alehra had to let them go. They did not trust to shoot down the path from here, knowing that the Tafer line was invisible on the other side of the fog. If the Kutel turned away they would shoot them. Four of them were coming strait up the path.

Lantid threw three knives in rapid succession, one high and two low. The Kutel caught the first two on its shield. The third one dug into its calf. Its shield was still low when it got to Fargus. 'The Crusher' slammed his mace down on the bridge of its nose and the Kutel's face disappeared in an explosion of blood. It was a lucky blow, but the other Kutel did not know that. As Blorfindel and Alehra were drawing their swords the other three turned to run shouting, "Cruska!"

Fargus leaped forward and struck another Kutel on the side of the head as it turned. Again the weapon proved stronger than a Kutel's skull. Some of the confused Kutel got a good look at its brains in the torchlight before they turned to run. Again, some of them shouted, "The Crusher!" as they bolted. Most of them ran back into the fog.

Blorfindel stopped to switch back to his bow. "Way to go, Crusher."

Alehra and Blorfindel got a few more shots into the panicked Kutel before the fog started to lift. There were desperate Kutel trying to break through the Tafer line. The archers put their bows down and charged at the backs of the Kutel.

The Tafer line was beginning to bend when they arrived. Lorten held his ground in the middle of the line, but both ends had been pushed back past the base of the stakes. Alehra ran in on the left side and Blorfindel on the right. Fargus went down the middle. Most of the Kutel never turned in time to see them. Those who did were killed by the Tafers in the line. When the last fighting Kutel dropped, Lantid said, "Now you can chase the Kutel."

Fargus stayed with the wounded Tafers in the line. Seven of the Tafers including Lorten went with Blorfindel, Alehra, Lantid and Nickadola to chase the Kutel down the canyon. The canyon was blind and Lantid held the others up while Blorfindel, Alehra, and Nickadola shot down Kutel that were trying to climb out. In the end the Kutel rallied. There were still twenty-five of them when they charged. Some of the Tafers were a bit panicky until the front line of Kutel fell on their faces, asleep. Lantid knocked out the second row with another sleep spell. One of them landed at Blorfindel's feet.

Suddenly, the Kutel were outnumbered. Seven Tafers, a Taforam, a Timble, and a Fitheran counter-charged the nine remaining Kutel. Lantid stayed behind to kill the sleepers. The battle was quick and decisive. Lorten dropped one, then Blorfindel, then Alehra. Once those three broke through the Kutel line it was over quickly. They were done in time to help Lantid finish the sleeping Kutel.

They went over the bodies before they returned to the path. Then the Tafers went back to their line to go over the other Kutel bodies there. Blorfindel, Alehra, Lantid and Nickadola went up the path. As much as anything Blorfindel and Alehra were looking to recover arrows.

When they got back to the Kutel leaders Blorfindel took the time to look them over. The first one they came to was the big-headed one. While Alehra was trying to work the arrows out of its shield without breaking them, Blorfindel saw that his arrows in its head and throat were both broken off. When they rolled it over he saw for the first time that Alehra had also hit it in the right arm. "This one took some punishment. He was still shouting after I hit him in the eye."

The other Kutel leader had a heavy leather collar that had saved it from Blorfindel's first arrow, though the arrow did some damage: there was blood under the collar. Its armor likewise stopped the arrow in its thigh. The arrow in its foot came out intact. The fourth arrow was stuck in its spine and it broke when Blorfindel tried to work it free.

Lantid was hoping that the Kutel brought food. They did. The Kutel had dropped their packs before the battle. They had enough supplies to keep the refugees going for a few days. Lantid went back to get Tafers to help carry. When they came back Fargus told them the damage. "One Tafer is dead. One will be before morning. Three were seriously wounded, but I healed them."

Alehra asked, "You couldn't save the other one?"

Fargus looked down, "I can only heal three. I used the spells on the others because I thought they could walk afterwards. We can't stay here, can we?"

"I guess not."

Lantid shook his head. "We can't even carry him."

"It would kill him anyway."

When they put the Kutel body count together they came up just short of Blorfindel's original estimate of ninety.

Nickadola asked, "Did you count four in the river?"

"No."

Lantid said, "It doesn't matter. It would be a miracle if we got all of them. This time it may not be so bad that some got away. Maybe they'll scare the Kutel into staying on the other side of the pass for a little while."

One of the former captives asked Blorfindel, "What does 'Guh Tithkut' mean?"

"'The Crusher.' The Kutel are afraid of Fargus."

"Why?"

"I don't know."

Fargus had a theory. "I think they saw bodies of the last group. Most of the sleeping ones got their brains bashed out."

"So?"

"These Kutel had no way of knowing they were asleep at the time, did they?"

"Most of them were killed with swords and arrows and things."

Lantid agreed with Fargus. "They were all pretty spread out, though. In that one spot it looks like The Crusher took on a half dozen Kutel at once and split all their skulls open. You remember what it looked like? It makes me sick just to think about it."

Fargus started to say, "You said–"

"You did the right thing. It just looked bad. Who knows, maybe that saved some lives tonight."

They left everything that did not look edible, even coins. Everyone was packing heavy and Lantid was in a hurry. "We have to catch up with the rest of the group as soon as possible."

"Meaning we march tonight through tomorrow?" Fargus asked.

"And into tomorrow night if we have to."

"We'll be passing out from exhaustion."

"Even if none of the surviving Kutel made it east, Nickadola killed four in the river. Odds are fair that the fishing group will know about our little skirmish here very soon. We need to get between them and the non-combatants before they come up river."

Fargus shook his head. "You can't do it to them. They're not going to make it. Even if we get there we'll be no good in battle. All we could do is die next to them."

"Then we're saying the Taforam, the children, and the wounded are all at the mercy of the Kutel that rallied by the river?"

"Can't Nickadola send a bird to tell the others to stop or something?"

"Who would listen to it? Do you think any of them speak bird?"

Blorfindel slapped them both on the shoulder. "I'll go. Someone will have to take the extra stuff I was packing, but I can manage all of my own kit and still move twice as fast as they're going. Raise the trees, they're so slow I may catch them before they break camp."

"Be careful. We don't know if there are any Kutel down the path."

Alehra said, "I'll go with you."

"You can't see, remember? You'll slow me down too much until the horizon gets out of the way of the sun." He smiled. "Besides, someone's got to carry all this junk."

He resettled his kit and started down the path. At first he moved cautiously, looking for Kutel that might have escaped from the battle. After two miles he picked up the pace. *Any Kutel who made it this far would have to be moving quickly, too.* On the way he saw two Kutel corpses hung up on snags in the river. *Maybe none of them will make it down to the fish-camp.*

Dawn colored the morning sky when he caught up with the other group. They were just waking up. They were surprised that the Kutel had been stopped upriver. He was embarrassed that he did not know the names of the Tafers who died. Most of them were not interested in the details of the battle, though they all recognized that it was not Lorten's style. None of them believed him when he told the number of dead Kutel, thought their lookout had seen two bodies float down the river. Blorfindel did not argue. He just got out of his armor and went to sleep.

When Blorfindel woke up the sun was still high. The rest of the combatants had not caught up yet. It took him a few minutes to realize that all the Taforam were busy with some project. His curiosity waited until after he washed and drank some water from the river. He was wading out, soaking wet, when one of the Taforam shouted to him, "Well, give us a hand!"

It was a raft. "We're going to float down the river, not walk. We can carry all the stuff they're bringing back and rest the wounded. It was Sodri's idea." Sodri, unfortunately, had little skill in actually building a raft. Apart from Blorfindel, the entire group's experience was with the raft they built to pull the Kutel leader up the river. By the time Blorfindel had disabused them of their Kutel design the rest of the fighters caught up.

Even Nickadola thought it was a good idea, if done properly. "We can't go all the way to the fishing camp on it, though."

"We should just make it big enough for the people who can't keep up, and the baggage. That should speed us up." Lantid frowned at the sun, "Maybe we can make up for the time we're losing building it. We'll probably catch them in a single day."

Nickadola had the most experience with rafts, so he stayed awake to help with the construction. Blorfindel, of course, helped also. All of the other combatants went to sleep.

Chapter 11

Nugrot

In consideration for their confused schedules they moved Blorfindel and Nickadola to the last two watches. They added one Tafer to each watch as well. Blorfindel found that his watch-mate was named Orrenc.

"So, are you from The Hunt?"

"Naw, I was sentenced there."

"What for?"

"Falling asleep on watch."

"You've got to be kidding me."

"Naw, actually I got caught dueling. I thought it was only illegal inside the city wall."

"At least you won."

"Naw, they broke us up before we could sort it out. I guess I should call myself lucky, if I'd have killed him they'd have executed me."

"What was it about?"

"I was young and stupid. I thought I was in love and he was in the way. After twelve years at The Hunt I can't even remember what she looked like. I messed up my whole life for her." There was a thoughtful pause. "What are you doing out here?"

"Messing up my whole life. I'm young and stupid and in love. I'm trying to collect enough money so her father will let me marry her."

"Congratulations, what's her name?"

"Afinlia."

"Well, I hope it works out better for you than it did for me."

There was a long moment of silence, then Blorfindel laughed.

"What is it?"

"The last suitor to get between me and Afinlia in a way lost the duel."

"You kill 'im?"

"Broke his spine. He drank poison afterward."

"That's not illegal where you're from?"

"Normally, yes, but– it's a long story. The law was on my side at the time."

"Lucky you. You could have been stuck fighting Kutel at The Hunt."

Blorfindel laughed. "I am stuck fighting Kutel."

"Yeah, but not at The Hunt. You don't have to take orders from Lorten."

"Is he always this bad?"

"Naw, he's awright most of the time. He's just a little direct is all. He doesn't like stratagems 'n' stuff. Straight at 'em and get it over with – that's Lorten. Except, this time the Kutel had a plan for that. Lantid's just the opposite, I guess."

"He likes to have a plan. Do you know what happened between him and Lorten?"

"Yesterday? I don't know but it must have been good. Lorten's belted right up."

"No, years ago."

"Oh, I wasn't there. The word at the barracks was that Lorten was embarrassed by Lantid. Lorten wanted a soldier-son to charge into battle next to him. I guess that's not Lantid."

"He had a bad cough, too."

"Yeah, I heard that. I heard he kept trying to tell Lorten what to do, too – you know giving advice where it's not wanted, but he wasn't fit to fight, so Lorten threw him out. Rumor is that Sodri's been paying his bills."

"I don't know about that. Lantid's been self-sufficient since I met him."

"Yeah, now, but someone put him through wizard school or whatever. Naw, I didn't mean she was still payin' for 'im. Crushk, most of 'em thought he was dead by now – the cough, you know."

"He sounded like he was going to die any day when I met him, and that was only a couple of weeks ago."

"What happened?"

"He got healed at the temple of Feadin in Kingstone."

"That must have cost a small fortune."

"Thirty malstren is the going rate, but the high priest is an old friend of mine."

"Must be nice."

"That's a long story, too."

They fell into silence for most of the watch. Late in the watch Blorfindel heard footsteps. He snuck up beside Orrenc and put a hand on his mouth, "Wake Nickadola, quietly. And Lantid. Crushka, wake all of us – you know, us. Something's coming. I'm going to take a look."

The Fitheran moved into the shadows on the uphill side of the path and worked his way downriver. At every piece of cover he would stop and listen. Soon it became clear that a large group was headed up the path toward camp. When he got closer he saw a Kutel. He realized that it was an advanced scout. *Kutel never do that. It's almost like – a beater! They're trying to get us to reveal our position.* Blorfindel remained hidden. A second Kutel came into view, almost parallel to the first but on the other side of the path. *That makes sense. They're checking both sides of the path for an ambush. Lantid will be planning an ambush if he can.*

The first Kutel was getting closer. Blorfindel's mind was racing, *If I run, they'll hear me and probably charge. How fast can Orrenc wake everyone? If I stay here, it might find me. If I do nothing these two are going to find the Tafers and Lantid isn't planning on them. He thinks it's just something they do when they attack Fitherani. It's something they do when their leader is smart enough.* He set his bow down, drew his dagger and hid himself. *Maybe it will walk close enough.*

The first row of Kutel was just visible when the scout walked up to Blorfindel's hiding place. The Fitheran froze in place until it walked past, then he picked up his bow. He could see three ranks of Kutel, five across, coming up the path and he could hear more behind them. *Which one is the leader? Maybe none of these.* The farther scout was moving away now and would soon be out of sight in the cover by the river.

Blorfindel made up his mind. He shot the far scout in the back of the neck. The nearer scout heard the arrow go by and turned its head. It was all the time that it had. Blorfindel's second arrow hit it between the shoulder blades. At this range its armor could not stop the arrow point until it was on the way out. Blorfindel could not make them fall quietly, however. The first one landed in the river with a splash and the second crashed through the undergrowth on the way down.

Blorfindel turned toward the approaching Kutel and fired five arrows as fast as he could aim them, one at each of the front rank. Two of the Kutel were fast enough to raise their shields. The other three got an arrow in the face. The second rank also raised their shields and the Kutel lines stopped.

Blorfindel kept shooting. They were stationary targets now. He put an arrow in the ankle of three more Kutel. From somewhere behind a Kutel voice shouted, "Charge! You idiots! If you stand there they'll shoot you all night!"

Blorfindel did not wait for their reaction. He ran. After fifty yards he stopped and turned behind cover. Two black-shafted arrows flew past. He stepped out to shoot. The archers were standing behind a row of Kutel who had their shields up. This was supposed to put their shields in the path of his return shots. Blorfindel put an arrow in the eye of one of the Kutel archers and ran again. This time he was careful to put the tree between himself and the Kutel as he ran.

He could hear, rather than see, other Kutel running up the sides of the path. They had not stopped when he shot and they were close. He concentrated on the broken ground in front of him and put on all the speed he dared. *Just like the start of the obstacle course.* Suddenly the timing candle did not seem like such a terrible opponent. He poured on the speed and the Kutel could not keep up. Eventually they worked their way to the path where the going was easier.

As he got closer to camp Blorfindel could hear Tafer voices over the tramping feet.

"Get ready! Line up!"

"What is it?"

"I don't know."

Blorfindel turned to take another shot. A Kutel shot first and their arrows passed in flight. A black-shafted arrow struck Blorfindel's shoulder and shattered on his armor. He got a small splinter under his chin but there was not enough poison on it to do him much harm. He turned and ran before he saw if his own arrow hit. He could still hear the voices of the Tafers ahead.

"What's the plan?"

"No time for that now! Get lined up! We have to stop them before they get through to the others!"

"How many are there?"

"How should I know?"

"Blorfindel's out there."

"Maybe he knows."

Blorfindel could recognize Lantid's voice. "It doesn't matter. We're not going to have time to change anything. For the love of Feadin! Leave that stuff! Just get out of here! You too, kid!"

Then Lorten, "Where do you want me?"

"Front and center. You're the anchor. Nickadola! Use your spells to keep them on the path. Don't let them go around us! Al, if you've got targets then start shooting!"

"It's too dark."

Blorfindel shouted back, "Don't shoot! I'm coming through," and he broke into sight of the line. It was not much of a line yet. Lorten and a half-dozen Tafers were in place. The rest were running around trying to find their weapons or their place. Someone handed Lantid a lighted lantern.

"Thanks, Ritt. Now get out of here!"

Blorfindel shouted back, "Put the lantern down! They've got archers!" He turned to shoot. Three Kutel archers were setting up to shoot at Lantid. Blorfindel shot at one of them for a scratch hit. It ran into the one beside it and the third flinched away unnecessarily. Blorfindel had to turn and run away. All three shot at Lantid a moment later.

Blorfindel watched Lantid standing still and defiant as the three black shafts flew toward him. He glared at them as if he dared them to do him harm. Blorfindel wanted to yell, "Duck," but there was no time. Even the Fitheran could see that all three arrows were well-aimed. Then they got there. All three arrows were targeted for Lantid's unarmored chest. All three arrows were perfectly aimed. All three arrows bounced off without so much as disturbing his robe.

Lantid shouted at the Kutel, "That's right! You got any more for me? You'll have to do better than that!" He threw two knives at a ridiculously high arc. They went past Blorfindel but the Kutel behind him did not sound injured. Lantid turned behind him, "Fargus, stay back and patch the line – we can't risk you in front without your armor. We'll need those heals."

Blorfindel crossed the line and turned to shoot. Three more arrows came up the path, all aimed at Lantid. One missed high. The other two would have struck him in the face, but again they bounced off. Blorfindel shot down one of the archers. Nickadola hit one in the bow hand with a sling bullet. It dropped the bow.

Lantid was shouting at the Kutel again. To Blorfindel's shock and amazement he stepped forward of the battle line. "C'mon! Your mama shoots better than that! I'm waiting!"

The rest of the Tafers filled in the line while he was shouting. Alehra shot the first Kutel to break into the lamp light. It fell back screaming and trying to hold the blood inside its neck. The second one jumped at Lantid with a battleaxe. Again, he just stood there and stared it down. Again, it worked. This time the Kutel never finished the swing. Lantid stepped aside as it fell on its face. There was a black-shafted arrow in its back. Blorfindel shot the archer twice. Both arrows hit its armor but it did not shoot again.

Lantid stepped back through the line as the first wave of Kutel attacked. Their shock staggered the line of Tafers but did not break them. In the center, Lorten did not move an inch. Even with a clumsy Kutel sword and no armor, he was more than a match for the first three Kutel in center of the line. Only one of them was whole enough to withdraw after facing him.

Blorfindel was on the far right of the line. When the Kutel on that side realized that he was a Fitheran they all tried to attack him. The result was that two of them turned their unprotected right sides to the Tafers in the line. One fell back, wounded, another was dead. The Kutel on the edge tried to run Blorfindel down. The Fitheran's sword went just over its shield and under its chin. Though the Kutel was dying its momentum carried it into Blorfindel. The shock pushed him back a step.

From the second rank a Kutel with a spear stabbed at the Fitheran. He turned slightly and the point grazed across his armor and under his right arm. He hooked the spear shaft with his arm and flicked his sword at its nearest wrist, opening a small cut. Then he lunged with his dagger under the spear and into the Kutel's gut. It fell back, seriously wounded. The right side of the line held.

The left side of the line was buckling. Alehra was on the far left and used her shield to shove the Kutel opposite her toward the middle. It collided with the Kutel next to it and tangled feet. Her sword thrust went all the way through the first one. The Tafer to her right stabbed a spear at the other off-balance Kutel but could not penetrate its armor. As the second line of Kutel filled in, Alehra and the Tafer were forced to step back to make space to defend themselves.

The Kutel pushed the whole left side of the line back. Fargus started casting his healing spell. The spell that was quick under normal situations seemed to take forever in combat. Where spaces appeared between the Tafers in line Lantid threw his knives. They did little damage but caused some confusion.

Blorfindel could hear the Kutel leader shouting, "Push on the right! Break through and we'll have them!"

The Fitheran shouted back, "Is that you Nugrot? I've been looking all over for you!"

When the Kutel heard his voice they started to shout, "Fitheran!" Most of the next wave turned away to charge at him instead of the weakened section of the Tafer line. The Tafers on the left side of the line threw back the first wave as the second wave was running past. They ran into each other and tangled together. Tafers began to score quick kills.

Blorfindel turned his attention to the Kutel in front of him. He parried a sword and stabbed between the bones of the Kutel's knee. As it was going down he ducked under a flail ball. Before it could react, the Tafer to Blorfindel's left shoved it over the knee-wounded one. That Tafer was in turn attacked by the next Kutel over. Blorfindel hooked its shield with both arms and jerked it towards him. This gave the Tafer an opening and he cut its shield arm off with his battleaxe.

Blorfindel threw the shield, arm and all, into the crowd of advancing Kutel. He took a moment to stab each of the prone Kutel at his feet and shouted to the Kutel leader at the same time, "Nugrot! I've got something special for you, Nugrot! Why don't you come and get it?"

Suddenly the trees and shrubs to the Fitheran's right came to life. Blorfindel could hear Kutel voices panicking on the other side. He kept on shouting, "That's not going to work, Nugrot. You're going to have to collect in person!"

Finally the Kutel leader responded, "What have you got for me, Fitheran? Your mother's too dried up and skinny for my taste. Did you bring your little sister along?" The battle up front was getting out of his control. The group Nugrot had sent around to flank them was now hung up in the trees. The second wave did not attack where he had ordered them. Nugrot thought, *If I push hard enough their left side will break, then we'll have them.*

Blorfindel shouted back, "I've got an old-fashioned Fithern butt-whippin' here just for you! Why don't you come and get it!"

Nugrot thought, *That might be just the cover I need.* He pretended to be incensed. "Come on boys! We'll show him what an ass-whippin' means!" He took the last of his reserves and charged but as they approached the line he turned them away from the Fitheran and toward the Tafers' left.

Lantid had been waiting for the final wave. He centered his sleep spell just behind the first row of Kutel. Five of the Kutel from the first wave went down and three in the third. Tafers charged back into the gap and met the remaining Kutel with equal force.

As the left side was being shored-up the right was beginning to advance. Blorfindel and the Tafer next to him curled around and began to press the Kutel from the side. The Kutel tried to fall back but Nugrot would not allow it. He shoved some back into the battle line and threw his spear through one that turned to run. He shouted, "Hold the line!" then drew his new sword and rushed to reinforce his crumpling left side.

Blorfindel finally saw the leader speak. It was only average height, but a bit broader than most Kutel, maybe twice the Fitheran's weight. Unlike the layered hides that most Kutel wore, Nugrot's armor much like Blorfindel's own. It had a sword with an unusually ornate hilt for a Kutel. The sword was half again bigger in every dimension than the Fitheran's. Its shield was smaller than average for a Kutel, round and covered with brass on the face. Even it the low light, it was clear that it was ornately carved. A sling bullet hit the cheek piece of Nugrot's helmet as it approached. Blorfindel smiled and stepped to the side to get a little more fighting room. "Here we go."

Nugrot feinted at Blorfindel's head and whipped his sword around to his thigh with a speed that surprised the Fitheran. He caught the sword with his dagger. He could not get his sword past the Kutel's shield and they locked up with sword and dagger crossed low and shield to sword handle high.

The Kutel flexed, intending to send the lighter Fitheran sprawling. Blorfindel got low and pushed back hard. For a moment there was no movement at all. Blorfindel's left leg was bearing all of the strain. He lifted his right high and stomped down on the inside of the Kutel's right knee. It buckled and sent the Kutel to the ground. Blorfindel stabbed at it but its armor turned his sword point. It rolled back to its feet and on guard just in time to turn the Fitheran's second thrust with its shield. It had to turn its sword awkwardly across its body to parry his dagger. Again the Fitheran pushed and this time the Kutel had to step back.

Blorfindel followed up with a thrust at its leg. It parried with its sword. The Fitheran stepped wide around to the left to stab it with his dagger. Nugrot spun around to meet the dagger with his shield. They were both too slow. Blorfindel's dagger opened a cut on Nugrot's upper arm. Nugrot's shield smashed into Blorfindel's forearm edge-first. Neither paused. Nugrot brought his sword around in a continuous arc carrying all the force of his spin. Blorfindel tried to slash at the back of its calves while ducking under the Kutel's sword. The Kutel redirected its sword at the

Fitheran and hit a glancing blow to his armor that knocked Blorfindel off his feet. Blorfindel's sword did not harm the Kutel leader, but cut the straps that held its left greave.

Blorfindel rolled to his knees and caught the Kutel's overhead chop with his sword and dagger crossed. The Kutel tried to kick him in the head but the Fitheran swung his dagger in a circle, catching the Kutel's leg and inadvertently sitting its foot on his shoulder. Blorfindel stood up and lunged forward while holding his dagger over the Kutel's leg. Nugrot stopped the sword with his shield and swung his own sword under his own leg. Blorfindel was forced to drop the Kutel's leg to parry the sword with his dagger, but on the way he cut its foot open. The shield strike on his forearm had weakened Blorfindel's left hand too much, and he could not hold his dagger against the sword strike. He took a step back and drew his war hammer with his left hand. The hammer felt heavy and slow and Blorfindel wondered how long he would be able to hold on to it. Nugrot was too off balance to follow up immediately.

As the two squared off again Nugrot's greave fell, dragging awkwardly in the dirt. Blorfindel stepped back to make the Kutel move toward him. He ran into Fargus. The Tafer grabbed the Fitheran on the shoulder and healed him. Suddenly his arm was strong again. Fargus ran back behind the line.

Nugrot started to say something but Blorfindel attacked at that moment. He engaged the Kutel's sword with his own and brought his war hammer down in what would have been a killing blow. The Kutel took it on the shield, too flatly. The shield rang with a solid crash and the Kutel's wounded arm would not hold. The back of Nugrot's own shield hit it in the face. Instinctively it slashed with the sword to force Blorfindel back but the Fitheran's blade was already resting against it. Nugrot's sword was too long for him to pull away and it had to give ground to come back on guard. Blorfindel pressed hard and stayed close, hammering again and again with more ferocity than style. The shock of each stroke went through the shield and onto the Kutel's head until it finally angled the shield enough to turn the blow. Blorfindel had to leap back to keep his follow-through from catching on the swords.

When they squared off again Nugrot was bleeding from his nose and under the rim of his helmet. Blood was running down his shield arm and he was dragging a greave on the ground. Someone was shouting but neither combatant was paying attention. Nugrot launched his own desperate attack raining blows with its sword as fast as Blorfindel could parry. It fell into a rhythm. Blorfindel turned its sword with his own and swung his hammer sideways at its right shoulder. Nugrot was too slow to get its shield over. A single spark flew from its armor which bent and twisted under the hammer-blow. Nugrot staggered for a moment and Alehra threw herself at the back of its legs, knocking it over and saving it from Blorfindel's stab to the head.

"Lantid wants him alive! For questioning!"

Blorfindel followed his sword thrust and jumped on top of the Kutel leader. With one knee on its shield and the other on its sword arm he punched it in the face five times before someone caught his arm. "Alive, Blorfindel! Leave him alive!" It was Alehra again.

Blorfindel looked up and saw that Nugrot would soon be the only Kutel alive here. Lorten and the Tafers had the last five Kutel surrounded. Blorfindel watched the Shieldmaster hack the head off one to bring the total down to four. Nickadola was humming tunelessly as he slug bullets into the trees. Fargus, his spells long spent, was tending to the wounded with river-washed rags.

Lantid was standing nearby. He stepped over and kicked the sword away from Nugrot's nerveless hand. As he picked it up he said, "Al, you probably ought to set this shield aside. I'll check it out later." He stood up, put the sword across his shoulder, and shouted, "Someone bring us a rope here!" Ritt found a rope and came running. Nugrot did not stir when Lantid bound its hands and feet.

Chapter 12

Family

Blorfindel, Alehra and Nickadola were finishing off Kutel that were caught in the trees when three Tafers came walking back up the path. Blorfindel asked, "Where did you come from?"

"We were chasing the ones that ran away."

"How many did you get?"

"Two who ran and seven wounded who were trying to get away."

Just then the trees stopped moving. One lone Kutel dropped and started running. Two arrows and a sling bullet hit it in the back. Alehra said, "Damn, we might have gotten all of them this time."

All of the captives were back at camp when Blorfindel, Alehra, and Nickadola arrived. Nickadola asked Fargus, "How did we do?"

"Three more wounded than I can heal, no deaths – better than last time. How many were there? It wasn't as many, was it?"

"No count, yet. Maybe forty or so."

Blorfindel said, "I got some on the way."

"Call it fifty, then."

Lantid still had the sword on his shoulder when he walked over to Lorten. He lifted it between them and said, "I think you lost this."

Lorten dropped the Kutel sword to take his ancestral blade from Lantid. He stared at it for a moment and then handed it back. "Maybe you should keep it, Lantid. You know, a lot has happened since you left The Hunt. I think you're worthy of it."

The crowd drew a collective breath. Lantid turned the sword so that one of the gemstones on the hilt was pointing up. He spoke as if to the sword. "A red spinel, for the blood spilled in defense of The Hunt and The Shield Valley. There's been a lot of that. You know, someone told me that Talor spent one hundred fifty malstren on this one stone."

"That's right, and there's the diamond on the other side for purity," Lorten said quickly. "It's a priceless heirloom."

Lantid looked Lorten in the eyes. "Only a few weeks ago, three people who I had known for less than a month, each volunteered to front me the money to get my cough cured. Do you know how much that was? Thirty malstren. For the price of this one gem you could have had all of your sons cured. I'd have two brothers, and probably still have a sister." Lantid dropped the sword on the bloody ground. "I don't need to be a part of any family that values its heirlooms more than its heirs."

Everyone stood in shock for a moment. When Lorten recovered he cuffed Lantid in the face. Lantid stared him in the eyes and did not flinch. The Shieldmaster's beefy hand stopped as if Lantid were made of steel. Lorten was holding his wrist when he drew it back. Lantid kept staring. "We've got a lot of work to do to get these people home. Let's get it done."

Lantid walked back to Nugrot. "We can't interrogate him until he comes to. He is going to live, right?"

Blorfindel looked down at the Kutel's pulped face and shrugged, "I don't know."

"We need to find out who sent the orders to the Kutel at Dath. If it was Nugrot, then he can tell us all about what we're in for when we go back. Dath's our staging base for an assault on Foralis, right?"

"Right, that makes sense."

"If Nugrot was taking orders from someone else, then we need to find out who that is. He'll still probably know about the force that went to reinforce the Kutel at Dath."

"I know you want to interrogate him. I can't heal him."

"Just make sure he doesn't drown in his own blood, will you?"

"Yes, that I can do. Oh, Lantid, how did you do the thing with the arrows? I thought you were dead for sure."

"It's the shield spell. Almost anything that I can concentrate on I can stop."

"You should do that more often."

"It's one more sleep spell I can't cast, besides, there's not much I can do in physical combat even with the shield on. It just seemed like a good idea to keep the archers occupied. Thanks, by the way, I wouldn't have had time to cast it if you hadn't distracted them."

"You're welcome."

"Oh, and thanks for inviting me on your quest to clear Foralis. It helped. It helped to know that I had something better to do than be Shieldmaster of The Hunt."

Fargus tapped Lantid on the shoulder and spoke softly, "You should talk to Sodri, Lantid. She's pretty upset."

"I wish– I guess I should have expect it, though. I owe her better than that." He took two steps away and turned. "Blorfindel, what was the name of the princess? You know, the one with the kitchen?"

"Shandi."

"Shandi, right, thanks!"

Blorfindel watched him walk away, but his thoughts were interrupted by Ritt, the Tafer child. "Will you play a song for us again? Please?" Blorfindel looked around and saw three or four other Tafers watching with hopeful eyes. He went to unpack his cittern.

As he tuned, he tried to listen in on Lantid and Sodri. Lantid was saying, "Yes, he took a step. Is that supposed to make up for all the times he told me I wasn't good enough?" Blorfindel tuned another string. "I never even knew Sural, really. Now I never will." He tuned another string. "True, the Kutel are to blame, but it's not their fault that I had to arrange secret meetings with my own family." Blorfindel realized that he was taking too long tuning and focused his efforts on the instrument.

When he stopped and tried to think of a song to play, he heard Sodri, "I just want to have a family again. You and your father are all I have left now."

"The only reason he is ready to consider me part of the family is because we defeated the Kutel. I'm nothing to him if I'm not a warrior."

Blorfindel forced himself to stop listening to their conversation and play. It was a short, bright, Fithern song about sunlight on raindrops. He did not even try to sing the lyrics – only Nickadola might have understood them, and he could not see the Timble nearby. When he stopped, he could hear Sodri again. "Shandi? I don't know. How long ago?"

"Eighty or a hundred years," Lantid replied.

"That would make her Talor's daughter, wouldn't it? I think there's a song with that name in it."

Blorfindel walked slowly toward them. He felt like he was intruding, but he saw other Tafers around who were clearly listening to them. He could hear Lantid, "That's right! How does it go? Something about winning the Shieldmaster's daughter in battle?"

"You remember it as well as I do, then. It's a long song, and a sad one if I remember."

"I don't know. I just remember that they didn't give up. I had sort-of forgotten the song. They don't give up, right? That's the ending – even though they can't win they don't give up."

Blorfindel adjusted his tuning as quickly as he could.

"Are you sure? I thought they died in the end."

"Maybe."

"How do you know it was Shandi's kitchen?"

"Blorfindel lived there."

Blorfindel interrupted, "I'm in the song."

Lantid looked over at him. "I didn't know that."

"Nobody knows that. My name's not in it."

Sodri asked, "But you know the song?"

By way of answering Blorfindel sang:

> Ammoss came unto The Hunt
> The Kutel there to slaughter
> and in the battles proudly fought
> he won the shieldmaster's daughter.
>
> Shandi was a princess fine
> born to the wooded frontier,
> And Ammoss took her back to Dath.
> He said, "We'll build a home here."
>
> Together then in Dath they lived,
> but Ammoss oft' would wander.
> He followed print and broken twig
> the Kutel paths to ponder.
>
> Then once a Kutel troop he found
> A-heading for Foralis.
> He begged Shieldmaster Roun for aid,
> but he stayed in his palace.
>
> Alone went Ammoss down the path
> to aid his Fithern neighbors.

Alone to face the Kutel horde,
the bravest of the Tafers.

Fitheran Child climbed up a tree
pursued by vicious Kutel.
Ammoss chose that place to stand
and there his sword make useful.

Like reaper to the waiving wheat,
Ammoss' sword laid waste.
By twos and threes the Kutel fell.
He thinned their ranks in haste.

The Fitheran Child, he brought along
from Foralis fateful
to his own most pleasant home
and Shandi's ladened table.

But Fitheran will no Tafer be,
and ran from home and safety.
He longed for woods and brook and field;
for bushes and for great trees.

In her heart poor Shandi ached
for her ward gone missing,
and to his trail she Ammoss sent
with weeping and with kissing.

In forest glen Ammoss found
Kutel took the Fitheran
and so to them he battle brought
to win back the child again.

When the forest floor was foul
with Kutel corpses crushed,
to Lalru was the Fitheran bound,
and to Bur-Droo he was rushed.

Though score of Kutel him harassed,
Ammoss still gave chase.

By streambed found he Lalru dead
with arrow in his waist.

To Bur-Droo then did Ammoss speed
with aspect cruel as steel.
For Fitheran was force marched there
with chains upon his heels.

But Bur-Droo is a fortress town
with Kutel, Cral, and Varr.
Yet Ammoss would have storm'd the gates
'cept Shandi's love afar.

Bitter were the Kutel's ends
who 'cross his path did roam.
But love for Shandi turned him 'round
and gently pulled him home.

With heavy heart and sagging head
he crossed his own threshold,
and through the night in Shandi's ear
his bitter tale he told.

Shandi's answer sent him back
for cruel revenge and grim.
For pots and cakes she packed a few
and traveled back with him.

She forsook her country home,
warm and safe and dry,
to stew wild squirrels in a pot
beneath a brooding sky.

And in the darkest Kutel vale
they made their erstwhile home
only for a week or two
then again they'd roam.

Together the seething town they 'sieged
the soldier and his lady

> And Kutel learned that death did walk
> down in the valley shady.
>
> Now Shunku brags his Varro found
> the soldier and his lady,
> but the Kutel know, 'tis death to go
> down in their valley shady.

Sodri sighed. "I told you it was a sad song."

"But they don't give up. I wonder if this is the valley? Bur-Droo is on the other side of the pass – at least I think that's Bur-Droo."

"It doesn't say anything about a river."

Blorfindel laughed. "The bard didn't know the whole story, anyway. I never went to Bur-Droo."

Lantid said, "You know, once you've avenged your Fithern parents maybe you should come back and avenge your Tafer parents, too."

Sodri asked, "Tafer parents?"

"Ammoss and Shandi took me in when my parents died."

"Her ward, the song says. If they died trying to rescue Blorfindel from Bur-Droo, then there is another score to settle. Shunku was the name of the wizard-king of Kutel. For all I know, it still is."

Sodri was still thinking of the past. "There weren't a lot of sons born into Talor's line. A few were disowned." She paused for a deep sigh. "I wonder how close that makes you to being heir?"

Alehra had been standing unnoticed but nearby. "If it means anything to you, my dad won't talk to me, either. He wanted a son."

"It means something," Lantid said quietly. "Your mother?"

"She raised me. When I was young, my father used to tell people that I was a boy – that's how my training started. When I got old enough that it couldn't be hidden, he threw us out. Even before then, it was only mom. I don't know him well enough to hate him, but if I ever go home, I don't know what I'll do."

They looked over at Fargus. "Don't look at me. My parents are alive and well in Kingstone, and I'll be happy to see them again when this is over. There's enough bitterness and revenge going around without my getting involved. I'm just here to help. Nickadola?"

"My folks are happy farmers and falcon trainers. My older brother stands to inherit, but there's no bad blood."

Sodri said, "If Shandi adopted Blorfindel, then that makes him family. Talor's sword is his birthright, too, after a fashion."

"I'm heir to Lalliam Steelhand." Blorfindel patted his sword hilt. "If I have a birthright, it's in Foralis. The Kutel killed my parents there. It's strange, in Sekri Timbrali I sort-of forgot... lost sight of how much the Kutel took from me. I don't know if I'll ever avenge all of that."

Sodri asked, "Sing another song, a happy song. The cittern is better for happy songs, anyway."

Borfindel chose a Shield translation of a Timbrali spring song, but when he started to sing a voice shouted out, "Baett! Kill me, but don't make me listen to a Fitheran sing!" It was Nugrot. Lantid, Alehra, Nickadola, and Blorfindel walked over to the Kutel leader. They all stared down at it for a moment. Nugrot got impatient. "Will you just kill me and get it over with?"

Lantid said, "I want some answers out of you first."

"What? You wanna know how I scared the princess to death? You wanna know what I did to her after she died?" For the second time that night Alehra saved the Kutel's life: Lantid drew his dagger, but she held his wrist. Nugrot kept talking, "What did you stop him for, do you want some too? I got some left for you." Alehra drew her war hammer.

Nickadola stepped on the Kutel's head and said, "He's trying to get you angry enough to kill him."

"I was just going to smash his–" She looked over her shoulder at the children. They were staring. "–stuff."

The Timble took his foot away. "Since he speaks Shield and we don't have to go through a translator, we can do this the easy way." He smiled. "If you wait a little while we can do this magically."

Blorfindel asked, "What are you going to do, kill him and interrogate his shade?"

"No. Wow, no," Nickadola sputtered, "Remind me never to let a Fitheran take me prisoner. I thought you were hard on the last one."

Nugrot interrupted, "He's just jealous 'cause he hasn't got one."

Alehra asked, "Hasn't got what?"

"A soul."

"Really?"

Blorfindel shrugged. "That's what they say."

Nickadola continued as if he had not been interrupted, "No, Dhu doesn't do much with spirits. In the morning he'll be happy to tell me anything I ask. We're not going anywhere for a while, right?"

Lantid looked around, "I don't know. It all depends on how much stuff these Kutel were carrying."

Nugrot kept talking. "More that you can manage, stick-boy. Did they carry you over the mountains or did you just grow here from a seed?"

Lantid cut a dirty strip of cloth from the Kutel's hem and tied it as tight as he could around Nugrot's bruised face. He looked at it for a minute, then he took it off, removed the Kutel's helmet and tied it again.

They put a guard on Nugrot and went about collecting the goods from the Kutel band. Near the place where Blorfindel made contact they found bags full of dried fish. Lantid figured that with that and the food from the other Kutel group they might have enough to get all of the refugees out of the mountains, if they could carry it. He had them put most of it on the raft.

After loading up and taking an early lunch Nickadola was ready. He had them untie Nugrot while he cast his spell, and the spell was done before they got the gag off. The Timble waved for them to step back and spoke directly to the Kutel, "Why don't you take that armor off? You don't need it now, and it's just extra weight."

Without a word Nugrot began to take his armor off.

Lantid said, "Ask him about Jun."

"Slowly. Give him a chance. He's on our side now."

Blorfindel said, "On our side? That's some spell! Why didn't you use it on the last prisoner?"

"Two reasons: first, he's my friend, not yours, so when you had to translate it wouldn't really work. He's still a Kutel. I don't think he'll ever like a Fitheran."

Lantid asked, "What's the other reason?"

"Dhu wouldn't let me use the spell until after we relocated the wolves."

"That's funny, I'm sure I could cast the spell if I could find the instructions or someone to teach it to me, but I can't. You could have but you weren't allowed. It seems less frustrating to be in my position than yours."

"Then you picked the right path when you became a wizard."

Alehra asked, "Can't you teach him the spell, Nickadola?"

Lantid shook his head. "He only knows how to get Dhu to cast it, not how to do it himself. The difference is huge." He turned to Nickadola, "How long does it last?"

"It depends on how strong his mind is. A regular Kutel might break free in a month. This one, maybe a week, but its freedom is never guaranteed — that is, the spell doesn't wear off until his ego breaks through it. I can guarantee three days. There's no way he's strong enough to break out in less than three days."

"We'll be done with him long before then."

"Not so fast, he's got a strong back and we've got a lot of stuff to haul over these mountains." He spoke to Nugrot, "Now, why don't you go down to the river and clean yourself up. And clean up the armor. We'll see if we can get someone else to carry that for you."

The Kutel staggered off. Blorfindel followed to guard it but Nickadola said, "Al, why don't you look after him. A Fitheran might make him… nervous. Oh! and everyone remember he speaks Shield. He won't forget what he's heard when he breaks the spell."

By noon they were moving east again. They put the bulk of their supplies and a few of the slowest people on the raft. For the moment that included Nugrot, so Nickadola sat with the Kutel on back of the raft. The Timble let his feet dangle in the cool, clean water and spoke quietly with his new comrade.

The sun was setting on the mountaintops when Lantid called a halt. Nickadola shouted back to the shore, "The Kutel fishing camp is just a little ways further!"

Lantid looked at the others walking down the path. None of them looked as weary as he felt. He shrugged, adjusted his pack, and waved them forward. They went one more mile to the camp.

Chapter 13

Sad Road Home

Lantid lay in the river and let the water cool off the bruises from his pack straps. He shouted to the shore, "Al, bring me that shield so I can have a look at it!"

"Are you wearing anything down there?"

Rather than wait for a reply Blorfindel took the shield and walked it down to the river. Alehra followed but stopped a few feet from the riverbank. Lantid cast a spell without getting up. "I thought so. It's enchanted."

Alehra frowned, "What good does that do? The shield didn't save it from Blorfindel. What if it's cursed or something?"

Blorfindel said, "I don't know, maybe it did save Nugrot. I was pounding him with the war hammer for a while and the shield was the only thing between his face and the hammer head."

Lantid looked at the shield for a moment. "Your night vision is better than mine, can you see where the hammer hit it?" He handed the shield back to Blorfindel.

"Yes, there it is. See all the little crescent moon shapes in the brass?" Lantid didn't seem interested in looking, but Alehra looked at the marks when Blorfindel took it back to her.

Lantid said, "Not much damage for brass that's been hit by an iron hammer head, is it? How heavy does it feel to you, Al?"

"It's about the same as my shield, but it's smaller."

"By what, two inches? Yours is mostly wood, this one is wood covered with brass, and in places the brass is thick. It ought to be heavier. I don't recognize the wood, do you?"

Blorfindel said, "It's... I don't know its name in Shield. Its name means 'axe-duller' or 'axe-blunter' in Timbrali. It's a tough, strong, heavy wood, but the grain is usually too confused to use for much. It's a weed, mostly, not even good firewood – you have to keep the fire hot to burn it. You're right, though, the wood ought to be heavier than Al's oak shield."

Alehra asked, "A weed? I thought it was a tree?"

"Trees can be weeds."

Lantid said, "Axe-Duller isn't a bad name for a shield, either. If I were you, Al, I'd give away your old shield and use this one. Besides, your old one has taken a pounding. How much longer before it falls apart?"

"It's still got some life in it." Alehra looked at the brass covered shield. "All right, I'll try it out."

"You can practice with it tomorrow. We're staying here."

"I thought you were in a hurry?"

"I am, but remember the Kutel leader and his raft? If he had stayed in camp and healed for a day or two he probably could have gone back to full speed. In the end, he would have gotten to Bur-Droo sooner – faster than we could catch him. If we rest tomorrow we will make up the time by going faster afterwards. Fargus can accelerate the healing process for us. Besides, we have more food than we can carry right now. We'll spend some of it getting healthy. The only risk is, are there other Kutel around? I guess I've put off talking to Nugrot long enough." Lantid stood up. Alehra used her new shield for the first time: to shield her eyes.

It turned out that Nickadola's conversation on the raft had given him most of the answers that Lantid was looking for. All of the Kutel from Nugrot's war band were supposed to return to the fish camp if anything went wrong. Lantid expected that there would be some deserters, but not many, and if they were not brave enough to join with Nugrot they certainly were not going to start a fight without him. Nugrot could not say anything about Kutel coming over the pass, but he and Lantid agreed that the three battle sites between here and Bur-Droo would discourage all but the strongest or most foolish of groups. He also confirmed that the city on the other side of the pass was, indeed, Bur-Droo.

Nickadola had also learned a bit about Jun. It was a big Kutel town now. Nugrot was not in charge, but his war band had been strong enough to put him on equal footing with Jun's chief. Jun was basically self-sufficient, but it did not have enough food stores to support itself and an army. The Kutel were mining coal out of the mountains and using it to smelt iron from the local bogs. Many of Jun's Kutel lived in the mines so that they did not have to go out into the daylight. Nugrot thought that this made them weak.

The iron got worked into weapons, of course. According to Nugrot, weapons and food were the two most important things for Kutel chiefs. Jun had lots of weapons but was food-poor. Dath had farms, and that's why the Kutel wanted it. Putting Dath and Jun together would make them a military power. In moments of pride Nugrot would refer to them as the new Kutel nation. He saw himself ruling Dath, if not both towns, in the future.

The one thing that the Kutel never had a shortage of was warriors. So long as a chief could feed them and keep them in line, a Kutel population would grow. Most of the Kutel armies were just overflow from cities and towns that could no longer support them. Kutel who were not strong enough to be in the armies got killed. For this reason, Kutel commanders could largely ignore their losses, especially if they were close to a breeding town.

The attack on The Hunt was also based on these Kutel economics: Bur-Droo could not feed Nugrot's soldiers through the summer. He attacked The Hunt with the intention of stealing their food stores or getting enough of his soldiers killed so that he could feed the rest from what he had. He had done both effectively. He even had another plan for taking The Hunt and holding it next year. The group that went to Jun after the battle was carrying provisions and was largely slaves – Kutel slaves who could be turned into soldiers by simply handing them a weapon.

Nugrot had sent the note that they intercepted. He guessed that Jun's chief, too, was raising an army or that he was going to arm his farmers and miners for the attack. Anyone who could hold Dath and Jun would be a very big Kutel indeed. Nugrot guessed that Jun by itself could field three hundred soldiers. Since he did not have his war band to go take them back, those slaves that he sent now belonged to Jun as well, bringing the ranks to four hundred and probably well over the number that the farms there could support. That was very bad news for Dath.

Jun also had a small population of Varren who fed themselves largely by hunting. The town could not afford the food to raise Cral so it had to buy them. Nugrot knew that there were Cral working in the mines, but he did not know how many. Lantid guessed that it was more than a few.

"Why?" Blorfindel asked.

"Because they have to dig bigger mine shafts to fit them in. It's hardly worth it for just a handful of Cral, is it?"

"One Cral can be more than a handful."

"You know what I mean."

Nickadola had another interesting bit of information. "You know, Nugrot doesn't consider himself to be a Kutel?"

"What does he think he is, a tree snake?"

"He considers himself to be from a superior race. He calls himself a Kushotel."

Alehra asked, "I've never heard of a Kushotel. What's the difference?"

Lantid said, "He's smarter, for one thing."

Blorfindel said, "'Sho' is the Kutel word for strong or strength or muscle."

"So you put 'muscle' in 'Kutel' and you get 'Kushotel'?"

"I guess so. He's strong enough, stronger than I am. I had to get really low to stop him."

Nickadola continued, "He says a bunch of Kushotel were sent north up the spine to join the Kutel here. The smart ones, like Nugrot, took over Kutel bands. The rest are still together in their own little groups."

Lantid did not like that. "If they start breeding Nugrots up here, we've got troubles."

"I don't think so. Nugrot was raised by males. He doesn't know of Kushotel females. I think they're an abomination."

"Kutel are an abomination, too," Alehra said, "What has that got to do with the Kushotel having no females?"

"What I mean is, I don't think they're bred. I think they're built – or at least bred from more than two kinds of parents, like maybe his grandparents were four different types of creatures."

Alehra grimaced. "You can't do that."

Lantid said, "Not naturally, but maybe magically."

Nickadola was less certain. "Tafers can interbreed with Kutel or Fitherani, though the latter is very rare. Maybe there are other combinations that we just don't know."

Alehra said, "Great! The world's not bad enough now, so someone had to cook up a recipe for Kushotel."

That night a gentle rain started. It was still raining in the morning. The Tafers cooked food caught by Kutel over firewood that the Kutel had forced them to cut. They all rested. They had large silk tents taken from the Kutel, and they were as comfortable as they could reasonably be.

Fargus made his rounds to the wounded but he was very careful where he applied his healing magic. "Blorfindel, are you injured?"

"Yeah, a bit. My knuckles are cut up from Nugrot's teeth. I got a bruise on my back. I got a scratch under my chin and my left wrist is still a bit sore. Hey, you healed that. Shouldn't that be better?"

"Wounds have strengths as well as severity. Maybe you could call it a toughness, or anti-toughness. Your toughness works against the wounds toughness; the result is how you feel. My healing is like the silverseeds, it has to work against the wound's toughness, too. Like the bruise on your wrist, you came away cut and sore, but maybe someone like me would have gotten the bone broken. It's not because my bones are softer than yours, but because you're a better fighter you pulled your hand back quicker than I would have. That's part of your toughness. Feadin's healing or the silverseeds power has to overcome the power of the wound, which was enough to break a bone, not just the damage that you feel, which is the bruise. Do you understand?"

"No, but I guess it doesn't really matter; it's what I have to live with. I thought your spells healed everything?"

"Oh, no. My spells have very limited power, though they will get stronger if I'm good. They're maybe equivalent to two days of bed rest and silverseeds right now – though that might add up to a week of camping in the rain. In any case, it sounds like you need another one." He cast his spell.

The rain kept falling. On the morning of their third day in camp Lantid stared at the gray skies and tried to decide whether to keep waiting or to move on. Fargus put his hand on his shoulder. "Wait. By tomorrow morning everyone will be able to walk, and all the fighters will be ready to fight. Besides, we still have more food than we can carry."

"Something's wrong. We may have to go back by another route. Who knows how long that will take?"

"What's wrong? Apart from the weather, this is about as good as things have been since I left Kingstone."

"Where are the knights?"

"What?"

"The Knights Of the Circle were supposed to come looking. Where are they?"

"Maybe they're still waiting for their tracker?"

"Maybe, but they had to expect him before now or they wouldn't have bothered. Think about it: we barely made it. We've been moving towards The Hunt for days and the knights still haven't showed up. It took the

Kutel, what, five days to get here? It took us three on the way out. If the knights left The Hunt even on the day we went over the pass, they'd be here by now. I hope it's just a truant tracker, because if something has stopped the knights, we're not going to get through it."

"Maybe if it was a rockslide or something that would stop their horses. We could climb over that."

"Maybe."

Lantid shared his concern with the others. There was nothing to do about it until they found out for certain. The rain stopped in the first watch of the night. The next morning they were back on the trail. Blorfindel went out on point in case Lantid was right. Their speed picked up and their spirits rose as the former captives got closer to home.

Late in the afternoon of the third day Blorfindel got to the spot where they met the bear. He went back and told Lantid who immediately called a halt. "We don't want to camp in his territory."

That night Nugrot seemed to have an accident: the evidence indicated that he slipped and fell on a knife four times. It was unclear how it happened or where the knife was now. He was alive when Nickadola went to sleep and dead when Fargus made his first rounds, so it happened on either Blorfindel's or Alehra's watch, but they both said they did not see it. Neither of them seemed very concerned. Alehra was sharpening one of her daggers on a rock when she said, "We've eaten enough so we don't need him to carry for us, anyway."

That morning Nickadola made a quick search for the bear but could not find it. The Tafers of the Hunt were in a hurry to get started. They expected to be home before the sun set. Lantid's misgivings, however, had spread to the rest of the rescuers. "The knights should have been here. We'll go slow today."

Nickadola said, "I wish I could talk to the bear! I'm sure he would know. His territory has to got to cover a lot of area."

Blorfindel said, "I'll just have to be extra careful on point. That means I'll be slow."

The Timble volunteered, "I'll go with you."

"Stay back, though. Stay where you can see me, but if something sees me it won't see you, you know."

"Right."

Lantid said, "Fargus, Al, I'm going to need help slowing the pace – these people want to get home."

"I can tell Sturdifoot to play lame."

"They'd just leave him at this point. It's only fifteen miles or so. Some of them have started discarding food to lighten their packs. I've caught two, I'm sure there's more."

Fargus said, "We've made it this far, we can stay careful for one more day."

Blorfindel jerked his thumb over his shoulder. "Tell that to them!" The former captives were packed up and on the trail.

Five miles down the trail Blorfindel signed to Nickadola, 'Stop. I'm going right to look. You stop the ones behind us.' Nickadola tossed his head Fithern-style and disappeared back up the trail.

Something was wrong. There were black arrows on the trail ahead, just beyond the first Kutel campsite that they had found on the way out of The Hunt. Some of the arrows stuck into the ground at a very steep angle. Their inclination indicated they had come from the cliff to the right. They had not been there when they examined this area on the way out.

Blorfindel remembered that only a short distance ahead the trail got very narrow, maybe even narrow enough to keep the sun out this late in the morning. To the west – his right – there was a cliff that would stop the afternoon sun. He doubled back until he could find a place to climb.

He did not climb to the top. The mountain rose at least a thousand feet over the cliff. It would be a pointless climb since all he wanted was to see the top of an eighty foot cliff. He circled around so that he would approach the cliff from the west, which meant from above.

He was quietly making his way down the mountain when he saw another figure moving similarly from right to left, paralleling the trail. The figure stopped behind cover, hiding himself from every direction but one: the one where Blorfindel was. Blorfindel whispered, "Ichassi."

The figure turned and put his back to a tree, scanning the mountain above. Blorfindel showed his face for a second then signed, 'Come.'

The two Fitherani had a detailed conversation in their sign language. Blorfindel gave Ichassi the composition of the group returning to The Hunt. Ichassi explained that the knights were stuck on the other side of the pass. There were Kutel on both sides, fifty or so on the far side, nearly a hundred on this side. They could shoot down on the path or even just drop rocks from that height. When the conversation was finished they each retreated back to their own groups.

Everyone was disappointed to hear the news, except Lantid. "Now it makes sense. They knights did not abandon us, they just can't get to us. That's fine, we'll get to them."

"We can't run these people under that cliff!" Fargus realized that Lantid was smarter than that as soon as he said it.

Lantid shook his head, "We won't."

Blorfindel said, "We can probably take out the groups one at a time. They can't really support each other."

Alehra agreed, "We should be able to get above them and shoot down on them. We can do a lot of damage if we can just slow them up – just like on the hill, only with more support."

Lantid held up his hand. "We don't have to. We'll go around. It's like you said, Fargus: it's something that just stops the knights. They can't bring their horses over the mountain, and they can't climb mountains in their armor. Without their horses and their armor what good are they? We don't have that problem."

Lorten asked, "Don't you want to kill the Kutel up there?"

"Not that badly, no. We came to bring these people home and we're going to do that. I'd rather walk a little further than take a chance on getting someone else killed."

"So we go around?"

"We go around. We're not in the high mountain passes anymore. We're almost at The Hunt. I bet the other side of that mountain is a lot easier than some of the terrain that we've already covered."

So it was. The sun was shining on the tops of the mountains, but not in the valleys below when the entire group came around the mountain and met up with the knights camped there. The knights held their position as the weary refugees made their way home in the dark. By midnight they were cold, weary, sore, dirty, hungry, thirsty, happy and home.

Chapter 14

Return to Dath

The homecoming was dampened by the realization that home was not the same. Both the returning captives and the Tafers who stayed at The Hunt were still discovering who lived and who died. It was most difficult for the families of those missing Tafers who were not in the group of captives. Much of the town had been burnt. Almost every home was damaged in some way. Some of the returning captives found that their accommodations for the night were little better than the tents they had on the trail.

In spite of all of this, it was a happy homecoming. The afternoon following their arrival, the town assembled to thank the rescuers formally. There was no food for a feast or money for any kind of celebration or reward. They just came out and said their thanks, even the Tafers whose loved-ones did not return. All of the knights stationed at The Hunt gave credit and honor to the returning heroes as well, though they did it in turns so that the bulk of them were always ready to repel an attack.

Even before the handshaking, backslapping, and tears were over, the adventurers were talking about leaving. "There's not much we can really do here, anyway," Alehra said.

Lantid looked over the wreckage of his home town. "We should get to Dath. Maybe… maybe this doesn't have to happen there."

Blorfindel said, "They were going to wait until the harvest was in."

"Nugrot was going to wait until the harvest was in. Who knows what the Jun chief is thinking." Lantid held out his hand to Fargus, "It's been special working with you. I don't think we could have done it without you."

"Definitely," Alehra agreed.

"That's true," said Blorfindel

"And you'll take back some appreciation for the world that isn't Tafer-made," Nickadola said. "I must confess I have more respect for Feadin after working with you."

Fargus took a deep breath. "I'm coming with you – that is, if you'll have me."

They broke out in general celebration. When things calmed down a bit Alehra asked, "I thought you were dying to get back to Kingstone?"

"It's like Lantid said, maybe we can prevent this from happening again. I mean, I came out from Kingstone to help these people who were suffering. If I can go and prevent the people of Dath from suffering, isn't that better?"

Nickadola laughed. "Admit it, you just got used to clean water and you can't bear to go back."

"And I far prefer rocks and sticks to a stuffed mattress."

The Timble laughed at that, too. "You know, after the trip through the mountains I'm looking forward to the accommodations at Dath."

Blorfindel said, "I thought you were going home? I mean, before we found out about The Hunt you were planning on going home."

"I want to go check on the wolf pups anyway, and besides, I'd never sleep nights wondering how it came out. Then there's Foralis. They say the trees remember Fitherani for a long time. I'd like to hear what they have to say."

The Fitheran laughed. "Trees are miserable gossips. You shouldn't believe them."

They were so happy that they would all be together and so anxious to get on their way that they packed up and started down the road that very evening. They spent one night on the side of the road but the next evening found them in the Howling Wind Inn at Across. They all ate and drank too much. Nickadola made certain that even Sturdifoot was pampered in the stables – two copper stowsaw to the stable-boy saw to that. When a fight broke out in the common room all five of them stood up. Immediately the combatants backed away. One of them even asked Blorfindel for a tune, and the Tafer danced.

The following morning they got passage on a boat headed for Taferford. Fargus was sick all that morning, but no one could tell if it was the revelry or just the motion of the boat, but the second day of the boat trip he was not ill. In the end they paid the master of the boat extra to take them all the way to Dath. The current was strongly against them and for the last two days they could have made better time on foot, but their feet were very much enjoying the rest.

Their return to Dath was somewhat of a surprise. The news of their arrival ran ahead of them and long before they had walked to the Shieldmaster's residence, the Tafers of the town were out in the streets shaking their hands, slapping their backs, and handing them mugs full of river-cooled local ale. None of the locals knew anything about The Hunt, of course, they were celebrating the victory over the Kutel locally. In the last few weeks the raids had begun again and everyone was glad to see the Kutel-fighters come back to town. They spoke over each other.

"They came back!"

"Did you think they'd abandon us?"

"We're so happy. We never got a chance to say thanks before."

"You're all welcome back at the barn, of course."

"Who's this, then?"

"It's Feadin sending her help, can't you see?"

"Of course she'll take our side!"

"Where are the wolves? Nothin' happened, I hope."

"Where have you been? We were worried about you!"

"No we weren't! We knew you'd come through!"

"Give 'em some air! You're like to smother them to death!"

The adventurers had no hope of responding to all of the shouts. Eventually everyone settled down to a victory-homecoming celebration. Blorfindel met more of the Tafers of Dath in that one night than he had in all of the time that they were defending the town.

Before long Shieldmaster Terak joined them. "I'm glad you're back. I was wrong and I admit it: we need you. We can't even handle the little raids as it is. They've only come into town three times since you left, in groups of four or six. They do some damage, but mostly they've been looking to steal things. I can give you the same deal as before, maybe. I don't know how long our little town can support you. If we have to lose all we have, I'd rather spend it on you than let the Kutel steal it."

Blorfindel said, "This time we're not here to defend the town. We've come to attack the Kutel."

"What's the difference?"

Lantid stepped in, "One difference is that we're not going to be staying in town any longer than we have to."

Alehra said, "Which means that you'll still have to deal with the little raids for a while."

Fargus said, "But, when we have beaten them back a bit, I expect they raids will stop."

Lantid picked up the thread again, "At least they won't be able to replace the Kutel that you kill during the raids."

Terak was getting confused trying to follow them all. "Stop! One of you, are you here to help us or not?"

Blorfindel answered, "We're here on our way to Foralis. When we're done at Foralis the Kutel won't be able to come through there to get here. If we find Kutel that might attack Dath, we'll stop them if we can, but we probably won't get them all before they attack here."

Nickadola added, "Perhaps its time the Tafers of Dath learned to use their axes on something other than trees?"

"These people aren't warriors."

Lantid said, "They are now." Terak started to object but Fargus held up his hand so that Lantid could continue. "The Kutel are coming, and we're not going to stop them. You have one choice to make: you can fight, or you can give the Kutel what they want. I recommend fighting, because what they want may well be these people. Start training them. You can use the weapons that you take off the Kutel. You would be amazed at what a bunch of Tafers can do when they're fighting for their lives and the lives of their families and neighbors. All you have to do is hold out for a while. We will cut off their lines of support and reinforcement. We've already destroyed one group that was coming to take over Dath."

"Some of these people aren't fit to fight."

Lantid shook his head. "Don't talk to me about fit. Who's not fit? Who's in worse shape than I was when I came here?"

"But you're a wizard."

"I wasn't born a wizard; I became one after I realized that I would never be fit to fight, as you say. Anyone who can't fight in hand-to-hand can find some other way to help. There will be weapons to sharpen, shields to make and mend, watches to keep, and probably wounds to bind."

"What about all the work that needs to get done?"

Nickadola said, "You've got your planting done by now, right? So the plants are going to grow without your help. What work needs to be done? You're going to kill more trees? For what?"

"Lumber is the way we make money around here."

Fargus put his hand on Nickadola's shoulder and spoke to Terak, "Forget about the money. If you spend your time making money you won't be able to keep it – the Kutel will take it away. If you spend your time getting ready to fight off the Kutel you'll at least get to keep what little you have."

Terak hesitated, but the crowd was for it. Unknown voices started to chime in:

"He's right."

"They won't burn my farm without a fight!"

"That's right!"

"We'll make it up next year."

"Or the year after."

Terak held up his hands. "So you are just stopping by to tell me to train these people to fight?"

Lantid said, "If you teach them to answer an alarm and hold a line in battle, you've done a lot, maybe enough. These raids aren't Kutel war-bands, they're little groups of Kutel who think they can go bully the local Tafers. When they find out that you're ready to fight them, they'll run."

"What if they don't?"

"Then you fight them, but they'll run."

Alehra said, "Do what you want. We're not staying. It would be nice if Dath was still here when we came back, but that's not up to us."

Blorfindel said, "We're going to fight the Kutel where they live. We're going to get rid of their town. We won't get you a peaceful summer, but we may secure a peaceful decade to come."

Lantid said, "An army is coming. You're not going to stop it here, not even with us helping and all of your people fighting. Your town is probably the hardest place to defend in the entire Shield Valley. If the Kutel take over Dath and can use this place as a rally point for their armies, Taforford will fall, too. That splits the Sheild Valley in half. All they have to do is sit on the rivers to starve Kingstone. They could attack the Timbles if they wanted or they could strike south to Sekri Timbrali. If a Kutel army comes down that path it will probably overrun the entire Valley. They have to be pushed back over the mountains to their own lands."

"The King will fight back."

"The King will fight back, and lose. He has to hold the pass at The Hunt and defend Eastower, too. After the defeat at The Hunt that just got harder than ever before. That means more troops. Everyone is thinking that the Kutel will attack in the east again because that's what they've always done. There are some smarter Kutel in charge now and they already know that this is the soft spot. They're holding the pass north of The Hunt with a significant force, but they're only holding. They're keeping open the path from Bur-Droo to right here. We cut it off for a while, but it's open again now. Any Kutel leader who can round up enough food can march his troops to within a few miles of here in perfect safety. He doesn't even have to arm them all, because somewhere up the path is a Kutel town with Kutel smiths making weapons for the Kutel army. We're going to try to stop that. Maybe with the King's help you can stop an army armed with sticks and stones."

Someone in the crowd shouted, "Why are they coming?"

"Yeah! Why don't they just stay home?"

Fargus answered, "They're starving. I know they don't look like they're starving, but there just isn't enough food for all of them. The weak ones die. The strong ones take what they want and all of the Kutel in between join up with the war bands coming here. The Shield Valley has food."

Lantid picked up the explanation. "And every Kutel leader wants to be bigger. They all dream of being the new chief here, or maybe even the new king of The Shield Valley."

"What chance have you got against an army?"

"None, but we don't have to fight the whole army at once. We're counting on the fact that they're not ready yet."

They spent the night in the barn. They wanted to take a prisoner, but the Kutel did not raid that night. The next morning they made their way, very cautiously, to the house outside of town. They expected to find a sentry. There was none.

"Maybe they're not here."

Lantid shook his head. "They're here. Where else would they be? This is the perfect base to launch attacks on Dath."

"Let's go around," Nickadola suggested, "If I can get to the ruins of the smokehouse the wolves might be there. They'll know."

"I forgot they were staying here. I hope they got away. I don't think the Kutel would be afraid of two wolves."

They went around the clearing as stealthily as they could. They were not stealthy enough. They had only made it to the north side of the house when Blorfindel heard voices from within. He stopped the others and listened, but he could not make out what was said.

"They're alert, anyway," he whispered. "I don't know if they've seen us or heard us or both."

They each took cover and waited. They waited for a long time. Nothing happened. Finally Lantid whispered, "They can make us wait here all day if they want to."

Blorfindel looked back at the little Tafer. "I could try to get closer so that I could hear. I'd have to go down to my leather armor, though."

Fargus said, "Don't you dare take that armor off."

Nickadola pointed. "Something moved in the window!"

"Which one?"

"West… that is, the one on the right." There were only two windows on the north side of the house, both on the second floor.

"What do we do about it?"

Lantid slid his pack off. "Has anyone got a torch?"

Blorfindel asked, "What are you going to do with a torch?"

Fargus said, "Burn the house?"

"You can't burn that house down!"

"They don't know that."

Blorfindel shrugged off his own pack. "There are two torches in there – on the left side."

Lantid started striking flint and iron as soon as he found a torch, but it was a long wait before he got one lit. Blorfindel, Nickadola and Alehra each spotted movement in the windows while they waited. "That's metal!"

"A sword?"

"Maybe."

When the torch was lit Lantid held it over his head and started walking toward the clearing. Alehra stopped him with an outstretched arm. "That's dumb. Let me do it, I've got armor. Besides, you don't look like the type to burn a house down."

Lantid had only just handed her the torch when Fargus snatched it away from her. "Don't be foolish. I'll go. My armor is better than yours and my shield is bigger. Besides, you have a bow. Everyone get your ranged attacks ready." He waited for Alehra to get her bow ready. Blorfindel's bow and Nickadola's sling were already at hand. He waited until she nodded then the cleric jogged toward the house with his shield over his head. When he broke into the clearing he shouted, "Kingstone! The Shield! and Feadin!"

When Fargus closed within one hundred yards of the house Blorfindel shot an arrow at the west window. Alehra followed immediately with an arrow at the east window. His arrow disappeared in the darkness beyond the window. Hers struck the wall below and to the left of the mark. The Fitheran said, "You missed."

"You had all that time to aim! I was just following your lead!"

"Fine, you take the right and I'll get the left this time."

Blorfindel let Alehra shoot first. Blorfindel's arrow followed immediately. Two black arrows came out of the windows at Fargus and all four were in the air at once. Alehra's arrow was on target and they could hear the unseen archer cry out. Blorfindel had forced his shot and his arrow struck the edge of the window, splintering the wood but clearly causing no harm within. "Maybe it's the window," Nickadola offered sarcastically. He slung a bullet at the window and hit the wall above. "See?"

Neither of the black arrows came close to Fargus.

When he was about thirty yards from the building they all got a surprise. Kutel started coming around the building. The first one to come around the corner turned to face Fargus, grounded its spear and raised its large shield. The next one around the corner stepped past the first and did exactly the same. Very quickly the Kutel put up a row of seven shields and seven spears on the east side of the house. They were, however, doing nothing that might prevent Fargus from lighting a fire.

Blorfindel could see more Kutel moving behind their line. He timed his shot to coincide with the next Kutel taking position. It had its shield up, however, and the arrow glanced off.

Lantid swore, "Chrushk!" and ran into the clearing. Blorfindel followed. Alehra and Nickadola shot once before they joined the charge. Their missiles did no harm.

"What's wrong?" the Fitheran asked, "You wanted them to show themselves, right?"

"What's Fargus going to do when he gets there, talk to them sternly?"

"Cruska!"

Lantid's cough was gone but his lungs were still not up to the task. Blorfindel passed him when he started flagging. The next Kutel to take a place in the line was wearing a bow in addition to the spear and shield. Reflexively Blorfindel stopped to shoot at it. His arrow glanced off its greave. "They've got metal armor!" Lantid, Alehra and Nickadola passed him as he spoke.

Fargus continued his ruse right up to the wall. He did not try to engage the Kutel at all. Instead, he ran up to the wall between the windows. Fortunately the Kutel did not man the murder holes in the overhanging second story. He pressed his back against the wall, stuck the torch in the ground and drew his mace.

Twelve Kutel had lined up with spears and shields when the first one pulled out of the line and ran to take up the next position. Blorfindel tried to time a shot at it and realized he was looking at too many feet. "There's someone in back!"

Lantid huffed, "They're guarding someone."

Blorfindel's arrow went between the shields but he could not tell if it struck anything painful. The Kutel held the line. "Two people! Four extra feet!"

Three Varren came around the other side of the building. Alehra and Nickadola each shot one down. The remaining Varro turned and ran even before Fargus raised his mace.

Another Kutel came around the corner and shot wildly though the gap between the building and the shield line. The black shaft was so ill-aimed that Blorfindel could not guess who the intended target might have been. The Kutel kept its head low and ran behind the line. Blorfindel stopped running a moment before it came past the line of shields. He shot an arrow just past the last shield The Kutel archer stepped out to shoot just as Blorfindel's arrow arrived. The arrowhead sparked on its armor but penetrated a little. The Kutel stumbled and Blorfindel shot again. Now that the Kutel was fully visible and barely moving, it had little hope. The arrow struck its face and it did not rise.

Lantid stopped to cast his spell. Fargus ran out to shield him while he was casting, but the spell was complete before the cleric arrived. Only three Kutel fell asleep. The two Kutel nearest the house were now separate from the rest of the line. They turned to run behind the line.

Blorfindel was not ready to shoot until they were concealed by the shield row. Instead, he ran to close the distance and to join up with Lantid and Fargus. Nickadola and Alehra did the same. As he ran he could hear Kutel shouting from behind the shield wall.

"We should turn and fight! There are only a few of them!"

"You fight, if you want to! I'll tell your boys how you died bravely!"

"Coward!"

"They killed all of Gronuk's band, including Gronuk and his Cral!"

"Gronuk was a fool!"

"So are you!" The one Kutel tripped the other and pushed him to the ground, then shouted, "Leave him! Let him fight if he wants to!" Two of the Kutel stopped to help the one on the ground. The other seven shield-Kutel continued their orderly retreat with the other speaker.

Blorfindel shot at the Kutel on the ground. Its armor – a combination of mail and small plates – stopped the arrow.

Alehra, Nickadola, and Fargus finished the three sleeping Kutel. Alehra said, "Only three? You're slipping."

"That means their tough. Remember what I said, it works better on the stupid and the weak."

The three Kutel that were not running away turned and marched toward Lantid. The two with spears threw them. Lantid ducked one but the other cut a crease across his chest. All three drew matching, heavy-bladed swords.

Blorfindel shot one in the foot before he drew sword and dagger. The Kutel paused a step to pull the arrow out, but let the wound bleed.

Lantid waited until they were very close, then cast his fire spell. All three burst briefly into flames, but the damage was light and the flames had nothing to catch on, and quickly burned out. Lantid backed away as fast as he could, holding the wound on his chest.

Blorfindel approached the Kutel on the left. Alehra closed on the one to the right. Nickadola drew scimitar and shield and stepped into the middle. Fargus started toward Lantid, but the wizard shouted, "Save it! Help Nickadola!"

Blorfindel slashed over the Kutel's shield, but it raised the shield and deflected the sword. It stabbed with its sword but he turned it with his dagger. He stomped down on its wounded foot and it shouted, but swung its shield down and struck his greave with the edge of its shield. Now that it's shield was down again Blorfindel stabbed over the top, but it's mail held and Blorfindel had to pull hard to free his sword from the link. There was blood on the tip of the sword. The Kutel chopped down. Its blow overpowered Blorfindel's awkward parry with the dagger and struck his shoulder but did not penetrate his armor. Blorfindel slashed at its arm with his sword as he retreated. The blade struck its armored sleeve first but drew across its exposed wrist and opened another small wound.

The Kutel tried to press its attack as Blorfindel withdrew. Blorfindel parried its sword with his own sword. It shoved forward with its shield to try to knock him off balance. Blorfindel twisted and got his dagger inside its shield. He staked its wrist to its own shield and left his dagger there. With his free left hand he grasped the Kutel's sword arm. The Kutel was trying to draw its sword blade against his armor, but could not break free from the Fitheran's grip. Blorfindel swung his sword around in a half circle overhead, but rather than strike down against its armored shoulder he turned the edge against its throat and drew it across. He held it in place while it bled.

While he was waiting for it to bleed to death he looked over across the battle. Nickadola was wounded. Fargus was raining blows on the Kutel's armor and shield but doing little harm. Nickadola himself was doing all that he could to keep the Kutel's sword away.

Alehra seemed to be uninjured, but giving ground before the Kutel in front of her. It had a small wound on its cheek and another just below its knee at the top of its greave, neither was serious. As Blorfindel was watching, three throwing knives flashed in. The first glanced harmlessly off its helmet. The second cut its shield arm on its way past. The third stuck in its hip. It tried to push Alehra away with its shield, but its hip did not have the strength and she turned it to her left with her own shield. It rolled on the ground and came back to its feet. It raised its sword just in time to save its life from Alehra's sword point. The sword scratched open its forehead and caught under its helmet which guided the weapon against its own scalp.

The struggling against Blorfindel's grip became weak as the Kutel bled out. He snatched his dagger away and went to help Nickadola and Fargus. He looked for an opening in the Kutel's armor, but it was covered head to toe in mail and over that had metal plates reinforcing the vital areas. Blorfindel knew that it must have eyeholes in its helmet, but he was behind it. He drove his sword point into the back of its knee. Its armor held and again he had to pull hard to get his sword out. He jabbed his heavy-bladed dagger in the mail under its armpit. Still the mail held, though the combination of the attacks to the back of its right knee and left armpit caused it to stumble.

When it regained its balance it turned to face Blorfindel. He tried to stab it in the eye, but it turned its helmet at the last moment and the sword was turned away. Nickadola was so wounded that rather than attack its exposed back he withdrew and Fargus went with him to heal him.

The Kutel and the Fitheran went back and forth in a classic duel for a moment. During that exchange their armor was not needed as they parried every attack with sword, dagger or shield. Eventually the Kutel made a mistake. It put his right fist against the inside of its shield and tried to overbear Blorfindel, expecting his own strength to be greater than that of the Fitheran. Blorfindel shoved back against the shield with his left forearm for a moment as he reversed his grip on his dagger, at the same time drawing back his sword as if to stab over the shield. When the Kutel took his right hand off the shield to attack Blorfindel's leg, the Fitheran hooked the Kutel's shield with his dagger and turned it away, exposing the Kutel's back. Blorfindel hesitated, returning his dagger to its normal grip. The Kutel spun around to its right, both freeing its shield and adding extra force to its sword blow. When it snapped its head around Blorfindel again stabbed at its eyes. It flinched away from the blade and again its helmet saved it, but now it was not looking at Blorfindel. Its sword continued to arc around with great force. Rather than parrying the weapon, Blorfindel stabbed the Kutel's sword wrist with his dagger. Even with the added force of the Kutel's own attack its armor showed its worth; a few links broke and the dagger opened only a small wound. Still, the links could not protect the Kutel's wrist from the force of the collision. Its sword flew away and struck Blorfindel's armor, causing a spark but no harm.

The Kutel leaped back and drew another sword, this one short and light after the fashion favored by some Fithern archers. Blorfindel paused for a moment as he looked at both the blade and the blood running freely from the Kutel's wrist. "I know that blade."

"You'll know it when I prick your guts with it!" The Kutel stabbed at Blorfindel, but it was an idle threat. He parried easily and gave a lightning stab under the Kutel's helmet. This also drew blood, though the wound was neither deep nor vital. The Fitheran retrieved his sword as quickly and the Kutel's shield struck only the air.

"Where did you get it, I wonder? Can you still speak?"

"I can speak! It was a gift from that cowardly Lurshod! To prove our lasting friendship, that's why he gave it! See my great friend Lurshod anywhere?" The Kutel attacked again. This time there was even less strength in its wrist. Blorfindel parried easily with his sword and stepped around the Kutel far enough to shove it behind the shoulder. It fell to the ground but rolled to its feet.

"It will betray you, you know. It already has, in fact. That's why you're here, facing me. Did he tell you whose sword it was?"

"It was the Fitheran chief's sword, if you can believe Lurshod." The Kutel did not try to attack again. Instead, it stayed on guard hoping that the Fitheran would leave an opening when he attacked. "Legend says that Solsung himself took it from the Fitheran's cold, dead hand."

Nickadola and Fargus flanked the Kutel but Blorfindel waved them off. "Leave him!" He had to say it again in Shield, "Leave him! He's mine." They went to help Alehra. "Lurshod lied. The sword you bear came from his left hand." Blorfindel raised his own sword as if in salute. "This is the one from his right."

The Kutel squinted for a moment. Its day vision was not so good, but the weapons did seem to match. "How did you get that?"

"It is mine by right." He stepped back into a fighting stance. "I am Blorfindel Brigtheyes, son of Lalliam Steelhand, and the rightful bearer of both my blade and the one you carry."

"Then come and take it away from me!" The Kutel beckoned with the sword.

Blorfindel laughed. "It will fall from your hand if you were to strike me with it. Do you think it would do me harm?"

"Why not?"

"Lalliam Steelhand was not chieftain of Foralis, but he was its greatest warrior, my father, and the commissioner of the blade you now wave. I have come to take back what is rightfully mine, and you see, the sword came to meet me. Don't feel too badly about it though, I would have come to kill you sooner or later."

"Will you kill Lurshod, too?"

"Is he at Foralis?"

"I don't know Foralis. He's at Jun. He's the chief there, and he wanted my help so he gave me this useless Fithern peace of Chruska! Wait! Foralis was the Fithern town, yes? Foralis is Jun, and there's more–" The Kutel lunged at Blorfindel, hoping the narrative had distracted him. It did not. He parried again with his dagger and drew his sword across the Kutel's eye-slit.

At the same time Alehra arrived. The Kutel's flexible mail armor was no protection at all as she smashed her war hammer into its side again and again. Finally, she pierced its helmet with the spike on other side of the hammer.

Chapter 15

Lessons Learned

Blorfindel dropped his dagger and caught his father's short sword before it fell to the ground. "I was talking to him!"

"I know. I thought I was going to fall asleep waiting for you."

"It was going to bleed to death talking."

"There are a bunch of other Kutel running away, remember?"

"Oh, yeah."

"They got away," Lantid said flatly.

"They can't be far."

"Can't they? Maybe Blorfindel could catch them, but I can't. Personally, I'm glad we didn't have to fight all of them together. We might not have made it." Lantid was holding a rag to his chest to slow the bleeding.

Fargus cast a spell that made the rag unnecessary. "How is that? We fought scores of them in the mountains and now we're nearly killed by–" he looked around "–seven?"

"Armor," was Blorfindel's immediate response.

Alehra said, "Skill. Did you see their retreat? We couldn't have done that – not as well as they did."

"Lots of things," Lantid said, "Nickadola didn't get a single spell off. The terrain here is flat and open and they had the only cover. Don't discount Lorten and his soldiers."

"The captives?"

"Some of them have years of experience fighting Kutel. That didn't just disappear when they were captured. Blorfindel and Al are correct as well, of course: these Kutel were much tougher than the ones we fought in the mountains."

"Except Nugrot," Blorfindel said.

Lantid lifted an eyebrow. "You fought Nugrot more or less on your own. It didn't look like you had this much trouble with him."

"You weren't watching that closely. I think he had me if Fargus didn't heal my wrist." Blorfindel gestured toward the cleric.

Fargus nodded to Blorfindel before saying, "If all of the Kutel here are this tough, we're in for a rough summer."

Blorfindel dipped his head 'no'. "They won't all be as tough as the leaders and their guard. If they were they'd all go get war bands of their own."

"These can't have been the leaders, they wouldn't have been the ones to stand and fight."

"Oh, I forgot, you don't speak the language. There were two leaders here. They argued about whether to fight us or run away. They had some sort of league, but I didn't get to why they were here before Al crushed it." Blorfindel waved the short sword at her, "That was good thinking, by the way, to use the hammer to defeat his armor."

"It wasn't a tough decision." She picked her sword up from the ground. The tip was bent sharply in two places. "I got it caught between this one's helmet and skull when he hit it with his shield." Fargus handed her one of the Kutel's swords. She looked at it and felt the weight. "No, it's really not the same at all. These were made to hack, not to stab."

Blorfindel offered her the short sword, "You'll be giving up a lot of reach, but you can use the same style. It's got more flex to it than your blade and it comes back to true."

She took it from him. "This is nice. The Kutel had this? Damn, it is really short, though, and blunt."

"It takes an edge quickly. The Kutel have been neglecting it." She looked at him under lowered eyebrows. "It was my father's. The other Kutel leader gave it to this hone as a present to seal their friendship. That was before he tripped him and left him to die, of course." He held his own sword next to it. "See, they're a matched set."

Alehra handed the short sword back to him. "You'd better keep it, then. I'll just use my war hammer until I can straighten mine out, or get a replacement. Besides, the flexible blade will work better for parrying than attacking."

Fargus offered the Kutel sword again. "Don't you think you ought to have a real sword?"

"Don't discount the value of a war hammer. Between the bludgeoning head and the spike on the back it can penetrate most armor. The only problem is the reach. You should try it sometime."

Blorfindel agreed. "That's right. If you were hitting it with a war hammer instead of that mace you might have finished it yourself."

Fargus said, "I bet I bruised him pretty badly."

"There's a big difference between bruises and broken bones, and you can throw a war hammer if you have to and really expect to do some harm."

"Enough! When you're ready to give lessons, I'll try it. Now is not the time."

Lantid shrugged. "I don't know, maybe it is. We should either plan on staying here or going back to town. I need some time before I can cast spells again. How about you, have you got anything left?"

"One. Is anyone else hurt?"

Blorfindel rolled his right arm, "I got popped on the shoulder pretty good, but it's nothing serious."

"If nothing else happens I'll heal you before I go to sleep. That is, if Nickadola's feeling all right." They looked around but the Timble was not with them. He was over by the wreckage of the smokehouse. Fargus shouted to him, "Nickadola! Are you all right? Do you need another heal?"

"I'm fine now, thank you. Well, no, not fine, my ribs are still sore." He looked back at the ruins. "They're gone. They've been gone for a while now. I can't tell if they left on their own or if the Kutel got them. I guess there is nothing we can do now but keep a lookout for them."

Fargus looked confused. Blorfindel whispered, "The wolves."

"He got a pretty nasty crack on the head, too." Fargus shouted to Nickadola, "How's your head?"

"Sad." Nickadola felt his scalp, "I've got a knot, too."

Lantid turned to the house. "Shall we see what the Kutel have left us?"

Blorfindel waited for Nickadola while the Tafers walked to the front door. "They probably left on their own when the Kutel started coming back. Remember, the first groups were little raiding parties. They wouldn't want to take the pups."

The Timble was not convinced. "They make armor out of wolf pelts, too. It's my fault. I brought them here. They would never have been in harm's way if I didn't ask them to help fight the Kutel."

"They were in harm's way when we found them, remember?"

"But they would have been safe if we had just left them."

"You think so? I think the Kutel would have recaptured the pups right after they killed us. We would never have survived the battle on the hill without the wolves."

"Maybe…"

Nickadola was interrupted by a shout from Fargus. "Don't open the door!" Blorfindel and Nickadola came running.

Lantid backed away, "What?"

"There's blood on the threshold."

Alehra waved at him dismissively. "There's blood everywhere. Even you've got blood on you."

Lantid said, "He's right. That isn't from today."

"We fought a battle here before, remember?"

"Not in the doorway. And see it's been scrubbed around the bottom, but not higher up. The Kutel were trying to hide this."

Alehra asked, "So what do you think it is?"

"I don't know. I don't think the Kutel cleaned it up just to be tidy, though."

Nickadola picked up one of the Kutel spears on the way to the door. "Stand aside." The Tafers all stepped to the left of the door. Blorfindel waited on the right with his bow trained on the door. When everyone was ready Nickadola tried to open the door with the spear. He could not. He could not hold the latch and pry it open. Fargus reached around the corner with his mace to hold the latch up. Nickadola pried the door open with the spear point.

Something struck out from the darkness of the doorway. Blorfindel's first impression was that it was a claw of some huge creature. He shot an arrow in the door opening behind it. It was, in fact, three hooks and a spike attached to a single pole. After the dust settled Alehra put her foot on the 'arm' and looked in the doorway. Wound cords had been used as the spring to power the trap. She looked around inside. "Good call, Fargus."

Lantid began to examine the workings of the trap. "Nasty and clever. They had to rig it so that the door swung out of the way before it came down or it would just scratch the door, and they had to have a way to set it when they left, because they used this door. There must have been a way to get in without triggering it, though."

"The back door?"

"That will be locked and barricaded, very likely. Remember, Fargus was charging at it?"

Fargus asked, "Are you certain that you want to stay here? There may be more traps."

"I don't think so, but we do need to be very careful – especially if anything looks out of place."

"Valuable," Fargus said, "If anything looks valuable, it's probably bait. They had plenty of time to pack up anything that they wanted to take with them."

Nickadola spun around and pulled out his sling. "The Varro!"

Blorfindel turned and drew another arrow. "Where?"

"I don't know, but one of them got away, right? It didn't go with the Kutel; I bet it was here waiting! It knew about the door, why not see if the trap got one of us? It had plenty of time to hide while we fought the others."

Lantid ran out of the house. "We have to catch it! If it's been watching all of this then it knows a lot!"

Alehra asked, "What does it know?" but no one stopped to explain.

Blorfindel looked for a good piece of cover and ran towards it. On the way he thought, *It's not there anymore. If it was there, where did it go? Where is it now?* He tried to guess three pieces of cover ahead and ran there. He could hear the Tafers running behind him. The Varro was not where he looked, of course. *That would be too easy.* There were many, many places that something as small as a Varro could hide. *How fast do they run? How fast can it move and stay hidden?* Blorfindel did not know. Without this information his search became indiscriminate and hopeless. Still, he searched.

A moment later a flock of crows passed overhead, fanning out as they went. One called, then a few more. The flock turned toward the call and they all started cawing and circling. After watching for a moment Blorfindel realized that the circle of crows was moving east. Nickadola shouted, "Follow the crows!"

Once again Blorfindel took off running. When he got within the circle of crows he saw a Varro duck under a fallen tree. Blorfindel jumped over the trunk and trained his bow underneath. Alehra, Fargus and Lantid were coming up quickly. They had it boxed in. The crows kept circling and calling. Alehra shouted at them, "I know! We've got him! Shut up!"

The Varro ran out from under the log and straight at Blorfindel. It had no chance. His arrow staked its head to the ground. It was still kicking when Nickadola arrived. Fargus raised his mace to crush it but Nickadola shouted, "Don't break its eyes! The crows want them!"

Alehra shook her head and walked away. "That's just nasty."

Blorfindel had to agree. He fixed his eyes on Nickadola rather than watch the Varro. "You got the crows to hunt for us?"

"I promised them that they could have all the corpses afterwards, even the eyes."

"They were going to get them anyway."

"They don't know that. Almost everything else that kills wants to eat the carcass itself and will chase the crows off until it's done."

They left the Varro and went back to the house. Blorfindel and Alehra started going over the Kutel bodies and stripping their armor. Fargus and Lantid went through the house looking for more traps. When Nickadola came back he said, "The crows are angry. They think your breaking our bargain."

"Tell them we're just shelling them, they can have the insides."

The crows perched in a solemn array and watched to be certain that they were not being cheated. Blorfindel had to laugh. Alehra looked over to see what could make him laugh while stripping a Kutel carcass. When she saw the dour jury of crows inspecting their work, she laughed too. When they got back to the house, Lantid wanted to know what they were laughing about.

"You had to be there." Alehra dumped the armor on the floor.

Blorfindel changed the subject. "What did the Varro know that was so important?"

Alehra jumped in. "Yeah! And how did you know what it knew?"

"It was watching us. It saw that I cast spells. It saw Fargus heal. It saw how much trouble we had with the last three. Maybe it saw enough to encourage the Kutel to come back and attack tonight. Right now the scared Kutel leader doesn't know much about us."

Blorfindel said, "He knows we killed the other group here."

"How would he know that?"

"That's what he said."

"I bet he doesn't know how long it took us to recover afterwards. As far as he knows we can do this all day long. I think he saw me get creased by the spear, but even then he doesn't know how bad it was. Ignorance is fear. So long as he is afraid of us we have an advantage."

"The Varro didn't see very much. They don't like sunlight either."

Nickadola answered before Lantid, "Varren don't care very much about what they see. What they smell is another issue. It knows which of us bled and by how much. It knows if you were working hard during the fight. It could easily have found out that we came from Dath and by which path. Even if it didn't learn anything else, it knows what we each smell like.

When the Varren at Jun smelled your trail after that, they would know it was you – not just some Fitheran, but Blorfindel Brighteyes. Varren are very dangerous scouts."

Chapter 16

Message

They spent two nights and a day at the house before Fargus was satisfied that everyone was completely healed. During that time they cleaned out the house and planned their next move. Alehra hammered her sword straight enough to use, though both she and Blorfindel were concerned that it would bend again if she tried to stab with it.

Everyone agreed that their next step included taking a look at Jun. Blorfindel was the obvious choice for scout. Late the following afternoon while the rest of the group and his armor waited under cover nearby, Blorfindel sprinted silently from tree to tree and approached the Kutel town that had once been his home. He was happy to see that many of the trees he knew were still there. That became rarer as he got closer to town.

The Kutel town of Jun was bigger than Foralis had ever been. Most of the expansion was north and east of the old town. The mines were clearly to the north. Black smoke filtered from foundries and smithies but no sound of a hammer rang in the daylight.

The Kutel had sentries, but they were too few to watch a town of this size. Blorfindel did not attempt to enter the town because of the warnings about the Varren and their noses. After circling the town once he returned to the group. Rather than answering their questions he moved them to a stand of trees on the slope of a hill northwest of town. From there they could see down into most of the town. The sun was setting when they arrived.

"It's big – eighty-two buildings."

Fargus frowned. "That's not big."

"Then you stroll down there and evict them."

"It's big for us. It's not a big town."

"Look at the farms," Lantid said. "How many Kutel do you think they can feed with those?"

Fargus shrugged.

"Nickadola?"

"It depends on what they're growing. I can't see from here."

"It's fair to guess that they are trying to get as much food per acre as they can, regardless of flavor or variety."

"They ought to be self-sufficient at least, but then who knows if Kutel make good farmers? I wouldn't think so."

"We can't even raid that. I mean, if they pin us down in town we have no chance. We'll have to find a way to get to some of them far enough away from town so they can't get help."

"What about the mines?" Blorfindel pointed east. "You can't see the entrances from here, but they're right over there."

Fargus shook his head. "Only if we have to. Kutel have every advantage underground and even more chance of boxing us in."

Lantid said, "Not every advantage. They can't use their numbers against us in a narrow mine shaft. Still, let's look for a better way."

As they were watching Jun began to come to life. A slow trickle of Kutel turned into a flood in minutes. Every house seemed to have at least a dozen Kutel in it. Groups started forming up to work in the fields or elsewhere. The metal industry woke noisily as well. Kutel with black sacks on their backs started coming out of the mines.

Lantid said, "I almost forgot about that. There are more living in the mines."

Blorfindel was watching one group in particular. They were forming up at the door to a large building. The door was large enough to make Blorfindel think that it was a barn of some sort, though it was not near a farm. There were four heavily armed Kutel in this group, in addition to about twenty that looked like regular Kutel soldiers. Once the elite Kutel had some sort of order the others opened the big door. Blorfindel whistled softly through his teeth and pointed as a Cral stepped out of the door. The others strained to see in the failing light as a box on poles followed the Cral out. Another Cral held the poles at the other end. To Blorfindel, it looked like a deep coffin. The Kutel closed the door and the entire procession moved east away from the center of town.

Alehra said, "Is that what I think it is?"

Fargus said, "A state funeral for a Kutel? Maybe. Do the Kutel bury their dead?" He looked around but none of them knew.

Lantid asked, "Blorfindel, what do the other Kutel look like. I can't see well enough."

"They look like regular soldiers, except for four of them which look more like the ones we fought the other day."

"Are they carrying anything other than their weapons and armor?"

"They have packs – satchels, that sort of thing. They look just like any other Kutel group."

"You mean just like any other Kutel war band." He snapped his fingers. "It's not a funeral. It's a payment! That's our target."

Nickadola frowned, "Two Cral backed up by four of those armored Kutel? Are you sure that's a good idea?"

"Not in the open. Not without surprise. Not without terrain. But they don't know we're here, and they can't be expecting us."

Fargus said, "Tomorrow. They're going slow and we can catch them in the daylight tomorrow. We want them to be the ones that are tired."

"Right," Lantid agreed, "but we still have to get away from here. We're too close to town to spend the night."

They moved northwest and spent the night. The next morning they circled around Jun to pick up the Kutel trail. Blorfindel bit his lip. "We should have watched longer. We don't even know where they went. They could have just gone to one of the farms or something."

Lantid shook his head. "They went east down a path. Two Cral carrying a box aren't going for a stroll to a farm. They're going to Bur-Droo or someplace like that. They need to sell their weapons and buy more workers or food or soldiers or whatever. The Kutel are packing satchels; that means they plan to be away for a while."

The trail was a well-worn path, but heavy Cral footprints were still visible here and there. They followed cautiously, with Blorfindel well in front of the group and Nickadola as a relay between. It was so late in the afternoon when Blorfindel sighted the Kutel that he had to be careful not to cast a shadow over them. They were in camp and getting ready for another night's journey.

When Blorfindel reported back Lantid, said, "Let them go for today. We'll rest and be on them all the earlier tomorrow."

Alehra said, "But we aren't catching them."

"We are. We had to go further than they did to walk around the town."

Lantid woke them before first light. The sun was still behind the mountains when they started down the path. By noon they had caught the Kutel once more. They had camped well off to the south of the trail at the base of a mountain. For most of the day the mountain would give them shade, but now the sun was high and filtered through the leaves of the trees that struggled to live in this rocky, sun-starved place. Again, Blorfindel directed the group to a place where they could see from a distance – this time the opposing hillside on the north side of the trail.

Lantid liked it. "Nice. All we have to do is take out three sentries and we can deal with the rest in their sleep."

Blorfindel dashed to another tree. As the stealthiest, he was responsible for the sentry furthest away. It took him only a moment to get into a good shooting position. He could see Alehra and Lantid were ready. Nickadola would be hidden somewhere near Lantid, and Fargus was further back. He watched his sentry and waited for Lantid's signal. It seemed like a long time coming, and indeed it was nearly five minutes before Blorfindel heard Lantid begin his spell. He shot immediately. The arrow struck the sentry's throat just under the jawline and the Kutel flopped to the ground. It was unable to shout out, but Blorfindel worried whether its struggling would disturb the Kutel sleeping nearby.

He did not hear Alehra's bow. After a moment he looked over to see why not. Both of the other sentries were on the ground. Lantid had waited until they were close enough to get both within the area of his sleep spell. Blorfindel's lip curled into a smile.

"Ambush!" one of the Kutel shouted.

Twang! Alehra's bow sounded.

Blorfindel turned his head to see that one of the other Kutel was awake. It was rolling to its feet and raised its shield. Blorfindel shot it in the back. As it fell he saw that Alehra's arrow was embedded in its chest, but all too late.

Nickadola and Lantid shouted together, "Fall back! Rally here!"

Alehra and Blorfindel abandoned their shooting positions to join them. At the same time Fargus came running up from behind. Nickadola's sling bullet hit one of the sleeping Kutel in the face. It curled its knees up and held its head, screaming.

As soon as Alehra and Blorfindel got back they began shooting. Alehra shot two Kutel back to the ground as soon as they stirred. Blorfindel saw one start to put on a mail shirt and aimed an arrow just above its naval. The arrow arrived before the mail covered.

Kutel were starting to get up faster than Blorfindel and Alehra could shoot. Blorfindel saw one try to crawl behind the box. He shot it in the leg but could not stop it from reaching cover. Alehra targeted Kutel that were closer. Lantid shouted, "Keep them away from the sleeping ones if you can! They can't break the spell with sound, only touch!"

One of the Cral started to rise. When Blorfindel turned to aim at it Lantid shouted at him, "Get the Kutel down first! The Cral take too long!" He shot down another Kutel instead.

As soon as the Kutel realized what was happening they ran for cover. Some of them found rocks and trees, but most ran behind the Crals. Blorfindel and Alehra shot the same one in the back as it neared the sleeping Cral. Nickadola hit another with a sling bullet but its helmet saved it. It jumped on the Cral's stomach and ran for the mountain behind. Alehra shot it in the back as the Cral started to rise.

Lantid dashed forward, bent over almost double to stay out of the way of the arrows. He went to the sleeping Kutel and began to cut their throats one by one with his dagger.

Blorfindel and Alehra each shot one more Kutel as they took cover. Alehra's arrow lodged between the Kutel's skull and spine. Blorfindel's arrow pierced the Kutel's thigh and caused it to fall behind the narrow tree that it had chosen for cover. As it landed its head was exposed on the other side of the trunk and Nickadola hit it with a sling bullet.

Then the Cral got to their feet. Immediately the Kutel cheered and fell in behind them. Blorfindel could hear the Kutel leader shouting orders but could not pick him out. He shot at a Kutel leg but a shield covered before the arrow arrived. Fargus ran forward and crushed the skull of a sleeping Kutel. At the same time he said to Lantid through clenched teeth, "We've got to get out of here!"

Nickadola cast a spell. Suddenly all of the trees in front of Fargus and Lantid began to grab at the Kutel and the Crals. Many of the Kutel were snatched up but Cral arms proved stronger than tree branches and they wrestled their way through followed by two of the armored Kutel.

Alehra grit her teeth as she drew her sword and swung her shield around. To her right Blorfindel looked equally happy as he drew his father's swords and steadied himself against the approaching Cral.

Each of the Cral had a Kutel behind it. Lantid threw knives at the one closest to Alehra. They did no visible harm, but the Kutel turned to run him down. Fargus attacked the Kutel closer to Blorfindel. His mace stuck soundly on its back, but it did not fall. Instead, it turned and chopped at his legs with a battle axe. Fargus managed to get his shield in the way of the axe handle but could not prevent the blade from opening a cut on his calf. Nickadola threw himself between Lantid and the Kutel that was charging the wizard. The heavily armored Kutel tripped over the Timble but got up immediately.

When the Cral got close, Blorfindel's thoughts distilled down to survival. He studied his opponent. Its skin was colored differently than the other Cral, and differently than the one they fought before. *I wonder if that means anything?* It was coppery-red with large black blotches. It had a ring of light blue hair from ear to ear, but it was bald on top like some Tafers get. The other was purple with white hair. They each wore a heavily soiled silk sarong that had once been dark blue. It seemed odd on the huge and stupid Cral. For a weapon it had a tree trunk that was over twice the Fitheran's height which it wielded like a staff. The heavy end was as big around as Blorfindel's neck. The other Cral had an identical staff. *They are the poles that they used to carry the box.*

The red Cral took a huge swing with the pole. Blorfindel waited until the last moment to duck under it. He touched his short sword to it on the way by, not that he could deflect the blow in any way, but he could feel where it was without watching it pass. While he was still bent over Blorfindel stabbed between the Cral's toes. He hit nothing but dirt. The Cral reversed its swing and dipped the staff low. Blorfindel sprung over the staff. He stabbed the short sword between its knuckles. The shock of the collision nearly knocked the sword from his hand. Even so, the sword's point did not draw blood.

Blorfindel looked over quickly when he heard Lantid cast his sleep spell again. Fargus, Nickadola, and both Kutel fell over, asleep.

The Cral jabbed at Blorfindel with the end of the pole as if it were a spear. The Fitheran stepped aside, but not quite quickly enough. The pole caught on one of the seams in his armor and spun him around. At the same time Blorfindel stabbed at one of the black blotches on the Cral's chest, but the darker skin was just as tough as all the rest and the point did not penetrate.

It took one hand off the staff as it spun it around, hoping to catch the Fitheran's sword. When its elbow raised over Blorfindel's head he stepped inside its reach and stabbed up into its armpit with the short sword. It opened a small cut, and for the first time the Cral started bleeding. He stepped underneath and tried to drive his long sword into the same wound but the Cral turned and the blade slid harmlessly across the thick hide of its upper arm. The Cral's swing would have flattened the Fitheran's head, helmet and all, if he had not ducked. His helmet stripped some bark off the pole as it went by. Even with that little contact Blorfindel's head jolted to the right.

The Cral bent its leg during the follow-through. Blorfindel jammed the short sword behind its knee even before he straightened his own neck. Again, the Cral's hide was too strong. The Cral struck at Blorfindel's head with its elbow. He leaped back and stabbed at the elbow with his long sword. The sword blade bent snake-like for an instant before the point cut through the Cral's skin. The sword sprung straight and drove its point between the bones of the monster's elbow. The Cral staggered with the pain and used its pole to steady itself. Blorfindel pulled hard to extract his sword from the arm but it stuck. He switched the short sword to his right hand and drew his dagger. The Cral was still leaning on its pole when he attacked. He tried to stab just behind its kneecap but before he could get that close it slapped him with the back of its limp arm. Instinctively he tried to parry the attack with his dagger. All of his strength just took some of the power off the Cral's clumsy blow. His armor gave a muffled clank as the Cral's hand sent him backward coughing and trying to suck wind back into his lung.

The Cral plucked Blorfindel's sword from its elbow and threw it away. Blood started to run from the wound as it regained its footing and its two-handed grip on the pole. Blorfindel took three running steps toward the Cral and dove over the pole as it swung at him again. He got a scratch on his thigh from the rough bark. As he rolled he left the short sword on the ground and picked up his long sword. As he came on guard a sling bullet hit the Cral in the side of the face just below its left eye. The Cral was in the motion of jabbing with the pole again when he looked away to see where the stone had come from. Blorfindel leaped onto the end of the pole and ran down it toward the Cral. Somewhere in the back of his consciousness he wondered how strong it had to be to take the full weight of him and his armor unexpectedly and without even bending. He aimed to stab his sword point into its eye, but the Cral raised the staff at the last moment, catapulting the Fitheran over its head. Then it spun to strike him in mid-air.

Blorfindel found himself flying over the purple Cral. He punched down on the top of its head with his left hand and landed on his feet between its arms. The red Cral's blind swing struck the purple on the side of the head. Before it could recover Blorfindel stabbed under its jaw. At first his sword did not penetrate. At the same time Alehra used the distraction to drive the spike of her war hammer into a purple foot. The full force of the hammer blow pierced its hide and wedged the bones of its foot apart. The Cral winced in pain. The added force of the wince pushed Blorfindel's sword through its skin and into its palette. Fargus struck the back of its knee with his mace and its leg buckled, adding extra force against the sword point. Blorfindel pushed up on the sword as hard as he could but the Cral's weight quickly forced him to the ground. Fargus' mace slammed down on the beast's head four times as Blorfindel struggled to lift the Cral's arm off him and pull his sword free. Even the thick skull of an eight-foot Cral could not take that much abuse: it caved in.

Blorfindel came on guard just in time to watch the red Cral jab at Alehra with the pole. She deflected the attack with her shield. Blorfindel expected that her shield arm would break, but she let the angle of the shield push her to the right and bruised its kneecap with her war hammer on the way by. As it started to swing at her a sling bullet hit it in the eye. Again she deflected the pole with her shield, this time allowing herself to be pushed down as the pole passed over her shield.

Blorfindel rushed at the Cral again. It reversed its swing and dipped its pole low to catch Alehra before she could rise. Before the pole could hit her, Blorfindel stabbed with his sword to the inside of the Cral's left elbow while he jabbed his broad-bladed dagger into the wound on the outside of its right elbow. Surprising the Cral, Alehra rolled onto its feet and inside the blow, once again driving her hammer into its kneecap. The Cral twisted, trying to take the pressure off all three points, and staggered sideways. Alehra drove the spike of her war hammer into this one's foot, too. Blorfindel saw the small cut under its armpit and stabbed his sword in as he had intended to do earlier in the battle. The point slid along the Cral's hide until it slipped into the wound and dug deep into its shoulder. As it stood tall to try to climb off the sword's point, Alehra and Fargus shattered its knee with her whirling hammer blow to the kneecap sandwiched against his mace strike to the back of the knee. The Cral came crashing down. Blorfindel stuck his sword in its ear and met little resistance until the tip hit the other side of its skull. They all moved away as quickly as they could to be clear of the Cral's death throws.

As they stood aside catching their breath Nickadola shouted, "There's still Kutel in the trees! The spell won't last forever!" Blorfindel raced for his bow. Alehra had a little limp as she went for hers. Together they killed four Kutel before the trees let go. There was only one foe left and it was one of the armored Kutel. It took one step. An arrow hit it in thigh. It fell to one knee. A sling bullet hit it in the side of the head. It reeled. An arrow pierced the mail covering its heart. It fell.

Lantid had one more sleeping Kutel with one more throat to cut after that arrow. He got to his feet and surveyed the scene. While he was still taking it in, Blorfindel said, "Just like we planned it, right?"

"Well, except for the waking up and fighting part, yes."

Alehra limped one step toward Lantid and turned to Blorfindel, "Could you slap him in the head for me? I'm too tired to limp over there."

Blorfindel was more concerned for her wound. "What happened to your leg?"

"The Cral stepped on my foot."

"How did you get out of that?"

"I hit him in the stones with my war hammer."

Fargus started casting a healing spell on Alehra. Blorfindel did not wait for him to finish before he asked Lantid, "Why did you put Nickadola and Fargus to sleep?"

"I didn't like the odds. Nickadola, Fargus and I taking on two of those heavily armored Kutel while you two danced with the Crals? No, I don't think so, so I cast my sleep spell. These two were too close to the Kutel – the spell can't tell friend from foe. After the Kutel were dead I woke them."

Blorfindel could feel the muscles in his neck tightening and his wrist was beginning to throb. He gestured to Fargus, "I'll take one of those spells, please." Nickadola, Lantid, and Alehra walked over to the box while Fargus cast his spell. By the time Blorfindel had collected his short sword Alehra was pounding the lock with her war hammer.

Fargus shouted at them, "Wait! What are you doing?"

"It's locked."

"So, one of the Kutel has the key somewhere, right?"

"Oh, yeah."

A short search produced the key and they opened the box. They laid over the undyed cloth covering inside and frowned at the contents. It was full of gritty bread and dried tubers. After a moment Lantid snapped his fingers. "Of course! Unpack it!"

"You're hungry?"

"No. How much do you think a Cral eats on a long journey? Would the Kutel carry it for them? Of course not, so they pile the Cral food on top of the rest of their burden."

Underneath they found a second door, also locked, which opened with the same key. Under the second door they found a piece of parchment and a blue silk wrapping. Lantid snatched away the parchment before Alehra pulled the cloth out. She started unwrapping something from the blue silk. Nickadola was too short to see that deep into the box. "So what is it?"

Fargus said, "Weapons."

Blorfindel carefully pulled one of the swords out. "It looks like broad swords, mostly." He drew it from the scabbard and felt the balance. "Not bad for a Kutel. You might even mistake this for Tafer-made."

Fargus smiled, "But not Fithern?"

"No–"

Alehra interrupted, "I've got the Fithern one. Take a look." She held the scabbard within the silk and drew out the fine, light sword. She handed it pommel-first to Blorfindel, "Do you recognize it?"

"No. This is a Fithern sword, though. Fargus, even you can see the difference."

Fargus waved at the blade. "Surely a Tafer could make a sword like that?"

"I don't know."

Alehra said, "They can and they do. There's a maker's mark. Is that a Fithern character? I'm surprised you don't recognize it. I expected you to tell me it was your uncle's cousin's friend's father's or something."

"I don't recognize it. Lots of Fitherani carry swords like that. It's a good replacement for your bent one, though."

"Are you certain no one's going to roll over in their grave if I take it?"

"How? We don't have souls, remember?"

Lantid asked, "Can you read it?"

"It's just a mark, maybe an initial." Blorfindel did not want to admit that he could not read a single character of his own language. "Even if he's not dead he's probably changed his name by now anyway. What's on the parchment?"

"Kutel writing. I'll have to cast a spell to read it, but not here, not today."

Blorfindel started unpacking the box. There were many swords, but also complete spears and spear heads, and heads for various other pole arms. He held one particularly strange one up, "What do you do with this?"

Alehra took one look at it and said, "Give it back to them. I want to fight the Kutel who's trying to use that."

There were maces and axes of varying sizes, including a few heavy double-bitted axes. Blorfindel frowned and gave one a test swing. It nearly took him off his feet as he staggered to catch up with it. *Who is going to use that?* He found two single edged swords like giant knives. Fargus reached in and picked up a war hammer. Blorfindel pulled a few more out and dropped them on the ground, followed by two dozen daggers in their scabbards.

Near the bottom were two swords big enough for Cral. They each weighed about thirty pounds in their scabbards and their total length was about seven feet with a handle big enough for two Cral hands. Blorfindel drew one far enough to see the blade. It was much like the smaller Kutel swords.

Fargus stared at it. "It's a good thing they didn't stop to unpack. Why wouldn't they be carrying these as ready weapons?"

Blorfindel tossed the sword over the box to the ground, "Thank Arienic for small gifts."

Lantid stepped back as it landed at his feet. "They probably are gifts. Maybe the note says."

Alehra disagreed. "I don't think these two were smart enough to use swords."

Nickadola said, "That means that somewhere there are Cral smart enough?"

No one knew.

At the bottom were piled eight mail shirts and one complete suit of mail with plates over vital areas. As Blorfindel started pulling them out arrowheads fell out of them. By the time he got all of the armor out he could see that the bottom the box was nearly covered with arrowheads. "Why would you pack arrowheads in armor?"

Lantid pulled one out of a chain link, "They probably just poured them in and they settled to the bottom of the box. They look normal to me." He tossed the arrowhead back into the box. "I expected they'd do something different to carry the poison."

Fargus asked, "So what do we do with it? We can't carry it all, even with the mule, and we don't want the Kutel to have it."

Blorfindel squatted and lifted one end of the box. It was heavy even empty.

Lantid said, "Take what you want. Bury the rest."

Nickadola shook his head, "We could be a long time trying to dig a hole big enough for all this."

Blorfindel shrugged. "I'm going to try to carry back as much as I can. I need the money. How much do you think we can make on Kutel armor? That one set would cost forty malstren in Kingstone."

Fargus said, "Herik the armorer might get forty for a suit like that in the Kingstone market. No one will pay that for Kutel-made armor. If you get a dozen you'll be doing well."

Nickadola said, "If Terak understood what Lurshod has planned, he'd buy the armor for himself."

Fargus advised, "We should take the Cral swords. We want to make certain that they don't get to their destination."

They all agreed to help carry the best of the weapons and armor. Lantid made an inventory of the contents of the box. Blorfindel folded one of the pieces of cloth into a bag and put a few handfuls of arrowheads in it for future use. Alehra added a light throwing axe to her kit as well. Packing heavy, and with the help of Sturdifoot, they still had to leave more than half of it. Blorfindel said, "We can hide the rest."

Alehra wanted to know, "Where are we going to hide all this?"

Blorfindel shrugged. "Here and there. Not together."

They spent the afternoon finding hiding places for various weapons. It became like a game as one would hide it and the others would check to see if it was too easy to find.

"What about the box?"

Nickadola asked, "Where did all of those axes go? It would make good firewood."

"It's too hot for a camp fire."

"Rain is coming."

They withdrew to the north side of the path and made a camp complete with a campfire. Lantid had kept some of the Kutel silk tents on Sturdifoot. Thunder was rumbling when Alehra and Blorfindel started breaking up the box. As they tore one side off she exclaimed, "Hey! Look at all of the iron nails!"

Fargus looked at it. "They must have a lot of iron to waste it like that."

Lantid was less certain. "Maybe, but I think it was done for a reason. All of this was going somewhere. I think the box and the silk clad Cral were supposed to look expensive."

Blorfindel said, "The Kutel use slaves to make silk. It's not expensive for them."

"Still, I think its all for show."

They left three sides of the box intact and put it over the fire to shelter it. The clouds started pouring rain on them while they were preparing dinner. Even so, they had a hot stew and dry tents. When the initial deluge let up, the steady rain felt good after a hot, dirty and very active day. There was even a rainbow. The storm was over before the sun set.

With a little stealth and a lot of hiking they by-passed Jun and went back to Dath. Shieldmaster Terak did buy the armor and the weapons. He gave each of the adventurers eight malstren. He was handing the weapons out to some of the townsfolk before Blorfindel finished his arithmetic. *Twenty-five... it will take twenty-five hauls like this to get enough money to win Afinlia.*

The group returned to Amoss and Shandi's house. In the two days it took them to return, Fargus' spells healed their wounds completely. The trap on the door had not been reset. It was beginning to feel like home again.

When they settled in, Lantid cast his spell and translated the parchment. "This is beautiful! Brilliant!" He started copying the translation into a little book.

Blorfindel and Fargus were in the kitchen with him, working on dinner. Blorfindel asked, "A brilliant Kutel? That doesn't sound good."

"He's probably a Kushotel. Listen to this: 'On this day...' yeah, yeah... oh, here we go, '...in memory of Jorshnu who died defending his liege lord from Fitherani during a surprise attack... The Fithern arrows were unable to penetrate his Jun armor... when the Kutel charged the Fitherani ran. One cowardly Fitheran hid in the trees and stabbed him in the back as he passed. The Kutel war band easily cut through the Fithern mail with their heavy swords and dismembered the assassin... All of the Fitherani in the ambush were tracked down and killed. I have included the Fithern sword that killed Jorshnu and this package of arms and armor for his family since Jun now has more weapons and armor than soldiers. If you find any soldiers who are fit to use like weapons and armor, and are keen to fight the Tafers and Fitherani here, send them on. Soldiers are welcome at Jun...' Blah, blah, blah."

Blorfindel frowned. "Too bad we couldn't join up with the Fitherani before they got killed."

Lantid was confused for a moment. "What? What Fitherani? No, it's all lies. Jorshnu is probably the Kutel leader we killed here – the one with your father's other sword. They're just good lies."

Fargus asked, "How are lies good?"

"Think about it. What if you were a Kutel with nothing to do? Or better yet, one with too many mouths to feed? Here comes this message that says Jun wants soldiers and better still – unimaginable – they pay when the soldier gets killed! The Kutel in Bur-Droo would be scrounging for soldiers to send. And the soldiers! They get to wear iron mail and use new steel swords. What Kutel wouldn't want to fight Fitherani in arrow-proof armor?"

"It doesn't work like that."

"They don't know that! Your average Kutel probably believes all this Crushk. I'm just surprised it doesn't say anything about sex or food."

Blorfindel asked, "What about the sword? It's definitely a Fithern sword."

"They probably had it lying around, just like your father's short sword. He made up a story to make it seem important then gave away a sword that he was never going to use otherwise. It's a good thing this message didn't get through."

Fargus said, "I wonder if there are others."

"Maybe, but he needed an excuse to send the gifts. That's the clincher. How many times can he send a box full of weapons and armor with two Cral? Not often, I hope."

Fargus stirred the fire. "So what does this tell us?"

"That Lurshod wants soldiers, and soon. It's a long walk to Bur-Droo, assuming they weren't going as far as Shonu or Droo, and they weren't moving too quickly. Figure on a three week round trip, maybe four. It will take some time for the Kutel there to get ready to march to Jun. I expect he can't feed them for long, so he's planning to attack as soon as he gathers his forces. I guess the plan was to attack in four to seven weeks."

Fargus said, "But the message didn't get through."

Nickadola observed, "The harvest won't be in yet, at least not much of it."

"He can use the surviving soldiers or Tafer slaves to get the harvest in."

Blorfindel said, "It's a mistake. Nugrot had a better plan."

"Why?"

"If he waited until just before the winter rains then The Shield Valley wouldn't have a chance to counter-attack until spring."

"He's right," Lantid agreed. "If they waited until late in the year and kept their forces at Jun, the king wouldn't even know the town was in danger until it was too late. It's a good thing he's a better liar than strategist."

Fargus said, "He might be good enough. Two groups like the one he sent with the box might be enough to take over the town now. How are we going to stop them?"

Lantid thought about that while they worked on dinner. They took it upstairs so they could eat together while Alehra stood watch. Lantid started to form a strategy. "He doesn't have armor for everyone, not even for all of the Kutel in the group with the box. He would have sent all armored Kutel if he could have; it would have looked very impressive. That means they're still working. Nugrot said that they were getting iron from the bogs. That means work groups, and probably spread out. We should be able to knock them out one at a time, at least for a while."

Blorfindel said, "If they're down in a bog then we would have to be attacking from higher ground."

"Right. Every load of raw iron that doesn't come through delays them. We should also keep an eye on the path when we can. If we can knock off the reinforcements before they get to town it will be easier on us, and we don't want any of these messages getting through. If we can do that, Lurshod will have to do something that he doesn't want to do."

"Like what?"

"Either attack with a smaller force than he planned on or wait longer for his forces to build. They'll also probably do something about protecting the groups in the bogs. We should be able to choose to ambush them or maybe attack the town when it's weaker."

Nickadola took a long drink of water. "They may hunt us down with Varren, too."

Alehra said, "I'm not afraid of a Varro."

"One Varro can lead a hundred Kutel to us, or a dozen Cral."

Lantid nodded. "We should start to look into that, soon. Nugrot said they tolerated the Varren because they hunted their own food. We should be able to ambush them. What do you think, Nickadola? Could you get some of your furry friends to lead the Varren into an ambush?"

"Maybe. Oh, they'll agree to help, but when they're being chased by a Varro they may forget the plan. Rabbits and squirrels are not famous for their brilliant tactics."

"Then we'll keep it simple."

Chapter 17

Muckrakers

The next evening found them two miles south of Foralis, the town that the Kutel called Jun. Nickadola was having a conversation with an owl while the others waited at a respectful distance. He rejoined them in a few minutes.

"What's the deal?"

"She'll help us find them. The Varren have been running her game out of the area. It sounds like there are a lot of 'em."

The owl took off.

Alehra said, "What? Now?"

"Did you expect an owl to wait until daylight? The Varren hunt at night, too."

Blorfindel followed the bird. "Just follow me and try to be quiet."

Nickadola jogged after the owl. "And remember that the Varren can smell you if the wind is right."

It turned out that the Tafers were merely baggage. Each time the owl caught a Varro, Blorfindel would kill it with a single arrow. The Varren were not wary at all. They thought they were hunting, not hunted. Three generations of Varren had hunted here without a threat from anything but the Kutel themselves. Blorfindel only paused long enough for Nickadola to feed some Varro meat to the owl now and then. By the end of the night seventeen Varren were dead.

When the sun rose they said goodbye to the owl and withdrew to make a hidden camp. Blorfindel marveled at how easy the hunt went. "That was too easy. It's like stealing. There must be something wrong."

Lantid said, "There is, but I won't think of it until I've had some sleep."

Nickadola massaged his feet, "I guess I've got first watch, again."

Fargus rolled his head on his neck and yawned, "I'll take it if you're too tired."

"I won't fall asleep on watch. It's good to get in the habit of sleeping through the days. If we're going to ambush Kutel work parties we're going to have to be up nights." Two hours later Nickadola woke Blorfindel for watch. "It's going to be a hot one, maybe a good day to sleep under a silk tent." Blorfindel decided not to put on his metal armor in the heat.

Only a few minutes into his watch Blorfindel heard quiet footsteps approaching. *Why is it always on my watch?* He woke Alehra quietly and signed to her, 'Be quiet. Shake the others. I'm going to check something I hear over there.' He slipped silently into the trees.

He found a string of Varren sniffing the ground and moving toward the hidden camp. He stepped back until he had a line of sight into camp. He caught Fargus' eye and signed, 'Twenty five little ones moving toward you.'

He could hear the cleric whisper to the others, "Twenty five… Varren, I think, coming towards us."

Lantid signed back to Blorfindel, 'You circle. Shoot them when they run.' Then he whispered to the others, "You three move back. They will try to surround the camp. When they attack I'll run back to you. That will put them all in front."

Alehra put her hand over his mouth. She shook her head and signed, 'No. I'll wait. I have armor and a bow. I'll run to you.'

The others were barely ahead of the Varren when they came to circle the camp. Alehra hung her bow over her shoulder and readied her shield and new sword. When the Varren broke cover and charged her she turned and ran. They had her surrounded. The Varren in her path set spears to stop her. She knocked two spears out of the way with her shield and slashed the snout off one Varro on her way by.

Two of the Varren behind her started to throw their spears at her. Blorfindel shot one in the back. The other's spear hit her armor and bounced back.

Nickadola and Fargus stepped up to meet the first two Varren. The others were charging and did not yet realize they were running into an ambush. When they saw Lantid, Nickadola and Fargus they slowed their charge and bunched up. Blorfindel could see Lantid smile as he cast his spell. More than half of them fell asleep even as Nickadola slashed open the Varro in front of him. Alehra spun and stabbed the one in front of Fargus.

The Varren hesitated for a moment. Lantid laughed as he cast the sleep spell a second time. The only Varro still on its feet after the second spell was the one that threw the spear at Alehra. It turned to run away, straight at Blorfindel. He shot it through the heart.

The battle then turned into a race to see if they could butcher all the Varren before the spell wore off. They could not: the last two died on their feet.

Alehra smiled at Lantid and wiped the blood off her cheek. "A dozen at a time, that's got to be some sort of record."

Lantid shook his head at the carnage. "I told you the spell works better on weaker targets. I bet I could have got more if they stood closer together."

Nickadola was already staggering towards the tents. "That's what we forgot. They followed our scent here. We were lucky that it didn't take them too long to find us. I bet if it had been one of you Tafers on watch they'd have been in the camp before we knew it."

Alehra said, "What's eatin' him? I thought he'd be happy to finally fight someone his own size."

Fargus said, "Sleep, or lack of it. He stood first watch. He's had about five minutes sleep since we got up yesterday morning."

Lantid let them sleep in. The summer sun was low by the time they were all awake. "We should move the camp. The heat isn't doing the dead Varren any favors. You have to expect that they hit us with all they could last night. There can't be many Varren. The real question is why did they come alone?"

Fargus observed, "There were twenty-seven of them."

"But they didn't bring any Kutel or Cral," Lantid explained.

Nickadola said, "The Kutel give the Varren orders, not the other way around."

Lantid nodded, "But when forty-four of them go missing the Kutel just might notice."

The Timble thought out load, "The surviving Varren are going to go crying to the Kutel for protection. Why else would they put up with the Kutel?"

"Can your owl friend find out if there are any left?"

"She'd have to fly over the town, probably a few times. It's too dangerous. The Kutel would shoot an owl if they could."

Lantid looked around as if for a plan. "We can't just let them hunt us down."

Nickadola said, "Scent trackers can be beaten, too."

Blorfindel said, "If we are going to delay Lurshod's plan, shouldn't we by trying to stop the iron? I mean, it's good that there aren't so many Varren tracking us, but the goal is to get him and his treasure."

"Treasure?" Fargus said, "There's a town full of Tafers about to be overrun."

"Same thing," Lantid said. "If the leader and the treasure are gone, the there will be no army attacking Dath for their harvest. That aside, unless Lurshod's an idiot, we're going to have to weaken his position before he's exposed."

"Let's see if we can hit one of the Kutel groups in the bogs," Alehra suggested.

Lantid shrugged, "We'll have to find one."

"This is my home town." Blorfindel smiled. "I remember where there's a bog or two."

Fargus asked, "How long do bogs last? It's been a long time."

Nickadola laughed.

Blorfindel said, "Bogs can live longer than Fitherani; that I know."

A few hours later they were on the side of a hill watching Kutel who were waist deep in muck and digging in the moonlight. Blorfindel climbed a tree for a better view.

Fargus said, "It looks miserable. Are you sure they're Kutel and not slaves doing the work? Isn't that a guard over there?"

Blorfindel said, "They're Kutel. I see three guards watching them work."

Lantid said, "The difference between a Kutel slave and a Kutel warrior is one weapon. In fact, I would expect the Jun chief to arm them for the attack on Dath if he can. He's not going to have them digging then."

Blorfindel continued, "Four, four guards, one just stepped out of the woods. I count thirty in the work party, but they're unarmed."

Alehra said, "Those shovels will make fine clubs in a pinch."

"Still, it doesn't get any easier than this," Lantid said, "Let's do it."

"Wait!" Blorfindel held up his hand. As they waited two Cral and four armed Kutel came out of the trees to the edge of the bog. Blorfindel watched as the Cral picked up the bags of drying mud and trudged back the way they came.

Fargus sighed, "That could have been ugly."

Lantid frowned, "The question now is do we hit the bog group or ambush the Cral?"

Alehra did not like their chances with the second group. "Two Cral backed up by four Kutel? These aren't Varren, you know. Do you remember what happened last time we fought two Cral?"

"We won. Listen, do you think we're ever going to get them in smaller groups?"

Nickadola advised, "We're ready to fight the bog group. Let's wait for the Cral to get farther away, then hit the diggers. Next time we can set up an ambush for the Cral, if you like."

"Agreed."

The bog battle was ugly and one-sided. They got as close as they could before breaking cover and had two of the guards down before they could raise the alarm. Fargus, Nickadola and Lantid engaged one of the remaining guards. Alehra eliminated the other. Blorfindel jumped up on a stump at the edge of the bog and picked off Kutel with his bow. By the time the workers figured out that their only hope was to fight their way out the last guard was dead. Alehra, Nickadola and Fargus held the bank while Blorfindel continued to shoot the slow moving Kutel. Before long all of the Kutel were dead.

Lantid was pleased with their performance. "Thirty-five Kutel down, no wounds taken, and without expending a single spell."

Blorfindel counted his remaining arrows. "Twenty arrows spent. I'm not going in there after them."

"You can replace them from the bundles on Sturdifoot."

They went back to the hill to collect the mule. On the trail Fargus asked, "Are we getting better or are they getting worse?"

Lantid said, "We haven't gotten that much better since the battle at the house, except at picking our battles. I bet those Cral would have given us a fight." As Blorfindel was unpacking the arrows a thought occurred to him. "No one knows about this battle but us, yet."

"Right, so?"

"So those Cral will be coming back for another load."

Blorfindel made eye contact with Alehra. She swallowed hard but nodded. He tossed his head. They turned to Nickadola and Fargus, respectively. The Timble sighed.

Fargus said, "Only if we find a good spot, and have a good plan."

Blorfindel said, "The place is easy. Follow me." He brought them back down to the bog and followed a stream that trickled out. The drippings from the muddy bags and the heavy footsteps of the mud-Cral were unmistakable. Ahead the stream got wide and shallow, with thorny berry bushes growing out of it. Blorfindel had them cross the stream before the bushes and climb a steep hill. They moved along the edge of the hill where they could keep the stream in sight. He stopped on top of a small rock outcropping, about twenty feet above the stream. Blorfindel waved down at the path.

Lantid looked around. "They can come around the rock. They're stupid, but they're not that stupid."

"It's still steep everywhere for a hundred yards in both directions, and they'll have to go through the bushes. The bushes run a good long way, too. Can you see?"

Nickadola frowned, "Those bushes won't slow down a Cral at all. Their hide is too tough."

Alehra said, "We're not going to find a better place unless we build a castle. Do you want to fight them or not?"

Fargus dropped his pack. "I don't want to fight them at all, but since we have to, you're right, here is about as good as it gets."

They took their places and waited for the Crals' return. Alehra fretted about the time. "I hope they come soon, the white moon's going to set."

Blorfindel said, "The blue moon won't set until after daybreak. You can see by its light."

"Not well enough for archery, it's not nearly as bright. Can't you see the difference?"

"Well, yes, but I didn't think it mattered so much."

Nickadola interrupted them, "Ssst! Something's coming!"

Two Cral followed by four Kutel walked up the path below. Alehra and Blorfindel separated just a bit more as they both tried to get the angle on their designated target. Nickadola retreated undetected from his position as lookout. Fargus and Lantid waited, lying prone on the rock both out of sight and out of harm's way. They were all nervous. The advantages of position and surprise would not stop the Crals. They did not expect to be able to kill or even harm them before they climbed the slope. The best they could hope for was to eliminate the Kutel before the Crals closed, after that the plan got a bit scary. They could not hope for one Cral to hit the other in the head or for Blorfindel's flying sneak attack like the last time. They hoped to trick one of them into falling down the hill so that they could fight them one at a time.

Blorfindel waited for Alehra. He knew that in the dark she would have more difficulty aiming. As soon as he heard her bowstring he released his own. Her arrow hit the Kutel in the side between two ribs. It spent the last few minutes of its life coughing up bloody foam. Blorfindel's target turned to face the sound of the arrows. Instead of piercing its eye, Blorfindel's arrow grazed its cheek and lodged inside its helmet. Blorfindel followed up with another arrow that stuck in its throat and finished it off. Alehra's second arrow hit another Kutel in the chest. The night was warm and the Kutel was not wearing its armor the one time that it really needed it.

The last Kutel hid behind a Cral and shouted, "Run!" Rather than turn and run back the way they came, the Cral simply broke into a run in the same direction that they had been going.

Blorfindel took two steps back, dropped his bow, then took three running steps over the edge. As he left the rock he drew both swords. In a moment of strange clarity he heard Nickadola say, "That wasn't in the plan." An arrow passed underneath him and struck the remaining Kutel in the back. The Kutel staggered forward and held on to the Cral.

Blorfindel misjudged his leap. Rather than coming down on the back of the first Cral he was falling in front of the second one. He twisted in mid air and tried to drive both of his swords into the Cral. His long sword slid along its hide, cutting a small furrow, but drawing no blood. His short sword struck just above its collarbone and stuck. With the added force of the fall the point pierced the Cral's tough blue hide and sank in to the cross guard. Blorfindel could not hang on. Losing his grip he fell awkwardly and would have landed on his face in the path.

He did not land in the path because the Cral swatted at him with its left hand. It struck high on his back and flipped him into the thorny bushes on the side of the trail. He lay there for a moment trying to determine if he was healthy enough to rise when he got a surprise of his own. Looking up, he saw two throwing knives come over the rock and sink into the back of the remaining Kutel. One of them drew a fountain of blood that was clearly fatal. This was not the surprise.

The surprising thing was that two more figures jumped off the rock. First Fargus leaped off and smashed his mace down on the head of the wounded Cral. The mace spun out of his hand but the Cral was reeling. Fargus landed poorly: feet, hands, backside, and head. Not a second later, Alehra came down on the Cral's head, hammer spike first. She swung by the handle and let go; landing with more grace on one hand, two feet, and the edge of her shield.

Blorfindel struggled out of he bushes with a hundred small cuts on all of his exposed flesh. He drew his dagger and stood in the path to defend his friends from the Cral, which had still not fallen. Cral stood there as if frozen with a sword hilt protruding from one shoulder and a hammer hanging from its head. Then, ever so slowly, it began to fall over backwards. Fargus scrambled crab-like on his hands and feet to get out of the way before the Cral fell dead on the spot where the cleric had landed.

Alehra was already charging after the remaining Cral. "Coward!"

Blorfindel surprised himself by following. He translated for Alehra, "She called you a coward!"

The Cral's long strides were keeping it ahead of Alehra and Blorfindel. Lantid gasped from behind, "Bow!" and when Blorfindel turned to look his bow was flying towards him. He dropped his dagger and caught the bow out of the air. He drew one of the three arrows that had not fallen from his quivers when he landed. For a moment he hesitated, trying to find a target that would slow the Cral down. He shot the Cral between the buttocks. The first arrow did not seem to have any effect, but after a second struck the Cral started limping.

Alehra caught up. She stuck her new sword into the back of its knee. It barely opened a scratch, but the Cral turned around. It swung a short hook at her which she easily turned on her shield. Blorfindel shot it in the eye with his last arrow. Even before it clapped its hand over its face he snatched up his dagger and was running toward the monster. Immediately a sling bullet hit the back of its hand as it plucked at the arrow.

Alehra used the opening to stab its armpit. Blood ran freely from the wound. She had to step back quickly to avoid the hook. She stabbed its chest as the maddened monster stepped towards her, but the point would not penetrate. The Cral's reverse swing caught on Alehra's shield and sent her flying off the path. Single-mindedly the Cral followed to finish her.

Blorfindel arrived before the Cral and braced himself. He held his dagger out in the path of the Cral's weapon arm. The light Fitheran and his small dagger could not stop the blow, of course, but the added strength of the Cral's attack drove the point through the sinews of its wrist. With the strength cut off from its hand, the Cral's hook stuck in Alehra's armor but went no further. She was back on her feet when Blorfindel stabbed it in its remaining eye with his sword. She shoved him out of the way with her shield as the Cral swatted down at him. The Cral's arm hit the edge of her shield and knocked her to her knees. When the shield's edge hit the rocky path it proved itself stronger than the Cral's arm. The crunch sounded like a tree breaking in a gale.

Nickadola shouted from above, "Just back off! It will die on its own now!" In spite of his own advice he slung another bullet which skipped off the top of the Cral's head.

Blorfindel and Alehra scrambled out of the Cral's reach. As it flailed around trying to find them, its blood flew in huge arcs. They continued to back away just to get out of the foul spray. Fargus caught up to them. By the time he cast a healing spell on each of them the Cral had fallen to its knees. They still had a long wait for it to bleed out. By then Nickadola and Lantid joined them on the path.

Lantid looked at Blorfindel. "Did I sleep through the part of the plan that involved jumping off a cliff, because I don't remember that part? Weren't we supposed to wait for them to climb the hill?"

"They were running away. They weren't going to climb the hill."

Fargus said, "You should have just let them go."

Lantid turned to the cleric. "You're one to talk. Were you the second one over the cliff or did you wait for Alehra?"

Alehra said, "I had to toss my bow and draw the hammer."

"Once Blorfindel jumped the die was cast, so to speak." Fargus laughed.

"What's funny about that?"

Fargus was still laughing when he replied. "No, it's something my mother used to say: 'If your friends jumped off a cliff would you jump off too?'" He spoke up into the night air, "Yes, mom, I would." He laughed again. Alehra laughed, too. After a moment Blorfindel joined in. After the adrenaline rush and desperate battle they needed the release. In a few minutes Fargus was crying and gasping for air, but showed no signs of stopping.

Lantid was not amused. "When you three are done, we ought to get out of here before these Cral are missed." He turned to Fargus, "I suppose you've already healed them? They still look like they jumped off a cliff into a thorn bush – oh, yeah, they did."

Blorfindel wiped his eyes. "Do we draw straws to see who gets the last spell?"

Fargus held his hand up until he got his breathing under control. "I used it on myself before I got to you two."

While they collected their weapons, Nickadola went into the bushes and found most of Blorfindel's missing arrows. He came out remarkably unscathed. "Thorn bushes can be friends, too."

Chapter 18

Hide and Seek

They packed up and left the path. Alehra asked, "Where are we going?"

"We need to find a place that we can defend when they hunt us down."

Fargus observed, "I guess they'll be pretty motivated now."

"Forty-five Varren, nearly forty Kutel, and two Cral? Yes, they can't ignore that," Lantid agreed. "The question is: what do they do about it? They could hunt us down tomorrow, that is, today during the daylight, or wait for tomorrow night. We need to get far enough away so they can't catch us tonight. We should be able to do that with our head start, but there's no way of knowing how long it takes them to muster a search party."

"Or how many they'll send," Nickadola observed.

"Not a few, unless they're complete fools," Fargus said. "Would you send fifty Kutel to do what two Crals could not?"

Lantid said, "Maybe with five Crals backing them up."

Alehra grimaced. "Keep thinking those happy thoughts."

Nickadola took Sturdifood's lead, stepped up his pace, and moved to the front of the group. "You'd better follow me, and try to do what I do."

They fell in line and followed before Alehra asked, "Why?"

"We need to break our scent trail, and our visible track if we can. We're not ready to ambush the hunters now, and they could catch us in a few hours if they're willing to run."

Blorfindel asked, "Can they track us that fast?"

"A Varro could, if there are any left."

After a few miles of relatively straight travel the Timble detoured to pick some leaves. He waved the rest of the group on. When he caught back up and took the lead he was obviously looking for something. Blorfindel asked, "What is it? What are you looking for?"

"Running water, hopefully with a strong breeze, but I want to pick it out well in advance. A cold, fast stream will carry enough air with it. We've been heading downhill, but not straight down, we should find one soon."

A few minutes later Blorfindel spotted a stream. Nickadola made everyone stop and went forward to examine it. When he came back he lead them all north, parallel to the stream, until they came to a place where the stream had worn a shallow groove in the exposed bedrock. "This is it. Stay on the rocks until you get in the stream, then turn downstream and stay in the water. If you feel the wind blow side to side stop there and wait for me. I'll catch up as quickly as I can." He turned back the way they had come.

They were waiting in a small clearing, standing in the cold stream and watching the sunrise with a gentle breeze at their backs when Nickadola returned. "This is the tricky bit." He had them all exit the stream one-by-one, then return walking backwards and using the same footprints. He had to guide Sturdifoot's hooves into his old prints.

When they were all done he took his hand and smoothed out the first few footprints in the muddy bank. Then he crushed a few leaves and sprinkled them over the path. Fargus asked, "Why did we go through that if you're just going to cover the track?"

Blorfindel replied as Nickadola set a few twigs over the false trail. "If they're bad trackers, we lost them at the stream. If they're good enough to still be on us, they're good enough to see that this trail has been covered. He wants them to think that they've outsmarted us here."

Nickadola rinsed his hands then took Sturdifoot's lead and led them all downstream. "If it was too easy they might be suspicious."

He continued downstream until he found the rockiest, most difficult bank that they had seen in this stream. He led them out there. "Don't worry about the water, but wash the mud off your feet before you step on the dry rocks. Remember, the rocks won't leave footprints, but the dirt and leaves will. If we're careful they won't even look here to see if we came out."

When they were away from the stream Lantid asked, "Now what?"

"Now we go wherever we want to. If they can follow that, we're not going to lose them."

"What were the leaves for?"

"They have a strong scent when crushed. They can overpower a Varro's nose for a little while."

The morning sun felt good as it drove away the chill of the stream. Fargus said, "It's odd, but in the sunlight I don't feel so tired."

Alehra smiled. "Are you ready to march all the way back to the house?"

"We shouldn't go to the house, anyway. Won't they look there first?"

Lantid agreed. "After they lose the track, probably."

Blorfindel said, "It would be nice to be able to see if they were trying to follow us."

They turned north and camped on the east side of a hill thirty yards from the top. From the rocky top of the hill they could see down into the clearing where they created the false trail, but their own camp was invisible from more than a few yards away. The trees provided protection from both prying eyes and the sun's summer heat. When the wind blew across the hill they had relief from the local insects, but only when the wind blew.

When Nickadola woke Blorfindel for watch he said, "They took the false trail maybe half an hour ago. I haven't seen them since."

"Varren?"

"Two, and a bunch of lightly armed Kutel – maybe twenty-five."

"You should have woken us, we could have ambushed that group."

"I thought it was a trick, like they were keeping their main force a ways behind them, but I haven't seen anything."

"If Lantid is right they should be headed to the house."

"Lovely day for it."

"Too hot. Too sunny for Kutel."

"Well, too bad for them, then."

Blorfindel's watch was uneventful. He woke Alehra and went to sleep. When he awoke Nickadola was on watch again. The Timble told him, "We're not going anywhere today, unless Fargus has a lot more healing power we may be here for a while. It's a good spot."

"Is there water?"

"That's the one bad part. You can see the stream from here, but we shouldn't leave a trail for the Varrento follow back to our camp."

"I guess I'll go back the way we came."

"Get all the water skins if you go, and don't go alone. Oh, and don't forget, you've got next watch."

"What happened to Lantid?"

"Nothing, except he went back to sleep. You slept through his watch. We're starting over."

Blorfindel went back to the tents, "Fargus, are you ready to take a little walk? I want to refill the water skins."

Alehra volunteered, "I'll go."

"Thanks, but I don't want to leave camp without a real fighter in case something happens. No offense, Fargus."

"None taken." The cleric started walking with Blorfindel. "I think I broke my wrist when I hit that thing's head."

"Let me see it."

"It's better now. The healing spell set the bone, though I am still sore. That has got to be about the most foolish thing I've ever done in my life."

"We won."

"We were lucky."

"Lucky and smart and quick and brave and stealthy and strong; you've got to put them together somehow if you're going to win."

"Is that how your people always fight? Fitherani, I mean."

"I don't know. I'd never seen a Cral until this spring."

"This spring? I thought you all were grizzled veterans."

"Fitherani don't get grizzled, not until they're well over twelve centuries, anyway. No, I just passed my archery test this spring. I don't know about Alehra and Lantid, it doesn't seem like they have a lot more experience." They walked in silence for a few steps. "No, I don't think so – that is, I don't think most Fitherani would jump off a cliff to attack a Cral. I think they'd shoot and run when it got close."

"Can arrows kill a Cral?"

"I don't know. I didn't say they'd win."

They laughed.

On the way back Fargus struggled a bit with the weight of the extra water skins. When Blorfindel offered to take one he waved him off. "I can manage. If we have to keep doing this, though, I think I'm going to save the trip and ask Feadin to deliver the water."

"Can you do that? I mean, I know anyone can ask, but will she give us water?"

"She would, but it would be one less cure for the day, and we need our healing now."

"What, does she just give you a spell ration or something?"

"More or less, yes, though I never thought of it like that. I can do anything she lets me do, and nothing more. Maybe if I keep fighting the good fight she'll give me more power, but it's up to her."

"That's strange. Like, when I play the cittern Arienic helps me play, but I'm the one who's playing and I'm the one who gets the notes right or wrong."

"What Nickadola and I do is different – not really a skill like playing an instrument. If Litne were to teach me all of the incantations and motions of his disease curing spell, I still wouldn't be able to cast it, even if I could imitate his voice."

"Can you?"

"Imitate his voice? Everyone at the temple did a Litne impression at one time or another, but no, I don't have any real talent there." He stumbled over something. "Do you ever get used to walking in the dark?"

"It's not dark, the white moon is up."

"Half full behind the haze. It's dark."

"It's not even dark enough for me to see heat."

"I've heard about that. What's that like?"

"What's blue like? What's orange like? I don't know how to describe it. It's just that they aren't very strong and when there's too much light I can't see them. It's like lighting a candle when the sun is bright: the candle is still burning, but the light doesn't really shine."

When they returned to the camp Blorfindel went on watch at the top of the hill. When Alehra came to relieve him the others came with her. Fargus cast a healing spell on Alehra and Blorfindel then asked, "How do you feel?"

Blorfindel shrugged. Alehra said, "Good enough."

"But not completely healed? We should wait until we're completely healed. One day won't kill us. A sore wrist might." Fargus massaged his own wrist.

Lantid nodded. "So long as they don't find us, we can wait."

Blorfindel said, "If it's the group Nickadola saw hunting us we should let them find us. We should be able to wipe them out without too much trouble."

Lantid said, "I don't think they'd fight if they found us. I think they're all supposed to run home and report."

"But we could just move again."

"I didn't say it was a good plan. They can't be coming to attack us, unless they have a major surprise for us, or they're completely stupid. They have to know about the two work groups and the Varren by now.

They don't know all that much, though. Maybe the Varren can tell that it was all the same group, maybe not."

Nickadola said, "They should be able to follow our scent from the bog to the cliff at least."

"That still doesn't tell them what happened. They can tell the Kutel were shot, maybe, but there's no trail from the bog to the dead Cral, at least not for all of us. They can't guess the attack came from the cliff, not the way it really happened. I can barely imagine it, and I was there. That makes us look like two groups, maybe three if they think someone else killed the Varren. We have to expect that the Varren smelled your blood, Blorfindel, you had thorn cuts all over. Since the Kutel hate Fitherani the most they probably think that it was a Fithern raid. I think they're looking for a big camp full of Fitherani. Whoever sent them expects them to get ambushed, he just wants one of them to survive so that they can tell him where the camp is."

Fargus asked, "Besides making us all feel clever and dangerous, what good does it do us to know that?"

"Well, we shouldn't ambush the scouts unless we can box them in somehow." Lantid looked pointedly at Blorfindel.

"I don't know any place around here where we could do that."

Alehra said, "What if they find us?"

"Well then–"

"–because they just did." As the others turned Alehra's bow sang. The arrow hit a tree branch on the way and was deflected.

They could see glimpses of three different Kutel running way. Blorfindel never got an arrow off. He started to chase them but both Nickadola and Fargus shouted, "Wait!" When Blorfindel stopped Fargus continued, "They could have their own ambush set up. We only saw three. Where are the others?"

"So we let them go?"

Lantid said, "You just told me that we can't catch them all."

Sturdifoot brayed.

Lantid shouted, "Crushk!" as they all turned back to the camp. One Kutel was pulling down a tent. Another was chasing the mule around the camp with an axe. Blorfindel shot the axe-Kutel. The arrow stuck in the hide armor which protected its torso. It abandoned its axe to run but got only one step before Alehra's arrow hit it in the calf. The other Kutel let go of the tent and ran.

Blorfindel did not shoot again because Nickadola, Lantid, and Fargus had passed him and were now down range. He ran after them. Nickadola got to the limping Kutel first and hamstrung it with his scimitar. Fargus crushed its head into the ground when it fell.

Lantid stopped to look around. The other Kutel was gone. The heavy cover that hid the camp also protected the Kutel running from it. Lantid looked over at Sturdifoot.

Alehra said, "What do we do now?"

Lantid frowned at the trees. "You keep watch. The rest of us need to pack up. We've got to get out of here before they get back to Lurshod."

Fargus asked, "Where are we going?"

Blorfindel said, "How about Foralis?"

"What?"

Lantid nodded. "I like it. They can't be strong everywhere. If they send an army out after us, they'll have to leave something unprotected at home."

Blorfindel held him in his gaze. "It's not their home. It's mine."

Chapter 19

Pigs

They reached Jun after midnight. From their hiding places Fargus whispered, "So much for weakened defenses."

Alehra said, "What are they? All I see are shadows."

Blorfindel whispered, "Kutel, for the most part. You should be able to pick out six Cral over by the barn." He had to repeat himself, Fargus and Alehra couldn't hear him through their helmets.

Lantid said, "Wait and watch. Blorfindel, try to get numbers and how many have good armor, if you can see that well."

"Two of the Cral have swords–"

"Feadin save us!"

"I think at least one has a spear, it could be two, or they could just be poles. Eight Kutel in armor, mail shirts, that is; one in full mail with plates, like the one at the house. I think that one's giving orders."

"That makes sense."

"I can't count the regular soldiers; they're moving around too much."

Lantid was having the same trouble counting the shadows. "It's got to be fifty, though."

"At least – I would have said seventy. Wait! They're moving."

"I can see that." Lantid smiled. "There going after us. That's the war band they're going to try to catch us with."

"The leader didn't go. I think only one… no, two of the armored Kutel are going."

"Varren?"

"I can't see any."

"Good, then they won't track us out of camp until they go back and get one. It's a mistake. Let's pull back where we can talk."

They backed away far enough so that they could not be seen from town. Fargus said, "If we hadn't seen them at the camp, we'd be in a lot of trouble."

Alehra said, "Damn, that would be a hell of a way to wake up."

Lantid was more concerned about what to do next. "So, what do we have left in town?"

Blorfindel said, "For certain, we have the leader and six bodyguards, or lieutenants, or whatever. There are still some Kutel at work. Can you hear the hammers?"

"I'll have to take your word on it. I expect they keep the Cral in that big building – the barn, as you said. They could have another six in there, it's big enough."

Nickadola said, "But probably not. They had to have room for the four we've already killed."

"Even two Cal puts them out of our league. The leader is probably about as strong as Nugrot. Didn't Nugrot say something like that?"

"I think so."

Blorfindel said, "If that's true then we may not be ready for just the leader and his guards."

Lantid said, "If I could guarantee that it was only them I'd try it, but we can't."

Alehra offered, "Farms, mines, or bogs?"

Fargus shook his head. "You've got to expect that they're watching for us at the bogs now, and walking into a mineshaft that only opens into a Kutel town sounds like a death trap."

She shrugged. "I guess that leaves the farms, unless you want to go downtown."

Lantid said, "Not with these odds."

An hour later they were on the other side of town looking down at the farms. "What if those barns have Cral in them?"

Blorfindel said, "Then they've got Cral that sound like pigs."

Nickadola said, "Pigs, that's right. I was trying to think of what kind of livestock they'd raise. I should have known the smell but I thought that was just the Kutel. Pigs are pretty smart. I might be able to reason with pigs."

"They're not as smart as Kutel," Blorfindel said.

"Are you sure?"

"A shapetaker told me, and he ought to know."

Alehra shook her head. "Damn, and I thought my life was strange."

Lantid asked the Timble, "What can you do with pigs?"

"I can't make them fly, or anything."

"What if all the pigs got free, could you get them to go east up the path?"

"I guess so, I mean, I could talk them into it. What good would that do?"

Blorfindel said, "The Kutel will try to round them up."

Alehra caught on. "But not with six Cral. They'll come out alone or in small groups."

Lantid shrugged. "Maybe they won't come out at all. Maybe they're too frightened."

Nickadola shrugged too. "Then we've freed the pigs."

"That's right, and that's not a bad thing. I mean, that way the Kutel don't get to eat them."

Nickadola liked it. "Good for the pigs, bad for the Kutel, let's do it."

Blorfindel crept towards the farmhouse. He had stripped off his metal armor and made no sound. The others were waiting at a safe distance in case he needed backup. He made a detour to the barn and peaked in though a knothole. It was very dark in the barn at night, but he could see the heat rising from a number of pigs in the low stalls. *Cral would not look like that,* he reassured himself.

He ran and put his back to the farmhouse wall. He heard the sounds of digging. He poked his head around the corner and quickly pulled it back. There were three young Kutel hauling bags away from a hole in the ground. The digging sound continued. *They must be digging a well. That explains why they are not out working in the fields at this time of night.* He could still hear digging. *There are probably two more in the hole.* The Kutel with bags walked far enough away from the hole so that he could see them again. Their backs were to him as they walked toward a pond full of sewage.

He stood and looked around the corner. These Kutel were no threat. He had an arrow set to string, but he did not draw. The three Kutel reached the pond. Two of them looked at each other and shouted, "Now!" then threw the third, the smallest, into the pond of pig sewage.

Blorfindel hurried quietly to the edge of the hole and saw two young Kutel digging. He withdrew to a rubble pile and waved to his friends. They were still out in the field when he heard a Kutel voice from inside the house, "I better hear some digging out there! You'll be sleeping in that hole until it's done! All of you! Pushi, go see what your brothers are doing!"

"I don' wanna sleep in the hole!"

<Whack!> Then crying.

When the door opened an even smaller Kutel came out. Behind it, there was a pregnant female in the house.

The group arrived at the rubble pile. Blorfindel whispered, "What are we doing here? There's got to be another way."

Alehra stared at the naked little Kutel who was shouting into the hole. "What is she, four?" She, too had an arrow on her bowstring, but did not draw.

Nickadola said, "Younger – the Kutel grow quickly, even quicker than Tafers."

Lantid sighed. "We can just try to steal the pigs, if you like; hope that the Kutel don't raise the alarm. That way they can starve to death when you're not watching."

Blorfindel had to fight to keep his voice down. "Raiden, Lantid! Kids and pregnant females?"

"You're one to invoke Raiden, I'm the one whose soul he's going to punish if we kill them." He closed his eyes. "Listen, either all of these Kutel children die, or all of the Tafer children at Dath die, it's that simple. If we only kill soldiers, if we could just stop the army without causing any more harm at all, all of the Kutel in this town would still die. Any of them that are strong enough to make the trek back to Bur-Droo are strong enough to get a spear and shield and get sent into battle. They can't go back. They'll starve or die of exposure when the rains come. If we let them stay here they'll just grow up to be a new crop of raiders in a couple of years. You know that little girl would kill you and eat you if she could?"

"I know it."

"As soon as food starts getting tight around here non-combatants are going to start to die. Even if the chief doesn't give the order, soldiers will sneak out and murder so that they can have more."

Nickadola said softly, "They'll eat the little girl, too."

Alehra shivered. "I didn't need to hear that."

Fargus said, "Me either."

When Lantid finally opened his eyes a fire shown there. His whisper was fierce, barely controlled. "Yes you did! We all did. We have to remember, these aren't Tafers or Timbles or Fitherani or even pigs. They want us all dead, especially you, Blorfindel. As soon as they're off the nipple they'd rather be eating Fitherani. It's in their blood, or their souls or whatever. Do you know why there isn't another Kutel here younger than this one? They killed it. There's no way they let three years go by between children. The Kutel decided something was wrong with it – maybe just because it was female or it cried too much – and they killed it. This town exists only to produce soldiers. Every Kutel in this town is part of the war effort. It's not like they all have plans for a peaceful life after the war is over. When Dath is gone they'll move on to Taferford, and so on. They're evil and they live to fight. We have to fight to live."

"I don't have to like it."

Nickadola held up his hands for peace. "We can free the pigs tonight. Just sneak into the farms, free the pigs, and kill only the Kutel that we have to."

Fargus said, "He's right. This night is nearly spent and we need to get done and get away before that hunting party gets back."

They snuck into the barn, but the pigs would not be quiet. The Kutel offered no resistance; they hid. The group went to three more farms rounding up a herd of skinny, sleepy pigs. The Kutel in surrounding farms were raising an alarm. As the Kutel messenger rushed to the chief's house Nickadola gave the pigs a little speech. Blorfindel watched the Kutel start to assemble in the center of town. When the door to the Cral barn opened he said in the Timble's language, "Hurry it up."

"… so we have come to free you from the Kutel oppressors, their cruel staves and their butchering knives. Flee with us to the shady forest, with acorns and mushrooms for all!"

The herd raised their rallying squeal and nearly ran over the little Timble on their way out the gate. Nickadola mounted a big hog and rode out of town like some surrealistic hero. The rest of the group followed with a close eye for pursuit.

A short distance out of town the group began to wonder if Nickadola was leading the pigs, or just riding one that happened near the front. The herd flowed over the forest like a squealing flood. They turned here and there without apparent reason, though their direction was generally east. Almost immediately after sunrise they came to a stop in a valley under some tall oak trees where the pigs stopped to eat. Nickadola dismounted and ran to meet the others.

"Well, that was refreshing."

"Maybe for you," Blorfindel said, "I had to run back to get Sturdifoot."

"Not the ride, freeing the pigs."

Lantid shook his head. "Four farms worth of pigs and a half-dozen dead Kutel. It was hardly worth exposing ourselves for."

"You're wrong this time, Lantid." The Timble smiled brightly. "Now we have an ally to defeat the Varren!"

Alehra wondered if something was wrong with Nickadola's mind. "You mean the pigs are going to hunt the Varren for us? What are they going to do, trample them?"

"They could, you know. No, they're not going to hunt anything more dangerous than mushrooms, but they can break our scent trail whenever we want."

"I had not though of that," Lantid confessed.

Fargus said, "But surely the Kutel are still following us."

"They're following the pigs, but right now that's the same thing."

Blorfindel suggested, "The col we came over to get into this valley would be a good place for an ambush."

The cleric asked, "What's a col?"

Alehra said, "The saddle-like pass between the two mountains."

"How did you, a foreigner, know that and I didn't?"

"It's the best place for an ambush that we passed." She turned and started walking back towards it. "I never heard the word before in my life."

"I just hope I get to sleep before I have to climb that col a third time."

Nickadola said, "Wait!" He picked a leaf from a young oak and started an incantation. During the incantation the leaf turned yellow, then brown, then brittle, and finally fell to dust. When the spell was completed they all felt as though they had slept for a few hours. They were still tired, but it was enough to keep them going for a while longer.

Lantid said, "You mean, you've been able to do that all along? When we were dragging through the mountains with the captives?"

The Timble's smile brightened. "No, I couldn't have cast it then. Think of it as a bonus for saving the pigs: Dhu is pleased. Even if I could have done it then, it gets diluted by the number of people affected. It could have been as good as a night's sleep for one, but instead it was a nap for all of us."

Chapter 20

Cral in the Col

Fir and spruce trees grew thick and short in the col. The pigs' trail ran under the tallest of them, and only those were clear of low branches. The result was a sort of path that the pigs could run through. Many of the branches obscured the view at five feet or so – normal height for Kutel eyes. A Cral would have to break through the tree limbs to get here at all.

Blorfindel and Nickadola put the Tafers in their hiding places. Because of the dense cover they could all be within thirty feet of the path, with decent running or shooting lanes, and still be totally invisible. They were all close to each other, with Nickadola a bit further away, toward the Kutel. Blorfindel was the most exposed on the northwest side. He moved down-slope far enough so that the trees were taller and the view longer.

He did not have long to wait. First came two Kutel with large shields and spears warding a Varro. A short distance behind them followed a group of forty or fifty Kutel. The Kutel scampered to stay out of the way of the three Crals smashing through tree-limbs behind them. Behind the Crals was the group's leader, the only Kutel in mail. A rearguard of eight to ten Kutel followed closely behind.

Blorfindel weighed the idea of shooting at range. *They don't know where we are right now. We do not want to fight those three Crals. If I shoot they will know that we are here. If the Varro smells us then we lose all surprise. We are too tired to run for long. We cannot hide from a Varro, not when it's this close.* He gauged the wind. It was light but variable and swirling. *That is bad. We cannot tell when the Varro might smell us. It has got to die.*

He moved swiftly from tree to tree. He was acutely aware of his iron armor rattling at each step. As soon as he got a clean shot at the Varro he took it. The two shield-Kutel fell behind, leaving the Varro exposed and nose-down on the edge of the trail. Blorfindel's arrow stuck fletchings-deep in its chest.

He did not wait for the Kutels' reaction. He ran immediately for cover, then turned back to the group. He paused at his original position to see where the Kutel had gone. The Kutel had stopped in their tracks, but the Cral kept moving, passing through their ranks as if nothing had happened. The leader was waiving them all up the pig trail. Blorfindel dashed back to report.

"Fifty or sixty Kutel, one in armor, and three Cral, all coming this way. They know we're here."

Lantid wanted to know, "How do they know that?"

"They had a Varro with them. I shot it."

Fargus said, "We have to get out of here."

Nickadola disagreed. "Where are you going to go? We can't run far. This probably the best hiding place for miles. Just stay quiet and stay still. They'll walk right by."

Lantid said, "They can fan out and hunt us once they find out the trail only leads to pigs."

Blorfindel said, "They won't hunt us without a leader. It's at the back and only guarded by maybe ten regular Kutel. If we let the others go by and knock off the leader the hunt is over."

"If those Cral catch us, the hunt is over, too."

Alehra disagreed. "Not in here. Even without Nickadola's spell those Cral will be nearly blinded by the trees. We can easily evade them, or even fight them one at a time."

Blorfindel could hear footsteps. "We're out of time!"

Alehra waved him back to his hiding place. "We'll ambush the leader. Lantid, we need you to drop his guards, then Blorfindel and I will take him out. Nickadola, if you can give us some kind of barrier between us and the main force of Kutel – good. Fargus, watch the trees, they'll tell where the Crals are. If they're getting close, yell. Now everyone hide until they go by."

Blorfindel stayed in the thick cover near the top of the col. He could still hear the Tafers taking positions when the first two Kutel went by. They were on either side of the trail now, like beaters. *This is probably their punishment for letting the Varro die.* One passed within ten feet of the Fitheran but the green needles obscured him completely. The Kutel were spending more effort looking out for low branches than ambushers, anyway.

The main force was sixty feet behind them. They passed neatly single-file. Nearly half of them had passed when Blorfindel thought to himself, *I should have counted them.* The Cral followed, also single file. They pushed their way through the tree branches effortlessly and the springy trees closed behind each. They were followed by the leader and his rearguard, who at least made a show of being alert. This time Blorfindel did count. *Eight guards plus the leader.* He hid his bow near his pack, drew his swords, and fell in line about fifty feet behind them, crouching below the tree limbs as he went. If the Kutel had only bent down they could have seen him clearly. They did not.

Blorfindel could see Lantid laying on the forest floor for a better view. When Blorfindel drew next to Alehra, the wizard began his spell. Blorfindel knew from experience that the sleep spell took Lantid only about three seconds. Right now, three seconds seemed like a long time. He forced himself to be patient. *Don't get too close. The spell can't tell friend from foe.*

The Kutel leader heard Lantid and shouted, "Ambush!" Blorfindel forced himself to wait one more second before charging. The Kutel in the rearguard turned to see a Fitheran and a Taforam charging with swords drawn. They pushed aside the low tree limbs and tried to form a line. Blorfindel was three steps away from a wall of spearheads when the middle of the Kutel line fell asleep leaving a huge gap. He was half a step ahead of Alehra as they vaulted the sleeping guards to attack the leader.

The Kutel leader had been facing the Cral, shouting, and trying to get them turned around. It heard the crash of falling Kutel behind it and turned to see what had happened. What it saw was two attackers in mid-air about eight feet away. Reflexively it raised its shield and reached for its sword. "Cruska!"

The Kutel's shield deflected Blorfindel's long sword away. Blorfindel's short sword struck the Kutel in the chest after the shield passed. The sword point was narrow and strong and the rings of the Kutel's armor expanded to let it pass. Even as the point was piercing the padding underneath, Alehra's sword point touched its neck. Both swords' points passed completely through the Kutel. Its own sword cleared its scabbard as it was falling from the Kutel's lifeless hand.

Alehra and Blorfindel spun in opposite directions as they pulled their swords from the corpse. Each turned to face one of the rearguards. The two Kutel on the extreme left and right of the line had not fallen asleep. They each tried to engage the assassins with their spears. Blorfindel turned one Kutel's spear point away and under his own right arm with his short sword, using the spear as a lever to push the Kutel's shield aside in the same circular motion. He stabbed over the shield with his long sword, piercing the Kutel below its right shoulder. As he withdrew his sword a branch slapped back into position between them. The Kutel fell. Alehra was pulling her sword out of the other Kutel when he turned around.

Each of them stabbed one of the sleeping Kutel before Lantid joined them. To their complete surprise he picked up the leader's sword and with three frantic two-handed chops, he cut its head off.

Alehra recovered soonest. "What? He's dead already!"

"The other Kutel don't know that!"

Blorfindel stuck his sword into a sleeping Kutel's chest, left it standing there, and picked up the leader's head by the helmet. He swung around a three-quarter circle and flung it as far as he could up the trail, shouting the Kutel word for "death" as he released it. "They know now!" When he faced Lantid and Alehra he saw that he had sprayed them both with blood.

One of the sleeping Kutel woke up – Blorfindel had stepped on its spear – but Alehra stabbed it in the eye before it could rise. Lantid and Blorfindel made certain that the other sleeping Kutel never woke up.

Unseen, Fargus shouted, "Cral! There's a Cral coming!"

Lantid and Alehra ran off the path. Blorfindel had to pull his sword out of a Kutel before he moved. He could see the Cral's purple foot crush Kutel leader's right arm before he dashed away. He did not even look up at it. He knew that he was within its reach.

The Cral could not see him. The tree limbs made a barrier which obscured its view. It could push them out of the way, but when it let go they would spring back. It flailed at them with its club and its free hand, but most branches were too tough and springy to break.

Blorfindel dashed back into the path and snatched up one of the Kutel spears. He braced the butt against a nearby tree trunk and tried to move the point into the path of the Cral's hand as if fought with the trees. Alehra saw what he was doing and did the same. Hers was the first spear struck. The spear shaft broke, but not before the point stuck in the back of Cral's hand. She ran back into cover before it could react.

The Cral pulled the point from its hand and bulled its way into the trees where Alehra had fled. Blorfindel dropped the spear and charged at its back. As he ran across the path another Cral was moving toward him. He trusted to the trees and ignored it.

The Cral chasing Alehra stopped short. Almost by accident Blorfindel ran his sword into the back of its knee. The shock of impact brought the Fitheran to a full stop, but his sword point penetrated. The Cral roared and swung its club blindly. The trees deflected it before it got near Blorfindel, but it opened a path for the Cral to see. The Fitheran did not wait for its reaction. As the Cral turned right to look, he dashed around its legs to the left and ducked under cover in a shower of needles. When the Cral whipped its head back around to the left, Alehra's sword point was in front of its right eye. The sword went deep. Even before it could cry out in pain she retreated, rolling under a low tree limb and crawling frantically away. The Cral looked around like a scared bird for a moment, then swooned and fell over dead.

When Blorfindel turned back toward the path he saw the second Cral crawling on its hands and knees, looking under the trees. He ran a circle behind it and waved for Alehra. As soon as she could get free of the trees herself, she followed. He circled around to its left, leaving her the shorter route to its right side. He stabbed its armpit with all of the force of his charge. Without so much as wondering whether the point penetrated he withdrew and dashed under the trees to the left. It rolled over to look for him and ruined Alehra's attack. Her sword grazed its back and shoulder on her way by. She stuck out her arm and clubbed it in the back of the head with the edge of her shield, more out of frustration for spoiling her attack than with any expectation that she might do it harm.

The Cral rolled all the way over on its back to swing at her. When it did so, its loins burst into flame. Predictably, the Cral ignored the retreating Taforam and reached for its own crotch. As Blorfindel charged at it he could hear Lantid say, "Cover that up!"

The Fitheran's long sword missed its eye and left a bloodless scratch on its forehead. As he jumped over its stomach his short sword found its way into the Cral's open mouth. He shoved the blade literally down the monsters throat as it doubled over and he had to withdraw his hand quickly to keep the Cral from biting it off. A second later he was hidden in the trees, wiping the Cral spit off his arm.

Fargus' voice blast through the trees, "A little help over here!"

Lantid broke cover and with both hands waved for Alehra and Blorfindel to go. They were already on the move.

Fargus was giving ground before the remaining Cral. Each time he would duck behind a tree the Cral would chop through it with its stone-bladed axe. It had now cleared a space big enough so that it could both see and fight. It did not turn away from the cleric to see Blorfindel and Alehra coming.

Blorfindel had to use his long sword to balance as he charged through the debris. He tried to stick his short sword into the side of its knee just behind the kneecap, but its hide was too strong. The Fitheran slammed face-first into its ribs under its left arm. In the copping motion, the Cral's upper arm struck Blorfindel and slapped him away.

The Cral's axe stuck in the tree trunk for an instant while Alehra ran underneath. She stabbed her sword up its bulbous nose. The point did not pass into its skull as she had hoped, but cut its nostril open and was deflected on its cheekbone.

When the Cral's axe came free its gaze fixed on the Fitheran sprawled out in the fresh cut boughs. It finally had a target that it could see – a target that was not running around. It swung the axe overhead to split the Fitheran in half.

Fargus broke cover and charged the Cral, but his foot got caught in the fresh cut tree limbs and he fell on his face.

Blorfindel lay on his back and watched the Cral raise its axe. It seemed to take forever. He noticed the springy, lumpy and yet somehow comfortable branches beneath him. He could feel the tiny scratches where he had brushed against the needles. He could smell the pitch that oozed from the broken trees. The Cral's axe started down. Behind the Cral's cruel and contorted orange face Blorfindel saw a little puffy white cloud in the clear blue sky. The monster was stepping forward now, into its swing. It blocked Blorfindel's view of the cloud.

Suddenly Blorfindel exploded to his feet and threw himself at the Cral. He thrust his sword into its navel and pushed up with both legs as if lifting a heavy weight. The blade was in nearly to the hilt when the Cral's axe handle hit him in the back. He remembered the ground getting rapidly closer.

When Blorfindel came to he was still face down in the spruce boughs. He could hear Fargus say, "Don't move him!"

And Alehra, "We can't leave him here!"

Blorfindel got to one knee. He lifted himself on his hands. The pain was remarkable, clouding his vision and his thoughts. Even his gums hurt. His left hand held his short sword. His right was empty. *Where did my sword go?* He looked to the right. *That's not my sword. What is that?* As the realization hit him he scrambled forward as fast as he could on all fours. It was the Cral's leg, and it was still standing.

Fargus and Alehra picked him up and set him on his feet. "Easy now," the cleric was saying, "don't hurt yourself."

Blorfindel snapped his head around to look at the Cral. The pain was so intense that his knees buckled. His friends held him up and turned him gently. The Cral was still standing, back to him, and leaning forward against the handle of its axe. The axe head was half buried in the ground. For a moment it looked to be urinating, but it was blood trickling out. The Cral did not move.

"My sword…"

Alehra said, "I'll get it. Can you hold him?"

Blorfindel gingerly started to take his weight on his own legs even as Fargus nodded. Alehra walked carefully around the Cral, pulled out the sword and retreated quickly. The trickle of blood became a torrent. It still did not move.

Blorfindel said, "One of those healing spells would be nice."

"You've already had one."

"How long was I out?" He wanted to look at the sun, but decided not to move his head.

"A moment, only – just long enough for me to get here and cast the spell. Can you walk?"

"I think so."

Alehra wiped off the sword and put it in Blorfindel's scabbard for him. She took the short sword from his hand and did the same. "Where's your bow?"

"I don't know. Uh, I haven't used it since… It must be where I started the ambush."

Lantid had arrived while Alehra was pulling the sword out of the Cral, but Blorfindel did not see him. Now he spoke. "I'll help him get it. Go see what's happening with the rest of the Kutel. Nickadola has been on his own for too long." He looked at the Cral, then picked up a sizable branch and struck it in the back of the knee. The knee buckled and the Cral fell over. The crash made Blorfindel jump. The pain made him whimper.

Alehra said, "Why don't you throw another heal on him?"

"After the battle; I don't want to run out. What if Nickadola's in the same condition when we find him?"

Lantid helped Blorfindel to his bow. He helped him to gently sit down in the shade and, more importantly, in the cover of the thick trees. Lantid moved to where he could see up the path and the Fitheran. Blorfindel lay back and tried not to move.

"Don't go to sleep on me, now. You know I can't lift you."

"You've got to be kidding me," Blorfindel mumbled. "I'd give ten malstren for one of your sleep spells right now."

A few minutes later the other three joined them. Fargus went immediately to Blorfindel and cast another healing spell on him. The pain dulled but the fog did not clear.

Lantid asked, "The Kutel?"

Nickadola shrugged, "Most of them got away. How's he doing?"

Blorfindel croaked, "I'll live."

Fargus said, "He needs rest, in a bed."

"That means going all the way back to the house."

Blorfindel said, "Camp today. We can go back tomorrow, can't we? I'm not getting any worse."

Nickadola looked down at him, "You're not getting better, either."

Fargus frowned but agreed with Blorfindel. "We need the rest. We'd probably be risking his life more by sleepwalking past Jun."

Alehra asked, "What about another spell?"

"That was the last. I used one on myself after the Cral dropped a tree on me."

"That's right, I thought you cast them all before we left our last camp?"

"I did. That was yesterday," Fargus waved at the sun, "and this is the morning of a bright new day."

She shook her head. "Yesterday they surprised us in camp and nearly killed the mule. Today Blorfindel nearly got killed. I can hardly wait for tomorrow."

"Let's get out of here."

Nickadola handed Blorfindel a Kutel spear. The Fitheran stared at it. "Walking stick." He climbed it hand over hand to get to his feet.

The trek down from the col was slow and largely a blur for Blorfindel. At some point Nickadola ran ahead and rounded up some pigs. He herded them across their path, and up and down it for nearly a quarter mile. "A Varro couldn't follow us through that."

They propped Blorfindel against a tree while they made camp. It was only then that he realized his pack was tied to Sturdifoot. Nickadola gathered leaves for his bed. Fargus helped him out of his armor. Blorfindel just tried not to move. They tried to get him to eat but he had no appetite. Finally, overcome by fatigue, he passed out.

When he woke up it was dark. He could hear Alehra and Fargus talking.

"I thought your spells were as good as bed rest."

"They are for moderate or even serious wounds. He's lucky to be alive at all. Without the healing magic I don't think we could have moved him – not without killing him. As it is he's lucky that all his limbs work. I'm sure his spine broke."

"Did you see how far into the ground the axe went after it hit him?"

"I'm just glad he wasn't under the blade – if that's what you call it. Is it still a blade when it's made of stone?"

"It's your language, Fargus, I'm just borrowing it."

"Can I have it back when you're done with it?" Fargus asked. She laughed. He continued, "It cut through the trees. I guess it's a blade."

"It's too bad. We were doing pretty well until we got to that one," she said. "I bet if it had a club like the others, or even a spear, we would have been fine."

Fargus replied, "We killed three Cral and nobody died – well, none of us died. Blorfindel will bounce back in a week or two. We're winning."

"I think you're right. Anyway, I'm going to try to sleep. Be careful. A lot of those Kutel got away. They're probably all lost by now." She laughed again. "That probably means there more likely to stumble into camp than if they knew where we were. I don't think they want any part of us."

"Good night."

Blorfindel lay still and listened to Fargus walk around the camp. It seemed like a long time before he could fall asleep again, but he did not hear the next watch change.

Chapter 21

Rest and Recuperation

The next thing Blorfindel knew, daylight turned his black tent purple. *I should get up. We have to move today.* He sat up. The pain was so intense that he was nauseous. *It's a good thing I didn't eat.* He took the tiniest of sips from his water skin. *Frenlias' gift! When was the last time I had any of them? That was probably why they wanted me to eat.* Slowly and carefully he unpacked his backpack until he found the bag of seeds. He chewed three of the tiny seeds and washed them down with another mouthful of water.

He could hear Fargus outside whispering, "I think he's awake."

"I'm awake. I just wish I wasn't."

Lantid opened the tent flap. Blorfindel could see Fargus behind him, bent over to look in. The wizard said, "I was going to ask how you feel, but I guess I know. Do you think you can stand?"

"I think I can walk. Where's the latrine?"

Fargus and Lantid helped him up and walked with him, one on either side. He turned to Fargus. "A week or two, even with Frenlias' gift and magic healing?"

"I think so. I don't have much experience with Cral-inflicted wounds, but my spells and the silverseeds – that is, Frenlias' gift – they won't affect some of the damage. Your body has to heal that. The seeds will speed things along, of course. I'm really not sure how it works. I just know that's the way it is."

Lantid said, "You're walking pretty well."

"I just hope I can walk all the way back to the house."

"Do you think you're up to it?"

"Does it matter?"

"Yes. We'll camp on the way if we have to."

Fargus smiled. "Maybe we can rig up some kind of litter? I'm sure Nickadola could talk some pigs into carrying you."

Lantid snorted and Blorfindel chuckled. "Oooh, don't make me laugh. Laughing hurts."

On the way back he noticed the morning sun was still low. "When did we get here? How long was I out?"

"We were back before noon. We all needed a long night's sleep."

They made him rest and eat while the Tafers broke camp. Nickadola kept watch.

Fargus and Alehra divided the essentials from Blorfindel's kit between them. Alehra shook her head, "No, this isn't going to work. We'll put his armor on Sturdifoot. We can unload the Kutel armor."

"I'll wear my armor." Blorfindel stood up.

"You can hardly walk as it is."

"I'll wear it, and the swords."

"You're not going into battle, even if they jump us."

"If they jump us I may not have a choice. Besides, without it I'm one black arrow away from being a corpse."

Fargus shrugged. "If he can wear it, it will be safer for him."

"Isn't he swollen?"

"No, the spells will take care of that." Fargus cast another heal on Blorfindel. "Even the bruising should be mostly gone by now. He'll still be weak, though, and that armor is heavy – even worse than mine because of the heavy layering."

"The pack is heavy, too, and I won't be carrying that."

Fargus said, "If we have to stop for him to take it off we're no worse off than we are now." He shouted, "Nickadola, I hope you have one of your fatigue spells handy."

"I took one this morning. Are you tired already?"

"Blorfindel's going to wear his armor."

"You know, if you want to rig something up I can probably get some of the pigs to help."

Blorfindel held up his hand. "No, ow, don't make me laugh."

"It's a long way back to Dath."

"Dath? I thought we were going to the house."

"The Kutel chief has to know we've been using that. Raise the trees, we met him there once."

"Don't say 'raise the trees' in Shield. It doesn't sound right."

It was a very long, mind-numbing day for Blorfindel. Even when they walked around Jun he could hardly lift his feet to get over roots, rocks and branches – normal forest obstacles. Nickadola hit him full force with his refreshing spell at noon. It was not enough. When he stumbled into Dath the horizon in front of them had just covered the sun. Fargus and Alehra were on each shoulder and practically carried him to bed.

When he woke up he did not know where he was, but it was a soft bed under a wooden roof. It appeared to be a small, private room. The two windows were shuttered, but shafts of sunlight cut through the cracks and lit up the dust specks floating in the air. Sounds of a mid-summer day filtered through the windows as well. The lumber smelled fresh. There was an 'x' scratched in the door where the handle ought to be.

He lay still.

After a short while he heard Fargus speaking. "I'm here to see the patient."

A Taforam responded, "Of course, come in." He heard steps coming closer. "What happened to him?"

"A Cral hit him in the back with an axe."

"Grailsin's gold! It's a miracle he's alive!"

Fargus' head was turned away when he opened the door to Blorfindel's room. "Yes, a miracle." He turned to face the Fitheran. "Fortunately, I'm getting the hang of miracles." He smiled and cast a healing spell before he continued, "How are we feeling this morning?"

"We feel about half dead. Guess which half is mine?"

Fargus opened the shutters. "You should try to rest as much as possible. One of us will be around all the time, but we're going to try to let you sleep, so we may be outside. Just shout if you need anything."

"Thanks Fargus. I guess you saved my life up there."

"You've saved Alehra. Alehra's saved me. Lantid has saved all of us. I expect Nickadola has too, in his own special way. We're going to have to get used to it if we keep up this line of work."

Without a handle he had to scratch at the door to get it open. On his way out the Taforam spoke with him again. "So there are really Cral out there? I'm going to have nightmares about a Cral with an axe!"

"Don't lose any sleep over that one. Blorfindel killed it."

"Are they as big as they say?"

"No, but they're big enough. The Cral that hit him wasn't tall enough to see over your rooftop, but he wouldn't have to jump much. You have to be a hero just to cut through their skin. He was orange as a pumpkin and dirty as a…" Fargus' voice quickened, "As a coal mine!"

Blorfindel learned that he was in the home of Threpon and Canfoli, Tafers of Dath. Threpon had built the room for Canfoli's mother who still lived in Taferford. They decided not to send for her while the threat of Kutel raids remained, so the room was vacant. Late that afternoon Threpon attached a handle to the door. "Sorry 'bout the noise."

"It's your house. Thank you for taking me in."

"I hear you fought a Cral."

"I think we're up to seven now – no, eight."

"Now that's a tall tale if ever I heard one."

"Not all at once!"

"Are they coming to town?"

"I don't know, not those eight. We never left one alive. I guess they mean to come."

"Eight Cral would smash this town into a pile of splinters. Are there any left?"

"I've seen six more."

"Then you're over half done!" He picked up his things, "Careful with the handle. The trunnel should hold, but the glue won't set up for a while." He smiled as he left. Blorfindel could not help but notice that the new door handle was not on straight.

Blorfindel spent most of the next ten days in that little room. The most effort he spent was for short walks around town in the evenings or early mornings. In the heat of the day he watched through the windows as Alehra drilled Fargus on the proper use of a war hammer. Many of the town's children gathered to watch and laugh, too. Blorfindel tried not to laugh.

On the eleventh day Blorfindel belted on his swords for his morning walk. He sprinted the last quarter mile. There was no pain. He was sitting in the sun when Alehra and Fargus arrived for practice. "What happened to my armor?"

Alehra answered, "It's in the barn. Do you want it? I had the blacksmith in town straighten out the worst of the damage – and clean the pine needles out. He's slow as time, but his work isn't bad for a blacksmith and he works cheap. You're bow's in the barn, too. I nearly pulled a muscle unstringing it."

Fargus asked, "Are you sure you're ready? You don't want to re-injure yourself."

"I'll know when I string the bow and put on the armor." They all started towards the barn. "Where's my cittern? I should have been practicing all this time!"

"We, ah, I'll have to look," Alehra said awkwardly. "I"m sure it's around the barn somewhere."

"There's no time for songs now. We've wasted enough time here."

"Not completely wasted," Fargus said. "We've got some practice in."

"I noticed."

"And Lantid got someone to fit your arrowheads to shafts. I don't know if he's got feathers–"

"Fletchings."

"–fletchings on them yet."

Alehra said, "And I think the trees that the locals replanted have grown a foot since Nickadola started tending them."

Fargus agreed. "That's no joke: a foot."

"We also got them to make you a new backpack. It might be too big, though. I think she forgot you were a Fitheran."

"It'll be fine. I owe someone some coin for all this."

"We took it out of the spoils. The change from the last few battles covered everything."

"It's got to be more than my share."

Fargus smiled. "We really didn't keep track. The blacksmith charged us for all of our armor repairs together, and we've been spending a bit more on ourselves while you had to stay in bed. Regardless, we decided it was more reasonable to cover all expenses before we cut the money."

"Which is to say, Lantid doesn't want us thinking about how much an arrow costs before we shoot them," Alehra said.

"Not much danger of that."

Lantid was sitting in the shade beside the barn writing when they arrived. "Feeling better? I saw your run this morning."

"You did?"

"It's still my watch. You look like you're ready to go."

"I think so."

Fargus said, "Wait until you've tried your armor on. You may feel differently with another fifty pounds."

"And pull that bow a couple of times," Alehra said. "That's more than fifty pounds. What is the draw weight on that, a hundred pounds, more?"

"I don't know. Fitherani fit the bow to the archer. We don't generally measure the draw weight. Since no one uses anyone else's bow, it doesn't really matter." He shrugged. "I split more arrows than most."

Fully armed, Blorfindel felt ready. Adjusting the straps on the new backpack took some time. "I think I'm ready."

"We'll go tomorrow, then."

"It's still early."

Lantid shook his head. "Nickadola won't be ready. He's been using a lot of spells on the local trees. He'll need to rest and change to battle spells. How about you, Fargus?"

"I've been carrying healing spells all the time. We should give Blorfindel's wound one more day, though."

Blorfindel did not rest that day. He started with archery practice. He could not set up a Fithern course in Dath, but he did the best that he could. Alehra followed him through the exercises with her own bow. She did fairly well for her first time in the Fithern style. By the time they stopped for water it was clear that she was no match for the Fitheran.

"You're really good at this. Is this how Fitherani practice?"

"We don't have the pendulums – moving targets – here. They're the worst, at least for me."

She joked with him, "What, do you miss them, you know, like maybe once in a dozen arrows?"

"Maybe."

"That must really knock down your score in the 'Best Archer In the World' competition."

He frowned and fingered his archer's talisman. "I'm just barely qualified to wear this. I might be the worst Fithern archer." Her look was incredulous. "No kidding, I just barely passed, and the weather was perfect for my test."

"Fithern archers are legendary, but damn!"

The crowd of Tafer children who had been used to watching Alehra teach Fargus with the war hammer had followed the archers around as well. Now that they had stopped, all of the children wanted a chance to try the bows. Alehra let them try hers. A few of them could draw the bow full, but they were all too shaky to give them an arrow.

"I bet I can draw a Fitheran bow! Fitherans aren't as big as Tafers."

Blorfindel smiled at the child, "That's <u>Fithern</u> bow, and <u>Fitherani</u> sure are smaller than Tafers, though I think I might be a bit bigger than you are." The child was a head short of Blorfindel's five and a half feet. He held up the bow, "Be careful, it's older than your father."

Alehra laughed.

"What?"

"I've seen you use that bow. What in– what's this kid going to do to it that you haven't?"

Like Alehra's bow, his bow was too long for the child to hold upright. He could only move the string about four inches. All of them had to have a turn, but none could draw it. Blorfindel retrieved his bow when their fingers got sore. He held it up for Alehra.

"I can't draw it either. I had to work to unstring it."

After a morning of archery, the afternoon became sword practice. This time Alehra faced Blorfindel in direct competition. At first it was just a series of exercises, and most of them at slow speed. As the afternoon progressed their competitive natures began to take over.

As exercises turned to bouts, both combatants had to adjust their fighting styles. Blorfindel was used to big, slow opponents who frequently underestimated his strength. Alehra was not as quick as Biolmi had been, but much quicker than anyone he had fought since then. She knew him too well to be fooled by his small stature. Alehra's adjustment was more difficult. She was used to being lighter and quicker than her opponents. Blorfindel's heavy armor brought them to about the same weight, but he was much quicker. Her flexible mail allowed her to move more freely, but it only seemed to get her in trouble with the lightning-fast Fitheran. It was not until she learned to use her shield's mass to overpower his light weapons that things started to level out.

Without the fencers noticing, the crowd of onlookers began to grow. The Tafers of Dath had just begun learning to fight for themselves. At first it was an opportunity to see how the professionals did it. As the intensity level rose, so did the attention of the crowd. Before long money started changing hands.

As Blorfindel started to get used to her new shield tactic he baited her. When she tried to block his swords he crossed them on her shield and shoved her backwards. It was only good balance born of hard training that allowed her to keep her feet, but he pressed the advantage and she was stuck on the defensive.

Blorfindel could hear two of the Tafers in the crowd.

"I wouldn't 'ave thought the Fitheran would be able to push her around like that."

"Course he can. She's just a Taforam, after all."

"She's done pretty well."

"What? Has she won two of seven? Anybody can get lucky."

Alehra heard him, too. She was angry with the comment and also frustrated that she had not done better. She was a bit embarrassed to be shown up so badly at archery earlier. She had promised herself that she would make up for it with the sword and that was not coming true.

Blorfindel slacked off just enough for her to recover and win the bout. He had expected that no one would notice. *Three to five is no disgrace to anyone.*

Alehra swooshed her sword through the air and stomped off after the bout. Three steps away she turned on him and pointed her sword accusingly. "You let me go!" She made an angry little flick with the sword tip.

He whispered, "I didn't want the crowd to think you weren't as good."

She used her full voice. "I heard him." She flicked the sword tip at each of them as she spoke. "To Raiden with him, and you too if you're going to treat me like some novice with fragile feelings. Before long, maybe tomorrow, I'm going to have to fight for my life. What good does it do if I haven't learned what really works and what doesn't? How am I supposed to learn if you won't fight hard?"

"I'm sorry. I thought... I know you're good. I mean, we've fought side-by-side. I'm no better than you."

"Yes you are. You're faster than I am and you're stronger than I am and you have that insane Fithern archer training." She took a deep breath. "I can live with that, it doesn't matter. I'm not out to prove I'm the best warrior in the world. The thing that eats me up is that I'm out there risking life and limb so that this loud-mouthed plow jockey can have a peaceful summer, but do I get any respect? Oh, no."

A fiendish smile crawled across Blorfindel's face. "That's easily solved." He strode toward the Tafer who made the offending comment. The crowd quietly moved away from him. Wild panic lit his eyes when Blorfindel stepped up to him. The crowd held its breath until Blorfindel reversed his sword, offering the hilt to the Tafer. "Your turn."

The hail of hoots and derisive laughter from the crowd gave the Tafer time to think up an excuse. "Uh, I'm really more of an axe Tafer, myself."

Blorfindel was not letting him off that easily. He resumed his normal grip on the sword and tapped the Tafer on the shoulder. "Go get it, then. We'll be down by the river, you know, just upstream of the mill where the water's clean." He turned to walk away. When he turned back, the crowd was still laughing and the Tafer had not taken a step. "If you're not there by sunset I'm going to have to assume something happened to you. I guess

I'd have to go looking for you, then. You're not going to make me go looking for you... after sunset?"

They were not long in the river when the Tafer arrived with his axe. He brought the crowd along with him, or perhaps it was the other way around. Coming out of the river Alehra was cooler both in body and in temperament. The bout was quick and predictable, yet amicable. Some of the crowd derided him for losing to a Taforam. Soaking wet and without her armor she looked more like a Taforam than ever; not all of the comments were about her fighting prowess. She ignored them and started going over some of the mistakes that the Tafer had made in the bout. Blorfindel joined in and the rest of the evening was a teaching session for all of the Tafers of Dath.

Nickadola diverted his walk back from the forest to see why the Tafers were gathered by the river. He stayed when the sun set and all of the Tafers went home. The night was still warm, and the Timble, the Fitheran, and the Taforam relaxed in the river. They talked about very little and watched the stars appear. The blue moon rose large and full over the forest. Alehra said, "The lover's moon."

"The what?"

"In Mikenura, when the blue moon is alone and full on a summer night it's called a lover's moon."

Blorfindel asked, "What does that mean?"

"I wish I knew."

Nickadola asked, "No Tafer for you?"

"I don't know. Who wants a sword Taforam anyway?"

Blorfindel said, "From the sound of the crowd, plenty of them."

"Maybe for a few minutes in the woods, not for a lifetime. Most of them are all talk, anyway. What about your lady-love? Is she an archer?"

"No, Fitheressi don't have to be archers if they don't want to."

"See what I mean?"

"No."

"Tafers want to rule the roost. At least they want to feel that way. You heard them all today, they shrivel up if they see a Taforam that's tougher than they are."

"Not everyone feels that way, at least not Fitherani."

"Then why aren't Fitheressi archers? Probably because they don't want to hurt their chances with the Fitherani."

"My mother was an archer – the second archer of Foralis."

"And who was the first, your dad?"

"He was better with his swords. I guess I take after him more."

"So she found someone who wasn't threatened by her. Good for her, but it's not easy."

Nickadola said, "Most Timble mothers are strong-willed, and the girls grow up that way. Anyone can sling a rock. We're just used to it, I guess."

Blorfindel asked, "What about Fargus? He's not threatened. You seem to get along."

"I don't even know if Fargus is allowed, you know, by Feadin." She paused. "No, Fargus… I don't know how to say it. It's not that he isn't brave, because he is. It's just that there's no adventure in him."

"He's here."

"He's here because he thinks he should be. If he had a wife he'd think that he should be at home. He does what he thinks he should, all the time. It makes for a great friend, but… I don't know. When I sailed around The Spine I didn't know there was a town called Dath that needed my help. I didn't know anything. I just knew that there was a lot more to see than the beach at Sami, and I wanted to see it. I still do. I always will."

Blorfindel looked up at the stars. "When you fall in love, all of that doesn't seem so important."

"How did it happen? I mean, how did you know she was the one?"

"When I met her she was playing her flute in the forest."

"And you knew right away?"

"Yes. No. I don't know, really. I knew I wanted to be with her, but for the rest of my life? I guess that took time."

"How much time?"

"More than two decades."

She laughed, "I haven't even been alive that long."

Nickadola was surprised. "How old are you?"

Blorfindel said, "You should never ask a Taforam that question. They get really sensitive about their age. You'd think they spoiled like milk."

Alehra said, "That's because Tafers think we spoil like milk. I'm twenty years old."

The Timble said, "You're young! You've got plenty of time."

"I bet every Taforam in this town had a baby before she was my age."

"A Timble is usually thirty, more often thirty-five before she's married."

Blorfindel shook his head. "It's odd, but even though Tafers live nearly as long as Timbles, they grow up faster. It's more like a Fitheran, they spend more of their lives as adults."

"That's too bad. Childhood's a lot of fun."

Alehra asked, "Are you still a child?"

"Sort-of. I won't grow any taller, just wider. I'm thirty-four, but no one expects me to be responsible for another year or two. How about you, Blorfindel? You're an archer, you must be an adult?"

"I'm seventeen."

"Decades!"

Alehra said, "But you Fitherani live to be a thousand or more, so you're younger than I am, in your own people."

"It's hard to compare. Certainly Afinlia's father thinks I'm too young. You're young to pass your test at fourteen, at eighteen you're too old."

Alehra said, "It's about the same with Taforam, just in years, not decades. If you're not married by the time your eighteen, you're too old."

Nickadola changed the subject. "We call the blue moon Serbin. The white one is Rirowen. They're the same in Timbrali, right?"

"The pronunciation is different."

They talked about the moons and stars for a short while and then headed in for the night. Blorfindel thought for a moment before joining them in the barn. *What does it say about me when I would rather sleep in a barn than a bed? I would rather be with my friends.*

Chapter 22

Black Squirrel

It was raining at dawn. They decided to wait out the rain and left late in the morning. The sun was bright and the rain-washed forest seemed content. The Tafers could enjoy the day, but Nickadola and Blorfindel reveled in it. The Timble said, "You can almost see the trees smiling. The whole forest got to sleep in this morning." He inhaled deeply through his nose. "If I live to be a hundred I'll never see too many mornings like today."

Blorfindel laughed. "A thousand."

The late start meant that they were not going to make it all the way around Jun that day. They spent much of the afternoon searching for a campsite. They worked hard to find a place that was hidden, defensible, and had a good view. No one wanted to get surprised again. The night passed without other event.

In the morning Fargus said, "Shouldn't we start going back to our nocturnal schedule?"

Alehra did not know the word. "Our what schedule?"

Lantid answered, "If we mean to attack work parties again, yes, we should start sleeping days."

"You sound like you don't want to go back to attacking work parties."

"I keep thinking about those mines."

"Thinking about dying like a trapped rat in the dark?"

"Lurshod thinks the iron makes Jun special. He's probably correct. The harder it is for him to arm his Kutel, the longer we have before they can attack Dath. The muckrakers should be scared, the porters should be scared, the farmers should be scared, the scouts should be scared, and the soldiers should be scared. That leaves the miners. They're not scared yet."

"I'm scared. All they have to do is put a couple of Crals in front of the openings and we're not coming out."

"Blorfindel, you got the best look at the mines, how big are they?"

"The openings were nearly square. The Kutel could walk straight and had room over their heads. Seven, maybe eight feet."

"Ten at the biggest?"

"That's a stretch."

"The only way they can use two Crals to block that is if they stand outside. The Crals are too big."

Fargus shrugged. "Or they can just bury us alive in there."

Alehra whistled. "Keep thinking those happy thoughts."

Lantid shook his head. "They need that mine. They're not going to close it."

"They can reopen it in a couple of days, after we're all dead."

Nickadola held his hands up. "Let's take a look at the mines." He turned a palm towards Fargus before he could object. "Let's not go in, just look around. We can knock off a work party if the opportunity arises, and we can see how difficult it would be to trap us in there. Maybe we can put a scare in the miners without risking getting trapped."

Blorfindel was less sure. "We can move around behind the mines without being seen, yes. We should be trying to get to Lurshod. Without a strong leader, the Kutel will fight among themselves. Besides, he's going to be the one with the money – isn't that what you said, Lantid?"

"Lurshod is still surrounded by guards," Lantid replied. "We're not going to get at him or his strongbox until he's forced to move. I think we're going to have to go in that mine sooner or later."

They moved cautiously to the back side of the mountain without being seen. They then began climbing. From about two-thirds of the way up Blorfindel turned and pointed out another bog. "They might be working that one, too."

From the top of the ridge they looked down on the town. From this height in the full daylight Jun was an eyesore. It was a dirty, ramshackle town at best. Refuse was everywhere. The mines looked like wounds that bled blackly down the mountainside and into the town. Where the black coal dirt began to thin the sewage ponds began, steaming in the summer heat.

Kutel patrols moved through town. For the most part they went from shadow to shadow, trying to stay out of the summer heat. Blorfindel could not shake the image of maggots on an old corpse. After a short while he went about fifty feet back down the mountainside and looked out at the clean, summer-fresh forest. Nickadola followed him.

"I just can't look at it."

"I know what you mean. You used to live there?"

"Not there, not like that. I don't even recognize any of the old trees. They've all been cut down. One of the stumps is built into the corner of a house. I guess it's a house."

For a short while they watched a hawk circling below them. It caught an updraft and for a moment they looked it in the eye. Nickadola said, "It must be horrible for him."

"Why?"

"His eyesight is so much better than ours. Besides, he has to live here."

"I should live here."

The hawk dove. It was so instant that Blorfindel and Nickadola jumped up in surprise. It came up empty.

Nickadola shook his head. "A miss."

"There's lots of good cover on the mountain."

"I wonder what it was."

The others came down the hill. They were arguing again. Blorfindel ignored them and watched the hawk. It dove again. Again it came up empty. This time the hawk moved on. "Whatever it was, it got away." He started down the mountain a few steps ahead of the others.

Lantid said, "We can get to the mine entrances under cover. Once we're in, they'll never hear about it in town unless we let one out."

"What if the mines are connected? They can come out one of the other holes."

"Then they can't block us in all of them."

"It's a death trap, Lantid."

Blorfindel turned to the arguing Tafers. "Listen, could you please be quiet? Half the Kutel in Jun could be sneaking up on us now and I'd never hear it."

Nickadola agreed. "You're not coming to any conclusions anyway."

They walked in relative quiet until they were halfway down. Suddenly Blorfindel pointed. After a heartbeat he whispered, "Nickadola, did you see that?"

"No, what?"

"A black squirrel."

Alehra looked to the sky. "You've got to be kidding me! Have you two lost your minds? Did you forget where we are? A black squirrel! I thought we were being ambushed or something."

Nickadola stalked soundlessly toward the tree where Blorfindel sighted the squirrel while Blorfindel hushed the rest of the group. Nickadola stepped sideways around the tree about ten feet away, then he stopped to cast his spell. A moment later he came back with a squirrel on his shoulder. It seemed occupied with cleaning itself.

Blorfindel whispered to the others, "Black squirrels are very rare around here, or anywhere Fitherani have lived. You see, this one isn't really black, it's just dirty."

Alehra had the courtesy to whisper, but her temper was getting short. "Fascinating, but don't we have better things to do?"

Lantid caught on. He also whispered, "Wait! How did it get blackened?"

Nickadola smiled and spoke softly, "Coal dust. She got covered in coal dust when she hid from the hawk."

"Does that mean what I think it means?"

"Maybe. She's going to show us. Follow me, but easy, please don't scare her. She's already had a tough morning, and she might forget where she was."

The squirrel scurried down the Timble as easily as any tree and darted off. She paused on a rock while they followed as smoothly as they could. After a short distance of this strange chase the squirrel disappeared into a bush. It darted back out and chattered at Nickadola.

"She tried to hide under the bush, but the hawk dove. See, there's a little bit of feather on the bush. Anyway, she ran into a hole underneath and that's where she got dirty." The squirrel darted up onto his shoulder as he parted the little bush. It stayed there as Blorfindel crept up behind.

"It's a tunnel." He reached in and broke off a piece of rock with his hand. He held his palm up for the others to see. It was black. "They must have followed the coal seam here and stopped when they broke through."

Fargus started to speak and dropped his voice to a whisper, "We... we can't get in through a squirrel-hole."

Blorfindel backed away and unshouldered his pack. He started rummaging through, looking for something.

Lantid said, "We could enlarge the hole, now that we know there is one."

"With war hammers and daggers?"

Alehra said, "I bet we can persuade some of the mining Kutel to loan us some tools."

Lantid said, "They can't box us in now. They don't even know where this goes."

"We don't know that." Fargus sighed. "All right, they probably don't know. We can get tools from dead miners to enlarge the hole. You're right, if we can make a back door that changes things."

Blorfindel found what he was looking for. He unwrapped a cloth and took out three black walnuts. "Just the thing for a blackened squirrel having a bad morning." He held his hand out to the squirrel. It scrambled away and hung on the other side of Nickadola. He put them on the ground and took two steps back.

The Timble giggled as the squirrel ran down his bare foot to the ground. After a quick sniff it gnawed into a rock-hard shell. It was still stuffing its mouth full when Blorfindel swung his pack back on and they were ready to go. Nickadola made a quick scan of the sky before they left. He warned the squirrel, "The hawk could be back anytime. Be careful." The squirrel looked up quickly then went back to the walnut.

As they were walking away Alehra asked, "Where did you get black walnuts?"

"There's a tree in Dath. They're last year's. I dug them out of the ground on my morning walks. The local Tafers don't know they're edible."

Lantid stuck out his tongue. "Bleah, maybe for Fitherani and squirrels."

She disagreed. "No, they're good. The hard part is pounding the shells open without scattering the insides everywhere."

When the sun started to sink below the horizon they were only a few hundred yards away from a mine entrance, partially hidden but for the most part just resting. As the light faded they prepared for their hit-and-run on the miners.

Fargus went over the objective again. "We're going to hit the first group we see–"

Lantid interrupted, "Fast and hard."

"–fast and hard, and we're going to grab some mining tools and run away. Even if we only get one pick, we're going to run away."

Lantid picked up the narrative. "If we get separated, we'll meet back here if we can. If not, we'll go back to the pig-camp."

"We're going back to the pigs, anyway, in case the Varren try to follow us."

"Right, but hopefully all together."

"Right."

They moved into position too late. Blorfindel could hear that the Kutel were already at work. No one was coming or going from the mines. "Now what?"

"We wait. If we don't see someone in an hour or two, we'll have to go in to hit a mining group." Blorfindel looked at Fargus who nodded in agreement. Alehra and Nickadola nodded as well.

Before too long a group of six Kutel came out of the mine. The group prepared to charge them but stopped when Blorfindel realized that they were not carrying tools. They had black bags on their backs, presumably full of coal, that they carried into town. He pointed out the different buildings they went to. *It might be good to know where they are using the coal.* Four of them went to a strange oven. When they emptied their bags another Kutel shoveled coal from a different pile back into them. He followed their movements to three other buildings. It seemed so odd he nearly missed what they were looking for. One of the other Kutel left his building with an empty sack and a pick. Another picked up two buckets of water. They were together walking to the mine, but well ahead of the other four.

"One pick, coming up."

The two Kutel had no chance at all. Blorfindel and Alehra each shot one as Fargus dashed out. He grabbed the pick and dashed back. He was running back before the other four Kutel even noticed what happened. They ran away, toward the center of town.

The adventurers retreated to their northeastern camp. Nickadola had to wake up some pigs to cover their trail. They kept watches and slept until noon.

Alehra said, "Time to go mining?"

Without another word they formed up and moved out. They were back at the hole before dark. They cleared away the plants and some of the dirt cover, but they did not begin on the rocks right away.

Blorfindel said, "They'll hear us for certain, if there's anyone in there. It shouldn't be long before the Kutel start work. We can start then."

Instead, they gathered materials for Nickadola. He wove them into a covering that they could put over the enlarged opening so that it was hidden from both inside and out. He could not make it look like a rock face, but at least the sunlight would not be pouring in.

When the time came, Blorfindel, Alehra and Fargus took turns with the pick to enlarge the hole. The job was easier than they expected. The Kutel had opened a mine shaft nearly to the edge of the mountain. The actual work, on the other hand, was worse. Even with all three of them working in shifts it took them hours to cut through the few inches of rock. Lantid hauled the big chunks away and scattered them so that they did not show off the dig site. Nickadola kept watch.

When the hole was big enough Lantid lit his lamp and slithered in. After a quick look around he came back out. "All clear."

"We need a bigger hole than that." Fargus wiped the sweat from his brow. "We may have to leave in a hurry." So they kept digging. It was midnight before the opening was big enough for his satisfaction. "We should just leave it for tonight. We're all tired."

Lantid was disappointed but could not argue. Blorfindel and Alehra were nearly as far spent as the cleric. "It's a long walk back to camp."

Blorfindel said, "We should be there for the sunrise. Besides, Sturdifoot would miss you if you stayed away."

"With all of those pigs for company?"

"He likes you."

Chapter 23

Mine

It was noon the following day when they finally entered the mine. Blorfindel went first, followed by Lantid and his lamp, but when the shaft got smaller Nickadola went to the front. Only the Timble could stand up straight in the tight shaft. They followed for what seemed a very long distance before the shaft opened up both in height and width. Suddenly they could all stand straight and even have some space over their heads.

Lantid whispered, "Do you know what this means?"

Alehra responded, "Nickadola shouldn't be on point anymore."

"Besides that. They made the tunnel bigger for a reason. It wasn't just to ease our backs, or theirs. It's Cral-sized now."

They crept forward with redoubled caution for a short distance before Fargus said, "This is no good. They'll see our light long before we ever see them."

"What do you suggest, stumbling around in the dark?"

Blorfindel agreed with the cleric. "He's right, if they don't see us coming they'll hear our echoes. We should move quickly and try to catch them off guard."

"It's daytime. They're not at work."

Nickadola said, "Nugrot mentioned that some of them were living in the mines. We ought to be able to catch them."

Alehra joined in. "And if the mines really are empty during the day then we should be able to set up some sort of ambush for the work crews."

They picked up their speed, slowing only at intersections for Lantid to scratch out a rough map. Suddenly they burst into a large gallery. The roof was still low and supported by irregular timber supports and pillars of the natural stone that had been left during the excavation. Some were as big as seven feet thick. The room itself was wide enough so that they could not see clearly side to side or end to end in the lantern light. The group did not stop to marvel at the architecture, however. The room was occupied.

Sleeping Kutel littered the floor. Between them were their tools, laid down to define each Kutel's space. Across the room they could see some larger mounds: there were Cral sleeping here as well.

The invaders all stood in wonder for a moment. Suddenly Alehra stuck her sword into the chest of a nearby Kutel. They burst into action. It was a race to see how many they could kill before they awoke. Blorfindel, Alehra, Nickadola and Fargus swarmed into the room stabbing, slashing and smashing with no thought to formation or defense. Lantid held the light and followed. As they started to fan out he hissed, "Cut a path to the Cral. We want to kill them as soon as possible."

Not all of the Kutel were asleep. Blorfindel saw one trying to sneak out of a side tunnel, presumably leaving its comrades to die. Blorfindel let it go so that he could deal with the Cral. They carved a path through the sleeping Kutel until Blorfindel and Alehra could get to the Cral without stepping on any of the sleepers. He stuck his short sword under the nearest Cral's eyelid and fished for its undersized brain. In its death throws it kicked the Cral beside it. Alehra's sword went in that one's ear even as its eyes opened. Its mouth opened as if to shout, then it was still. Suddenly there were Kutel shouting everywhere. In the enclosed space the noise was incredible. Blorfindel and Alehra each dealt a fatal blow to another Cral as they were waking.

Before they could get any further the remaining two Crals were on their feet. The one on the left seemed to be purple-skinned underneath the coal dust. On the right, the Cral was blotchy pink and white. Each had an oversized mining pick. Dozens of Kutel were also awake and panicking, and many of them tried to hide behind the two Crals.

Blorfindel and Alehra were more than seventy feet from the doorway, with only Nickadola and Fargus to hold the Kutel at bay. Lantid quickly realized how easily the Kutel could cut off their escape. "Fall back! To me! To the doorway!"

They withdrew at a run while Lantid held the lantern for them. The few Kutel that blundered into their path were cut down. The Kutel who had their wits rallied on the other side of the room, behind the Cral. Blorfindel could see only faint movements in the darkness as he and Alehra stood in the room and waited for Fargus and Nickadola to pass.

Lantid stepped into the tunnel and beckoned. "Back out of the room before they cut us off."

When Fargus got to Lantid, he asked, "What about those cross tunnels? If they're not dead-ends they'll be able to circle around and attack us from the rear."

Blorfindel and Alehra got two panting breaths in the doorway before the Crals roared and changed. At least forty Kutel followed on their flanks. In answer Blorfindel shouted, "Foralis!" and charged at the purple Cral.

Alehra shouted, "Idiot!" but charged the pink and white Cral. Nickadola and Fargus rushed back into the room a few steps behind, trying to keep the Kutel from flanking. Lantid stood in the opening to the tunnel with his mouth open.

A seven-foot thick natural stone pillar stood between them and the Crals, forcing the Crals to separate. Blorfindel flashed in front of Alehra so that he was now on the right. She followed his lead and swung to the left. The Crals, each intent on its own victim, tried to cross as well. Their slow minds did not take into account the stone pillar in the way. They both ran into it face-first. The shock caused pieces of the ceiling to rain down all over the room. The mountain proved stronger than the Crals, and they both fell, dazed, to the rough stone floor.

The Kutel engaged Blorfindel before he could get to the Cral. He dove over a pick aimed at his chest and rolled to his feet behind the Kutel line. He was on guard before he realized that the handle had bruised his thigh just above his right knee. When the Kutel turned to follow up on the attack Fargus smashed it in the back of the head. Almost as quickly all of the other Kutel nearby fell asleep.

The pink and white Cral was struggling to get off its back. Blorfindel wedged his short sword behind its neck with the pommel scraping sparks across the stone floor. Fargus turned, leaped, and came down with his mace on the Cral's face. The monster fell backward onto the sword, it's own weight delivering a blow that no Tafer or Fitheran ever could have. Blorfindel left the short sword in its throat and drew his war hammer with his left hand.

The remaining Cral did not attempt to rise before taking a swing at Alehra with its pick. She easily hopped over the ankle-high attack. Blorfindel thrust at one of the Kutel facing her with his sword, but only to back it off. His attention was focused on driving his war hammer down on the Cral's already-mangled nose. Its fleshy purple nose exploded as if it were a rotten apple, but its thick skull was unharmed.

The Cral, still on its back, swung at the Fitheran. He leaped back out of reach but was suddenly beset by Kutel. They had neither armor nor shields, but their picks were furious. Blorfindel reflexively stabbed at two of them. His sword pierced one Kutel's heart. The flat top of his war hammer did little harm to the other. Withdrawing his sword he struck yet a third in the side of the head with the pommel.

Suddenly the Kutel routed. Blorfindel slashed the throat of one on its way past and turned to the Cral. Alehra was just pulling her sword out of its eye. Nickadola finished off a Kutel that was struggling on the floor. Fargus and Lantid were killing sleeping Kutel.

Blorfindel struggled to pull his short sword from the pink Cral's corpse. When he stood up the only Kutel in the room were dead. Blorfindel made one limping step before Fargus cast a healing spell on him; suddenly the limp was gone. "Do we follow?"

Lantid shook his head, "They scattered. We'd never catch them down here, anyway. They're running scared and they know these tunnels."

Nickadola wiped his scimitar on a corpse. "Time to go, then." The others turned towards the way they came in. The Timble stopped them, "Wait! Follow the breeze!"

"The breeze?"

"We opened a hole on the other side of the mountain. The breeze must come out at Jun. We can follow them out and maybe they won't guess that we have another way in."

The others fell in behind Nickadola again. They only slowed when they came to an intersection, and then only long enough to check the wind. They passed one more Kutel corpse on the way. Alehra stabbed it anyway, just to be sure, before leaving it behind them. They were very close to Jun. After only a few turns the blinding light of the summer sun shown in front of them. They held up for just a few moments, long enough for their eyes to adjust a bit while Lantid extinguished his lamp, then they dashed out.

Many of the surviving Kutel miners had reached town before them. Jun was waking to the alarm. Kutel ran around seemingly without direction. Some were readying weapons. Others ran to hide. Covered with equal parts coal dust and blood the figures exiting the mines were nightmarish even to a Kutel.

When Alehra saw them in disarray she shouted to the others, "Come on!" and dashed down the hill toward town.

Blorfindel was faster and passed her on the way. A Kutel with a spear stepped out of a building, blinking in the light. It tried to level its spear at the half-seen Fitheran barreling down at it. Blorfindel turned its spear with his short sword and stabbed it in the throat with his long sword. He was not far beyond when Lantid shouted, "Hold up!"

Blorfindel and Alehra stood ready in the wide street while the wizard made a torch from the Kutel's clothing, spear, and some of his own lamp oil. He waved them into the building.

Blorfindel was first in. It was a forge. In one movement, Lantid lit his torch and pulled some of the live coals out of the fire. The fire-dried wood at the base of the wall caught immediately. "Let's go!"

They went from one building to the next, pausing only long enough to make certain that the fires were lit. Any Kutel who were too slow answering the alarm escaped into a street held by fierce foes. Some of the Kutel pleaded but Blorfindel was the only one who understood, and he was not merciful. *Was there mercy from the Kutel when Foralis burned?*

Blorfindel sheathed his short sword and pulled a burning brand from one of the buildings. Alehra and Fargus followed suit. With each new torch they accelerated the burning. Before long half of the town was on fire.

In the center of town Lurshod, the Kutel leader, tried to assemble his forces. His personal guard was there and ready, but the other Kutel were panicked and only a handful rallied to him. He had put his Cral in the mines for safekeeping, but that meant now he did not have them at hand, and some of the miners were screaming that they were dead. *They cost me a fortune!* he thought.

Lurshod watched as his town burned. He was not concerned for the loss of the homes or lives, but all of the forges and foundries were near the mines and ablaze. In spite of his own raging and that of his lieutenants, most of his soldiers were running scared. The summer sun and the growing smoke conspired against his vision and he could not see more than fleeting glimpses of the raiders. *There cannot be many of them,* he thought. *There are enough Kutel living here to surround and destroy them if I can put them in order!* Chaos reigned. About thirty Kutel rallied to his standard. *It's not enough. Gronuk's band was twice this many and had a Cral.* "Cruska! Thornat! Muuk! Go get my strongbox! We're leaving!"

The adventurers kept spreading fires and slaying tardy Kutel. Eventually they were forced out of town, but not by the Kutel. Their own fires blazed too hot and barred their way. They had to escape down the western path toward Dath. For the second time in his life, Blorfindel ran down that path away from a burning town on a hot summer night. The tears in his eyes were not from the smoke.

The others began to slow as they left the burning town behind them, but Blorfindel continued to run and pulled ahead of them. They all looked at each other for a moment and chased after him. "What is it?"

He did not hear them. In his mind he was eighty-one again. His strides were longer and heavier now as he flew down the path. At once tears dropped from his eyes and for a moment he could see clearly. An ancient maple tree stood to the right side of the path in front of him. His run turned into a stagger as he ran over and hugged the giant trunk. "I remember you." He pressed his face into the rough bark and cried.

The others caught up and stared. Lantid caught Nickadola's eye and held up his palms and shrugged as if to ask a question. There were no words. Nickadola spread his own hands and shook his head. He had no idea. Fargus said quietly, "Blorfindel?"

"Ghinlihil." He sniffed and gasped. "I was Ghinlihil... when they burned Foralis... I hid in a tree... this tree."

They all stood there, Nickadola and Fargus in reverence, Lantid in shock, Alehra just at loss for words. Eventually the Timble stepped around to the other side of the tree. He said to the others, "They say the trees will remember Fitherani for a long time." He cast a spell, closed his eyes and put his hand to the tree bark. "It remembers you. It remembers the fires. It was a night like tonight, only not as dry. The Kutel came with fire. The town burned. The Kutel came and you climbed high. It remembers your touch. There was a Tafer."

"Ammoss!"

"He fought the Kutel. You left with him. The tree could taste Kutel blood in the soil until the winter rains came."

"I'm sorry." He said it in Timbrali – his apology to the tree. Then he let go, wiped his eyes, and said it again in Shield, "I'm sorry. It all came back in a rush. I never thought it would be like that." He sniffed. "We should go. We need to collect our stuff and get away before the Kutel get organized."

Lantid nodded. Alehra sighed. They all formed up and circled around to the hole in the back of the mountain. They each kept their thoughts to themselves as they covered the hole, picked up their packs, and moved on. The town was still burning as they headed back toward their northeastern camp. They paused only long enough to clean up at a stream on the way.

It seemed as though no words were spoken until Nickadola woke Blorfindel for watch. "Are you all right?"

"I can stand watch, if that's what you mean."

"We were afraid you came unwoven on us back there."

"I did. I've seen it happen to my cousin, Jerhalli, a couple of times. He was there, too. I didn't think it would happen to me. It was all the same: the fires, the smoke, the summer heat, the smell of Kutel and blood. Then we ran down the path, just like I did nine decades ago. I never saw my parents again."

"I know. I can't imagine what that's like."

"I hated them for so long. I thought they had abandoned me, but they were dead." Blorfindel thought he was past tears.

"You didn't know. You were a kid."

"Then Ammoss came and rescued me, and I got him killed."

"I thought you lived with him at the house near Dath?"

"I did, but then I went into the woods and got caught by a Kutel. Both Ammoss and Shandi went to the Kutel lands to try to get me back. The Kutel killed them, but it's my fault: they never would have been there if it wasn't for me."

"Hey, that's not right. You can't blame yourself for that."

"But–"

"No, listen: when we went after the Tafers from The Hunt we all put our lives on the line. If something had happened, if one of us had died, you wouldn't blame them?"

"It's different–"

"No, it's not. You just think it's different. You were a Kutel captive just like they were. Yes, you probably could have done something differently and avoided being a captive, but so could they. I bet if you asked them everyone could think of something they could have done differently to avoid capture. They did the best they could at the time. It's not their fault. You didn't run to the Kutel to get Ammoss and… ah… Shandi trapped, did you?"

"Of course not."

"Then it's not your fault either. You did the best you could at the time. If, in the mine, if I didn't distract the Kutel next to Al, and he killed her, would you blame me?"

"Of course not."

"Good. It's just the same. We all do the best that we can, but there's danger here. There's danger all around. Sometimes even when we do our best something bad happens. We can't feel guilty about that, we can't carry that around all our lives."

Blorfindel said nothing but tossed his head.

Nickadola woke Alehra. "I think we'd better skip Blorfindel's watch. You can have Lantid wake me again for last watch to make up the time."

Blorfindel said, "I'll be fine."

"Don't argue, just go to sleep."

Sleep was a long time coming. The dawn was starting to brighten the tent before Blorfindel could stop rehearsing his childhood in his mind. Eventually he forced himself to remember the sound of Afinlia's flute and that finally let him rest.

Chapter 24

Scarred Elm

When Blorfindel awoke the sun was high. All of the others were waiting for him. Fargus asked, "How are you feeling?"

"I'm fine!"

"How's the leg?"

"Oh, that, I think the spell healed it. What's the plan for today?"

Lantid answered, "Reconnaissance. We hurt them yesterday. We hurt them very badly, no question."

"We must have burned most of the town."

"Except the east side and the outlying farms. I didn't see any Cral get out of the barn, did you?"

"No, I thought we got the last six in the mines."

Lantid stared into the distance. "Six Cral – I can hardly believe it myself, but we don't know if they were the last – at least I don't."

Alehra said, "They can't have much left. They didn't counterattack."

Fargus said, "They were scared. I don't think their leaders had control, not even after we left. There was a lot of shouting. Blorfindel, did you hear what they said?"

"It was too confused."

Lantid continued, "So we need to find out what they have left and what they're doing."

Fargus asked, "Do you think they'll come back? It looked like they abandoned the town."

"We didn't do any harm to the mine or the bogs, or even the farms. That's what they really want. What will it take for them to rebuild?"

Nickadola said, "More dead trees."

"And time. Every day they delay is another day the Tafers of Dath train to defend themselves."

Blorfindel strung his bow. "Lurshod needs troops. Every couple of days, two weeks at the longest, a bunch of them die. Even if he is just trying to hold Jun, there's got to be a lot of deserters."

Alehra swung on her pack. "Well, let's go find out."

It was less than a mile before they scared up a Kutel. It was alone, apparently hiding, then burst into a run. One arrow killed it. Their trip to Jun was slowed by numerous stops along the way. Once they started looking, it seemed that every quarter mile they turned up a Kutel or two trying to hide. Whether they were trying to hide from the adventurers, the Kutel leader, or the summer sun it was difficult to tell. Few of them even woke up before they were discovered. Some of the Kutel ran, but none of them could outrun an arrow. By the time the group reached the clearing at the edge of Jun another thirty-four Kutel were dead.

The town appeared to be abandoned. The summer sun was hazy and low in front of them but somehow Jun did not appear to be asleep. It looked dead. Some of the fires were still burning, particularly near the mine. The smoke and the haze and the low sun gave the town a hellish aspect.

Blorfindel frowned. "That's odd: we lit the fires near the mines first. I would have expected them to burn out before the others."

"Piles of coal," Lantid responded. "Retteric only knows how long they'll burn."

Alehra asked, "Do we go door to door, or just light torches and finish the job?"

Fargus looked around. "Do you think it's a trap? It's awfully quiet."

They all studied the remains of the town for a moment. Blorfindel spoke. "Where would you put it? The trap, I mean. The farms – the barns, really – are the only place where you could hide a Cral anymore."

Lantid said, "The mines."

Nickadola smiled. "That worked out so well for them last time."

Blorfindel continued, "You can't put an ambush at every farm, they never had the troops for that, they certainly don't know. Where would you set up your defense, if you were the Kutel leader?" The question was directed at Lantid.

"Bur-Droo."

They all laughed, but Blorfindel pressed the question, "I'm serious. Lurshod is the real prize – or target or whatever – where is he?"

"He's lost over a dozen Cral. There are so many deserters that you can't walk a mile without tripping over one. He can't smelt iron, all his smelters are still burning. He can't forge weapons, the forges are burning too. All he's got left is the crop in the fields and the pigs we missed the first time, but like you said, he can't defend them. Even if he had weapons stored around town, they'd be damaged by the fires."

Fargus asked, "What if they're in buildings that didn't burn?"

"Then he can take them with him. He hasn't got soldiers to swing them, anyway. Maybe he can get a good price in Bur-Droo."

"You really think he's gone?"

Lantid nodded.

Alehra said, "I'd bait my ambush with the pigs. It's the most valuable thing they've got left."

Nickadola said, "I'm sure they'll be flattered to hear it." There was a long pause. "Lets break down some fences and open the barn doors. If there's an ambush, we'll find it."

"Yeah, when they jump out and surround us. No thanks."

"You can all stand back and watch. If they jump me, you counter-attack."

Blorfindel said, "I'll go. I can outrun them if they jump me." He started to take off his metal armor. "You stay hidden. I'll lead them back if they try anything. Just like the hill, I'll keep running if there's too many."

Alehra said, "There's a lot of open area out there. Keep your eyes open for archers."

"I will."

The barnyard raids met with no resistance. Some of the farmhouses still had Kutel in them, but they were not going to confront a raider; they were just glad not to be the target. All of the Kutel that saw him stayed hidden and hoped that he would not light any more fires. In an hour the pigs were free to roam. Few of them did.

When he came back Lantid said, "Lurshod's gone."

Fargus said, "Does that mean we've won? I mean, they can't be much of a threat to Dath now."

"Only if we're willing to let them go."

Blorfindel said, "You said the leader would have the best treasure."

"That's right, and he probably took it with him; all he could carry at least."

Fargus said, "Is that what this is about, money? I thought you were in it for Fithern pride or revenge."

"A bit of both now, but when I left Sekri Timbrali I didn't know I would be coming home. I need money. If I can get two hundred malstren then I can marry Afinlia and I'm not going back until I have it."

Alehra said, "I'm game. Let's go."

Lantid agreed, "I want the leader dead. If not, he may try to come back later. Is that a worthy enough cause for you, Fargus?"

The cleric sighed. "I'm not going to abandon you out here, anyway. If you're chasing, I'm chasing."

"Nickadola?"

"You went to the trouble to free the pigs for me. I can help run down the Kutel for you. Fair's fair, as they say. Besides, I still want to see how it ends."

"Back down the path, then."

They waited just long enough for Blorfindel to put his armor back on. As they walked away Lantid asked, "Can you make out any tracks?"

"Not on the path, it's too well worn. Do you think they went some other way?"

"Probably not, though it would be nice to know for sure. It's just possible that I'm wrong and they didn't go at all."

Alehra mocked him. "Just possible?"

He ignored her. "What I really want to know is how many are there and do they have any Cral with them?"

Nickadola said, "I'll ask."

"Not here. Let's go a little ways first. I don't want any of your small-brained friends to get confused by deserters and stragglers. Most of them can't count high enough, anyway."

If anyone expected Nickadola to be offended, he was not. "Let me know when you want to ask."

Less then half a mile down the path stood an ancient elm tree with a number of scars. In spite of the damage, it was still alive. The Tafers cringed when Nickadola asked, "Blorfindel, do you know this one?"

"It's old enough, but I don't remember the scars. They must be recent."

The Timble agreed. "None of them are very high up. Still, they've healed fairly well. They're certainly not new."

Lantid was trying to be patient. "I know you often come to a point eventually, but what is it?"

Nickadola asked, "Who scarred the tree?"

"The Kutel, who else? If it happened since Blorfindel left, it had to be the Kutel."

"How many scarred trees have we seen?"

"I don't know. The Kutel cut down trees all over the place."

"Right, they cut them down. They don't scar them. Even a giant like this is no match for a Kutel axe."

"So you want to talk to it?"

"Who knows, maybe it's learned to count better than a squirrel? It's had enough time to learn."

"Don't forget to ask about the Crals."

They all walked over to the tree with him. Blorfindel walked around, "Wow, the other side is worse. They're all about the same height though."

Lantid's curiosity got the better of him. "How long does it take a tree to grow that much?"

Blorfindel said, "When they're this old they don't grow much taller, just wider."

Nickadola looked at the other side. "It's hard to say. How high were they when they were made? If Blorfindel hadn't said otherwise, I might guess a hundred years." He cast his spell. "The Kutel went past last night, not long after the fires started. There were no Cral. Some were together, most were not."

"The ones that were together…"

"More than a tree-cutting party, maybe twice as many."

Alehra asked, "How many is that?"

Lantid was quick. "Sh! Fifteen to twenty per group. Armor? You know, like metal bark?"

Blorfindel said, "It's a tree, Lantid, not a fool."

"One for each of us. The Kutel did make the scars. It was before most of its neighbors emerged through the soil. The Fitherani were here then. The Kutel came and the Fitherani ran, all but one. One stayed to defend the tree. He shot many arrows, but when the Kutel shot the tree, the Fitheran gave up his bow and cut it in half. The blow marked the tree bark as well."

Alehra asked, "Why would he do that?"

This time it was Blorfindel. "Sh!"

Nickadola was only listening to the tree now, anyway. "The tree tried to protect him, but they all move too fast. It took some of the attacks for him. Then the Kutel surrounded him. The tree wanted to wrap its protective bark around him–"

"They can do that?"

"–but it happened too fast. It needed years, and the Kutel were done in seconds. They did not stay. Their leader ordered them away to light fires. The tree saved the bow. It has been watching the Kutel come and go ever since, waiting for the Fitherani to come back, wondering if they forgot."

"We haven't forgotten." Blorfindel spoke directly to the tree in Timbrali, "I haven't forgotten."

Nickadola continued to speak for the elm. "Have you come to stay?"

"Not yet. I'm alone. I can't come to stay yet."

"It is sad."

"I'm sorry."

Fargus asked Blorfindel, "Who was it? Did you know him?"

"I don't know. It could have been anyone."

Suddenly the tree bark split open, and a vertical seam of nearly six feet appeared. Even Nickadola gasped. His spell did not do that. Slowly, a wooden object flowed out through the seam. Blorfindel caught it as it fell. It was a bow. The bark closed leaving yet another scar.

"Ermingo Coldheart. This is his bow."

Alehra said, "I thought he cut it in half?"

Nickadola was still wide eyed, but he asked the tree and got an answer. "The tree grew it back together. It took years to grow it into its bark, and years more to put it together."

"I can't take this. He should keep it."

Nickadola was the tree's voice again. "Trees grow bows. Fitherani use them. The bow is made. Keep it from the Kutel, that was his wish." Nickadola shook his head and spoke for himself, "I'm sorry, my spell ran out."

Blorfindel held the bow in both hands like a plain branch. "I can't take it."

Fargus asked, "Why not?"

"It was Ermingo's. It wouldn't be right. Besides, I have a bow."

Lantid remarked, "Not one given to you by a tree."

"All bows are given by trees, or taken from them."

"You know what I mean!"

"All Fithern bows are given by trees, not taken. A Fitheran will search for years for a tree that wants to become a bow, or that grows a branch to become a bow. This tree is a little more dramatic than most, that's all. Some Fitherani will grow a tree to be a bow, but a lot of Fitherani think wild bows are better than domesticated. Mine is wild."

Fargus said, "Ermingo Coldheart; it doesn't sound very nice."

"No one told me why. I guess I was too young."

"Who was he?"

"He was the best archer in Foralis."

Alehra remembered the conversation in the river. "Better than your mother?"

"Yes, the only one. They didn't get along, I think – or maybe it was my father he didn't like. That's another reason why I can't take the bow."

Nickadola said, "We can't leave it. The Kutel might find it."

Alehra finally realized. "That's why he cut it in half! He didn't want the Kutel to get it!"

Lantid said, "I don't want the Kutel to get it, either. I don't want to get shot with it."

Alehra asked, "Any reason why I can't use it?"

Nickadola said, "The tree might object."

"It's not like I asked a tree if it wanted to be my old bow, you know?"

Blorfindel shrugged, "Why not take it? You're going to shoot Kutel with it anyway. You don't have to worry about Ermingo's ghost."

"Because he hasn't got one, I know." She unpacked a spare bowstring and strung the bow. She pulled it once before drawing an arrow. It was stronger than her bow, but not by a great deal. She could handle the extra pull. "It's going to take some getting used to." She ran her hand along it, "It feels new."

"It might be the oldest thing in the forest, after the rocks. Ermingo was not a young Fitheran. I don't know how long he could make a bow last."

"Not a young Fitheran as in…"

"They say that he walked in the unbroken shade of the trees from Sekri Timbrali to Foralis when the town was founded."

"But The Shield Valley is in between."

"It is now."

They all knew how old Fitherani could live to be, but they did not really understand what that meant. Even Lantid found it hard to imagine that Ermingo Coldheart might have shot this bow before his country, his culture, or his language was formed.

Blorfindel called them all back to the present, "We should go. The Kutel leader is getting away."

Lantid laughed. "You can bet he's not stopping to talk to the trees."

They walked into the night. When they got back to the point where they had hidden the Kutel weapons, Blorfindel looked for a spare dagger. "It's gone." The others checked some of the places they had hidden weapons. Most of them were gone.

Nickadola said, "They were here recently."

Alehra said, "We know that."

Lantid said, "But if they stopped to hunt for weapons that took time, time we can use to catch up."

They did not catch up that night. When morning dawned in front of them they set camp. Their eagerness could only push them so far, and they were spent. Sleep seemed to come and go in a blink. Lantid had them back up and moving long before the sun set.

Fargus asked, "How hard to you think the Kutel are pushing?"

Lantid replied, "We haven't passed a campsite, yet."

Blorfindel disagreed, "Yes, we did. They just don't have a camp to set. They slept among the corpses near the weapons. Didn't you notice?"

"I guess I didn't think to look there."

Alehra had her hand over her mouth. "Why would they camp there?"

Nickadola said, "To hide. They're hoping that we wouldn't look there, or maybe if we did we would think they were corpses, too."

"The Kutel are pretty nasty, but they don't look like a three-week-old corpse."

"That's where they spent the day."

The group walked all evening and into the night. Well before midnight they found three more Kutel corpses. Each had a great gash on its head or chest. These were fresh. Blorfindel said, "Three hours at most."

Nickadola was examining the area. "This is where they spent the day. If they waited until dark to move, then we're only a few hours behind them."

Alehra asked, "What killed them?"

Blorfindel was surprised. "I know its dark, but can't you see–"

"I can see their wounds, but who did it?"

Lantid said, "Probably Lurshod. He needs to get some discipline into his mob. He's lost a lot of soldiers and probably a lot of prestige, maybe someone thought they didn't have to take orders."

As they were walking away Fargus asked, "So what does that tell us?"

"His troops are unruly and he's getting them under control. No surprise there, I guess. Probably if we can split them off they'll run. They're just more afraid of him right now, but if it looks like he's going to lose…"

"I wonder if he knows he's being followed."

"He's got to at least suspect. If they slept next to those corpses, he knows the path isn't safe."

Within an hour they found another group of Kutel corpses lying around the path. They looked to be weeks-old as well. They certainly smelled that way, and it appeared that the vultures and crows had picked some of them over.

Blorfindel started to walk over to examine them. "Did they carry some of the corpses?"

"Maybe they think we are tracking them by scent?" Nickadola offered.

Even as he said it, the nearest corpse stood and took a step toward Blorfindel. It's head flopped backwards on a broken neck, but that did not seem to hinder it at all. The other six also stood and rushed to surround him. They held weapons, but it seemed that they had forgotten what do to with them.

Fargus' voice boomed through the trees: "Your power is gone!" The others were startled both by the strength of his voice and the words that he chose. More startling still, the corpses fell where they stood as if a puppeteer's strings had been cut. Blorfindel jumped back and drew his swords, but it seemed the danger was gone.

The others turned to Fargus. He said, "The Kutel have a priest with them – a Baett worshiper, very likely, but it could be their fire god, or lightning god... they have many whose names are not spoken in civilized places. Many of them will raise the dead to do their will."

Lantid was the first to speak, "What did you do? That wasn't a spell."

"These abominations cannot stand in Feadin's light. I am just a path for that light."

"What happens now?"

"We keep going. The power that animated them is broken. They will decay again."

They returned to their march.

"I knew it could be done," Nickadola said, "but I had never seen it. Dhu doesn't get involved in this sort of thing. It seems to belong to another word and Dhu is rooted in this one."

"It is the power of a dark world that animates them, and a light world that drives them back. Actually, I thought that they might just go away – leave us alone. I've never seen them before, but Litne told me what to do years ago."

Lantid thought a moment. "They were put here to stop us, or slow us down."

"That didn't work."

"No, but it does tell us that they expect us, and that they have some cleric with them. What can he do?"

Fargus answered, "He's probably making the poison for their arrows most of the time. Most of them don't heal – can't heal – I'm not certain. It probably varies with god and worshiper. Whatever he is, he's been there all along. Whatever he can do, he has been doing it the whole time. If you see him, he'll stand out – probably with a ceremonial weapon or headdress." Fargus touched the dove symbol on the brow of his helmet.

Chapter 25

Lurshod's Stand

Though they traveled well into the heat of the next morning, they did not catch the Kutel. Alehra shook her head. "How long can they keep this up?"

Of all of them, Lantid suffered from fatigue the worst. He was leaning on Sturdifoot. "How long can we keep this up?"

"Do you want to quit?"

"No, I want to rest."

They set a hasty camp on the spot. Blorfindel was too fatigued to even eat more than a bite. He could not remember laying down when Nickadola woke him for his watch. Less than an hour later, Blorfindel woke Alehra. He whispered, "I hear something. I'm going to go check it out." He waited until she was fully awake and armed before he snuck off into the trees. It was about an hour after noon.

When he came back he whispered, "Wake the others."

"What is it?"

"The Kutel are close."

When Lantid stumbled out of his tent he asked, "How close?"

Blorfindel clapped his hand over the wizards mouth and whispered in his ear, "Close enough to hear you if the wind dies down." It was true. They had made their camp within a hundred yards of the Kutel. The trees between them muffled and masked the sound, but two Kutel had broken out in an argument and Blorfindel's Fithern hearing had picked up their rough voices.

They moved a short distance away, took cover and spoke in whispers. They were all tired. At most, they had slept for less than three hours since their long march. Nickadola was the most fatigued, having stood first watch. He asked the leaf-lined ground, "Are we going to attack them now?"

Lantid answered, "If we wait, we run the risk of them finding us."

Without another word the Timble found a live oak leaf and cast his refreshing spell on everyone. It replaced an hour and a half of sleep that they did not have. When the spell was complete the others were ready to fight. For Nickadola it was just enough so that he could think properly.

Blorfindel explained what he saw, "They have a lot of sentries up – at least five, probably more. I didn't circle around. There was one in mail, but I don't think it was the leader. If I had to guess I'd say all of them are taking a watch, split five or six ways. It looks like all Kutel, no Crals or Varren."

Lantid said, "If the tree's count can be trusted, they had forty-five, maximum, when they left town. They killed three."

Fargus said, "They might have picked up some deserters along the way."

"Maybe. How far apart are the sentries?"

"Twenty to thirty feet to the one next to them, fifty or sixty between the farthest two I saw. The mailed one gave them impossible orders."

"How so?"

"They're all supposed to be hidden, but he wants to be able to see them to be sure they're not asleep."

"I can't hit an area that big. Nickadola?"

"What? A twenty yard circle? No, it's too big."

Blorfindel said, "Some of that fog would be really handy. Maybe we could knock off a couple before the others noticed."

Nickadola shook his head, "I didn't prepare for that spell today."

Alehra asked, "What if we bait them out, make them move to us?"

Fargus did not think it would work. "Why would they chase us? They're running away. They're more likely to go in the other direction."

Lantid said, "We won't catch any asleep that way, rather they charge or flee."

Blorfindel glanced in the direction of the Kutel camp. "I don't think we can knock all of the sentries down before they raise the alarm, anyway.

There's got to be at least one or two I didn't see, even if we could take all five."

"Which we can't," Alehra said.

Lantid had an idea. "Then we'll have to gamble a little."

Blorfindel was standing on a tree branch overlooking the Kutel camp. He was in plain view, but the Kutel on watch were scanning the ground. None of them wanted to look up into the bright sky beyond the shade of the leaves. The sun was high over his head. Nickadola and the Tafers were scattered and hidden across the path from the Kutel camp. Lantid's plan had spread his friends very thinly around the Kutel camp, but no one had a better idea.

Blorfindel had a rope secured to another sturdy branch above him. It was already wrapped around him so that he could rappel down any second. He was too easy to surround in the tree. He put arrow to string and waited. His first shot was the hardest, but it was also the only one that would have total surprise.

Yurthun, the Kutel lieutenant on duty for this watch, turned to look west. He had to be careful not to look up, the sun gave him a headache. He saw something odd hanging in the trees. *That looks like a rope.* When he squinted for a better look he heard a terrifying sound. A bowstring's song was the last thing he ever heard.

Blorfindel had been waiting for the Kutel to face him and stand still. He wanted to have a shot at its exposed face. Blorfindel's powerful bow drove the arrow through its skull. The Kutel's helmet could not even stop the arrow point on the way out.

A sentry on the eastern edge of the camp was first to turn to the sound. He saw an arrow head pointing grotesquely from the lieutenant's helmet. He couldn't understand why it would be a Kutel-made arrow point.

Blorfindel's second arrow hit the sentry across the camp. His aim was a bit lower and the arrow went though its slack jaw. Its death was not quick enough to suit either the Fitheran or the Kutel. Blorfindel had already drawn his third arrow before either Kutel hit the ground.

Most of the Kutel sentries had heard the bow. All of them heard the lieutenant hit the ground. Some shouted. Some ran. Some tried to take better cover. Only one had a good idea of where the attacker was. It pressed itself against a tree and screamed for help.

Blorfindel's third arrow hit another sentry in the back of the neck. It had taken cover from the wrong direction. The sleeping Kutel started to wake. He shot arrows into them as quickly as he could aim. Those Kutel who stood up started to fall from arrows from the northeast as Alehra added Ermingo's bow to the confusion.

Then the Kutel leader was awake. "Shields! You bog-heads, shields!" Blorfindel turned to shoot where the order came from, but all he could see was a shield. Alehra's view was obscured by a tree. The plan said that they should shoot the leader as soon as they could find him, but he was not playing along. Blorfindel loosed two more arrows before the Kutel camp turned into a wall of shields. *Time to go.* He started his rappel down the tree. Suddenly, everything went black. Rappelling on feel, he was down the tree in two bounds and hit the ground. At the base of the tree it was light again. Alehra stood ready with her bow as Blorfindel dashed across the path to where the others were waiting, but the Kutel were staring at the black blotch in the tree where the Fitheran used to be.

Lantid watched the Kutel react. Part one of the plan had been a success: they had seriously confused the Kutel and reduced their numbers. Part two had failed: the Kutel leader was still alive. Part three, panicking the rank and file, was not going to work until they silenced the leader.

Lurshod, the Kutel leader, knew that he was being ambushed. He tried not to do what the enemy expected. The arrows caused harm, but could not stop him. *They want me to charge them,* he thought as he shrugged on his mail. "Form a circle on me! Keep your shields up! Rungut, kill your darkness spell, it's not blinding them, it's hiding them! Muuk, how many do we have left?"

Lantid watched under the blotch as the Kutel formed a circle. He waved Blorfindel and Alehra to him, then cast his sleep spell just as the darkness dissipated. The Kutel shield wall came down as seven of them fell asleep. Two arrows immediately flew into the gap. One hit a Kutel in the back and killed it. The other knocked a little statue off a lieutenant's helmet. More shields filled in, but there were still gaps. Two more arrows followed, but they could not see what they hit.

Some of the Kutel panicked. "A wizard! We're all doomed! Run!"

"Shut up!" The leader punched one in the face. "They're just asleep!" He grabbed another by the shoulder, "Go wake them up! Muuk! I'm waiting!"

Blorfindel got a shot at a Kutel as it bent to wake the others. It woke two when its dead body fell on them. Alehra shot one of the sleeping Kutel. After a few spear-prods and the odd kick all of the other Kutel were awake.

Muuk, one of the Kutel lieutenants, finished his count, "Three, twenty-two, and seventeen. Yurthun's dead."

"I can see that! Put your armor on! Fool!"

Blorfindel reported to the others, "They still have more than forty left." His next arrow stuck in a shield.

Lantid said to himself, "They're not following the plan."

Blorfindel shot as a lieutenant raised its hands above the shield wall to put on its mail shirt. The arrow collected a finger bone on its way by.

The Kutel leader shrugged at his losses. *Yurthun might make a difference.* He did not care about the others; he had planned to kill them later anyway. *I wonder how many arrows they have?* He dismissed the idea. *We can't just stand here and soak up arrows. We cannot charge them without fighting in trees.* "Ready the bows! Thornak, get a group to go around to the left – no, left is that way! Rungut, get a group to go right! Send them! I want you two here with me! Muuk! Pay attention!" He drew his sword and cut the mangled finger from his lieutenant's hand, "Wrap it up! And pay attention! Get the archers going! Anything in front, if it moves, it dies!"

Blorfindel tried to shoot a Kutel in the foot. The arrow hit a root and fluttered sideways into its neighbor's shield. "They're trying to flank us."

Alehra shot, "I've got fifteen–" <Twang-vss-thock> "–fourteen, coming right!"

Lantid cast a spell and jumped into the path, "Arrows!" One struck his shield spell. Another put a hole in his robe below his knee. He could feel it burn on its way past. "Crushk!" He had to see them to stop them. Blorfindel put an arrow into another shield gap. Again, he had no way of knowing if it did any harm.

Arrows were shot in both directions for no effect. Two more bounced off Lantid's spell. Blorfindel and Alehra sent arrows into the Kutel groups, but none dropped. There was another quick exchange of poorly aimed arrows while Nickadola convinced the trees to stop the flankers, first on the left, then on the right. The nearest Kutel was ten feet from Alehra when an oak snatched it up.

Lantid took that as his cue. For the first time in his life he cast a third spell in a single day. The shields in front of the Kutel archers dropped again. Alehra and Blorfindel shot at the two Kutel archers who were now exposed. They both hit the same one, in the arm and in the thigh.

Lurshod raised his own shield and shouted, "Wake them up!" There was no time. Two arrows struck the second Kutel archer in the back as it turned to run. It was still spinning when it hit the ground.

With the front line down the adventurers could see that the back line of Kutel had been stripped to make the flanking groups. Nickadola ran around the moving trees and moved to flank the Kutel. Fargus saw him going and charged straight at the Kutel. "Feadin!" He hoped to distract them long enough for the Timble to cross the path unseen.

Blorfindel and Alehra were as shocked as the Kutel when Fargus charged. None of this was in the plan. Both dropped their bows and drew steel as they charged. Fargus arrived first.

Muuk stepped up to face the crazy Tafer. Thornak and Rungut were on his flanks. He raised his shield to block the mace and stabbed with his sword. The bandage made his grip awkward.

Fargus knocked the sword aside with his shield and swung his mace in a hook that crushed both of the Kutel's knees. He shoved the Kutel over backwards and kept on moving. He stepped on its face on the way by and tripped when its neck snapped.

Thornak and Rungut had no time to attack the Tafer's back. They had to defend themselves against a Fitheran and a Taforam. Still, they were happy to be in sword range. *You've had your chance with your tricks and your little arrows. Now it's our turn.* The first engagement did not dampen their enthusiasm. They both stopped the on-rushers cold and threw them back with their heavy shields. Thornak's sword skipped off the top of a round shield. Rungut's struck armor but did not penetrate.

Fargus got up and started crushing sleeping Kutel. He was shocked when he looked up and saw the Kutel leader standing very near, kicking them. For a moment it was a race, but Fargus had the advantage. He crushed two Kutel as they were waking up. They both reached the last sleeper together. The Kutel leader hacked at Fargus while he kicked. Fargus took the blow on the shield as he crushed the last of the sleeping Kutel. Then the Kutel leader hit him in the right side with its shield and sent him sprawling.

Alehra made a feint to her opponent's face and struck the Kutel leader in the side of the head with edge of her shield. She knocked it off its feet and saved Fargus, but in doing so she left herself wide open. She gave ground and parried frantically, trying to recover while the Kutel attacking her pressed its advantage.

Blorfindel saw none of this. The elite Kutel had surprised him with both its strength and skill. The Fitheran had another card to play: speed. The Kutel jumped at him with an overhead stroke. Blorfindel waited until the last instant to step aside. While he guided the Kutel's sword past with his own, he jabbed his short sword at its ribs on its right side. The Kutel parried with its shield. *That's done it.* Blorfindel did not have time to smile. He held the Kutel's sword down with his own and looped his short sword around to the other side of its shield. The Kutel moved the shield enough to cover, but now its arms were crossed tightly against its body. Blorfindel hooked the shield and shoved it left.

Rungut had to disentangle himself. He jumped back and spun right. His sword sang through the air just above the Fitheran's waist height, but when his eyes came around the Fitheran was not there. Suddenly his extended right elbow exploded in pain. His eyes followed the sword point from his elbow to the Fitheran, somehow behind him and at full lunge. He reversed his spin and got his shield between its short sword and his kidney. He could barely hold onto his sword. He knew his end was near.

Blorfindel was surprised by how long the Kutel held out purely on defense. It had no strength to attack with its sword, that was clear, but its shield covered it from ankle to shoulders and was a heavy club if he let himself get too close. Eventually he caught its sword between his own and kicked the Kutel's wounded elbow. His shin was bruised on the side of the Kutel's shield, but the sword came away. From there it was a simple matter. He stabbed over the Kutel's shield with his short sword and down with his long sword. The Kutel could only block one and wisely protected its face, but the long sword staked its foot to the ground until Blorfindel withdrew. With a hole in its foot Blorfindel easily got behind it and delivered the final blow with his short sword. As before, the rings of the Kutel's armor could not stop the strong, narrow point.

Blorfindel turned to see Fargus trying to defend himself against the Kutel leader. He was clearly losing. The cleric's helmet was bent at the cheek piece and his face was bleeding. There was another cut on the back of his mace wrist. Alehra was still working hard to hold off the other Kutel's attacks, but she was catching up. Blorfindel saw a third Kutel coming at her from behind. "Cruska!" He made a running attack at it and slashed open its throat. He turned to help Fargus as quickly as he could, but now he was too far away.

As Blorfindel raced to aid his friends time seemed to compress and every step was an eternity. In horror, he watched his waking nightmare play out in a few running steps. He was seven steps from the Kutel leader when he saw Nickadola sneaking up behind it. He was five steps away when the other Kutel lieutenant saw the Timble. It shouted, "Behind d'aaah!" It's warning died as Alehra stuck her sword completely through its right thigh just left of the bone and with a flick hamstrung it from in front. It should never have taken its eyes off her.

Blorfindel was not looking at Alehra or her opponent. He was still three steps away. The Kutel leader stepped sideways, guiding Fargus' mace away with its shield. At the same time it swung its sword backwards at the half-glimpsed Timble. Nickadola raised his shield but he could not stop the powerful, unexpected blow. The sword struck him on the bridge of the nose and cut deep into his skull.

Even as the Kutel leader turned to face Blorfindel, the Fitheran knew that Nickadola would not rise. In his anger his attacks were blind fury. His long sword slid against the Kutel's shield, the short sword turned on the Kutel's sword. Blorfindel's charge carried him past the Kutel and the Kutel turned with him.

Fargus slammed his mace down on the Kutel's left shoulder with all his might. He did not even realize that the battle cry he heard was his own until after he felt the Kutel's collarbone give.

Lurshod threw his weight at the Tafer and once again knocked him off his feet, but it was too late. His shoulder would barely hold his shield anymore, and he could not turn it quickly enough. He turned and backpedaled toward the Taforam, dragging his shield. *At least I won't be killed by a Fitheran,* he thought. He was wrong.

Blorfindel launched himself at the Kutel again. He turned its sword away with his short sword. His long sword point was aimed at the eye slit in the Kutel's helmet, and this time it could not raise its shield fast enough. The Kutel flinched away, but Blorfindel expected that. He followed it and followed through as it fell backward until his sword point was pushing the back of the Kutel's skull into the ground. He could hear Alehra and Fargus behind him as he ground his teeth and grimly waited for the Kutel to die. He did not withdraw the blade until the Kutel stopped thrashing.

"Heal him!"

"It's too late."

"Damn it, try!"

Fargus' voice was low and quiet, "It doesn't work that way. He's gone. Even if I could put his… heal his flesh, I can't put life in him. Maybe Litne could do something if he was here, but I doubt it."

Blorfindel half turned and stared into space. He did not want to look. Suddenly he looked around, but not down. He could hear footsteps running away. He could see nothing moving. Finally his gaze was drawn down. Alehra and Fargus knelt by Nickadola with their heads bowed. Dead Kutel were strewn everywhere. All was still. Even the trees stopped. "Lantid!"

They found him face down in the path. He was alive, but unmoving. Fargus looked him over and found only a small cut on his calf. Blorfindel picked up a piece of a Kutel arrow which had broken on Lantid's spell, "Poison!"

Alehra asked Fargus, "Can you do anything about poison?"

"No, not really. I can heal the damage if he survives, but the poison's got to run its course. You really did need Litne here today, not me."

She grabbed the cleric by the armor and shook him. "You're what we've got! What do you know about Kutel poison?"

"Nothing." He crumpled to one knee, defeated. "Priests of Feadin don't handle poison: it's dangerous. Even the poisoner nicks himself every now and then– The Kutel Priest! If anyone has an antidote, he does!"

Alehra looked around frantically. "I didn't see a priest. Which one is it?"

"Look for a ceremonial headdress or weapon."

Blorfindel shook his head. "I didn't see anything like that. Do you think he got away?"

"Even if he did, he left his kit – they all did. Check the bags for a Totem. He has to have something for a shrine."

Alehra ran to the middle of the Kutel camp and started looking through the bags. Fargus was behind her. "Look for the best bags. He was probably the second most privileged Kutel in Jun.

Blorfindel surveyed the Kutel bodies, looking for the priest. What he found was a roughly-carved obsidian statue of a Kutel, about four inches tall with its feet broken off. He held it up. "What's this?"

"That's it! Where did that come from?" Fargus ran to Blorfindel but spoke to over his shoulder to Alehra, "Your looking for an unholy symbol of Baett."

"What does that mean?"

"The ugliest doll you've ever seen." He got to Blorfindel. "It's broken. It must have broken off something. The feet are probably still attached to whatever it came from." Blorfindel started looking at the Kutel on the ground. Fargus was torn, "It will have good armor."

Alehra shouted, "I found a metal box! It's heavy."

"Be careful! Don't open it!"

"It's locked, anyway." She shook it. "It sounds like coin."

Fargus cringed. "Don't do that! The antidote could well be in a glass vial. It will break!"

Blorfindel's search brought him to Rungut's corpse. The obsidian feet were still attached to his helmet. "Got it!"

Fargus came running. "A vial, or a pouch, or even a little water skin – maybe an animal bladder." Blorfindel was already stripping the body.

There were three bones hanging from its sword belt – parts of bones, really. They had been cut off cleanly, not broken, and the marrow-hole was plugged with a bone stopper covered with wax. Fargus reached for one then stopped short. His eyes fixed on the dead Kutel's chest. "That's got to be it!"

Rungut had a thong around his neck. Even his Kutel skin was raw from it. The rough thong held a jewel which was clearly not of the same make, or even Kutel-made. It had a diamond in the center which was set in a much larger red spinel, all surrounded by smaller diamonds in a gold setting in the shape of a teardrop. The teardrop point was bent over to accept the thong. Fargus pulled the thong over the dead Kutel's head.

"Are you sure that's it?" Blorfindel asked.

"Who hides jewelry? He wore it under his armor, under his clothes – he has marks on his chest from where it rubbed." Fargus ran to Lantid. "Diamond for purity; spinel for blood – just like his family sword! The gold isn't even scratched from the iron armor. Don't open the bones – they're probably full of poison!"

Fargus touched the jewel to Lantid's throat. Alehra stood over and looped the thong over his head.

Lantid mumbled, "Weak." They turned him over and sat him up. He looked like he just had a bad coughing fit, but his color was returning. "Did we win?"

No one wanted to answer that question. *Is this victory?* Blorfindel wondered.

Fargus said, "The Kutel leader is dead. The ones in the trees must have run away when the trees let go. We're the only ones alive here." He touched his cheek as if just noticing his own wound. A salty tear ran into the cut.

Even in his weakened state Lantid recognized that something was wrong. He looked at each of their faces and came up one short. "Nickadola?"

Chapter 26

Final Task

They helped Lantid over to Nickadola's body. All four of them stared at it for a time. Eventually Alehra slapped Fargus' armored shoulder. "You should heal yourself. You're bleeding." While the cleric was casting his spell she asked, "What to we do with him?"

Blorfindel brought the cleanest Kutel shield he could find. Fargus arranged the body on it. Blorfindel put his scimitar in its scabbard on his belt and took his sling. "It should go back to his parents, I think."

Lantid's head was already clearing, though he was still too weak to stand. "I guess we bury him. Have we still got the pick?"

Fargus asked, "Out here? This isn't hallowed ground or anything."

Blorfindel sighed. "I think it is to him – in the forest. The trees won't soon forget him." The others nodded.

"The pick is back at camp," Alehra said. "We can carry him that far. We shouldn't bury him with the Kutel, anyway. The tree said they foul the ground, remember?" She could hardly believe she remembered it.

Alehra and Fargus carried the shield with Nickadola. Blorfindel half-carried Lantid to camp. Lantid was leaning heavily on the Fitheran when he said softly, "I'm sorry, I know it's my fault. My plan didn't work–"

Blorfindel interrupted, "No. It's not your fault. You did the best you could."

"But it wasn't–"

"No! Nickadola told me himself, after my incident with the tree. He wouldn't blame you. He was clear on that. We all took the risks. He knew them as well as any of us. It's the Kutel's fault, and that's all."

"Bless him for that," Fargus said. They took a few steps in silence. "It's Baett's fault, too. Dhu isn't supposed to allow that."

They set Nickadola down next to a big oak tree. Sturdifoot pulled his lead free from the bush that held it, walked over, and nuzzled the body. By the time Alehra got the pick out of the baggage, seven wolves – two adult and five young – came plodding down the path. They sat in a group and stared. Alehra muttered bitterly as she started to break the earth between two large roots, "Where were you an hour ago?"

An owl flew in and landed in the tree. Blorfindel was surprised to see it out in the daylight. He was more surprised when it released a live squirrel from it's talons. The squirrel ran down the tree and stood on the root between Alehra and Nickadola. Blorfindel put his hand on her shoulder and pulled her gently away. "Something's happening." She let the pick fall from her hands as she backed away.

A murder of crows circled and landed in the oak tree. They looked down with a solemnity that only crows can master. A moment later, a duck landed noisily in the leaves nearby, waddled over, and hopped on the edge of the shield.

An enormous bear walked from behind the stunned adventurers and sat to their left, facing Nickadola. Lantid said, "That's the bear from the pass near The Hunt. How long was I unconscious?"

Fargus answered, "You haven't lost consciousness, or we all have. This is all very strange."

Clouds passed over the sun, dimming the forest slightly. Though they had seen it happen many, many times before, this time it seemed purposeful somehow. A gentle rain started to fall and each leaf had its own sound. Blorfindel felt that they were speaking, or singing, but the words did not come through.

Lantid said, "I feel like the old elm tree could come walking down the path any minute."

Alehra did not turn away from Nickadola when she replied, "It wouldn't make this any weirder."

Blorfindel took off his helmet and listened. "Something is coming." Almost as soon as he said it, the others could hear it, too. Before he could say, "Hoofbeats," it was there. It was gold and white, so bright it was hard to see clearly. The raindrops steamed from its pure white coat and splashed off a single golden horn.

The unicorn bowed and lightly touched its horn to Nicadola's mangled face. The light seemed drawn out of its body and into the horn, then the light passed into the Timble and rested in the wound on his face. Then the unicorn spoke. "There is one more thing that must be done–"

Already stunned, Blorfindel, Alehra and Fargus were even more shocked when Lantid interrupted. "In Dath, I know. I've been meaning to, but we've been busy."

The unicorn fixed him with its gaze. "You accept this task as your own?"

"Yes, certainly if it's going to get us Nickadola back. You are giving him back, right?"

The unicorn then nodded its head and turned. It pranced a half-circle around the group then galloped away into the forest like a streak of lightning.

"Hey, that's a unicorn!" It was Nickadola's voice.

They did not now whether to laugh or cry or hug or dance or sing or shout. They did all of that, in no particular order. They had to tell the story to Nickadola over and over again.

"An owl releasing a squirrel unharmed? That would be something to see! Look how the cubs have grown! I worried about you, you know? And you, bear, you came all this way? Did anyone show the crows to the dead Kutel?"

Apart from a silver-gray scar, or scab, across his face, Nickadola seemed unhurt. They walked together, through the rain, to the battle sight – from squirrel to bear, all of them. The adventurers picked over the Kutel corpses before the scavengers started on them. Alehra took a key from Lurshod's body and went to open the strong box.

"Wait! What are you doing?" Fargus rushed over.

"I'm opening it. Is that sacrilege or something?"

"No. Remember the door at the house? Be careful."

Blorfindel said, "Don't open it here, anyway. We can carry it back in the box." The crows had already stolen away a few of the bright coins that he had pulled from the Kutel.

The duck was the first to leave. Then they looked around and the squirrel was gone. The owl went to sleep on a tree branch nearby. The bear, the wolves, and even the crows ate their fill and moved on.

The group packed as much of the valuables as they could carry and walked as far down the path as their remaining strength allowed. They did not hurry, though they did not even look in on Jun; they could see the smoke was still rising. Nor did they stop at the house. They avoided it.

Although Fargus had long since healed their physical wounds, none of them wanted another battle. They took five days to return to Dath. They did not even announce themselves; they just went to the barn.

Finally, Fargus and Blorfindel let Alehra open the strongbox. It was trapped, but the trap was set to go off only if the lock was broken or picked, and they had the key. Before she set the trap out of the way it was clear that this was a big haul. Even Lantid, who had predicted the leader's riches, was surprised. Lantid had to light his lamp so that they could keep counting into the night. The wizard did the math. "Split five ways, it comes to just over two hundred twenty-six malstren each."

Alehra said to Blorfindel, "You got enough."

All Blorfindel could do was smile.

Lantid woke Blorfindel and Alehra that night. Nickadola was already awake. After nearly a week of healing spells, the mark on his face remained unchanged. The moonlight lit it like the bark of a silver birch.

Lantid whispered, "There's something I have to do. Don't wake Fargus. I don't think he'd understand."

They moved stealthily to the river. There was a Tafer lookout posted in town, but he was easily avoided. Lantid brought them to a halt at the sawmill. He opened the door quietly and said, "Make sure there's no one in there."

Blorfindel could see that the mill was deserted, but they checked every hiding place they could find, anyway. Nickadola escorted out a stray cat. When they were done Lantid sent them outside to keep watch. They could hear him cast a spell. Suddenly the mill burst into flames. His eyebrows were smoldering when he came out, but he could not help but smile. First Blorfindel, then Alehra smiled, too. Nickadola was weeping. They made no pretense of stealth as they walked away.

The watch could hardly miss the conflagration. The four sat on a slight rise overlooking the fire as the local Tafers poured out of their homes. Soon Shieldmaster Terak appeared and started organizing a bucket brigade. Lantid stood up. "We mustn't have that." The others followed.

Before the first splash of water hit the mill all twelve Tafers of the bucket brigade fell suddenly asleep. Lantid said, "Let it burn."

Alehra pulled the nearest Tafer away from the fire while Blorfindel stepped between Lantid and Terak. They could see Fargus running up in the darkness as well. Clearly the Shieldmaster did not understand. "We still might save it! I know it looks bad, but we have to try!"

Blorfindel drew his swords. "Let the tree-eating abomination burn to the sap-soaked ground."

Terak stood there with his mouth open. Lantid tried to explain, "He gave up his life for your little town. Your town can give up its sawmill for him."

"Who? What are you talking about?"

Nickadola spoke, "He's means me."

Lantid added, "He died saving your town from the Kutel. I made a deal to get him back: the sawmill must go."

"I told you, we need the mill."

Blorfindel did not raise his voice, but he Tafers standing around shrank from it. "Then your town is doomed. I will be back, Shieldmaster Terak, and if you, or your son, or your grandson, for a thousand years, if any of you rebuilt this mill there will be blood to go with the ashes. This I swear."

Fargus was uncomfortable with the situation, but there was only one side he could take. "The Kutel town is burnt. Their leader is dead. The Cral are all dead too, I think. If Nickadola hadn't come, the Kutel would have burned the mill, anyway – along with the rest of the town. One mill is a small price to pay. Lots of towns live without a sawmill. In fact, I've never heard of one before." He looked into the flames. "I hope I never hear of one again."

The adventurers returned to the barn. They kept watches for the rest of the night, but the Tafers of Dath stayed in their homes. In the morning they packed up to leave.

"Do you think there'll be trouble with the locals?" Lantid asked.

Alehra shook her head. "They'd have to be crazy."

Most of Dath was waiting outside the barn when they stepped out. Blorfindel and Alehra both drew their swords. The crowd cheered. Shieldmaster Terak was absent from the celebration, but very few others were. They did not care about the mill. They heard that they Kutel were gone. They heard that their homes were safe. They heard that their children were safe. They heard that they could harvest in peace. They heard that they could go back to normal life again. They heard that five heroes had done what the Shieldmaster and the King could not, or would not do.

The heroes were drawn into the celebration like a stream into a river. The local ale flowed, and they stayed one day longer than they had planned.

Two slow days later they were at Taferford. They sold the last of their Kutel goods in the little market there and spent the profits on anything that caught their eye. Nickadola talked them into eating at The Muskrat, a Timblish inn. The Tafers had never been to the Timble lands and they felt very awkward and out of place. Everyone and everything seemed to be in miniature. The only thing they could get in Tafer size was a meal. It was, they all agreed, the best meal they had ever had. The Timble-sized drinks, however, would not do. The party moved across the river to The Bee Hound, where a meed horns and ale mugs were taller than the chairs at The Muskrat.

After a the first round Alehra asked, "What happens next?"

"I'm going home," Blorfindel smiled a far away smile, "to get married and live happily ever after."

Fargus raised his glass with a short laugh, "I'm going home to get some sleep."

Nickadola followed suit and made it a toast, "Home!" They all drank.

Lantid said, "I think I will go back to The Hunt. What about you, Al?"

"I think I can find something to do. There's a lot of the world I haven't seen yet."

The wizard said, "You're welcome to come with me. There's never a shortage of action at The Hunt."

"Thanks, but I don't know. I think I should be moving on. I want to see the Conjinese Empire."

"Why?" Blorfindel asked.

"Because I haven't seen it yet."

Just then two newcomers entered the common room from the street. "Hollenwae!" Alehra said, "You're a long way from home! Come and join the party!"

The two Hollenwae set their burdens down and bowed stiffly. They would have been impossible to tell apart if they wore matching clothes. As it was, one wore more red and the other yellow. They were tall for Hollenwae, three inches over four feet, and like all of their race they were broad shouldered, barrel chested, and thick legged. Their coal-black hair was tucked under their helmets and coal-black beards hung over their black iron mail. Each had a battle axe whose long handle made the weapons nearly as tall as the wielders. Even under their mail sleeves their arms seemed thickly muscled.

"Hro-in," said the one in red.

"And Kro-in," said the one in yellow.

"Of Sturm Deop, to your aid," they concluded together.

Alehra bowed and responded correctly, "Alehra of Sami, to yours and your city's. My companions are Lantid of The Hunt, Fargus of the Temple of Feadin in Kingstone, Nickadola of the Forest, and Blorfindel Brighteyes of Foralis." They each bowed and were bowed to as they were introduced. "What brings you to Taferford, if it is business so public?"

Lantid waved them over to their table. "The beer is worth trying." He shouted for the barman, "Two more beers!"

"News has come to the Hollenwae that these lands are beset by our race-enemy, the Kutel. While Sturm Deop can not spare many from its own wars, my brother and I have come to represent our people in this most needful of struggles. I do not know the names of Sami or Foralis, but perhaps some of your companions know of the plight of a town called Dath, said to be north of here. Have you, too, come to lend aid in this time of need?"

Lantid responded, "You're too late."

"Alas, then perhaps we can extract a measure of revenge for the unfortunate Tafers who have lost their homes and property, or indeed, their lives."

"You misunderstand. It is the Kutel who have lost home and property and their lives. Dath is safe."

The Hollenwae almost looked more disappointed. "How do you know this?"

"We were there, as you said, to help out."

"We fired the Kutel town and killed their leader and their Crals."

"We were all headed home."

Alehra gave Lantid a wry look, but said nothing.

Hro-in spoke, "We should be happy for the fortune of Dath, and, indeed, for the destruction of Kutel and Crals we raise our cups–" they both toasted them, "–though it would seem we have made a wasted trip."

Lantid pulled up a chair and shouted to the waitress, "Wine for me, and a refill for the Hollenwae!" He sat down and smiled and put a silver paddiban on the table, "You can't go home now before the rains. There are Kutel to fight at The Hunt, always. I know they hold a pass just north of there. Will you come with me?"

The brothers looked at each other. Their faces were blank masks that revealed nothing to the outsiders, but they seemed to communicate between themselves. They sat down, "Well met, Lantid of The Hunt. You are a wizard, yes?"

Blorfindel, Nickadola, Alehra, and Fargus were all laughing when they got their drinks. The evening went very late, and Blorfindel was too drunk to pluck his cittern before it ended.

The sun was bright and punishing their eyes the next morning. Blorfindel found himself wishing he had been drinking one of Linxico's vintages instead of the Tafer wines. He found the same fisherman to ferry him across the river then said his goodbyes to his friends.

"We part on the Brewster River," Nickadola said, "You know the way to Thornhill? Find me when you can."

"Do you help getting across? I'm sure the fisherman would take you."

Nickadola laughed, "I can still weave a boat, you know."

Fargus looked at each of them. "Come and see me at the Temple some time."

Alehra said, "And before long I'm going to want a tour of Sekri Timbrali – and to meet the lucky bride, of course."

Lantid said, "I hope our paths cross again, Blorfindel Brighteyes. Send for me when you're ready to go back to Foralis."

"That may be a long time coming."

"Wizards can live long, too, if I can learn the right spells."

Even Hro-in and Kro-in said, "May the Kutel fear your coming, and be not when you leave."

Blorfindel smiled. "I hope you find Kutel to suit your axes at The Hunt."

Once on the other side of the Eastering river Blorfindel turned his thoughts from the friends now in his past to the Fitheresse of his future. Still, he would not let himself imagine that he would never see them again.

Appendix A

Glossary

Alath – Timbrali word for blessed or sacred.

Ammoss – Tafer warrior and tracker from Dath, Foster father of Ghinlihil.

Anagoth – god of Virtue, son of Feadin.

Ardiv – brass coin current in the Shield valley and surrounding areas. Worth 4 hauger of 1/6 of a stowsaw, one ardiv will usually buy two beers at a tavern.

Arienic – god of song and gifts.

Baett – Kutel god of hatred, believed to be the creator of Kutel.

Biolmi Yewstaff – master Fithern archery trainer.

Blorfindel Brighteyes – Fithern archer and adventurer (Blorfindel translates to "Child of Bondage").

Bur-Droo – literally "Cold Water" in the Kutel language; a Kutel city in the mountains near the Shield Valley.

Chuum – a crude fermented drink made by the Hollenwae when no other alcoholic beverages are available.

Conjinese Empire – the southernmost nation known to the Shield Valley.

Cral – a species of people aligned with the Kutel. They are large, averaging 9' and 850 lbs. Cral are less intelligent, on average, than Kutel. Their coloration varies widely.

Dath – Tafer vilage in the northwestern Shield Valley. Also the Timbrali word for the tree parts remaining after cutting a tree and taking the desired products.

Dell – Timbrali for "child" or "little one"; shortened to "-del" when used as a suffix.

Doutak – a small platinum coin current in the Shield Valley and surrounding areas. Worth 64 stowsaw, the dautak is not in common use. A single doutak will by a Fithern long sword. A large and well-trained warhorse might cost 20 doutak.

Dhu – god of nature, protector of all life that is unaligned with any other deity.

Feadin – goddess of righteousness.

Fitheran – species of people, or the male of the species. Fitherani (male) adults range from 4'6" to 5'5" and average around 100 lbs. The natural lifespan of the Fitherani can reach two thousand years, with 1200 being common. It is believed that the Fithern lifespan was created so that they could be gardeners of great trees.

Fitherani – plural of Fitheran or a mixed group of Fitherani (males) and Fitheressi (females).

Fitheresse – female Fitheran. They are generally smaller and lighter than males, averaging 4'10" and 85 lbs. 5'2" and 100 lbs is an exceptionally large Fitheresse.

Fitheressi – plural of Fitheresse.

Fithern – of or pertaining to Fitherani.

Fiz – Timbrali for water. Plural: Fizthe.

Frenlias – Fithern god of nature, believed to be the creator of Fitherani.

Frenlias' Gift – seeds from a number of common plants which speed healing. They are known as silverseeds and bloodweed seeds by cultures separated from Fitherani.

Foralis – Small village of Fitherani; Blorfindel's (FKA Ghinlihil) birthplace.

Fummer – Hollenwae word for someone who is not stupid but does something stupid.

Ghinlihil – childhood name of Blorfindel Brighteyes.

Hauger – bronze coin current in the Shield valley and surrounding areas, worth ¼ ardiv or 10 jertak. A hauger will buy a single simple arrow.

Hollenwae – species of people or plural of those people. Hollenwae males average 4' and 150 lbs, with females being somewhat smaller. Their lifespan can exceed 450 years, though the eldest are so sheltered by their own people that it is speculated that they might exceed 700 years in exceptional cases.

Hytrem – god of war.

Ichassi – Fithern archer and sometime commander.

Ilsorma – Goddess of passions, including romance and anger.

Jilwanis – Renowned Fitheresse archer; mother of Ghinlihil / Blorfindel and wife of Lallium Steelhand.

Jertak – iron coin current in the Shield valley and surrounding areas. 10 Jertaks are worth 1 hauger. A single jertak might buy a piece of bread.

Kraahg – Hollenwae word for making someone angry at someone else.

Karakak – Kutel god of lightning and random destruction.

Koraggen – A Hollenwae city-state east of Sekri Timbrali.

Krargle – Hollenwae word for a person who does not properly respect their own family, especially the parent-child relationship. Its use is offensive, and generally grounds for violence. In Hollenwae society it is a crime to use 'Krargle' without proof.

Kushotel – a Kutel-like creature, stronger and smarter than most Kutel.

Kutel – species or sub-species of people, or their language. Kutel average 5'6" and 150 lbs naturally, but due to culling the Kutel encountered are generally larger. The natural lifespan of a Kutel is thought to be 65 years, though their violent culture prevents virtually all Kutel from reaching their natural old age. Kutel religion insists that they were created from nothing by Baett, but their ability to interbreed with Tafers leads some to believe that they were derived from Tafers by some magical or supernatural process.

Lalliam Steelhand – Finthern archer and warrior, father of Ghinlihil, and husband of Jilwanis, killed by Kutel at Foralis.

Linxico Oldgrape – retired Fithern Wizard, vintner, restaurateur, and longtime friend of Biolmi Yewstaff.

Lufkora – Hollenwae word for lava.

Madrok – Hollenwae word for a fool of low moral character.

Malstren – gold coin current in the Shield Valley and surrounding areas worth 5 paddiban. One malstren will buy a serviceable sword or a good riding saddle. Two hundred malstren will buy 5 wagons, 10 oxen to pull them, and pay teamsters to run them for more than a year.

Manrachian Nomads – Tafers who live in clans on the plains south of Sekri Timbrali.

Order of the Circle – and group of knights based in Kingstone and pledged to Anagoth.

Paavruk – A Hollenwae shield similar to a pavise.

Paddiban – large silver coin current in the Shield valley and surrounding areas, worth 8 stowsaw or 1/5 of a malstren. A pair of boots or a private room at an inn might cost a paddiban. Skilled artisans are paid in paddiban.

Putnu – a species of seafaring people aligned with the Kutel. They average 3'8" and 80 lbs.

Raiden – God of vengeance and hard justice.

Radorak – alternative name for Rettoric, favored by Hollenwae who consider him to the creator of their species.

Rettoric – God of the forge, forger of the world.

Rirowen – the white, larger, brighter moon. Tafer calendars follow Rirowen.

Sekri Timbrali – Fithern city-state south of The Shield Valley.

Shandi – A Taforam princess of The Hunt, wife of Ammoss; foster mother of Ghinlihil

Shield – language of the Shield Valley.

Shieldmaster – Chief political figure in the cities and towns of the Shield Valley. The position is appointed and traditionally hereditary. The political power of a Shieldmaster varies widely, depending on the town.

Shield Valley – Tafer nation, also known as the Valley of the Shield, centered on the Eastering River.

Shonu – capital city of the Kutel nation.

Serbin – the smaller, darker, blue moon. Serbin has a larger effect on tides. Fithern calendars, and traditional Timble dates, follow Serbin.

Stowsaw – copper coin current in the Shield Valley and surrounding areas, worth 6 ardiv or 1/8 paddiban. A knife or a bottle of wine might cost a stowsaw. Most laborers are paid in stowsaw.

Tafer – species of people, or the male of the species. Tafers average 5'10" and 165 lbs, but vary widely. They also vary widely in temperament, morals, and intellect. A Tafer's natural lifespan can exceed 100 years in rare cases, though 60 is more common.

Taforam – female Tafer, averaging 5'6" and 130 lbs.

Timble – species of people. Timbles vary from 2'8" to 3'4". Weight is highly variable and generally considered a sign of status or well-being.

Tyuriaras – goddess of Iniquities – the antithesis and adversary of Feadin.

Valley of the Shield – Alternative name of Shield Valley

Varren – a species of people aligned with the Kutel. They are small, rarely exceeding 3' and 50 lbs, and have dog-like features, including an exceptional sense of smell.

Varro – one of the the Varren.

Wizard-King of Shonu – ruler of the Kutel.

Appendix B

Currency

Name	Metal	Weight	Value	Value
Doutak	platinum	9 grams	1.6 malstren	64 stowsaw
Malstren	gold	9 grams	5 paddiban	40 stowsaw
Paddiban	silver	22 grams	8 stowsaw	8 stowsaw
Stowsaw	copper	9 grams	6 ardiv	1 stowsaw
Ardiv	brass	9 grams	4 hauger	1/6 stowsaw
Hauger	bronze	9 grams	10 jertak	1/24 stowsaw
Jertak	iron	9 grams	1/15360 doutak	1/240 stowsaw